**Praise for *New York Times* bestselling author
Heather Graham**

"Graham stands at the top of the romantic suspense category."

—*Publishers Weekly*

"Will keep you glued to the pages. The danger, drama, and energy of this book will blow you away, and just when you think you got it figured out… wrong!"

—*Fresh Fiction* on *The Seekers*

"Graham is the queen of romantic suspense."

—*RT Book Reviews*

Praise for Jessica R. Patch

"If you like romantic suspense, you need to read [*A Cry in the Dark*]."

—Lynette Eason, award-winning and bestselling author of the Extreme Measures series

"Beautifully flawed characters face off against a deadly serial killer with a complex criminal psychology. This gritty thriller is one you won't want to miss!"

—*USA TODAY* and *Publishers Weekly* bestselling author Lisa Phillips on *Her Darkest Secret*

New York Times and *USA TODAY* bestselling author **Heather Graham** has written more than two hundred novels. She is pleased to have been published in over twenty-five languages, with sixty million books in print. Heather is a proud recipient of the Silver Bullet from Thriller Writers and was awarded the prestigious Thriller Master Award in 2016. She is also a recipient of Lifetime Achievement Awards from RWA and The Strand, and is the founder of The Slush Pile Players, an author band and theatrical group. An avid scuba diver, ballroom dancer and mother of five, she still enjoys her South Florida home, but also loves to travel. Heather is grateful every day for a career she loves so very much. For more information, check out her website, TheOriginalHeatherGraham.com, or find Heather on Facebook.

Jessica R. Patch is a *Publishers Weekly* bestselling author known for her dry wit, signature twists and complex characters. She loves reading true crime books, discussing cold cases over chips and salsa with her girlfriends, and hunting down serial killers in her romantic suspense novels and psychological thrillers. She resides in the Memphis area with her family and her spoiled Shetland sheepdog. You can join the Patched In community at her website: www.jessicarpatch.com.

New York Times **Bestselling Author**

HEATHER GRAHAM

SHADOWS IN THE NIGHT

**HARLEQUIN
BESTSELLING
AUTHOR
COLLECTION**

**HARLEQUIN®
BESTSELLING
AUTHOR
COLLECTION**

Recycling programs
for this product may
not exist in your area.

ISBN-13: 978-1-335-00825-1

Shadows in the Night
First published in 2017. This edition published in 2023.
Copyright © 2017 by Heather Graham Pozzessere

Fatal Reunion
First published in 2016. This edition published in 2023.
Copyright © 2016 by Jessica R. Patch

For questions and comments about the quality of this book,
please contact us at CustomerService@Harlequin.com.

Harlequin Enterprises ULC
22 Adelaide St. West, 41st Floor
Toronto, Ontario M5H 4E3, Canada
www.Harlequin.com

Printed in U.S.A.

CONTENTS

Visit her Author Profile page at Harlequin.com,
or theoriginalheathergraham.com, for more titles!

SHADOWS IN THE NIGHT

Heather Graham

Prologue

The Mummy
A Year Ago

"Sir!"

The word was spoken softly and with respect.

Dr. Henry Tomlinson, renowned Egyptologist, turned. One of the grad students had just slipped through the inner flap of the air-controlled prep tent and was smiling benignly, awaiting his attention.

He hadn't actually taught in about five years, but he still loved it—and working with students. He'd retired to spend all his time in the field, and he'd recently been hired by Alchemy, an Anglo-American sponsoring company, to head this dig. Alchemy was into all kinds of tech and had become a Fortune 500 company. Every year, they sponsored an exceptional archeological event, followed by a public exhibit. Recent ones had been centered around the Amazon River, central China—and now ancient Egypt. Their resources were phenomenal and Henry still couldn't believe his good fortune. But no matter what monetary resources had been offered, he was thrilled about having grad students involved.

This one was Harley Frasier. Just twenty-six, she was tall, shapely, honey blonde, with a face crafted in perfect classic symmetry and enormous green eyes that seemed to take in everything. She was serious and brilliant and could nail the crux of information with laser-like acuity. She also had a sense of humor and the most delightful laugh he had ever heard.

Of the five specialty graduate candidates, she was, beyond a doubt, his favorite. He often felt like a grandfatherly mentor to her—and the idea made him happy. He'd had no children of his own. He'd never even had a wife. No time for a family. He hadn't intended it be that way forever, but there was always so much to do. If he'd had the chance to be a father, he would've been pleased and proud to have had Harley as a granddaughter. She seemed to feel the same closeness to him.

Perhaps their bond was odd since, of the five grad students, she was the one who was different, the only one not majoring in Egyptology—though she was minoring in it. She had no plan to go into Egyptology or even archeology or history for her life's vocation.

Harley was with him, first of all, because of her knowledge regarding the field and her love for it. But she was also there because her work was going to be in criminal psychology and forensic science. Henry had been baffled when he was approached by her university. Professors at the Maryland college Harley was attending—which was arguably the top school for criminology and it also offered majors and minors in Egyptology and archeology—had explained to him the importance of having a student like Harley on this expedition. He had been on the hunt for the tomb of Amenmose for nearly a decade; for that entire decade, he'd been finding more and more clues about the location—and, of course, with the permission and blessing of the Egyptian government—finding other ancient tombs and treasures in the process. This allowed for his continued excavations. But the discovery of the tomb of Amenmose was the main focus of his work.

Many others had searched.

Some of them had died or disappeared in that effort.

History suggested that Amenmose had been murdered. As a criminology student, Harley was to be in on the discovery and would seek and find whatever evidence those who had managed his secret burial might have left behind.

Not that, to Henry's mind, Amenmose hadn't deserved murder. He had usurped power every step of the way. He'd abused officials below him. It had even been intimated that he had attempted to kill those in power above him.

"I think we've gotten all the manual labor done for the evening and we're going to pack it in, maybe drive to that little town for some dinner. Want to come with us? You should. You'd enjoy it. Or shall we bring you back something?" Harley asked him.

"Next time, Harley, I'll come with you all," he promised. "There's so much in here! I'm not going to go touching anything until we've had a chance to work with the preservation measures, but I do intend to look at everything."

Earlier that week, they had finally discovered the secret site of the tomb of Amenmose. And, of course, since then, Henry Tomlinson had been on cloud nine. This was a dream come true, a fantasy realized, the culmination of a lifetime of love and dedication.

Harley laughed softly. "Yes! You did it, Dr. Tomlinson."

"I did, didn't I?"

The Amenmose find was among the most important ancient Egyptian discoveries of the past few years; he couldn't have been more excited about being a major player in that discovery. And even now, at the end of an exhausting day—and even though he truly enjoyed the young people working with him—he was far too fascinated to leave. There were a dozen or so coffins to be studied, one of them presumably that of Amenmose; the group wouldn't consider opening them until everyone was back at the museum in Cairo. But he *could* study the canopic jars they'd found thus far. There were also other artifacts that had been carefully moved into the prep tent. So much to observe and to describe! And there were the broken coffins, which had probably been as meticulously set as any of the others, but had been in the section where a partial cave-in had taken place. Several of those outer and inner coffins had split and exposed their mummies. Henry Tomlinson was fascinated to see what study was possible before the mummies were packed and crated and prepared for the trip to Cairo, where options for preservation were far more sophisticated, and where the mummies could be X-rayed and DNA could be tested.

Oh! It was all so monumental.

Amenmose had been a priest in the days when another priest, Ay, had ruled Egypt as regent. Ay had done so for a well-known pharaoh, the boy king, Tutankhamen. As regent, Ay had wielded immense power. He'd gone on to become pharaoh in his own right—after the death of Tut at the age of nineteen.

Amenmose, according to ancient texts, had tried to usurp some of that power. And he'd had his own followers in the court, making him a dangerous man. Because of this he had feared for his immortal life—and his wife had kept his burial plans a complete secret, shared only with members of his family. Naturally, legend had it that many of his most loyal followers—rather than give away any secrets— had been willing to die with him, sealed alive in a grave for eternity.

"Dr. Tomlinson, you worked so hard. And wow! You triumphed. You should celebrate. Come out with us. Is there nothing I can do to convince you?" Harley asked. She still had that wonderful smile, as if she were the one who was far older and wiser. "Nothing's going to disappear. We'll go have some dinner and drinks and come on back. There are plenty of men on guard here. And," she added, "you really deserve a little celebration with us. Think of it—you researched and imagined and looked into the ancient Egyptian mind and you made the discovery. It's your shining moment. You're another Carter with his Tutankhamen, Dr. Tomlinson. Do you realize that?"

"Oh, no, no," Henry demurred. He shook his head firmly. "A celebration is tempting, but I couldn't leave. I couldn't. I do promise that I'll come with all of you on another day. Harley! Look at this! I feel like, as the song says, I have treasures untold."

Harley laughed. "You saw *The Little Mermaid*?" she asked.

He stared at her, feeling a bit chagrined. "Oh! Yes, I get it, you wouldn't think that I'd see a children's movie…" He laughed, too. "Remember, I do have great nieces and nephews! Anyway…"

He started walking as he spoke. "Harley, these are such treasures! This broken coffin." He gestured at it. "Damaged by time and by that cave-in, however many centuries ago. And this fellow, Harley. It almost looks as if he was buried alive. Wrapped up alive and screaming."

"I don't think you can embalm anyone and have that person come out of the process alive," Harley reminded him, amused. "That's only in fiction. We both know what was involved in Egyptian embalming, and just how many factors could've had an effect on the mummy's appearance. Screaming mummies belong to B movies, right? And when you think about it, weird mummies are all the more reason you should come with us."

"Why is that?"

Harley didn't answer. The flap opened again and Jensen Morrow, another of the students, poked his head in to answer.

He'd obviously heard the question.

"Ooh! 'Cause you shouldn't be alone with scary old stuff when you have cool kids like us to hang out with!" Jensen said.

They all laughed. Jensen was a good-looking, dark-haired young man who loved the study he was involved in, and Dr. Henry Tomlinson liked him very much, as well. Jensen played hard, but he worked harder. He came from money; his father was an inventor who'd come up with a special cleaning product. And yet Jensen never acted like money, never acted pretentious or entitled the way some rich kids did.

"Tempting, tempting, tempting," Henry said again. "But I'm going to stay."

Jensen raised his eyebrows at Harley. "Hey, girl, then it's you and me heading out. The old man here isn't coming. That's okay. We're bringing back the goods. Just the two of us, since Belinda Gray is waiting for a video chat with her fiancé—military, as we know!—in Iraq. Roger Eastman agreed to help one of the tech guys investigate some computer info they're picking up. I hate to say it, but we're getting chatter about an insurgent group starting up. And Joe Rosello said he wants to learn more about the excavation equipment. He's working with that pretty Egyptian girl, our translator, and learning about hoists."

"Hoists? Yeah, right!" Harley said. "Satima. She *is* pretty, and thank goodness we have her. I'm just grateful she filled in at the last minute when the older gentleman we'd hired wound up ill. If I know our friend Joe at all, I know he's very happy!" she said to Henry. "We won't go far, since we seem to be feeling a wee bit nervous! And we won't be late. We'll bring you something to eat and see if you want to be social when we get back, okay? If, and only if, you're absolutely positive you don't want to take a ride with this handsome, if ridiculous, guy and me?"

Henry laughed. "Oh, Harley, you're a sweetheart, but give it up. You know I'm not coming."

She grimaced, a delightful movement of her face. "Yes,

I do," she admitted. "But we—your devoted students—have to try. I'll bring you a special treat for dinner."

"Don't worry about me, guys. I'll be fine."

"Sorry, we *will* worry about you. At least we can make sure you eat. I'm willing to bet you're going to be up all night—and you won't even notice that you haven't slept," Harley said.

He smiled and made a shooing motion with his hands. "Go! Get on out with you. Be young and have fun and don't become an obsessive old curmudgeon like me. Jensen, get her out of here!"

"Yes, sir!" Jensen said.

Harley still hung back. "You're neither obsessive nor old," she insisted. "Okay, wait. Maybe you are obsessive. Anyway, we'll be back by nine or so, and like I said, I'll bring you something delicious."

"Sounds lovely! See you soon."

And at last, Harley and Jensen left.

Dr. Henry Tomlinson turned his attention back to Unknown Mummy #1 for several long moments. Many pharaohs and royalty and even esteemed but lesser men, like Amenmose, ended up with unknowns in their tombs—servants needed in the next life.

Almost the entire lid of the coffin had been torn open. That afternoon, two of the students had painstakingly cleared out the rubble around the mummy. But Henry felt as if he was indeed looking at remnants featured in a B horror flick; the thing really did appear to be a man who'd been wrapped up with his mouth open in horror, left to silently scream into eternity.

Mummies weren't wrapped like this alive. Unless, of course…

He'd never been intended to be a mummy?

He'd been a murder victim.

Could this unidentified mummy be Amenmose him-self? he wondered excitedly. They hadn't identified the man's tomb.

Great question, but it wasn't scientific to jump to conclusions. X-rays would give them an image of the insides—and that would probably tell them if the fa-cial contortions had happened because of some acci-dent in the drying process or if he *had* somehow been wrapped alive!

No, it couldn't be Amenmose, Henry decided. Ac-cording to the ancient texts and all the information at his disposal, Amenmose had died before burial. Besides, they'd discovered one coffin in an inner tomb, deep in a hidden recess—again, just as the ancient texts had said. Amenmose's enemies might have defiled his tomb if those who loved him hadn't concealed his remains. The mummy here, found in the outer chamber, couldn't be Amenmose—not unless there was a great deal they were missing! "Sorry, old boy. Lord only knows what happened to you," Henry told the mummy.

"Hey!"

The inner flap to the preparation tent opened again. Henry looked over to see that it was Alchemy's direc-tor at large, Ned Richter.

He was smiling. As he should have been. Their day had been fantastic.

"Hey," Henry said. He liked Richter okay. Although not an Egyptologist himself, the man was studious and yet always ready help out with manual labor when needed.

Henry didn't like Richter's wife, Vivian, so much. She was an Egyptologist, too—at least in her own mind, he thought with a snort. Okay, so she did have her master's degree from Brown; she was just annoying as hell and she didn't think clearly or reason anything out. She was an attractive enough woman with short dark hair and dark eyes, and she claimed the maternal side of her father's family had been Egyptian.

She liked to pretend that she knew what she was talking about.

She seldom did.

"Just checking on you!" Richter said.

Henry heard Vivian speaking behind her husband. "Tell him to come with us. We'll get some food and drinks."

"Hey, Viv!" Henry called out. "I'm good tonight. Going to work. And a couple of the students are picking me up something to eat. Listen," he added in a more affable voice, "can't wait till you and I have a chance to talk tomorrow. We can compare notes then!"

"Can't you make him come?" Henry heard Vivian whisper.

"No," Richter said flatly. "He's head of the examination and prep all the way through the removal to Cairo—by Alchemy and the Egyptian government. As you know," he muttered.

"See you in the morning!" Henry called pleasantly. Yes!

But he'd barely turned around before he heard the inner tent flap opening again.

This time, it was Arlo Hampton, the Egyptologist who'd been employed specifically by Alchemy to watch over their investment.

Arlo was young—tall, straight and a little skinny. He preferred his thick glasses to contact lenses. Good thing for Arlo that nerds were in; he was, beyond a doubt, a nerd. But a friendly and outgoing nerd. He loved Egyptology, and yet, unlike certain other people, he wasn't full of himself or convinced that he knew everything.

"Hey, I knew you'd be alone with the treasures, snug as a bug in a rug!" Arlo told him cheerfully. There was something slightly guilty in his voice. "I wanted to make sure you were okay, though."

"I'm great. And, of course, if you want to join me…"

"I'm beat, Henry. I'm what? Thirty years younger than you? I don't know how you do it. I'm going to have a sandwich with the grad students when Harley and Jensen get back, and then hit my bunk until tomorrow. If that's okay. I mean, I should be like you, hard at work… Oh, I did just meet Belinda's boyfriend on Skype. Seems like a decent guy. So Belinda, Roger and Joe are taking care of their personal business, and then we're all going to meet and after that—"

"I saw Harley and Jensen. They'll bring me food. You're fine, Arlo. Have a nice night."

"Yeah, thanks. Strange, though. Something doesn't feel right his evening. Am I just being paranoid?"

"Yes. And shoo. Go on, Arlo. You worked hard today. And I'm an obsessive old bastard. Get out of here!"

Arlo grinned. He lifted his hands. "I'm gone!"

And, at last, he was.

Henry was thrilled. He even began singing Ariel's song from the Disney movie *The Little Mermaid*.

He walked back over to Unknown Mummy #1. "Strange," he said, shaking his head with perplexity as he studied the mummy. "Just who was he? And what brought him here in this state?"

But then he shrugged. He'd found "natural" mummies at other sites—servants who'd stood guard after burial rites and died where they collapsed after the tombs were sealed and they slowly asphyxiated.

Henry walked back over to his desk to dictate notes into a recorder for the exhibit, which would one day be based on this project. "The earliest Egyptians buried their dead in small pits in the desert sand. The sand and the heat naturally 'mummified' the dead. Later, to prevent animals from digging up the bodies, they resorted to creating coffins. Coffins kept out animals, but they didn't allow for the natural mummification that had been occurring when the bodies had gone straight into the sand. So the Egyptians began to learn the art of embalming. They quickly discovered that the 'wet' parts of the body needed to be removed. That included the heart and lungs, brain and liver and other organs. These were stored in canopic jars, where they were guarded, just as the body was guarded, so the dead were protected and ready as they entered into the afterlife. The process became forty days of drying with natron, a form of salt. Of course, a body was never simply dried. It was adorned with oils at various stages and also treated with religious rites."

Henry stopped speaking; he thought he'd heard something moving in the preparation tent. That was odd. The local guards and the staff who worked for Alchemy were weary and bored with the findings. Egyptians had been unearthing mummies forever and ever, and even the security force of Americans and Brits was more bored by the ancient than intrigued. Most of them had worked around the world. They were, in a word, jaded—and far more interested in the pay scale than the work itself.

He looked around the tent. Nothing. Everything as it had been. Crates and boxes and mummies and treasures!

He shook his head, impatient with himself. He was incredibly lucky to have this time alone in the preparation tent. He'd been the one to do the research and the calculations; he'd been the one who'd garnered the sponsorship that had provided the money for this expedition. His papers had raised significant interest. It was—yes, indeed—his baby.

But eventually Dr. Arlo Hampton would want his time here, his chance to study these mummies, these treasures. So would Yolanda Akeem, their liaison with the Department of Antiquities. Then, of course, there was Ned Richter…and his wife. He'd bet that Richter couldn't care less if he got any time with the mummies and ancient treasures or not. Richter was there to guard Alchemy's interests and, Henry suspected, to ensure that they looked as if they were being incredibly magnanimous to the Egyptian government. After all, Alchemy financed these expeditions, he was almost certain, for tax breaks—and the media attention and promotion they provided.

Fine. The excavation was a great success. And this was *his* time. His time alone with all his treasures!

He started to go back to his work, but he could've sworn he'd seen movement from the corner of his eye.

He stood up and walked around.

Nothing.

Henry sat back down and continued his recording.

"Ancient Egypt—"

There *was* something behind him!

He tried to spin about.

And he saw nothing but binding, the linen binding that had been used on the ancient dead, saw it wrapped around fingers and a hand, saw the fingers and the hand circle his neck and—

Fingers, like wire, clutching his throat, so powerful, so strong...

He fought their hold. Wriggled and squirmed. He tried to rise; he couldn't. The pain was terrible. The world began to blacken before him; little dots of light exploded in the darkness. And all he could think was that—

The mummy!

The mummy had risen to kill him!

It was impossible. Impossible. Impossible...

He was a scientist. Rational. He didn't believe.

He was a scientist...

And as the last electrons exploded against the stygian pit of his dying mind, he couldn't help but think...

He was a scientist.

Being killed by an ancient Egyptian mummy.

It didn't make sense. It wasn't right.

Chapter 1

One Year Later
The New Museum of Antiquity
New York City, New York

The moon that shone down through the skylights in the temple region of the museum created a stunning vision. Opalescent light shimmered on the marble and made it appear that the ribbon of "Nile" river by the temple was created of crystal and glass. The lights in the area were dim, designed to look as if they were burning torches set along the walls.

The exhibit in the New Museum of Antiquity was impressive—even to Harley, despite all the time she'd spent in the real Sahara. In designing this space, the organizers had also borrowed heavily from another famous NYC museum, all to the benefit of the Egyptian displays. Harley felt a sudden breeze from an air-conditioning vent, and she shivered.

"Mummy thing getting to you, huh?"

"Pardon?" Harley turned quickly to see the speaker. The words had been teasing; they'd also been spoken in a pleasantly deep, masculine voice.

The voice aroused a strange memory she couldn't quite reach—and seemed to whisper to something inside her, far beneath her skin.

She hadn't seen the speaker before, despite the fact that his voice seemed oddly familiar. Here, on opening night, she should've known most of the invited crowd. But she didn't know him, and—as her chosen field of criminology had taught her—she studied anyone she didn't recognize in a situation such as this evening's event.

A soiree to celebrate the exhibition. This was opening night for the traveling exhibit that would, in the end, return to Egypt, where the precious artifacts of that country would then remain. But tonight they celebrated the very first time the exhibit had been seen! It would open to the public in the morning. It had, quite properly, been named in honor of Henry—the Henry Tomlinson Collection of Egyptian Culture and Art.

There would be toasts in his honor, of course.

This phenomenal display would not have been possible without him.

But Henry was gone, as much a part of history as his treasures.

She sensed that this man—with his deep, somehow familiar voice—was connected to Henry.

She definitely hadn't seen him before.

He wasn't the kind of man you forgot.

He was tall—well over six feet, she thought. Because she'd recently taken identification classes that taught criminologists to look for details to include in descriptions, she also noted that not only was he about six foot three, but he had excellent posture. Nicely muscled, too. She had no doubt that he was the kind of man who spent time in a gym, not to create impressive abs, but to train the complex human machine that was his most important tool.

How could she be so sure of this? she asked herself. And yet she was.

He wore a casual suit, no jewelry. He was freshly shaven, and kept his dark hair cropped close to his head.

Someone's bodyguard?

Beneath the glimmer of the moon that showed through the skylights, she couldn't quite ascertain the color of his eyes. She had a feeling they were light, despite the darkness of his hair.

Thirty-three to thirty-six years old, she estimated. Carefully nondescript clothing—dark blue suit, dark blue shirt, pin-striped tie in shades of blue and black. Sunglasses resting on head.

He moved closer to her; she was certain he'd been doing the same kind of study on her that she'd nearly completed on him.

No, she'd never seen him before, but she *had* heard his voice.

"Sorry. I didn't mean to interrupt. You're not afraid of mummies, right?" he asked again, his expression quizzical.

"No, not at all," she assured him. "Ah, well, that's a bit of a lie. I might be afraid of some of the bacteria that can be found in old tombs, but as for the mummies themselves…no. My dad was a cop, a very good one. He taught me to fear the living, not the dead."

"Sounds like a bright man," he said. He stepped toward her, offering his hand. "Micah. Micah Fox."

She shook his hand. "Harley Frasier. How do you do? And pardon me, but who are you? Do I know you?"

He smiled. "Yes, and no. I'm an old student of Dr. Tomlinson's," he said. "I was at Brown when he was teaching there. About twelve years ago, I was lucky enough to join him on one of his expeditions. Back then, he was looking for the tomb of a princess from the Old Kingdom, Fifth Dynasty." He paused, still smiling, and shrugged. "He found her, too—right now she's in one of the display cases in a room not far from here, near the temple." He stopped, studying her again, and asked, "Are you surprised by that?"

"No, no, I'm not. You don't look like an Egyptologist," Harley said. "Sorry! It's not that Egyptologists look a certain way. I just—"

"It's okay. I'm not an Egyptologist," he told her. "I meant is it surprising that he found his princess? No, of course not. Henry was the best. But even though I began in archeology, I changed my major. I'm with the government now."

"FBI?" Harley guessed.

He nodded.

"Something seems to be coming back. I'm not sure what," she said. "I know your voice, but I don't know *you*. I mean—"

"Yes, you know my voice. I guess I should start over. I called you soon after the incident when you were staying in Rome. Your group was shipped from place to place, and we were trying to get a handle on what happened. I'm the Fox from those phone calls. Special Agent Micah Fox—though I admit, I was working on my own, and not as assigned by the bureau. And I apologize, because I do know a lot about you, although it wasn't appropriate to bring that up at the time. You're Craig Frasier's first cousin, and Craig and I have actually worked together. Of course, we're in different offices now. Naturally, you've met a number of the men and women with the New York office. Craig told me you finished grad school, and you're deciding what to do with all your education—join up with NYPD's finest, remain with the private agency employing you now, or go into a federal agency. But tonight, you're here for the same reason I am, honoring our old professor. For one summer, you were an unofficial Egyptologist. And, as I just explained, you recognize my voice because we spoke on the phone. I'm Criminal Division, FBI. Right now, I'm assigned down in DC. I've taken some leave to be here."

"I…see," she said.

Did she?

No, not really.

Wait. Fox—yes, that was the name of the man she'd spoken with about Henry Tomlinson, just once, what now seemed like a lifetime ago.

These days, that time was mostly a blur. Maybe because she didn't *want* to think of it. But she couldn't stop her mind from rushing back to the night they'd returned to the camp, laughing and loaded down with food and drink for their professor, only to find him on the floor, along with the broken coffin and the "screaming" mummy. He'd been garroted by his own belt, eyes open and bulging, throat blackened and bruised, a swatch of ancient linen wrapped around it.

There'd been an immediate outcry. Security was convinced that no one from outside had been anywhere near the expedition tents; they kept a tight perimeter around the work area, which included the tents that had been set up for the staff. Egyptian police had come out, ready to help with the investigation.

Then, all hell had broken loose. The computer had picked up more chatter. And word had come that the fledgling, unaffiliated militant group calling themselves The Ancient Guard was bearing down on the expedition. Perhaps they intended to steal the artifacts to finance their cause. Not an uncommon scenario... It meant that everyone and everything needed to go as quickly as possible. Government forces were being sent out, but no one wanted scientists from around the world caught up in an exchange of gunfire.

Security forces from Alchemy, along with the Egyptian police, did their best to preserve what they could from the expedition, as well as the body of Henry Tomlinson so they could discover the circumstances of his death.

Much was lost. But at least no one else was killed. The final inquiry, conducted by the Egyptian police and the Alchemy security force, concluded that the brilliant archeologist Dr. Henry Tomlinson had driven himself mad and committed suicide. According to their conclusions, he believed a mummy had come to life with the intention of murdering him... It was suspected that some unknown bacteria had caused the temporary fit of insanity, and everything from the expedition would be scrutinized using proper precautions.

Harley had fought the verdict—vociferously. She was a criminology student; she knew what should have been done and a lot of it wasn't. Pretty much nothing had been done, really, not as far as a crime scene examination went.

Not in her opinion, anyway.

How many men committed suicide with their own belts in such a manner? She sure as hell hadn't seen or read about any. And she was *studying* criminology.

Nope, never heard of it!

Her friends backed her up, at first. And then, one by one, it seemed, they all decided that the poor professor—so caught up in his love and enthusiasm for his work—had gone mad, even if only temporarily. No one could find a motive for murdering him. Henry Tomlinson had been respected and dearly loved by everyone. No one could find a clue.

The police assigned to them had been incompetent, to Harley's mind. Authorities in Egypt and in the United States hadn't done enough.

And the Alchemy people...

They wanted it to be a suicide. They didn't want to deal with a murder. They accepted the verdict without a whimper.

They were so sorry and sad, they'd claimed, and in hindsight, they could see so many mistakes.

They should've known to be more careful!

Henry should've known to be more careful!

But in fact, they said, the professor's enthusiasm for the project had caused them all to bypass modern safety regulations that might have kept him alive.

A great company line, Harley thought in disgust.

And what was the matter with her? They might all

have been killed by a crazy insurgent group that hadn't defined exactly what it was fighting for or against. It was a miracle that they'd gotten out, that they were all alive.

Well, most of them. And Henry, poor Henry, he'd done himself in—according to the authorities and to Alchemy, who went on to say that now they'd never completely understand the biology of what had gone on. They weren't allowed back on the site; the Egyptian government had stamped a foot down hard.

And that night...

First, they were shuffled to Cairo, then, almost immediately—on the orders of the Egyptian authorities and the US State Department—they were put on planes to Rome, and from Rome they were flown to New York City.

But, thinking back, Harley recalled that it was while she'd been staying at the little Italian hotel near the Spanish Steps that she'd spoken with this man. Fox. He'd wanted to know whatever she knew about the situation, and she'd told him everything, adding that she didn't believe a word of the official explanation.

There was no way Henry had killed himself.

Special Agent Fox had seemed to accept her version, but apparently he'd been just as stonewalled as she had.

Like her, he'd been forced to realize in the end that no one was going to believe him. Or her.

And even if the authorities had believed him, they didn't care enough to make a killer pay!

Here, tonight, for the first time in a year, everything about that horrible occasion was suddenly coming back.

Tonight was about honoring Henry Tomlinson. This would be an event during which people would shake their heads sadly, missing the professor who'd done so much, declaring it tragic that he'd lost his mind because of what he'd loved so deeply.

"Ms. Frasier?"

She blinked, staring at the man in front of her, wondering how long she'd been lost in her own thoughts.

In a way, she did know him. They'd just never met in person. She'd left the Sahara before he reached it. Then she'd been flown out of Cairo, and soon after that she was back in New York.

"I'm sorry!" she said softly.

He shook his head. "Hey, it's all right. I know you really cared, and that you tried to do something. It must have been hard to maintain your own belief that he'd been murdered when everyone else was telling you otherwise," Micah Fox said.

It had been and still was. "Oh, don't you know?" she muttered. "'Henry went crazy. Bacteria in the wrappings. He just *had* to dig in before proper precautions were taken. It's so tragic—don't make it worse by rehashing every little thing!'"

Her tone, she knew, was heavy with sarcasm.

They were alone in the temple area—or so she believed. Still, she looked around and repeated, "I'm sorry. I tried… I do believe he was murdered. They did find bacteria, but not enough. Henry was murdered. And I couldn't do a damned thing to prove it."

Micah nodded at her. She liked his face. Hard-jawed, somewhat sharp-boned. His eyes, she saw now, were actually blue—sky blue—and they seemed to see a great deal.

"Remember, I was a student of his, too. And now I'm an FBI agent. And I couldn't do anything, either. You

have nothing to be sorry for." He paused. "I should explain. I knew about you through Craig, of course. And
also through Henry. We kept in touch when we could—
he'd let me know what was up, what was going on. I
went into law enforcement, but I still love Egyptology.
Henry thought the world of you." He shook his head. "I
can only imagine what it was like that last night. I hope
you're okay now. Time...heals, so they say."

"So they say."

"It heals when you're at peace with the past."

"And I'm not," she said grimly, and added, "And
neither are you."

"No. Anyway, I'd like to find out about the last time
you saw him. If you don't mind."

"There won't be a chance tonight," she said.

"I know. At a later date."

Harley nodded. "I'll be happy to speak with you. I'm
not sure what I can tell you, though."

"You found him."

"Yes."

"I'd just like you to go over it with me. I realize it's
painful, but..."

"The verdict was ridiculous! You know what the ME
said! That he killed himself."

"An Egyptian ME, who wanted out of there as
quickly as possible, with armed insurrectionists about
to attack the place."

True!

But then...

"The company, Alchemy, brought in a medical examiner, too. He agreed with the Egyptian ME's findings."

"I'm sure that all happened in about two minutes in
Cairo or Rome. And as soon as they made their deci-

sion, Henry was shot through with preservatives and packed into a box. So anything that could be construed as evidence was compromised. I could be way off base. *We* could be way off base. Thing is, I'd feel better if we could talk."

"Yes, of course," she said.

Of course?

She didn't want to remember that night!

And yet, here was someone—someone in law enforcement—who agreed with her, the only person who did. Like her, Fox believed there was a truth out there that everyone else had denied.

They looked at each other awkwardly for a moment.

"Well, a pleasure to meet you in person. I guess I'm going to head over to the party area," Micah said. His voice softened. "I didn't mean to interrupt you. You might want more time here. On your own. By the way, as I said, I really do know your cousin fairly well. We worked together years ago on a case in DC. He's a great guy."

"Yes. Craig's great," Harley agreed.

She sensed that he wanted to say more.

Like maybe when or where they could meet again?

But he didn't speak. They weren't alone anymore.

Jensen Morrow came striding through the temple area. He apparently saw Harley, but not Micah Fox, probably because he stood in the shadow of a carved obelisk.

"I knew I'd find you here!" Jensen told Harley, heading toward her for a huge hug.

He'd written his thesis, gotten his graduate degree and taken a job here as an assistant curator, making use of his doctorate in Egyptology. He'd been her friend through her suspicions, her anger, her demands—and her final defeat, when she'd realized that nothing was going to be done.

No one was ever going to make her believe that Henry Tomlinson had been convinced that a mummy was attacking him—while strangling himself with his own belt.

Jensen, she was certain, had just given up. He'd been told the lie so many times that to him, it had become truth.

Harley accepted Jensen's hug; she still cared about him. When they'd first met, they'd hit it off as friends. They might have become more at one time; he was fun, energetic and thoughtful, not to mention tall, dark and handsome. But everything had changed the night Henry Tomlinson died.

Even though she didn't see the friends she'd made in Egypt very often—they were all busy working, getting on with their lives—they had all stayed friends. They were, in fact, oddly close; they had shared the experience of the dig, Henry Tomlinson's death and the escape from the desert under dire circumstances in the middle of the night. All of that meant they had an emotional bond few people shared.

And yet it was a closeness stained with the loss of the man they'd all adored. Stained, too, by the way they'd fled on the very night he died, swept up in a reign of terror.

She'd gone on to finish her own graduate work, head bent to her studies, and had taken part-time work with a prestigious investigation firm in the city so that she could still take classes when she chose while deciding what path to take for her future. It felt right, for the time being. But she had to make some real decisions soon. And yet, even as she'd worked toward her educational and career goals, she had felt that she was waiting. A temporary post—with flexible hours!—was all she'd been willing to accept at the moment.

"They're about to start," Jensen said, pulling away from her to study her face. That was when he rather awkwardly noticed there was someone else in the temple exhibit.

He offered Micah Fox a hand. "I'm sorry. How rude. I didn't see you. I'm Jensen Morrow."

"Micah Fox," the other man returned. "And actually, we've spoken. Over the phone."

"Oh! Hey, that was you?" Jensen said. "Wow. Was I vague when I talked to you? Or worse, rude? If I was, I didn't mean to be. It's just that…well, you had to be there that night. We found Henry—or, I should say, Harley found Henry—and by the time the medical examiner arrived, they were screaming that the insurgents were a few miles out and we had to break camp ASAP! I know Harley and I were going crazy with concern and disbelief and…well…hey," he finished lamely.

"There wasn't anything you could have done to change the situation," Micah said.

"Well, you're FBI, right? I guess if you couldn't prove anything different from what was said or get anything done, Harley and I, who had no law enforcement power, couldn't have done more than complain and question. Which we did. Who knows? The thing is—thing that got me, anyway—we weren't in a closed or confined space. I mean if bacteria were going to get him, you might've thought someone else would've had a reaction or… Anyway, had you been assigned to the case—officially? The FBI works in Egypt? Or does it?"

"The FBI works all over the world, as necessary," Micah replied. "But… I was there because of Henry."

"Special Agent Fox was another of Henry's grad students, but years ago," Harley quickly explained.

"Ah," Jensen murmured. That was obviously enough of an explanation. "I guess you were crazy about him, too."

"I was. Brilliant man. Horrible circumstances."

Jensen glanced at Harley. "I think we were the last people who saw him. Alive, I mean. Harley was trying to get him to come out with us. But you knew him. There was no way he was going to leave his work that night."

"No, Henry wouldn't want to leave his work." He paused, clearing his throat. "Well, I think they must be about ready to start."

"Let's go." Harley slid her fingers into Jensen's and they left, nodding to Micah. It was ludicrous, but she was suddenly afraid to be too close to the man. He not only projected strength—he was someone warm when the world had been cold. Too confident, too attractive…

She could easily give in to her feelings of sadness and loss and even anger on a night like this. With a man like this.

She was aware of Micah watching them leave.

And she wondered what he was thinking.

Harley Frasier, Craig's cousin, was certainly a beautiful young woman, Micah thought, watching her leave, hand in hand with Jensen Morrow. He'd been studying her intently for some time before he'd spoken with her.

It was evident that she had really cared about Henry. And he knew how Henry had felt about her.

According to Craig, she had wonderful parents and a great older brother, living grandparents, all kinds of family life. Micah's parents had been lost in a bridge accident when he was a child; his aunt had raised him. Auntie Jane. He loved her and she was a talented and compassionate woman. But she was it as far as family went. He had no siblings, no cousins—no one else anywhere that he knew about. His family went far back in Virginia history; it had simply winnowed down to him and Jane.

His father had been FBI. People had feared the dangers of his job. They'd never imagined that he might die young because of a bridge collapse.

Henry Tomlinson had treated him like a son or grandson. He'd shared his enthusiasm for Egyptology with Micah. Henry had a family he adored. He hadn't married, but he had a loving niece and nephew-in-law, and he was crazy about their kids.

He'd send Micah pictures of an unusual canopic jar right alongside ones of the kids with their new puppy. That was Henry.

Micah followed the pair who'd just left, wondering if he was indulging himself in an exercise of futility. Was the truth about Henry Tomlinson's death ever going to be uncovered? Henry had been murdered, which was terrible enough, but it had happened on a night when both the Egyptian government and the US Department of State had been determined to get all the workers away from the site and out of the country. The group who'd planned the attack had called themselves The Ancient Guard.

Apparently, they hadn't believed that Alchemy intended that the treasures they'd found would merely go on loan to the United States and other countries—and that they'd remain Egyptian property. Maybe they hadn't cared. And maybe, like most militant groups, what The Ancient Guard wanted, religious and political ideology aside, was a chance to fight and stave off frustration. And probably steal the treasures to finance their fighting.

They'd either been beaten back or dissipated quickly when met with armed resistance.

Micah had gone to Cairo to investigate Henry's death on an unofficial basis, and then to Rome, where the Alchemy crew had briefly stayed. Their communication had been by phone—he'd been a day behind each time everyone had moved on. And by the time he'd reached the States, it had all been too long.

Henry had been cremated, just as he'd instructed his niece to arrange in the event of his death. Then, of course, it was too late to bring in any experts.

But Henry had never suspected that he might be murdered.

And why would he?

Why the hell kill an academic like Henry? The man had never wanted or kept anything for himself—he'd never tried to slip away with even the smallest, most insignificant artifact. His work had always been about sharing treasures with the world.

Tonight… Well, tonight, Micah could watch. He could see the people who'd been close to Henry in his last days.

The grand foyer of the museum had been chosen for the site of the private gala opening. The center monument here was a massive replica of a temple from Mesopotamia that sat in the center of a skylit rotunda. The museum was beautiful, and just down the street from its larger cousin, the Metropolitan. Many design ideas that worked well in the first had been used in this newer museum. The offices were deep in the basement, for the most part. The museum was dedicated to the ancient world; it was divided into sections that concentrated on the earliest humans to the rich, ancient civilizations of Greece, Egypt, Persia, Mesopotamia and more.

The exhibition hall that would open to the public in the morning was an admirable addition to the museum. Exhibits didn't stay forever, but the hall itself would continue to thrive because of the work of Henry and other archeologists and scholars; right now, however, it was all about Henry.

Men and women in pairs and groups stood around the room, chatting, while waiters and waitresses in white-and-black attire moved about with trays of hors d'oeuvres and flutes of champagne.

Many of those invited were here because they were sponsoring patrons of the museum. There were also a number of politicians, including the mayor.

None of them interested Micah.

He scanned the crowd, taking note of those he did find intriguing.

Arlo Hampton, young, pleasant, eager. Tall and slim, but handsomely boyish-looking in a suit, speaking with an Egyptian dignitary. Ned Richter and his wife, Vivian. He so robust, she so tiny, both smiling, standing close, chatting with the mayor. And there—between an aging Broadway director and his latest ingénue— Belinda Gray, sans her fiancé, who was still serving in the military. He saw Roger Eastman, wiry and lean, wearing thick-lensed glasses, talking with his hands as he loudly discussed a technical innovation for dealing with the security of priceless historic objects. Across the room, in the midst of a few young female museum apprentices, was Joe Rosello. Joe seemed electrically energetic; he was a square-shouldered guy who could've been a fullback. He had a full head of curly dark hair and a very white smile.

Micah had done research on everyone involved with the last stages of the dig. Every one of the workers who'd had access to the tent. It hadn't been easy finding out about the Egyptian workers. Since they weren't archeologists or preservation experts, they hadn't been allowed into the inner sanctum of the camp, where the preparation tent was located. Still, he'd done his best. But everything in him screamed that the guilty party was not Egyptian, but someone among those who should have loved and honored Henry.

Why? he asked himself again. Why the hell would anyone kill Henry? If he could come up with a *why...*

"Micah?"

He turned. He hadn't expected to know many people here tonight. His name had been softly voiced by one of the few people he did know, and he knew her fairly well.

Simone Bixby, Henry Tomlinson's niece.

Simone was in her midthirties, a sandy-haired woman who looked eternally like a girl. She was small and slim and wide-eyed. She was accompanied by her husband, Jerry, a banker, who was equally slim and wide-eyed.

Micah greeted them both.

"Thank you for coming. And thank you for caring

so much," Simone said. "It's still so hard to accept what they say."

"Yes, it is," Micah agreed.

"But tonight," Jerry said brightly, "tonight we honor his body of work."

"Yes. An incredible body of work," Micah said. "How are the girls?"

"Getting big!" Simone answered. "Ten, eight and five now."

He nodded. "I've seen pictures. They're beautiful."

"They are. Thank you. They loved their uncle Henry, too," Simone said.

"We all miss him."

"Oh, look—there's Arlo Hampton," Jerry said. "Micah, we'll talk later? Simone, we need to find out what he wants us to do when he speaks."

"Excuse us," Simone said.

"Of course!" Micah told them. They moved on.

He continued to survey the room.

Hail, hail, the gang's all here. Grad students. Administration staff. Egyptologists. City officials. Museum people. And there…

An exotic woman with dark skin and almost inky black hair was speaking with Simone and her family. Arlo stood beside them.

Yolanda Akeem. They'd met briefly—very briefly— in Cairo. She was the Egyptian liaison with the Department of Antiquities. Naturally, she'd be here tonight.

She saw him looking at her. She elegantly lifted her glass a few inches in acknowledgment.

She'd given him whatever information she'd had in Cairo; it hadn't been much. A two-second autopsy report and a lecture on the dangers of the Middle East.

He didn't listen to much of it. Henry's body was gone by then and the members of the expedition had been shuttled off. He'd been ready to follow them as quickly as possible when they'd been in Egypt—and through their escape from the trouble that had befallen the expedition that night.

Tonight, they were all here.

And there was Harley Frasier. She had a smile on her face as she spoke with Gordon Vincent, director at large for the museum. Her smile was forced. Jensen was with her, smiling and chatting, as well. He seemed to be putting a little too much effort into being charming.

Which didn't seem necessary, since he was already employed by the museum.

Harley didn't; she worked for Fillmore Investigations, a large security and investigation company that served the civilian market, but was known for its close affiliation with the New York City PD and other law enforcement agencies. The founder of the company, Edward Fillmore, had barely survived a kidnap-for-ransom scheme as a child. He had founded his company on the premise that all agencies, public or private, should work together for the benefit of victims. Since Micah's job with the FBI had come about because of similar circumstances, he liked the man without even knowing him. Micah was pleased that Harley Frasier had chosen such a reputable company. None of his business, of course. But…

He'd felt something for her, just from hearing her voice over the phone a year ago.

And now…he'd seen her.

Anyone awake and breathing would find her attractive and charming.

He was certainly charmed by her and impressed by her—and so much more.

Even though he hardly knew her…

He forced himself to look away from Harley and objectively observe the other people in the room.

He was standing back, watching, when he became aware that a friend had arrived.

"I have to admit I was definitely expecting you to be here," Craig Frasier told him.

Micah smiled without glancing over. "And I guess I'm not surprised that you're here," he said.

"I can't let you get into too much trouble," Craig murmured.

"I'm just here to honor an old friend," Micah said.

"Like hell." Craig smiled grimly, studying the crowd milling in the foyer. "But I don't know what you think you can discover at this late date."

Micah turned to face Craig at last, a rueful half smile on his face. "Right. Well, it would help if someone suddenly had a guilt attack and admitted going crazy— from the bacteria in the wrappings, of course—and murdering Henry."

"Not going to happen."

"I know."

"So?"

"Don't worry. I'm not going to harass your cousin," Micah said.

"I'm not worried. I think you two can actually do each other some good it you get a chance to really talk. Maybe you can figure something out, late as it might be. There was so much done so quickly and so politically. State Department, international bull. A cover-up. Yeah, it'll be good for the two of you to talk."

"You say that as if you doubt the official line, too," Micah said quietly.

"Because I do. I believe it was a cover-up."

"Not by the government," Micah said.

"By?"

Micah looked at him and said, "By Alchemy."

Craig didn't get a chance to respond.

Arlo Hampton took the microphone on a small portable dais set in the center of the foyer. He cleared his throat, then said, "Ladies and gentlemen, friends of the museum, friends of science and exploration, and friends of the City of New York!"

It took a moment for everyone to stop talking and start listening. Someone tapped a champagne flute with a fork or spoon. Then the room fell silent.

"We welcome you to our amazing new exhibit, brought to us through the genius of the man—the brilliant, kind, ever-giving man—whose name will now grace our museum walls, Dr. Henry Tomlinson. Those who knew Henry loved him. He was a scholar, but he was also a very human man who loved his family and friends. No one knew Egyptology the way Henry did…"

A sudden gasp from the crowd silenced him. Everyone turned.

Someone had come up from the basement steps, and was now staggering through the crowd.

Someone grotesquely dressed up in a mummy's linen bindings, staggering out as if acting in a very bad mummy movie.

A performance for the evening?

No.

Because Arlo grunted an angry "Excuse me!" and

exited the dais, walking toward the "mummy" now careening toward him.

"What the hell?" Micah and Craig were close enough to hear Arlo's words. "Richter, is that you? You idiot! Is that you?"

It wasn't Richter; Micah knew that right away. Richter was far too big a man to be the slight, lean person now dressed up.

Or at least Ned Richter was!

Micah burst forward, phone out and in his hand. As he neared the mummy, he was already dialing 9-1-1.

"Get those bindings off her! Get them off her fast!" he commanded.

The mummy collapsed.

Micah barely managed to catch the wrapped body sagging to the floor.

As quickly as he could, he began to remove the wrappings.

He heard the sound of a siren.

Then Vivian Richter looked up at him, shuddered and closed her eyes.

The wrappings, Micah knew, had been doused in some kind of poison.

Chapter 2

Chaos reigned.

Harley was stunned and horrified that Vivian Richter was so badly hurt—so close to death.

She was wrapped tightly. The outer wrappings were decayed and falling apart; they'd come from a historic mummy. The inner wrappings were contemporary linen, the kind the museum used in its demonstrations, made to look like the real deal.

Vivian was gasping and crying, completely incoherent. One woman in the room was a doctor—a podiatrist, but hey, she'd been to medical school. She was kneeling by Vivian, calling the shots, talking on the phone to the med techs who were on their way.

Special Agent Fox had already taken control of the room. No one was to leave; they were all in a lockdown.

She was incredibly glad that Craig was there. And,

of course, he was with his girlfriend or fiancée—Harley wasn't sure what Craig and Kieran called each other, but she *was* sure they were together for life. Kieran was standing near Harley, ready to comfort her, as the slightly older and very protective almost cousin-in-law. Harley appreciated that, even though she didn't really need it. She worked with criminals all the time, as well as people who weren't so bad but still wound up in the criminal justice system. She was calm and stoic; Micah and Craig were questioning people, grouping them, speaking to them, both digging for answers and assuring them all that they were safe.

"She's going to die! She's going to die!" Simone Bixby, Henry Tomlinson's niece, cried out. Harley saw that Micah Fox hurried over to her, placed a comforting arm around her shoulders and led her to a chair.

By then, of course, museum security had arrived. So had the police—New York City and state police.

People were talking everywhere. Micah and Craig had herded everyone into groups, depending on their relationship to the museum. Some were employees of the museum; some were special guests. The people who'd been on the expedition were in a corner. Harley was with Belinda Gray, Joe Rosello, Roger Eastman and Jensen Morrow, as well as the Alchemy Egyptologist, Arlo Hampton.

Ned Richter was crouched on the floor, at his wife's side.

All of this seemed to go on for a long time, yet it was a matter of minutes before more sirens screamed in the night and the EMTs were rushing in. Ned Richter was allowed to go with his wife; Arlo Hampton and others more closely associated with the exhibit were now gathered together in a new group. Guests who'd only recently made it through the doors were questioned and cleared.

Anyone who had anything to do with prep for the evening was in another group; every single person would be questioned before being permitted to leave for the night.

Officers and crime scene techs were crowding through the museum, heading to the Amenmose section—and to the staff office and prep chambers beyond.

"Too bad we couldn't continue the celebration," Joe said, hands locked behind his back, a look of disappointment on his face. "What a waste of great food and wine."

"Joe! What's the matter with you?" Belinda chastised.

"Come on! Vivian Richter's a drama queen," Joe said.

"She might die," Roger said very softly.

"You mark my words. She will not die," Joe insisted.

"They're saying it's poison," Roger pointed out. "Some kind of poison on the wrappings."

"She's going to be very, very sick," Jensen said. "Those wrappings decaying and falling all around her... Who the hell knows where they came from—or what might be on them?"

"Or if something was *put* on them," Roger said. "That's how she would have been poisoned."

They were all silent for a minute.

"And then dead—like Henry Tomlinson," Belinda said.

Again, they were silent.

"Great. But at least now, maybe someone besides me will start fighting to figure out what happened to Henry," Harley said quietly.

She'd actually discovered that night that someone *was* on her side. The agent with the great voice. Craig's friend. Micah Fox.

"Okay, okay," Belinda said. "I didn't push it a lot at the time. I mean, it didn't make any difference, did it? The cause of death—two medical examiners said— was the fact that bacteria made him crazy and he killed himself."

The reaction to her comment was yet another bout of silence.

"What were we going to do?" Belinda wailed. "We had no power. Insurgents were bearing down on the camp, and everyone wanted us out! So, what *could* we do? Henry was dead," Belinda said.

"And back then, none of us believed he killed himself," Jensen said at last.

"But we all let it go." Roger sounded sorrowful as he spoke. "Except Harley, and we all kind of shut her down," he added apologetically. "But, seriously, what were we going to do? There were some whacked-out insurrectionists coming our way. I'm sorry, but I've got to admit I didn't want to die. I really didn't care if anyone was collecting evidence properly—all I wanted was out of there! And in the end, I guess we bought into the official—" he made air quotes with his fingers "—version. It was just easier and—"

"Ms. Frasier!"

Harley was being summoned. She saw that it was the plainclothes detective who had apparently been assigned to the case. He was lean and hard-looking; his partner was broader and had almost a baby face and a great smile. They were McGrady and Rydell, Rydell being the guy with the smile.

She wasn't going anywhere alone. She was never sure how Craig could home in on her problems so quickly, and tonight he was with Micah Fox, the agent who had called her before—and approached her at the beginning of the evening. What if she *had* talked to him when he'd wanted to?

Could tonight's disaster have been avoided?

Did it have anything to do with what had happened before?

She was led into one of the museum offices that had been taken over by the police. She felt, rather than saw, her cousin Craig and the enigmatic Micah Fox come in.

They didn't sit; they took up stances behind her.

McGrady took the seat behind the desk and asked her sternly, "Ms. Frasier, what exactly is your association with the museum, the expedition—and the injured woman?"

"I was on the expedition. I don't really have an association with Vivian. It's not like we have coffee or hang around together and do girls' night," Harley said. "Vivian is married to Ned Richter, the CEO of Alchemy. Alchemy financed the expedition. Alchemy is the largest sponsor for this exhibition. We were all pretty close in the Sahara—not that we had much choice."

"So you did know her well!"

"I didn't say I knew her well. We were…colleagues."

"But you like mummies, right? All things ancient Egyptian?" McGrady asked.

"Yes, of course. I find the culture fascinating."

"And it would be a great prank to attack someone and lace her up in poisoned linen. Like a mummy?"

"What?" Harley exploded.

McGrady leaned forward, wagging a pencil at her.

"You were the one who discovered Henry Tomlinson—dead. Correct?"

Harley had never thought of herself as particularly strong, but his words, coming out like an accusation, were too much.

She heard a guttural exclamation from behind her. Craig or Micah Fox, she wasn't sure which.

But it didn't matter. She could—and would—fend for herself. She leaned forward, too.

"Yes. I found Henry. A beloved friend and mentor. I found him, and I raised an outcry you wouldn't believe. And no one in a position of power or authority gave a damn. First, it was oh, the insurgents were coming! Saving our lives was more important—and yes, of course, that was true—than learning the truth about the death of a good man. I could buy that! It's an obvious decision. But then, no decent autopsy, and his niece, bereft, had him cremated. And now you're asking me about Henry—and about Vivian Richter. You have nerve. I was here tonight in honor of Henry. I didn't see the exhibit before tonight. I haven't been associated with Alchemy since we returned. I suggest you speak with the people who *were* involved there and worked on the exhibit."

McGrady actually sat back.

Everyone in the room was silent.

Then Harley thought she heard a softly spoken "Bravo."

McGrady cleared his throat. "Sorry, Ms. Frasier, but you do realize that Vivian Richter is dangerously close to... Well, we might have a murder on our hands."

"You *do* have a murder on your hands. Dr. Henry Tomlinson was murdered. Now we have to pray that

Vivian comes out of this, but still, you've got a killer here. Do you have anything more to ask me?" Harley demanded. They did need to hope and pray for Vivian, but by now, surely they had to recognize the truth of what had happened to Henry!

"Did you see Vivian this evening?"

"No."

"But you arrived early, didn't you?"

"Only by a few minutes. I walked out to the temple area."

"Which is off-limits until after the exhibit officially opens tomorrow."

"I was allowed to go back there because I'd been on the expedition."

"And you were close to the backstage area where exhibits are prepared?"

"Yes."

"Where Vivian would have been?"

"Possibly."

"But you didn't see her. Who did you see?"

"Just Jensen. Jensen Morrow. He's working here, with the exhibit. This is actually his field of work. I saw Jensen—oh, and Special Agent Fox." She glanced back at him. He and Craig were flanked behind her like a pair of ancient Egyptian god-sentinels. They almost made her smile. Not quite. She couldn't believe that this detective was quizzing her—when she couldn't get any help before, no matter how she'd begged and pleaded!

"Special Agent Fox?" McGrady said.

"I arrived within minutes of Ms. Frasier. I was told she'd just headed for the temple. I wanted to speak to her about the death of Henry Tomlinson. I went straight there. We were speaking when her colleague Jensen

Morrow appeared. Exactly as she indicated," Micah Fox said.

McGrady stood up. "Fine. Ms. Frasier, you're free to go."

Harley stood up and glared at him. "I'm delighted to leave. But perhaps first you'd be kind enough to let me know how Vivian's doing. We might not be close, but we were serious associates."

McGrady sighed. "She's holding her own. The doctors are combatting the effects of the poisoning."

"What was the poison?"

"It's an ongoing investigation. That's information we can't give out right now, even if we had it."

"I see. Thank you."

Craig opened the door; she marched out. He and Micah followed. She thought she heard McGrady mutter, "And take your Feds with you."

"Not the usual helpful attitude, at least not in my association with the NYPD," Craig said. "Usually, we have an excellent working rapport."

"Maybe he's resentful because he's not sure what this is yet. It's impossible at this time to say what happened," Micah said.

Harley spun around to stare at him. "What are you, a fool?" she snapped. "We both know—not suspect, but *know*—that Henry Tomlinson was murdered. Then Vivian Richter comes out wrapped in mummy linens, screaming and poisoned with some kind of skin toxin, and we don't know what happened? Obviously, someone tried to kill her!"

Craig grabbed her by the shoulders. "Harley! Stop. Micah's on your side. What are you?" he asked. "A fool?"

She flushed uneasily. They were just outside the

door. The nicer cop, the quiet one with the baby face, Rydell, came out and approached Jensen Morrow. He was next on the block, Harley thought. And how stupid of the cops. Jensen had been with her, away from the camp, when Henry Tomlinson was killed. They just didn't seem bright enough to realize that there was a far bigger picture here. They needed to see it—before someone else died.

But Craig was right. She shouldn't be taking it out on Micah Fox.

Why was she being so hostile, so defensive?

Pushing him away on purpose.

He was trying to help her. He was…

He was a promise she was afraid to accept. He claimed he wanted the truth, and he seemed to have all the assets needed to get at that truth. He was too damned good to be true, and she didn't dare depend on someone like that when the very concept of an ally, someone to depend on, was still so…

Foreign to her! He was law enforcement—and on her side. It was good. After all this time, it felt rather amazing.

"Sorry," she murmured.

She'd barely spoken when Kieran Finnegan came hurrying up next to her. "I have a car outside. Come on, I'll get you home."

"But—"

"There's nothing else you can do here tonight, Harley," Micah said.

"Remember, you came to me."

"Yes. And there's nothing else you can do here tonight," he repeated.

Harley stiffened.

"Let's go," Kieran said gently.

So she nodded. "Thank you," she said to Craig and Micah, and then she allowed Kieran to lead her out the door, to the front of the museum.

A light-colored sedan was waiting, just as Kieran had promised. Kieran wasn't driving; Harley assumed the driver was FBI and that Micah or Craig had made the arrangements.

Once in the car beside Kieran, Harley regretted the fact that she'd already left. "I should still be there. I should be back with the exhibits. I should see the prep rooms. I was with them on that expedition and I know what we discovered. I saw the tomb when it was opened. And I... Lord, yes, I'm the one who found Henry."

"Logically, there isn't a damned thing you could've done tonight. They won't let anyone back by the exhibits, the prep rooms, the offices—anywhere!—until the crime scene people have gone through it all. Naturally, everyone's hoping that Vivian Richter pulls through. If she does, maybe she'll be able to remember something that will help. For now, well..."

"McGrady is NYPD. He isn't letting Craig and that Agent Fox in on anything."

"They'll get in on it. Trust me. Craig will talk to his director. His director will call the chief of police or the mayor or someone, but they'll get in on it," Kieran said with assurance.

Harley leaned back for a moment, suddenly very tired. She closed her eyes and then opened them again, looking over at Kieran. She liked her cousin's girlfriend. Really liked her. She wasn't sure why they weren't engaged or married yet, but...

Kieran, of course, knew all about what had gone on

during and after the expedition out to the Sahara in the search for Amenmose's tomb. Considering what she did for a living—a psychologist who worked with law enforcement—nothing much surprised her or rattled her. Besides, she'd met Craig during a period when the city was under siege with a spate of diamond heists.

"So tell me—what's your take on this?" Harley asked Kieran. "Who would kill Henry Tomlinson? Or rather, who'd dress up as a mummy to kill him, and then dress Vivian Richter like a mummy to try and kill her?"

"The incidents might not be related," Kieran said.

"Oh, please! Don't tell me Henry wasn't murdered! Don't tell me I want that to be the case because I don't want to believe he went crazy and committed suicide."

"I'm not saying that at all. Here's the thing. You were in the desert, so it had to be someone there. Henry's dead and maybe this would-be killer is playing on that. Or maybe the two are related. The problem is, I don't know anyone involved. It's hard enough to make judgment calls when you've had a chance to speak with people and question them."

"Yeah, yeah, I'm sorry."

"That said…"

"Yes?"

Kieran smiled and shrugged. "You've had as much education as me, if not more."

"Ah, but in different courses! I need more in psychology."

"Specifically in human emotions. Like jealousy."

"Jealousy? As in…someone who wanted to be a famed Egyptologist?"

"Possibly. Some people kill because they're deranged. They're psychotic, or they're sociopaths. Then, of course, you have the usual motives. Love, greed, hatred…jealousy. Think about everyone involved if you're convinced that the two situations are related. The rest of us weren't there. Only you know the dynamics among all the people who were on that expedition."

"I can't imagine anyone who would've wanted Henry dead. I just can't."

"It's not that you can't. It's that you don't want to," Kieran told her.

They'd reached Rector Street and the old warehouse apartment that legally belonged to Harley's uncle, who was mostly out of state now and had generously given the large, rent-controlled space to Harley while she finished her degree and decided on her permanent vocation.

The driver hopped out of the car, opening the door for Harley. Kieran leaned out to say goodbye and thank the man.

"Get on home, get into bed, go to sleep," Kieran said. "Much better to start fresh in the morning."

Harley gave her a quick hug and a peck on the cheek. "Thanks. Thanks for getting me here. But… I'll be back on it in the morning."

Kieran grinned. "We'd expect no less." She leaned back in the car and the driver shut the door. He offered Harley a grave nod, and waited until she was safely at the door to her building.

Harley keyed open the lock and waved to the night clerk on duty at the refurbished twenty-floor building. Then she took the ancient elevator to the tenth floor. It wheezed and moaned, and she wondered if Mr. Otis himself had seen it installed in the building. However, it worked smoothly, and she was soon on her floor and in the spacious area she knew she was incredibly lucky to have in New York City. The building had once housed textile machinery and storage. She had over a thousand square feet with massive wall-length windows that looked out on the city with a special view of Grace Church. Harley knew she was blessed to have this space, and reminded herself to send Uncle Theo another thank-you. A counter separated the kitchen from the dining area and living room, while wrought iron winding stairs led up to the open loft space that was her bedroom. Her mom had told her that the apartment had once been Uncle Theo's bachelor pad, but at the ripe old age of sixty-five, he'd met Helen, the love of his life, and they were happily enjoying the pleasures of Naples, Florida, year round. Helen, a spring chicken of fifty-five, was delighted that Harley was watching over the place, just so they'd have a place to crash when they came up to see friends.

Harley found herself staring out at her view of Grace Church.

Home, bed, sleep.

Impossible.

Henry Tomlinson, an Egyptologist by trade, had loved Grace Church. The church itself dated back over two hundred years, although the current building went back to the 1840s, with new sections added along with the decades. Gothic and beautiful, it was the kind of living history that Henry loved.

She wondered if Vivian Richter was still hanging on. She thought about calling the hospital, but they probably wouldn't give her any information.

Home, bed, sleep.

She could try.

Climbing up the stairs to her bedroom, she quickly changed into a cotton nightshirt and crawled beneath the covers. She realized she hadn't closed the drapes.

She stared out at the facade of Grace Church.

Yes, Henry would have loved a view like this.

What was Henry's niece, Simone, thinking tonight?

And Micah Fox? How had he arranged time off? How had he managed to be there? Would he figure something out?

She prayed for sleep, but her mind kept returning to that time in the Sahara. Being part of the expedition had been such a privilege. She remembered the way they'd all felt when they'd broken through to the tomb. Satima Mahmoud—the pretty Egyptian interpreter who had so enchanted Joe Rosello—had been the first to scream when the workers found the entry.

Of course, Henry Tomlinson was called then. He'd been there to break the seal. They'd all laughed and joked about the curses that came with such finds, about the stupid movies that had been made.

Yes, people had died during other expeditions—as if they *had* been cursed. The Tut story was one example—and yet, by all accounts, there had been scientific explanations for everything that'd happened.

Almost everything, anyway.

And their find...

There hadn't been any curses. Not written curses, at any rate.

But Henry had died. And Henry had broken the seal...

No mummy curse had gotten to them; someone had killed Henry. And that someone had gotten away with it because neither the American Department of State nor the Egyptian government had wanted the expedition caught in the crosshairs of an insurgency. Reasonably enough!

But now...

For some reason, the uneasy dreams that came with her restless sleep weren't filled with mummies, tombs, sarcophagi or canopic jars. No funerary objects whatsoever, no golden scepters, no jewelry, no treasures.

Instead, she saw the sand. The endless sand of the Sahara. And the sand was teeming, rising up from the ground, swirling in the air.

Someone was coming...

She braced, because there were rumors swirling, along with the sand. Their group could fall under attack—there was unrest in the area. Good Lord, they were in the Middle East!

But she found herself walking through the sand, toward whomever or whatever was coming.

She saw someone.

The killer?

She kept walking toward him. There was more upheaval behind the man, sand billowing dark and heavy like a twister of deadly granules.

Then she saw him.

And it was Micah Fox.

She woke with a start.

And she wondered if he was going to be her salvation...

Or a greater danger to her heart, a danger she hadn't yet seen.

Chapter 3

Micah did his best to remain calm and completely in control. That was definitely a hard-won skill from the academy.

It was the crack of dawn, the morning after the event, and he'd been called in to see Director Richard Egan. Alone.

Egan was Craig's immediate boss. The man was a hard-ass, Craig had told him, but in a good way. He had the ability to choose the right agent for the right case in the criminal division.

He'd also fight tooth and nail when he thought the agency should be involved. He'd take a giant step back, too, when he thought he'd be interfering with the local authorities.

They were often part of a task force, but it didn't seem there was going to be one in this situation. Hell, there might not even be any official FBI involvement. At the moment, they were looking at what might have been a murder thousands of miles away, and what might have been an attempted murder at a museum opening. It might also have been some kind of bizarre ritual or prank.

Several morning newspapers—among the few still available in print—were on Egan's desk. The front pages all held stories with headlines similar to the first one he read: Mummies Walk in New York City!

Egan glanced at the papers and shook his head, dismayed, Micah thought, more by people's readiness to believe such nonsense than he was by the disturbing headlines.

"You see? Everyone will be going crazy. Thank God that woman didn't die—thank God she didn't die, no matter what—but with this mummy craze…there'll be pressure. The press will not give it up. So. Let me get this straight," Egan said. "You have lots of leave time?"

"Yes, sir. I'm on leave now."

"But you started off taking some of that leave and traveling to Egypt."

"Yes, sir." He hesitated. "That was a year ago. I took several weeks then, and I'm taking several more now. I'm never sick. I've accrued other time as well and work with a great group. So, last year…"

Egan was waiting.

"I came back. I'd heard that Henry Tomlinson, an old friend, had died under unusual circumstances. I tried to reach the site, but when I got there, it had been cleared out. I tried to track down his body, but I was behind by several steps. But you know all this." He hesitated.

"I'm a bit of a workaholic, sir. Like I said. I put in a lot of time, and wind up owed a fair amount of time off."

"And you use your leave working, I see."

"I flew all over last year, being given the runaround. Our people in Cairo helped, but they were stonewalled, too. And a lot of the time, certain Egyptian officials acted as if I was an idiot and an annoyance. According to them, they were trying to keep people alive and I was making waves about a dead man. It was too late for them to do anything, of course. I pursued it as far as I could, but Henry's niece had been told that her beloved uncle had died in a horrible accident and, abiding by his wishes, had him cremated. Can't autopsy a pile of ashes."

"Our people in the Middle East would've done exactly what you did," Egan assured him.

"Yes, sir."

"But?"

"But I knew Henry Tomlinson," he said. "He was a friend. He was also a good man. His death deserved a decent investigation, which— due to the circumstances, I know—he did not get."

Egan was quiet for a minute.

Then he said, "And you just happened to be at the museum tonight when a woman, wrapped in would-be old linen tainted with nicotine poison, came crashing into the ceremony."

"So that was it, nicotine poisoning. Hmm. But I didn't just *happen* to be at the event, sir. I was there purposely. As I said, I knew Henry Tomlinson. I loved the guy. I was there to honor him."

"But Craig Frasier has an involvement because his cousin Harley was on the expedition."

Micah shrugged, but kept his eyes steady on Egan's.

"You're a good agent, Micah," Egan said after a moment. "I've seen your service record. I know your supervisor."

Micah lifted his hands. "Sir—"

"Yeah, whatever, forget about it," Egan said flatly.

"Begging your pardon, sir, but—"

"I heard the cop on the case is a dick." He grinned. "In more ways than one."

Startled, Micah raised his brows.

Egan laughed. "The guy's partner, Rydell, actually called me. He wanted to apologize for McGrady's behavior. I guess the guy was hoping it would turn into a murder case and that it would be his—and he wanted the FBI out of it."

"I see."

"Don't worry. The FBI is in. Taking lead."

"Really?" He'd decided to stay calm, so made a point of not betraying his surprise and delight.

Egan leaned back, studying him. "The case began in the Middle East. It entails far more than the City of New York."

Micah felt his pulse soar, but he still maintained his composure.

"That's excellent, sir. And…"

"Yes, I've spoken with your office. You and Craig can take lead on the case. Mike—you know, Craig's partner, Mike?—he needs some vacation time, and if you're here and we're taking this on, I'm going to go ahead and give it to him. So it'll be the two of you. Work with the cops, though, and any other agencies that may become entangled in this. We'll have State Department and embassies involved, too, I imagine. Anyway, our victim from last night regained consciousness thirty minutes ago. I've asked that they let you and Craig do the talking. You are no longer on leave. I suggest you get moving."

"Yes, sir, absolutely. Thank you."

"Just get the son of a bitch," Egan said.

Micah nodded and started out.

"Hey!" Egan called, stopping him.

"Sir?" Micah walked back.

"I didn't hear much about that whole mess in Egypt. What ever happened with the insurrection?"

"Over before it began, from what I understand," Micah told him. "By the time I landed in Cairo, the expedition people were on planes headed out. And the military had routed the coup—it was more of a student protest than anything else. Sadly, it's a fact that there's a lot of unrest in the Middle East, for various reasons. Anyway, it was over, but the expedition was gone. I went out to the site, but…by then, there was nothing to find. Everything had been cleaned out."

"And the insurgents?"

"A few arrests. Most of them dispersed when the military came on the scene."

"In retrospect it might look like overkill, but better safe than sorry," Egan said.

"Of course, always," Micah agreed.

But as he left Egan's office, he found himself wondering, for the first time, whether the insurgent event had been planned to ensure that Henry Tomlinson's death wasn't investigated.

Maybe he was pushing it, getting paranoid.

Maybe he was taking a conspiracy theory too far.

And yet…

Had there been some kind of conspiracy?

* * *

"What do you think?" Jensen asked Harley.

She was back at the museum, in the Amenmose exhibit; she hadn't been able to resist. Jensen had called her, saying that with Vivian in the hospital, he could use some extra help, so she'd come.

"They've delayed the opening by a day," he'd told her over the phone early that morning. "But with Vivian out of the picture—temporarily, of course!—and especially since you were there and have a memory like a camera, you can help me with loose ends, tying things up, paperwork."

She'd assured him that she'd be there.

Jensen had told her he'd never left the museum the night before. He didn't look tired, but he was one of those people who could work for days, then sleep twenty-four hours, party a night away, and work a full load again. Jensen could be absolutely tireless.

"I think the exhibit is so special. Just like Henry," she said quietly.

They were standing in the temple area, right where she'd stood the night before when Micah Fox had come upon her. But she wasn't staring at the exhibit, which was surrounded by the glass-and-concrete walk and the "river"; rather, she was looking back at the hall that led to the temple.

One broad corridor led here, with six smaller chambers off the main hall. The temple faced east, in the direction of the sunrise, since it was dedicated to the sun god, Ra. It wasn't filled with statues. Instead, it was open to the glass that revealed the sun.

"The earliest known temple to Ra," Harley said, smiling.

Jensen nodded. "Info on Ra, on Tutankhamen, Ay and Amenmose are on the side there. Near Amenmose's mummy." That was on display in a small room, which it had all to itself. "The hallways feature a lot of the fabulous funerary art we found," Jensen continued.

"Which is surprising, don't you think?" Harley asked.

"How do you mean? That we have anything left— after running out with our tails between our legs?"

"Running out with our tails between our legs was the only thing to do," Harley replied. "No, of course, the historical assumption is that Amenmose was murdered. By someone under Ay, who knew that Amenmose wanted to usurp his power with the boy king, Tutankhamen. Our discovery proved that he *was* murdered, once we were back in the States and the body was properly identified through the DNA testing."

"He'd been strangled!" Jensen said.

"Like Henry," Harley murmured.

"Well, we don't really know about Henry."

"I do."

Jensen shrugged. "In this case," he said, "when it comes to Amenmose, X-rays that show fractured hyoid bones don't lie."

"But we have no clue who did it."

"I'm willing to bet Ay did it himself."

"Oh, today, in one of our courts, Ay would be guilty. He'd be guilty of *conspiracy* to commit murder. It was his idea, I'm sure. But that's just it. Somehow, Amenmose still ended up being properly mummified and placed in an inner coffin and several sarcophagi and laid to rest in his tomb. So who killed him? And who got the body and managed to bury it with such honor?"

"Hey, I'm the Egyptologist here!" Jensen reminded her.

"Yes, and I'm the criminologist. We've got to know who did it and why," Harley said lightly.

"I think we can rest assured that the murderer has long since gone to his own reward," Jensen said, grinning.

"Amenmose's murderer."

"Ah! But not whoever murdered Henry, right? Is that what you mean?"

She nodded.

"Your cousin's FBI and that other guy, Micah, he is, too. They'll get to the truth. And now, because of what happened to Vivian, they'll keep going," he said with confidence. "And guess what? We sold out. We didn't open today as planned, obviously, but we will tomorrow…and it's a total sellout. Not that sales weren't good before, but now that we have mummies walking around, we're a real hit."

"I've seen the news and read a few of the papers. Yeah, what a great story. But there was no mummy walking around. That was Vivian. And speaking of her, how's she doing? Have you heard anything?" Harley asked.

"Doing well, I understand. Awake and aware and lording it over the hospital staff. She's going to be fine."

"Thank God. But what's she said?"

"Nothing. She remembers nothing. Who knows what'll happen eventually? They'll have shrinks in there and everything. At the moment, though…nothing."

"But she'll be okay. That's the most important thing."

"Of course," Jensen agreed. Then he said, "So, what are you doing tonight?"

"What am I doing?" Harley repeated. She felt a strange tension. She'd almost dated Jensen when they were on the expedition. Almost. There was nothing to dislike. He was good-looking, he was smart, he was alpha-fun and…

She did like him.

But she suddenly dreaded the fact that he might be asking her out. There wouldn't have been anything wrong with dating Jensen. They'd teased and they'd flirted and come close. But now she wanted to retreat; she wasn't sure why. It must be everything that had happened, that *was* happening…

She didn't want to turn him down. She wanted to be friends. Maybe she even wanted the relationship option left open.

"I'm, um… I'm not sure," she said. "I came here this morning because you said you needed me, and I want to help."

"This is social."

"Oh. Well, um—"

He laughed softly. "Don't worry. I'm not putting you on the spot. Not tonight. We wanted the whole group to get together. Those of us who were the last people with Henry," he added.

"Oh. Okay. Well, you know that my cousin's girlfriend owns a place and—"

"Yes! That's right. What a great idea! Finnegan's on Broadway. We were planning on meeting somewhere midtown, but once you're on the subway, who cares? We talked, Belinda and Joe and Roger and I. And we thought we owed it to ourselves and to Henry to have our own private little event. Can you get us a corner at Finnegan's? A reserved corner?"

"Anyone can make reservations. But—"

"But you'll be someone they care about when you make the reservation."

"It's a pub. That means hospitality. They care about everyone."

"But more about you."

She gave up. "No problem. I'll make the reservation."

"Cool. So you'll join us all?" Jensen asked her.

"Sure. It'll be great."

Would it be great? she wondered. What was going on with Vivian now? The woman hadn't died; she was doing well. If that had changed, surely they'd all know.

And the majority of the museum was open, although there was a little time left for the cops to come back and look over the new stuff for the Henry Tomlinson section. Still…

"Love ya!" Jensen said, grabbing her by the shoulders and planting a quick kiss on her lips. "I'm so glad you're in for tonight! I was afraid that you wouldn't be."

"Nope, I'm in," Harley assured him. "Anyway, I thought there was work you needed me to do?"

"Yeah, look around the exhibit. Some of the work here is yours, like the prep stuff you were writing up before we even found the tomb. For someone who was going into criminology, you were quite the Egyptologist."

"Hey, lots of people do more than one thing in life. I love Egyptology. It was my minor, just not my major."

"That's my point here. Thing is, check it all out. Make sure there are no imbecilic mistakes."

"Okay. But I'm not the most qualified person to be doing this."

"Oh, come on! You *should've* been an Egyptologist. You were so good at all the stuff we delved into. You knew who thought what, all about the argument over the gods, everything. And you cared about what we were doing. You just wanted to do more with finger-prints and DNA and the detecting part of it. But this exhibition is your baby, too. Check it out for me. You're going to love it!"

He waved and started walking in the direction of the temple, then apparently decided he should go the other way. The temple was a dead end, except, of course, for museum employees. There was a back hall that led to the stairway and a number of museum offices.

"Where are you going?" she asked.

"To clean up—after the cops!" he told her.

"Clean up what?"

He didn't hear her or pretended not to. But he wasn't heading to his office. She had no idea what he was up to.

She glanced at her watch.

That was all he wanted? For her to verify exhibits? He'd said he'd needed help because Vivian wasn't there. And yet he didn't really need much.

Did it matter? She'd never get a chance like this again.

She wasn't even part of it all anymore; she was Jensen's guest and she was a guest because once, she *had* been a part of it all. She didn't embrace Egyptology with the same wonder that drove some of the others, but she did love ancient Egyptian history.

Nope, she probably wouldn't have another opportunity to wander the exhibit entirely alone.

For a moment, she stood still, and then she smiled. She hurried to the right, slipping into one of the rooms where the social and political climate of Amenmose's life and times were explained. She'd done a great deal of the research work and prepared a number of the papers from which the story in the exhibit had been taken.

Entering the first room, she looked around. Display cases held many items of day-to-day life; sure, there were fantastic necklaces and beautiful jewelry, but Harley had always been most fascinated by the storage jars, the pans and other cooking implements that told more about a basic everyday lifestyle.

The center in this exhibit was an exceptionally fine statue of the god Ra, depicted with the head of a falcon, the sun disc above him.

She read softly aloud. "'Ra—ancient Egyptian sun god. By the fifth dynasty, in the 25th to 24th centuries BC, he had risen to prominence, and would be joined by others at various times. Tutankhamen's great changes after his father's reign and his own ascension to the throne involved bringing back the old religion. Under Akhenaten's rule, the old gods had been disrespected; many statues and other honorary sites were destroyed. His dedication to his religion—he wanted to see the deity Aten, the disc of Ra, the sun god, worshipped above all else—caused a weakness in the Egyptian military and a lack of action that was seen as a betrayal by a number of the kingdom's allies. Tutankhamen meant to undo the harm, as he saw it, his father had done. He wanted to bring back all the old gods, including Amun and Mut and others who made up the hierarchy of ancient Egyptian power. Amun-Ra, as Ra was often called, and the others would return. Tutankhamen felt his father's legacy was one of destruction, and under *his* rule, the world would improve. To that end, he looked to the priest Amenmose, despite the fact that the priest Ay was in power as the boy king's regent.'"

She let her words settle in the empty room. "Pretty good," she said with satisfaction.

There was an inner sarcophagus of a handmaiden, buried with Amenmose, in the last of the horseshoe-shaped displays. The woman, at least judging by the artist who had painted her face for the sarcophagus, had been beautiful.

"What do you think?" she asked the image of the long-dead woman. "The New Kingdom, Middle Kingdom, Old Kingdom—it can all be so confusing. Not to mention the dynasties! Anyway, I think the display works, and I had a lot to do with that. It's simple enough to be understood, without leaving out any important facts. Of course, in my view, young King Tut was probably murdered, too. But we'll never find out now, since Howard Carter found that tomb so long ago!"

She read the little note beneath the sarcophagus. The young woman's name had been Ser. She'd served Amenmose in his household. She hadn't been killed for the purpose of being placed in his tomb. She'd succumbed to a fever before his death, and had been moved here to lie with the man she had served so loyally.

Next to her was a servant, Namhi. Like Amenmose, Namhi had been strangled. There was no explanation anywhere on his wrappings or in the tomb. From all that she had read, Harley suspected that either Namhi had been used as an instrument of murder, or he had belonged to the cult of Aten-Aten, a secret society pretending to agree with Tutankhamen's return to the old religion while trying to undermine it at the same time. It had been suspected during Amenmose's lifetime that Namhi was a leader of the cult. That alone would make Ay want to murder him, as well as Amenmose.

But Amenmose might also have been murdered by Tutankhamen's half sister or brother-in-law.

Ay had actually been the grand vizier. And, upon Tutankhamen's death, he would become pharaoh.

"You all had motive," Harley murmured.

Yes, just as it seemed everyone did today in the murder of Henry Tomlinson and the attempted murder of Vivian Richter. No one had a solid motive—or, rather, they all had the same motives! Fame, position in life, in society. But…was that enough to make someone kill?

Harley turned to look at the case where mummified animals were displayed. She was staring at a mummified cat when she heard the bone-chilling sound of a cat screeching as if all four paws and its tail had been caught in a car door.

She froze; she felt goose bumps forming all over her body.

There were no cats in the museum. Not living cats, anyway!

A complete silence followed the sound. And then Harley became certain that she heard movement in one of the side rooms off the Amenmose exhibit main hall.

She remained still, listening.

She'd spent her life priding herself on her logic. Obviously, a mummified cat had not let out a yowl. It was more than possible that someone else was in the exhibit. And possible that a cat had somehow found its way in. There might well be police in the prep areas and in the offices behind the public areas of the museum.

Despite her logical reasoning, there was no way to explain the sensations she was feeling. They were different from anything she'd ever known.

She quickly slipped from the side room where she'd

been, the first one next to the temple. She thought she saw movement at the end of the hall.

A person, wearing something dark.

That hall was a dead end for visitors. There was a magnificent podium that held the giant-size lion sculptures that had guarded the inner door to the Amenmose tomb. You walked around it and saw the second side of the exhibit before exiting to the rest of the museum.

She told herself she had no reason to be afraid that someone was there. People worked here, for heaven's sake! The cops and crime scene techs were probably still trying to figure out how Vivian Richter had been assaulted with nicotine poison.

But…

There'd been something furtive about the dark figure.

Well, at least it hadn't been a mummy walking around. The person had definitely not been in decaying and frayed linen wrappings.

Whoever it was wore black. Head-to-toe black. Slinking around.

Crazy!

The room she was in displayed different stages of mummification. There was a life-size display in which a mannequin was being dried with natron on a prep table, while priests said their prayers and sprinkled him with some kind of herb water or oil. In the next window, the wrapping process itself was displayed.

The next room was filled with sarcophagi and mummies, wrapped, half-wrapped and unwrapped. And among them…

She paused again, gazing at Unknown Mummy #1. She suddenly, vividly, remembered the night Henry had died. She could see the interior of the prep tent, could see Henry, his face reflecting his enthusiasm.

Somebody brushed by something out in the hallway.

Anyone might have been there! Working, investigating, exploring.

No. The person was moving…

Furtively.

She hurried to the door and looked outside. She could run back to the statues and escape into the back to the offices and prep rooms behind the scenes.

She could demand that whoever it was show him or herself.

And wind up with a belt or other object around her neck, or poisoned linen wrapped around her body?

She realized that her heart was thundering. In a thousand years, she could never have imagined being so frightened in the middle of the day in a museum. She wasn't sure she'd been this frightened even when they were forced to flee the Sahara.

Harley flattened herself against the wall, waiting.

She was startled to hear the scream of a cat again.

That was no damned mummy! There was a living cat in the museum—fact!

But she wasn't staying to search for it.

She burst out into the hallway, racing toward the exit.

"Harley!"

She heard her name; it was a heated whisper. She sensed somehow that it wasn't a threat, but by then she was propelling herself forward at a frantic pace.

"Harley!"

That whisper of her name again.

She wasn't going to make the exit.

She turned and saw Micah Fox standing there.

One minute she was running, her feet barely touching the floor.

The next…

She'd fallen flat on her back, blinking up at the man straddling her.

"Harley! Damn!"

Fox. Micah Fox. Special Agent Micah Fox.

She stared at him blankly. For a moment, she wondered if *he'd* been stalking her through the Amenmose exhibit.

"There was someone in here!" she said. "Watching me."

"Yes," he said flatly. "And thanks to you, that someone has gotten away."

Micah rose to his feet and helped Harley to hers. "What?" she demanded. "How?"

"I had him—or her. I don't even know which it was. Then you made enough noise to raise a legion of the dead—"

"Oh, no, no, no! *You* were the one making the noise!" Harley told him.

"Harley, if you'd just stayed where you were…"

"And let someone get me? What a bright comment from a law enforcement officer!"

"Harley," he began, then broke off and halfway smiled, lowered his head and shook it slightly. "Sorry. I guess I think of you as Craig's cousin, and as a student of criminology, and I suppose…"

"You suppose what?"

"That you'll behave as if you were trained in criminal behavior and…well, working a case."

She stood there, still staring at him, pursing her lips. Then she offered him an icy smile. "Okay, let's put it this way. Take doctors. Some are great practitioners and others are diagnosticians. My training helps us to figure out what happened—not to bulldoze our way into a situation with guns blazing!"

He listened to her speak; his reaction was undeniable amusement.

"Okay, whatever. Let's go to the offices here and see who we can see, yes?" he asked her.

She turned and headed for the doors marked Cast Members Only—as if they were at a theme park rather than a museum—and pushed her way in. She feared for a moment that the doors would be locked. They were not.

A long hall stretched before her. To the left were offices; to the right were the labs and prep rooms.

She could see that one door was marked with the name Gordon Vincent. She hadn't really met him, she realized, and he wasn't just in charge of the Amenmose exhibit, but the entire museum. His appearance was perfect for the part; he was solid, about six feet even, gray-haired and entirely dignified. The office beside his bore a temporary name; that was obvious from the way the name placard had been slipped over another, the name being Arlo Hampton. Next to his office, the jerry-rigged nameplate read Vivian Richter.

Jensen Morrow had his own office, since he was now an employee of the museum.

No one was in the hall. Looking through the large plate-glass windows to the lab, they could see that Arlo wasn't in his office; he was in the lab. He was working with one of the unnamed mummies they'd found in the tomb, running the X-ray machine over the remains. Harley waited until he'd completed his task. Then she tapped on a window. Arlo raised his head, startled. He saw Harley and offered her a large smile—then noticed Micah and didn't seem quite so pleased. He disappeared for a moment as he walked through the changing area and then opened the hallway door to let them in.

He beamed; in fact, he seemed to come alive as he met Harley's gaze.

He did not seem concerned that a woman, a colleague, was in the hospital. That someone had attempted to murder her in a particularly grotesque manner.

"Harley, nice to see you. Jensen said he asked you to come in. I believe he was going to ask you to work with him on a few last additions we're thinking of adding. I'll tell you the truth, I wish you'd been one of ours. I want a room on what we've discovered from the mummies—and what we know about their deaths. Oh, the whole Tut thing is still speculation, and that's not ours to tear apart. This is!"

"Thanks," Harley said, wondering why Jensen hadn't mentioned that. "I'm happy to help with…whatever's needed."

"Great. And you, Agent Fox." Arlo turned to him. "Are you part of the police investigation? They were here all night. They found nothing. Of course, they still have Vivian's office closed off and we won't open this section until tomorrow, but…wow."

"Yeah, wow," Micah said, his tone flat. "So, what do *you* think happened to Vivian Richter?"

"Her husband's with her now," Arlo said. "I mean, needless to say, we care most about the living. It's just that…well, the world can't stop because something bad happened to someone."

"Yeah, but that bad thing happened right here," Micah reminded him.

"Of course," Arlo said. "But…it had to be a prank, right? She didn't die. I'm thinking some college student who suffered some kind of slight at our hands was in here and played a prank on her."

"Nicotine poisoning is no prank."

Arlo looked truly perplexed. "Someone definitely came in through the back, to get to her. Otherwise, whoever it was would've been on the cameras. The only people picked up on the security video cameras in this section were the two of you and Jensen Morrow. But, of course, there are entrances from the basement on up—a few secret entrances. Did you know the building itself was originally erected by Astor as a bank? That's why there's the gorgeous foyer and all. But speaking of secret entrances, the cops are looking at everything. Oh yeah, you're a cop. Okay, sort of a cop. Do you want a tour?"

"I would love a tour," Micah told him. "But first, who else is working today?"

"Well, define 'working.' I think everyone's been in. The only one not really part of the new exhibit is Harley. Belinda, Joe and Roger have been giving it about ten hours a week. Jensen is here full-time, which I'm sure you know. Joe and Belinda both have full-time jobs with two of the other major museums in the city, and Roger is teaching now. They were all in at one time or another this morning, checking out their space. The cops tore through everything, looking for the source of the wrapping and the poison. But honestly, I don't think we even have any natural linen back here. And any idiot knows that's not how you make an ancient Egyptian mummy. But—"

"So who else was here this morning, Arlo?"

"Let's see. Ned Richter was in. Left the hospital, popped over here and went back. But he was here."

"And the others?" Harley asked.

"Yes, like I said, at one time or another. I've been busy, as you can see. We still have a wealth of remains and artifacts. There was the mess with that so-called insurgent group, but then the company and the government sent guys with big trucks and equipment, and they emptied the tomb—including all the mummies—before thieves could. Oh yeah, some people see the Western world as one giant thief, but everything we have is cleared through the Egyptian government and will be returned, and that was common knowledge from the get-go."

Arlo seemed to consider it more important to honor international agreements than to worry about anything else.

Admirable.

But Henry had died. And Vivian might have died, too.

"I'd love that tour now," Micah said, smiling. Harley saw the way his face moved when he smiled. Obviously, despite his work, he smiled a lot. He had the kind of smile that made her wonder what it would be like if they were just talking together at a restaurant, in a class...

"I can't give you a tour of the entire place. We're going to concentrate on this exhibit. You'll notice that our offices are in this section with the directors, with Gordon Vincent. He's a very smart, well-educated and supportive guy. He purposely keeps his office over here. That way, whatever is new, he's in on it."

"So he might have been in his office before Vivian came out screaming?" Micah asked.

"I suppose so," Arlo replied. "But are you suggesting Gordon was involved? Really? I don't think so."

Harley didn't, either. He hadn't been on the expedition. She could tell that Micah didn't think Vincent was guilty of anything, either; he was just covering his bases.

"Show me around, please. That would be great," Micah said.

"Okay, let's go!"

Arlo ripped off his paper lab coat and set out. "As you can see, that's a lab—a 'clean room' lab, if you will. You have to coat up, glove up and mask up before going in. You never know what might've been in the ground for millennia! And over there, the museum offices. Now, we're on the ground floor, or so you'd think. Directly beneath us is the cafeteria and there's another rotunda-like area for international exhibits. That one's a bit different. International, of course, but Egyptology has always had a place in the higher echelon of what people find fascinating in a museum. And, sadly, museums are bottom-line—everyone needs donations and funding and numbers—and mummies are a draw. Always have been. Even though they were so plentiful in Victorian times that people used them for kindling! Yes, those good religious uptight folk used human remains as kindling."

He kept talking, pointing out different research rooms and more offices. Then he came to a staircase. It was an old stone circular staircase, high and steep. "This led down to the vaults at one time. It wouldn't have been easy to steal from this place when it was a bank!"

They followed him down to the basement and then the sub-basement.

"Does this bypass the actual basement?"

"Yes, these stairs do. And…" Arlo turned, shining a flashlight at them, although they were still receiving ample light from above. "It'll get dark in here!" he warned.

Harley took a penlight from her purse at the same time as Micah drew one from his pocket. She was rather proud of herself for never leaving home without one!

"You can still kind of see. There was emergency lighting put down here before the place went belly-up during the Great Depression," Arlo told them. "As you can tell, the design of the hallways is almost like a perfect cross, and each of them opens out to five vaults. The elite of the elite had their treasure down there. The museum will use the space eventually, but at this stage, it's not really needed yet. Anyway, the quality of the exhibits means more than the quantity."

Arlo was quite happy to keep talking. They saw what he meant about the cross design, and each section held vaults of slightly different sizes.

"And there's a way out?" Harley asked.

Arlo didn't get a chance to answer. There was a narrow area that simply looked like an empty space at the end of the vault area facing Central Park. Micah headed that way.

Harley followed Micah, and Arlo followed her.

"What's going on?" Arlo asked when Micah came to a stop.

Micah had found something. Harley could hear metal grating and squealing; she realized he'd come to a door. That he'd gotten it open.

She came up behind him and looked over his shoulder. All she saw was black.

"Abandoned subway tunnel. They're all over the city," he murmured.

"I guess that's one way out. Or you can just walk out the door that leads back up to the park and picnic area at the side of the museum," Arlo said, pointing to the right. "But an abandoned subway. I think I'd heard rumors, but never really knew if they were true of not. Cool!"

"Yeah. Cool," Micah said wryly. "So, does everyone know about that way out—to the park area?" he asked Arlo.

"Oh, I wouldn't think so," Arlo replied. "Just people who work here. And maybe people they've told."

"We might want to get a lock on the door to that exit," Micah said. "And to the subway tunnels. The info could easily have been tweeted across the country. Maybe it has." He paused, studying Harley. "We'll get a few of our people down here," he told her. "I need to go over to the hospital. I've been told that Vivian is conscious and speaking. But I'll need to find you later. Do you know where you'll be?"

Harley hesitated. Then she shrugged. "Finnegan's," she told him. "Finnegan's on Broadway."

"Kieran's family's place?" he asked her.

"It's the only Finnegan's on Broadway."

"You'll definitely be there?"

"Oh, yes. I'll be meeting my colleagues from the expedition."

"Including me!" Arlo said happily. He sighed. "Well, we won't have Vivian there, and I doubt we'll have Ned Richter with Viv in the hospital."

"Henry. We won't have Henry," Harley said.

"No, we won't have Henry," Arlo agreed. He tried an awkward smile. "But at least we won't have any mummies running around at Finnegan's. A banshee or two, maybe, but no mummies!"

Neither of them managed even a small smile for his attempt at humor.

As they left, Harley remembered the cat she'd heard earlier. There'd been no further sound after Micah had appeared—claiming she'd frightened off the person who'd apparently been stalking her. The person he, in turn, had followed. And lost.

Chapter 4

"I was in my office," Vivian Richter said. "I was in my office…"

Her voice trailed off. Her face was set in a concentrated frown.

"In my office and then…"

"And then?" Micah pushed gently.

Vivian was in her hospital bed, in a seated position. Craig Frasier and Micah stood at the foot of the bed, patiently waiting.

Micah knew that the local cops had already been in. But it had only been a short time since the lead on the investigation had been handed over to the federal government. Vivian had let them know that she'd spoken with McGrady and Rydell. The nurse in the hallway had informed them that McGrady had brought Vivian to tears, demanding that she remember what she just couldn't.

Micah had received a call from Rydell, since it was still a joint task force, if a small one. Rydell had apologized for his partner.

For the most part, I work with great people. No one is better than the NYPD, Rydell had assured him.

Micah had told him not to worry; any agency in the world could come with a jerk or two—and McGrady was that jerk. He hadn't said that in so many words when he'd spoken to Rydell, but they both knew exactly who he was talking about.

"I'll bet you were excited about the exhibit," Micah told Vivian. "All the work that had been done. And then the discovery—and the terror in the desert, with Henry Tomlinson dead and the fear of armed rebels coming at the camp. But now, here, you have the culmination of your dream of getting the Amenmose exhibit up!"

"Oh, I was excited. So excited. And we were going to have all our grad students and Henry's niece and her family at the opening. And…oh! Those children. Henry's great-nieces and nephews. And there were probably other children there. And they saw me coming out like—?"

"A mummy. Vivian, think. Did anyone come in to see you in your office when you were getting ready for the grand celebration?"

Her frown deepened.

"Everyone had been there. Everyone. Ned, of course. We were excited together. He's administration and I'm an Egyptologist, but we're a married couple, and that made it an incredible night for both of us. Arlo, darting in and out with last-minute things. The grad students…they were all there. Belinda wanted me to look at her dress and Joe—that boy is such a flirt!—asked if he looked both dignified and handsome. Let's see, Jensen. He's full-time here now, you know. He was in more than once. And then..."

She went silent, dead silent, her mouth falling open in an awkward O of horror.

"What?" Craig asked.

"One of the mummies came in. It was walking. Yes, yes, that was it! There was a mummy. Oh, my God! A mummy... I remember now. It...stared at me!"

She began to shake. Micah and Craig glanced at each other, deciding it might be time to hit the nurse-call button.

But first they both moved close to her, each man taking one of her hands.

"It's going to be all right," Micah said in a soothing voice.

She shook her head. "Mummies don't walk. Except in really bad movies. Okay, even good movies... *The Mummy* with Brendan Fraser was good." She paused. The shaking had stopped, and she looked at Craig. "You any relation?"

"I'm afraid not. My last name's actually Frasier," Craig told her.

Vivian suddenly stared hard at Micah. "That was it, yes. I saw the mummy. I stood up—I'd been at my desk. I stood up, and I couldn't believe what I was seeing. It had to be a joke, a prank...but then the thing came at me and I tried to scream, or I think I did, and it kept coming...and..."

"And?" Micah asked.

"That's it. That's all I remember. A mummy came to life," she whispered.

"Vivian, you of all people know that a mummy didn't

come to life. Whoever was pretending to be a mummy wrapped you in linens that had been soaked with nicotine. That person wasn't a real mummy," Micah said.

"But…it seemed so real. Or surreal. But terrifying!" Vivian said.

"Vivian, someone who was in the museum at the time dressed up as a mummy to attack you. Do you have any idea why? Were you having an argument with anyone? Is there any reason— Well, I'll be blunt," Craig said. "Is there any reason anyone would want you dead?"

Vivian gasped. "Oh, God!"

Micah glanced at Craig. She must have just realized that someone had tried to kill her.

"No, no, no!" Vivian said. "I know I'm not the nicest human being in the world. I'm not a Pollyanna of any kind, but… I don't hurt people. I've never fired anyone, not that I have that kind of power. I'm not mean to people, I don't scream at them to work harder. I'm a decent person, damn it! No, there's no reason anyone would want to kill me!" she declared.

"Did you have a fight with anyone—anyone at all?" Micah asked.

She sighed. "Every once in a while, I get into it with Arlo. But that's just because…well, when Henry was alive, we all acknowledged him as the real guru. He had the experience. He was chosen by Alchemy to head up the exhibition, and he was chosen because all his research on Amenmose was so good and so thorough. With Henry gone, I think maybe Arlo and I have a bit of a rivalry going. But a healthy rivalry!"

"Arlo was working today."

"Of course he was. There's still much to be done.

You have to understand that the tomb was *filled* with mummies, including that of Amenmose. And, as with Tut, some of the funerary objects appear to have been reused. We have every reason to believe that Amenmose was murdered—and it must've happened quite suddenly. He was entombed with all the rites by someone who really loved him, but it was all hush-hush and under the radar. Ay did become the ruler after Tut died. Anyway, there's still so much to determine about our find! I'm sure everyone's working." She was quiet for a minute. "Including my husband. Bless Ned. He was so torn! But I've assured him that I'm on the way to being just fine and that the museum—at this moment— is the most important thing in our lives right now. And I'm getting great care here, so it's fine that he's gone."

Micah wasn't sure she was telling the truth. He wasn't convinced she didn't feel hurt that her husband wasn't with her.

But he didn't want to rub salt into any wounds.

He glanced at Craig. They would move on. Craig was probably doubting her words, too, but they wouldn't get different answers to what they'd asked—not at the moment. Time to ask other questions.

"What about the grad students? Any arguments with any of them?"

"Well, they're not grad students anymore, are they?" Vivian asked a little sharply. "I told you, I saw Belinda and Joe and…" She paused, sighing deeply. "I was a bit worried about seeing your cousin, Agent Frasier. She was so committed to Henry. We all loved him, but it was as if he saw her as a grandchild and she saw him as a wonderfully brilliant grandpa. She never got over his death. Then, of course, there's Jensen, and he's taken a permanent position with the museum. He helped her fight for Henry up to the end, and then… Henry was cremated. We had two different medical examiners give verdicts that suggested suicide, possibly brought on by a delirium caused by bacteria. Anyway, we'll probably never know just what was going on in Henry's mind. And…" She broke off again, looking from Micah to Craig. "Someone wanted me dead, too. But how did I get out in the foyer? How did I get help? Oh, it's all so terrifying!"

She began sobbing quietly.

Micah squeezed her hand. "Hey, you're going to be fine. So if there's anything, anything at all, please call one of us. We intend to find the truth. We *will* find the truth."

She nodded and squeezed his hand back. "Thank you," she said.

"Of course," he told her.

He thought she smiled.

There was a lively crowd at Finnegan's on Broadway that night, but then again, it was Friday.

New Yorkers had a tendency to be "neighborhood" people. On the Upper East Side, you found an Upper East Side hangout. There were lots of bars and pubs around Cooper Union, St. Mark's Place, the Villages, East and West, and any other neighborhood you could think of in the giant metropolis.

But Finnegan's drew people from everywhere. For one thing, it was one of the longest-running pubs in the city, dating back to pre–Civil War days. For another, it was run with a family feel, and somehow, people knew the right time to bring their kids and the right time not to. The kitchen was as important as the bar. It was simply a unique place, and Harley was delighted with Craig's association with the Finnegan family—and through him, her own connection to them.

She'd been able to reserve a corner near the entrance, against the wall and across from the actual bar tables.

Jensen got there first, greeting her with a hug and a kiss on each cheek. She wasn't sure just how far he would have gone; a waitress—a lovely girl who'd just arrived from Ireland, came by to take their order. That was when Joe Rosello walked in.

He had to flirt. But he couldn't seem to decide whether to flirt with Harley or the waitress.

He opted for both, which got him a punch on the shoulder from Jensen. "Hell, you can't take him any-where."

"You are atrocious," Harley told him, shaking her head.

"Hey! I just admire people and make them happy. I don't do anything evil!" Joe protested.

"We'll let it slide this time," Jensen said. "Lay off Harley, eh? She's seen you with the ladies. She knows your MO."

"Harley, do you really mind me telling you that you're gorgeous and mysterious and desirable in black?" Joe asked, sounding wounded.

"No, just don't slobber on my hand, please."

"Slobber? That was an elegant kiss!"

"Ah-ha! A very wet and elegant kiss!" Jensen said. By now, Roger had come in; he listened to the ongoing conversation, rolling his eyes. "And every one of us has a doctorate!" he murmured. "Pathetic. What is this world coming to?"

"I think the world was a mess long before we came along!" Belinda said, joining them.

It was then that Harley noticed Micah Fox; she hadn't seen him come in. He was standing at the bar with her cousin Craig. The oldest Finnegan, Declan, who ran the family establishment, was talking to the two men.

She had a feeling they were all watching her and her friends.

A minute later, Micah walked over and joined the group.

Harley wasn't the first to greet him; Belinda was. Harley was busy greeting Arlo, who had just arrived, and Ned Richter, who had apparently chosen to join them rather than stay with his wife at the hospital.

They were seated around two of the big mahogany tables in the corner, Ned Richter, Arlo, Joe, Roger and Belinda crowded in against the wall, and Craig, Micah, Harley and Jensen perched on the chairs across from them. There was ordering of drinks and meals, with casual conversation at first. And then Ned Richter raised his glass and said, "In memory of Henry Tomlinson, the greatest Egyptologist I ever knew and one of the finest men to have ever walked this earth, as well."

"Hear, hear!" the others chimed in.

They all raised a glass to Henry, and then Ned continued with, "And to the bastard who hurt my Vivian—may these agents and cops find him, and may he rot in hell!"

"Hear, hear!" another cry went up.

"That's harsh," Jensen teased. "At least you're among friends."

"That's what an Irish pub is all about," Richter reminded them all, drawing a round of laughter. He went on, saying, "Sorry, I can't help it. I hope the bastard dies a hideous death."

Harley wondered why he wasn't with his wife, since he was so devastated by what had been done to her.

But she was wedged between Jensen and Micah, and she was very aware of both men being so close to her. She found herself wondering, too, just what connected people. She was seated between two very fine men. Both exceptionally good-looking and bright—and both engaged with the world…in completely different ways.

She liked them both.

And yet, sitting there, she knew why she wasn't with Jensen, why they hadn't gone out. Each man's interest was unmistakable.

But only one man's seemed to matter.

She was attracted to Micah Fox. She barely knew him, and yet when she'd seen him again, just the sound of his voice had aroused her senses.

"Seriously, who would've done such a thing? Harley, what do you remember?"

Harley realized that her mind had completely—and inappropriately—wandered. Belinda was staring at her, brown eyes wide, and waiting for an answer.

Harley took a sip of her drink—a Kaliber non-alcoholic beer by Guinness, since she'd decided she couldn't risk losing an ounce of control tonight. She hoped someone would say something that explained Belinda's question.

She felt Micah's eyes on her. Maybe he knew she'd been distracted. Hopefully, he didn't know that her mental absence at the table had been due to him.

"About that night…that night in the Sahara," he said.

"We were all so excited," she began, and around her, Jensen, Joe, Roger and Belinda all nodded.

"And we were rewarded!" Ned Richter said.

"A find beyond measure!" Arlo agreed.

"We'd started to bring some things from the tomb into the prep tent," Harley said. "It's a special tent, temperature-controlled. Everyone's careful there. Amenmose's tomb turned out to have more than a dozen mummies and sarcophagi—all in different states of disrepair and decay. We've proven that Amenmose was murdered, so after it happened, someone who loved him borrowed—or stole—funerary objects from the dead who'd passed on before him. They also brought together people, dead and alive, who'd served him."

"Why would they do that? Why go out and find people who'd already died to bury with him?" Micah asked her. "I studied Egyptology," he said sheepishly, "but, I don't understand—taking people who have already died and their things. It's like robbing the dead. It *is* robbing the dead."

"He would need servants in his next life. Servants, women… He would need people and animals, just as he'd need his bow and shield," Harley explained.

"I know about objects needed for the next life. I guess I never heard of them being taken from somewhere else…dead, or still alive."

Micah seemed to move even closer to her. She could feel his eyes; she could almost feel his touch. His elbow was on the table and his fingers dangled near her lap.

She forced herself to concentrate. "We worked really hard that day—for hours and hours. I'm pretty sure it was close to eight o'clock. There was a little village not far from the dig and the people there were incredibly nice. We'd go sometimes to have dinner and maybe sit with coffee at a place there, something like a family-run restaurant or cantina. But we decided in the end that Jensen and I would go by ourselves and bring back food. Jensen came to get me while I was trying to talk Henry into coming with us. We were all tired, of course." She glanced over at Belinda who was still watching her with wide brown eyes. "Belinda was Skyping with Al. he was in Iraq at the time, I think."

"Iraq, yes, just about to leave," Belinda said.

"And Roger was working on tech and communications because we were hearing rumors about an upstart hate group, so he didn't go." She turned to Joe and couldn't help grinning. "Joe was still moving some of the artifacts. We had a lovely young Egyptian as our interpreter. Satima Mahmoud. They were…working."

"Working, right!" Belinda mocked, then laughed affectionately. "Joe was flirting."

"What? I don't flirt!" Joe protested.

"You're a flirt!"

Harley was sure they all said the words at the same time.

Joe flushed and shrugged. "She's really pretty. And smart."

"That she is," Harley agreed.

"So, Jensen," Micah said, looking past Harley, "you and Harley went out together that night. How long were you gone?"

Jensen thought it over, raising a brow at Harley. "Hour and a half maybe?"

"Somewhere in there. An hour to an hour and a half," Harley said.

Micah nodded, then swiveled around to look at Ned

Richter and Arlo Hampton. "Neither of you checked on Henry during that time?"

"There was no need to check on Henry!" Ned Richter said. "We had security on the outskirts of the camp. Henry was completely in his element, like a kid in a candy store. I wouldn't have interrupted him."

"And you?" Micah asked Arlo. "Shouldn't you have been in there with him?"

"No, because I—"

Arlo turned beet red and stopped speaking.

"You what?"

"I was working," Arlo said.

"On what?" Ned Richter demanded.

Arlo looked guiltily around. "Well, I had one of the funerary tablets in my tent."

"You took a tablet from the find into your tent?" Ned repeated, his tone grating.

"Well, you see, I was interpreting, trying to figure out just what had happened at this site and how. It wasn't usual, having that many dead in a tomb. I was transcribing the tablet."

"What did it say?" Harley asked. She'd never heard about the tablet.

Arlo flushed miserably again. "I don't know."

"No artifacts in private tents," Ned told him, irritated. "I'm not going to fire your ass or anything over it, but damn it, that's the last time, Arlo. We follow the rules at Alchemy."

"What did the tablet say?" Harley persisted.

"I don't know," Arlo said again, his expression peevish.

"You didn't translate?" Harley asked.

"I didn't have time. I got through a zillion lines of

how wonderful Amenmose had been and then...you started screaming."

"I'd just found a friend—dead!"

"Well, yes, you screamed, and then everyone had to come and look at Henry. Then we heard we were about to be attacked, and *then* we were all helping when it came to loading up what we could, trying to get to the airport in Cairo."

"Yes, but where—"

"Harley, I haven't the faintest idea where the damned tablet ended up!" Arlo said. "I thought we were getting together tonight to be supportive, and you're all accusing me of terrible things!"

"We didn't *accuse* you," Ned pointed out drily. "You admitted you took an artifact."

Arlo sighed. "Where were *you*? What were you doing? Why wasn't Vivian with Henry? She's the one who loves it all so, so much!"

"I had gone to get dinner to bring with Jensen. And, then, of course, when we got back, we were busy making plans to get everyone and everything out of the desert! That was a nightmare. What the hell? We're going to attack one another now?"

"Hey, guys, you all came here to honor Henry!" Micah reminded them.

Jensen laughed. "You're the one who started this."

"Yes, I am," Micah said seriously. "Henry died out there that night. Now Vivian's been attacked. I wonder if you realize just how lethal nicotine poisoning can be."

"I certainly realize," Ned Richter said hoarsely.

"We all do. It's just that...we wouldn't have hurt Henry!" Belinda said. "And... I have no idea what went on with Vivian. No idea," she repeated softly.

"Nor do I. She was in her office," Jensen said.

"And you last saw her when?"

"I told the police—I told anyone who asked. I saw her about an hour before the celebration started. She was in her office, said hi, then waved me out. She seemed too busy to worry about the opening ceremonies, although she definitely showed up later. She loves the exhibit, you know."

"The rest of you? Did anyone see her before the celebration?" Micah asked.

"I saw her at about four o'clock," Ned Richter said. "She came to my office. She wanted permission for more expensive testing. I told her we had to hold off for a while." He paused and then added, "Every once in a while, I have to make her understand my position. I'm a CEO. I can't give in to her just because she's my wife. *Especially* because she's my wife. She's a highly qualified Egyptologist, but she didn't even work for Alchemy at first. She has her position due to me, so…"

"I waved to her," Arlo offered. "I was working in the lab. She didn't wave back. She was concentrating on whatever she was doing. Then again, that's Vivian's way."

"I didn't see her at all," Belinda said. "You know, not until…"

"Me, neither," Joe said.

"Nor me," Roger chimed in.

"Thanks." Micah lifted his glass. "So, to the evening, then, huh? To Henry, our mentor, a man we all loved dearly… I assume?"

Assent was quickly voiced by everyone in the group. "To Henry!"

Their waitress came by; Harley noted that Micah

made a point of dropping any questioning at that point. Instead, he ordered the pub's very popular shepherd's pie.

He clearly had the ability to be very charming when he chose. He got Belinda to speak about her upcoming marriage—she was supposed to have a Christmas wedding—and he got Arlo talking about the way he'd fallen in love with mummies at the Chicago Field Museum as a kid. Joe, in his turn, became enthusiastic and wistful talking about the beautiful Satima Mahmoud and what an excellent interpreter she'd been, helping whenever anyone needed it. They'd come this close to having an affair, he admitted, and then, of course, everything had gone to hell.

Roger talked about his love for the desert—and his happiness over the fact that they were home. There was no place like New York. He loved being home, he said; he loved his job.

Ned didn't stay more than an hour, since he was going back to the hospital to be with his wife.

No one else seemed to want to break up their get-together, but it was growing late. The fine Irish band playing that night announced their last number.

The evening inevitably came to an end.

"So who sees to it that our lovely companions get home okay?" Joe asked, rising and indicating Belinda and Harley.

"No need to worry about me," Harley assured them. "Seriously. The tall, dark, handsome and deadly-looking guy at the bar is my cousin."

"Oh, Craig's here! I didn't realize. He should've joined us," Belinda said.

"Maybe he didn't want this to look like an inquisition," Jensen said, staring at Micah.

"Maybe," Micah said casually. The two men were almost the same height, both about six-three. Micah was smiling, not about to get into it—and not about to back down.

"If you're tired, I can take you to your place," Jensen told Harley.

"I'm fine, really," she said. "My cousin, remember? Craig is my cousin."

"Yeah, he is," Jensen said. For a moment, his eyes fell on her, and she thought he might be feeling something like jealousy over her preference for Craig's company rather than his. But although they'd teased and flirted, they'd never dated; they'd never been more than friends. She liked that he was protective. However, he didn't have any grounds to be jealous. At least not of Craig…

"Fine. Belinda?" Jensen said.

She laughed. "I'm a native New Yorker. I've been taking the latest subway most of my life. But sure."

"Your fiancé is a man serving his nation, Belinda. It's my privilege to see you safely home. And," he added, "I'm damned good with the subways myself."

"Okay, thanks. Come on. I'll make tea when we get to my place—so you can get yourself safely home after that!" Belinda left with Jensen's arm around her.

Harley realized that, as the others trailed out, she was still standing near the exit with Micah.

"Strange," he muttered.

"What is?"

"He's the one person who can't be guilty."

"Who? You mean Jensen?"

Micah turned to look at her, studying her eyes

thoughtfully, his own pensive. "Yes. He was with you in the desert. The two of you saw Henry alive together, and then you left together, and when you came back, Henry was dead."

"Yes. Why do you find Jensen suspicious?"

"Something about him."

"They teach you that at the academy?" Harley asked.

"Actually, yes. But never mind." He took her elbow. She was startled by the way she reacted to his simple touch.

"Shall we join Craig?" he asked.

They did. Craig stood politely to offer Harley his bar stool, but almost on cue, the cuddling couple who'd been taking up the seats next to him rose, hand in hand, seeing nothing but each other. They began to wander from the bar and toward the exit. Craig gestured at the three stools conveniently left for them and they all sat down.

Micah went over the conversations at the bar and Harley knew that Jensen had been right; Micah really had been grilling all of them.

If Craig had joined them, it wouldn't have been a get-together.

It would've been an inquisition, just as he'd said.

Kieran came from the back office, sliding in comfortably with her back to Craig's chest, leaning against him on his bar stool.

"Make any headway?" she asked.

"Ah, yes, Special Agent Fox has had a gut feeling," Harley replied.

"I don't trust the guy," Micah said mildly. "Jensen."

"Hmm," Kieran murmured.

"The psychologist's deep, dark 'hmm'!" Craig said. "There must be a Freudian meaning there!"

"No, I don't think there's a rational explanation for

a gut feeling." Kieran shook her head. "But perhaps if there's dislike involved…"

"Don't dislike the guy. He seems okay. But I sense that he's not quite trustworthy," Micah said.

"Ah." Harley shrugged. "I have a hard time seeing Jensen as a criminal. And in our group, Joe's the one who tends to go off on tangents, not that it means he's guilty of anything. But he's easily distracted."

"By the beautiful Egyptian girl," Micah said. "Satima Mahmoud."

"Yes, and she's still in Egypt, so I doubt she had anything to do with last night," Harley said.

"You know for sure that she's still in Egypt?" Micah asked.

"I, um…"

Harley was forced to pause. "No. Of course I don't know *for sure* that she's in Egypt. I assume she is. It's where she lives and works."

"Worth checking on," Micah said. He was, however, aiming the remark at Craig, who nodded in agreement.

"I think I need to go home." Harley stood up, yawning.

"I've got a car today. We'll get you home," Craig said. "Kieran? You ready?"

"You guys go ahead. I promised Declan some help figuring out an invoice."

"No, it's okay! I go home alone all the time," Harley said. "You—"

"Micah, you take the car," Craig interrupted. "Pick me up in the morning. I'll wait here with Kieran. Declan can drop us off or we'll grab an Uber."

"I can grab an Uber, too. I'm really close, just by Grace Church," Harley said.

"No," Craig insisted. "Let Micah take you, please. This whole mummy thing is...creepy."

"I'm not afraid of mummies."

"You should be. But only of the living ones," Kieran said. "Living people who are pretending to be mummies. Or having other people dress up like mummies. Anyway, get home safely, okay?"

Arguing would make her appear...argumentative, Harley thought.

"Thanks," she said simply. She turned away, aware that she was trembling slightly. It was a ride—a ride home. She wasn't afraid of Micah. She was afraid of herself.

She felt intensely attracted to the man. She'd sat at their table in the bar, wondering how she could be seated between two men with all the right stuff—and feel such an attraction to one and not the other.

She knew nothing at all about Micah Fox, except that he was with the FBI, that he'd worked with Craig and that Craig seemed to like him. And that he'd also been a student of Henry's.

That was the sum total of her knowledge. Was it enough of a basis for...anything?

Or had she spent the past year drifting, trying to develop an interest in someone, and not managing to find any kind of spark, any reason to pursue a relationship, even just a sexual one?

But if this was sexual, did it matter?

It did! He'd loved Henry, too. He was friends with Craig.

What if she threw herself at him, and he turned her down?

She was afraid her thoughts were making her blush, so she kissed her cousin and Kieran good-night and led the way, with Micah right behind her. She explained that it was ridiculous that he felt he had to drive her; it was maybe a mile away at most.

"Yeah, but it's late," Micah said.

She knew that the cars Craig used that belonged to the bureau could be parked just about anywhere. Except that parking wasn't easy in Lower Manhattan—or pretty much anywhere in Manhattan!

"You can drop me off in front of the building, and thank you again," Harley told him.

"I don't think so." He gave her a smile. "Sorry, even if you weren't Craig's cousin, it wouldn't be my style."

"You'll never find parking."

"Yes, I will. The academy also taught us how to summon our individual parking witches," he said, his tone droll.

She pursed her lips and sighed. "Great. Witches? I thought people had parking fairies."

"Not in the academy. Witches are scarier. They get rid of the other cars, frighten them off, you know?"

He did have a parking witch—or damned good luck. She was surprised at how close he got to her building.

He walked her there, and stepped inside with her. He saw the security guard and nodded in approval.

And, of course, he could leave her right there. She was obviously safe; her building had keyed entry and security! The push of a button summoned the police in the event of any trouble.

She found herself staring at him, waiting.

"Good building," he told her.

"Thanks."

She hesitated. She wanted to kick herself. She was standing here so casually—surely she was standing casually; surely she could speak casually!——but she didn't want to let him go. Something was alive inside her, something burning, hot, shaking, nervous…something that made her feel as if she was in her teens again. She'd done very little except study and work over the past year, trying to struggle up from the strange void Henry's death had created.

"Did you want to come up for…tea?" she finally ventured. "Or something stronger? And a view of Grace Church?" she asked. She had to sound like an idiot. "I'm keyed up tonight. I don't know why. I keep thinking we should all be exhausted…"

"Yes."

"What?"

"Sure, I'd love to come up."

"Oh! Um, great." She turned and headed for the elevators, praying that her flushed face wouldn't betray the way she suddenly longed to forget every propriety, every word, and just fall into his arms.

Preferably naked!

Chapter 5

"This place is incredible!" Micah said, looking around her loft. He glanced at her with a curious frown. "Did I miss something about you? You're a trust fund baby?"

She laughed. "I happen to have an uncle who isn't living here right now. He was a snow bird, but these days he's spending most of his time in Florida. He's had the place for fifty years, and I'm pretty sure his dad had it before him. They were both in construction, so they did a great job with the space. However, only in NYC, Tokyo, Mexico City and a few other cities around the globe would this be considered a big space. You must've tried to rent in New York at some point."

He nodded, staring out the windows at Grace Church.

"I went to Brown, and then to Columbia University, so I lived here for a while," he told her. He grinned drily. "I think I lived in a closet."

"Ah, Columbia," she murmured. "But you knew Henry at Brown, right?"

"Yep. I knew Henry. I went on to Columbia, where I was a grad student. I didn't particularly intend to be an Egyptologist, but I was considering anthropology or archeology. And then…"

His voice trailed off. He shrugged and then turned to look at her again. "My senior year as an undergrad, a friend of mine was kidnapped. The FBI tracked down the kidnappers. My friend's family was rich, and yes, they were going for a ransom. But…well, one of the guys admitted after they were caught that they hadn't intended to let him live. I guess I kind of fell into a bit of hero worship for the FBI. So, I switched to criminology. I knew I wanted to do what those agents had done."

"I'm sure you made a great choice. I know how Craig feels. Of course, my whole family worries about him, but we all believe he made a great decision."

"Yeah. Sometimes, though, the bitter truth is that you lose, too. Things don't always work out the way you want them to."

"You didn't lose with Henry. You were never in the fight," Harley said quietly.

He nodded. "Yeah? Thanks. Well, I suppose I should get going."

"I'm still wide-awake. Um…can I get you something to drink? I was going to make tea. Oh, it's not decaffeinated. I mean, that's never made much of a difference to me, but…"

"Caffeine. Sounds good."

"Okay."

She turned in her little kitchen area and put the kettle on. He perched on one of the bar stools. Facing her, he also faced the kitchen. Spinning around on any of the stools, you'd still have the great view of Grace Church. She waited for the water to boil, aware that he watched her as she got out mugs and tea bags.

She needed to let him go. And she needed to let go of her interest in him—emotional and physical!

"How's it going with Officer Friendly?" she asked.

"McGrady?" he asked. "He's kind of irrelevant. The powers that be have gotten the NYC office put in charge," he told her. "Henry's death may not be related to what happened at the opening ceremony, but on the other hand, it might have been. That makes this not just national but international, and luckily the FBI does work out of an office in Cairo. It was my first avenue of investigation last year when I heard about Henry. I wasn't officially on the case, but I went to Cairo. I knew our guys would be sympathetic. This might be a terrible thing to say, but I think Detective McGrady might've been disappointed that he wound up with a live victim. He wanted a murder case."

"You still have to deal with him, though?"

"Yes, but he's not really interested now. Rydell's a good guy, and he keeps apologizing for his partner. We haven't made any complaints. We're trying to keep it all copacetic."

"Where would someone get nicotine for a poisoning like that? I gather the linens were soaked in it and only the fact that they got them off her so fast saved Vivian's life, right?"

"Right."

The kettle whistled, and Harley poured the water into two mugs. Their fingers nearly touched as she pushed his toward him, as they both dipped their tea bags in the hot water. She flushed, catching his eyes on her.

She really, really needed to let him go.

That or...

Give in. Spit out the truth that she was incredibly attracted to him. Totally inappropriate under the circumstances, but they *were* adults, after all. It could just be sex; she could handle that. And they could try to figure out what was going on between them after this case was solved.

"We have people looking into large purchases of nicotine, but—"

"Insecticide," Harley interrupted, thinking of the most obvious place to buy commercial nicotine.

He sipped his tea and nodded. "I forgot. Research for an investigation agency is what you've been doing."

"Part-time. I've been trying to sort out what to do with my career. And this job pays well." She shrugged. "Only a few of the cases I've worked on have actually been criminal. Mostly civil suits. A lot of my time's been spent monitoring bad behavior. People trying to get a relative to leave money to one person or another, husbands and wives behaving poorly and, very sadly, in one case that did become criminal—stopping a blood relative from preying on a young boy. The job's been interesting, but I haven't been sure what I want to do, which way I want to go. But since I met Kieran, I've come to like the psychology part. I think I'd like to get into profiling."

"You certainly have the right degrees."

"It all looks good on paper. I'd have to see how I do in practice."

"Want to practice?" he asked her.

"What do you mean?"

He was suddenly very serious. "Think of all the people you know who were involved with the Amenmose expedition and exhibit. Who would have a reason to kill Henry? Was money ever an issue?"

"Not that I know of—other than the fact that an archeologist's prestige means more money the next time he or she wants to go out on a project. But I'm sure you're aware of that."

Harley realized she was leaning against the counter. He was seated in one of the stools, so that meant she was leaning closer and closer to him. Their fingers, wrapped around their mugs, were only inches away.

It was hardly champagne and strawberries.

It was...

She needed to move back.

"Ye olde process of elimination," he murmured, apparently unaware of their closeness. "So, who can you eliminate?"

"Everyone!" Harley said.

He shook his head. "That won't work. You most probably know the killer."

"Any of the students would benefit from prestige. It would make a radical difference as far as their careers in Egyptology, archeology and anthropology are concerned," Harley said. "It was impressive to work with a man like Henry, but to take his place would be even more impressive. Still..."

"Process of elimination," he repeated, then abruptly stood up.

"I have to leave."

"Oh. Okay. If you have to."

"Yeah, I do."

But he was still standing there. He smiled suddenly. "Yeah, I have to go," he said again.

"You really don't."

His smile deepened. "I do."

"Because I'm Craig's cousin?"

He shook his head, his eyes never leaving hers. "Because you're you. I don't know what it is... I guess we can't define attraction, but... Anyway, I'm being presumptuous, but—"

"No, actually, you're not," Harley broke in. She wondered how you could *feel* someone so completely when you weren't even touching that person.

"We have to give it time and thought."

"I wasn't thinking everlasting commitment. I'm not FBI, but I can help a great deal and we're going to...be together. Differently. I—"

"That's not what I meant," Micah said.

"Yes, okay. I guess I know what you mean. I believe... I believe we'll see each other tomorrow and the next day, and if..."

"Yes," Micah said. Then, neither spoke; they looked at each other.

"We're adults," Harley whispered.

"Yes, and so... I'm heading out."

He walked to the door. Harley followed him, ready to lock up when he left. She stayed a short distance behind him. She felt as if her flesh and blood, muscle and bone, had come alive, as if neurons or atoms or other chemical entities were flashing through her system with tiny sparks of red-hot fire. He had to leave; otherwise, she'd embarrass herself.

But she didn't really care.

Still, he was right. They needed time. Just because they could hook up didn't mean they should forget that there were consequences to any deed, even if neither had any expectations.

At the door, he turned to her.

It could have all ended there—as it should have.

She could've stayed where she was.

But she didn't. She walked forward, her eyes on his, until she was touching him, and when she did, he backed into the door. At the same time, his arms came around her.

She touched his face. Stroked his cheek, felt the power in his arms as he drew her close. She let herself shudder with a delicious abandon as she felt the heat of his body, the texture and strength in his muscles. And then she felt his mouth, crushing hers, and she returned the kiss with equal open-mouthed passion. They stood in the doorway, fumbling with each other's clothing. Micah pulled away for a second, removing his holster and Glock from the back of his waistband, setting them down on the occasional table.

Then he paused, breathing heavily. "Wait. Is there… someone else? Is there that kind of reason?"

She shook her head. "No. No one else. There hasn't been anyone else in well over a year." She felt her cheeks turn a dozen shades of red. "But it's all right. I'm on the pill."

He drew her back into his arms for a very long, very wet, hot kiss.

Then they moved through the apartment, half disrobing themselves, half helping each other.

They stood in the center of the loft, next to the plate glass windows looking out on the night, on the gothic structure of Grace Church. They both hesitated a minute.

Not that anything was wrong; rather she felt blessed.

The light that came in and bathed them together was beautiful and romantic. Micah smiled and said, "I have this great image of me sweeping you into my arms and carrying you up the stairway...but it's winding and it's iron and..."

Harley laughed. She turned and ran up the winding stairway to the loft. He quickly joined her.

The loft seemed to be aglow with light in the most glorious colors—pastels with bursts of darker blue and mauve, probably from some vehicle moving down on the street. They found each other's mouths again, kissed forever, and then Harley rolled over and straddled him. They twined their fingers together and looked at each other again, and she couldn't help wondering if it was possible to not really know someone—but to believe that you did.

You could be fooling yourself! a voice nagged.

But she didn't care. She'd been spending the year since Henry's death biding time, waiting...

For what, she hadn't known.

Until now? Until this? And maybe it was just sex...

But at this point in her life, that was fine, too!

She felt his hands moving over her body, touching and teasing, exploring and giving. They turned on the bed, facing each other, laughing, kissing, their lips roaming, intimate. They shared kisses that caused sensation to soar, cries to escape into the night...

Then at last they were together, moving with the brilliant colors of the night. She caught his eyes and they were beautiful.

His hands were electric, his movement fierce and erotic, and it seemed that they'd joined in something wonderful that captured the pulse and beat of the city... agonizing in its wonder, lasting too long, and yet over too quickly.

She lay beside him, breathing desperately. She could

hear her own heartbeat as if it shook the very foundations of the building.

And she felt his knuckles, gentle on her cheek. He pulled her to him. She prayed her heartbeat would slow…

"What are you thinking?" he asked her quietly.

For some reason, she couldn't resist being honest.

"That you're very, very good. Or that everyone else in my life of the boyfriend variety has been bad. Disappointing, anyway. I mean, as a lover…"

He laughed. "I'm going to take the 'very, very good.'" He hesitated, drawing a line gently from her face to her collarbone. "Why?" he asked.

"Why are you good at this?" she murmured, perfectly aware that wasn't what he meant.

"Why have you been…alone?" he asked her.

She shook her head. "I haven't been alone. My world is very rich with family and friends. I'm lucky. I've been out there. I've even waited tables a few times at Finnegan's when they were short on people. And I actually like working for Fillmore Investigations. I'm not out on the street much. I like to think I'm kind of a little like Sherlock Holmes. Field agents with the company bring me information and I figure things out from the bits and pieces. I often talk to Kieran, and discuss my people with her, put them in hypothetical situations."

"That's work. Not personal."

"Yes, true. I've been to Florida to visit my family. And I've gone to tons of shows with Kieran's family. Her twin brother, Kevin, is an actor and—"

"I know. So why did you suddenly need me so badly?" he asked her.

She turned toward him, drawing the sheets to her

shoulders as she answered the question. "Why are *you* here—needed or just as needy?" she asked.

He laughed softly. "Ouch. Hmm."

"It's a fair question. I was in criminology, probably because of Craig. I've lost family members, but I hadn't ever seen anyone die the way Henry did. And I was so crazy about him, as if he'd been a relative. You know...yeah, you know what he was like. Anyway, I tried to do something about his death. I failed. I never expected this, though!"

"You mean me?"

"No, sorry! No, I meant Thursday night, at the gala. Vivian! Why kill Henry and wait all this time to attack Vivian?" Harley asked.

He rolled onto his back and stared at the ceiling. "Maybe the killer's triggered by events."

"You mean—"

"Henry died the day your team made the discovery. Vivian was attacked the day you were all about to celebrate that discovery."

"The mummy's curse?"

He groaned.

"No! I don't believe it, but... Micah, there were Egyptian workers who told us we were going to be cursed."

"None of the Egyptian workers were here at the gala," Micah reminded her.

"Yolanda. Yolanda Akeem," Harley said.

"Ah, Yolanda."

"You know her?"

"I do. I met her in Cairo."

"So...would you say you're friends?"

"Oh, I don't think that word describes our brief time together. No, she got me out of Egypt, helped me chase after you guys," Micah said. "We're having some problems reaching her, although I assume she's still in the country. McGrady tried to get her to stick around after the night of the celebration, and he managed to talk to her for a few minutes, but in my mind, she hadn't been properly questioned yet."

"What? Why?"

"She has some kind of diplomatic immunity. And, of course, she had nothing to do with what happened to Vivian."

"How do you know that?"

"She was always within range of cameras," Micah said. He smiled. "The FBI's taken the lead, so we have footage, prints, you name it. Sadly, even with all the crime scene evidence that was collected, we don't have answers. But as far as Yolanda goes, we're almost positive she wasn't anywhere near the museum before the gala. She arrived just in time for the party, and she was on camera the entire time. She didn't even take a trip to the ladies' room."

"Why do you think she doesn't want to talk to police?"

"Apparently, she believes that the entire expedition was run by a bunch of idiots, and she's tired of all the bad press involving archeological work in her country." He grinned suddenly, and ran a finger from her collarbone to her abdomen. "There's something wrong with this picture. I'm lying here, next to you, seeing you, feeling you and…"

"And we're talking about work. But with your kind of job, it's what you do all the time, right? Is that what you mean?"

"No," he said, laughing. "What I meant is that I'm obviously not so good or you'd be more intrigued by us being together here—naked in bed!—than by the puzzles that will return in the morning."

"Morning, evening…"

Harley felt almost giddy and worried about herself all at once. It was too natural to be here with him. Too easy, too sweet.

She crawled on top of him, her breasts just teasing his chest. "Don't worry. I'm not at all distracted. Like I said, you're very, very good. Of course, feel free to reinforce such a notion at any time."

"Of course!"

He drew her to him. They were locked in a hot, wet kiss again, then disengaged to shower each other with featherlight touches, brushing with their lips and fingertips, delicate brushes that turned urgent and became fierce, passionate lovemaking that left them both breathless, hearts pounding once again.

It was incredible. Being together was incredible. She lay curled next to him as he held her. They were both silent for a few minutes.

"Okay, we know that while Yolanda Akeem might conceivably have had something to do with Henry's death, she couldn't have had anything to do with what happened to Vivian," Micah murmured.

Harley laughed softly. "So, *I'm* not that good, eh?"

He turned to her. "Good? Good? 'Good' is a total understatement. You are spectacular. And beyond."

They both went on to prove just how much they appreciated each other.

When morning came, and they'd both showered and dressed, he sat on the bed next to her, adjusting his sleeves while she buttoned her blouse.

"Amazing, huh?" he said. "And that's not a word I use lightly."

"What is?" She grinned; she couldn't help herself.

"'Very, very, *very* good'? Now, as to amazing..."

"Hey!"

"Okay...amazing."

"I meant that it was special to have a night like this, to be focused entirely on another person, without losing focus on the rest of your life."

"But remember, neither of us has a hold on the other. How awkward! What I mean is...you didn't become forever committed."

He gently kissed her lips.

"No hold. I have to meet up with Craig at the office. I'll see you later, right?"

Harley nodded. "I'll be at Finnegan's this evening. I've gotten together with Kieran and Craig for Sunday roast the last few weeks. I imagine that if you're going to be with Craig, you'll end up there, as well."

"Excellent."

At the door, he lingered, kissing her goodbye.

He left and she leaned against the door.

Then she reminded herself that he'd been nothing but a forgotten voice until two nights ago. That she'd wanted to believe she'd be happy with just one night.

Except that now...

She wanted far more than a night.

Micah sat in the New York office with Craig and one of the computer techs.

He stared at the security footage from the museum over and over again.

It didn't matter how long he studied the footage, it didn't change. He saw everyone involved with the exhibit as they arrived that day. Administrators and other key people got there early, heading straight over to the area that was about to be unveiled.

He saw the coming and going of visitors to the main part of the museum during the day.

The caterers arrived. Everything looked just as it should for the evening that would welcome a special group for the official opening of the Henry Tomlinson Collection.

"Whatever went on with Vivian, it was planned way before the event. There are security cameras just about everywhere except for the offices, and they reveal nothing and no one out of the ordinary. Of course, there are the subterranean so-called 'secret access' areas that Arlo showed Harley and me," Micah said. "There's no question in my mind that whoever did this planned it well ahead of time. The linens would've been on hand in the prep room. Even before the Amenmose exhibit, the museum offered Egyptology and they have classes for high school kids in which the religious and funerary rituals are demonstrated. As to the nicotine poisoning, it's easy enough to get hold of insecticide."

"We'll need warrants," Craig said, "if we want to check out credit card purchases. Although I sincerely doubt we'd find what we're looking for. And I'm not sure we can even get warrants unless we have information or evidence we can use to designate suspects."

"Whoever bought the poison didn't use a credit card. And he or she didn't buy it all at the same place," Micah said. "It's one of them," he added. "I know that one of them killed Henry. The same person apparently tried to kill Vivian. Either that or..."

"Or?"

"We've been chasing the wrong dog," Micah said thoughtfully. He looked at Craig. "Everyone involved in that exhibit and in the expedition knows that a lot of people didn't believe a verdict of death by accident—that Henry killed himself in a state of delirium—no matter what official reports said. I realize that most eventually gave up and accepted the verdict, or pretended to."

"What if someone was trying to kill Vivian, and trying to make it *appear* that it was Henry's killer coming after her?" Craig suggested.

"I don't know," Micah said with a long sigh. "Maybe that's far-fetched. I'm still suspicious about the entire thing that went on in the desert. The insurgency—the supposedly violent insurgency that killed no one and led to nothing but a few demonstrators being arrested. Also, there's another name that keeps coming up, that of Satima Mahmoud. The translator."

"She's in Egypt."

"I'd like to talk to her. If we can reach someone in our Cairo office, perhaps they can arrange a meeting."

"All right. I'll give tech a call. We'll see if they can get through to our people over there now. And if so, if the staff can bring Satima in and set up a satellite call."

"That's great. Either a video meeting or, if I have to, I'll fly back over."

"Alone?" Craig asked him.

"You're welcome to join me."

"I wasn't thinking about me. To be honest, I don't like the idea of Harley going back there—not now, and not in relation to this case."

"I wouldn't bring Harley," Micah said quickly.

"You're going to make damned sure you keep her

out of danger, right? I know she'd say she can look after herself, and of course, that's true. But she's my cousin and I love her, so I can't help feeling this way. You understand?"

Micah nodded. He understood.

Craig was still looking at him. "Yeah, you do understand. Thank you," he said quietly.

And once again, Micah nodded.

Chapter 6

Edward Fillmore was an exceptional boss.

In many ways—although he was less on the slightly crazy academic side—he reminded her of Henry Tomlinson.

They were both decent men. Not on-a-pedestal wonderful; they had their moments. But they were both good people. Or, rather, Henry *had* been good until his unfair and untimely end.

Edward had founded his company years earlier. They handled private investigations, such as finding lost family members, searching for missing children and were certainly happy to participate in any "silver" alert, as well. He seldom took on divorce cases in which one spouse was trying to trap the other. In fact, he'd only take on such a case if he met with someone he saw as an injured party first, and then only if it meant getting suitable support for any children who might be affected.

When Harley had first gone to work for him, he'd told her to feel free to use her own time and whatever resources the company had to look into Henry's death. She'd never used work hours — say, when she was tracking down a credit card report or some lead on a missing person—to pursue her own investigation. But she'd accepted his offer, although she hadn't come up with anything yet. Henry was gone, had been cremated. And there was no lead to follow; it was all a stone wall. It was somewhat comforting to know that the FBI had encountered the same stone wall. No one had been able to crack the defenses established when the Amenmose expedition had ended, Henry had died and they'd all left the site.

Now, of course, she had a new crime to pursue—the poisoning of Vivian Richter.

She called Edward Fillmore and asked if she might have his blessing to head into the offices and search through info on various people.

Edward was quick to allow her access to his computers and databases.

So Harley spent her Sunday morning going through everything she could find on everyone she knew—including her colleagues on the expedition, the people she'd never suspected. Her search yielded little.

Ned Richter had been a CEO with a pharmaceutical company for nine years before joining Alchemy, where he'd been in charge of "Exploration" for over a decade.

His work record was spotless. He'd graduated from Harvard.

He'd married Vivian Clifford, a graduate of Cornell, a decade ago. When not working, the couple loved to vacation in historic places, including Peru, Mexico, Egypt and Greece. The couple had no children, but seemed devoted to each other.

Arlo Hampton had no criminal record, not even a parking ticket. He'd received his doctorate in Egyptology from Brown. He'd been with Alchemy for nearly eight years and had been hired by Ned Richter.

She looked up Jensen next. He'd gone to NYU. He was a New Yorker through and through.

He had a ton of parking tickets.

Nothing else on him.

Roger Eastman had been arrested once; he'd been protesting commercial testing on animals.

He'd received probation.

Belinda had no parking tickets—she didn't drive. She'd never been arrested. She'd been valedictorian of her high school class and had gone to Northwestern before arriving in New York for graduate work.

Joe—Joseph Rosello—had also been born in New York City, in the Bronx. He'd gone to Ithaca, in Syracuse, and then finished at Brown. However, she found something she hadn't known or even suspected. He'd paid his way through college by working as an extra in movies and doing a stand-up comedy gig at a place in Times Square.

According to his social media pages, he still enjoyed dressing up and playing parts.

She should have known this. And, of course, she would have—if she'd just spent more time on social media. So…he played roles.

Would that include the part of a mummy?

Harley wasn't even sure what she was doing at first when she reached for the phone; then she knew. She called Kieran and asked for Kevin's number, since Kevin was a working New York actor.

Naturally, Kieran wanted to know what was up. Harley told her.

"Kevin's performing at some kind of zombie walk today in Times Square. What's your guy's name? I can see if he's taking part," Kieran said.

But Harley didn't need Kieran to check it out for her; she'd keyed in some more information and had come up with Joe's status for the day.

"Yes!" she exclaimed. "They're both taking part in the zombie walk. The walk's for charity, and Joe's one of the performers doing pictures with people. Hey, do you feel like heading down to be in a zombie walk?"

"Sure," Kieran said. "I'll be a good sister. What the heck, we can support a charity and investigate what's going on. Sounds like a plan to me."

They agreed to meet at a restaurant off Times Square—quieter and not as much of a tourist attraction—and get lunch before joining the zombie walk.

And watching the players.

A waste of time? Harley wondered.

A lot of investigative work was a waste of time; that was part of the process of elimination, as Micah had described it. But Kieran was right. If nothing else, their entry fees would go toward charity.

Micah had no intention of denying anything; he really cared about Harley—and Harley certainly behaved as if she cared about him. Was it forever and ever? How could they tell? Did he want to see her again?

Touch her again, breathe in her scent, be with her again and feel her, naked, against him?

Well, yes. That was a definite yes.

But he'd never been in precisely this situation before.

Was Craig supposed to ask him about his intentions? Or maybe he was supposed to give Micah a good left hook to the jaw.

"You're sleeping with her, right?" Craig asked.

"Define sleeping," Micah said. "I only knew her as your cousin and a voice on the phone until two days ago. Last night, yes. We were together." He hesitated and then admitted. "I actually tried to leave. Probably not hard enough."

Craig lowered his head, obviously amused.

"Just keep her safe," he said.

And then, before either one of them could say any more, the phone in the conference room rang.

Craig picked it up and frowned as he listened to what was being said. He hung up slowly, rising as he did. "Come on, Egan's office. He's got a video call up with one of our agents in Cairo."

"Already? They have Satima Mahmoud?" Micah asked.

"No, but they have some kind of information," Craig replied.

They strode rapidly down the hall. Egan's secretary waved them in and they entered his office. He was speaking with someone via his computer; they both walked around behind his desk.

Micah had met the agent on the screen. His name was Sanford Wiley, and Micah quickly greeted him. Egan introduced him to Craig.

"So, we got your inquiry just now and I happened to be in the office," Wiley said. "I don't know whether it means anything or not, but I wanted to get back to you right away with what I have. The local police are look-ing for Satima Mahmoud. Now, they're not always en-tirely forthright with us, but from what I've been able to gather, she's suspected of having something to do with agitating trouble—and insurrection. She was under suspicion by the Egyptian police, who are now helping our people with the investigation, we believe, as well. They've been searching for her for several days. We'll start our own line of investigation, since she's a witness or person of interest to you all. Fox, I know you had some interaction with her. Do you suspect her of being involved in Henry Tomlinson's death?"

"When I saw her, she informed me that the others had left. She had just gotten to Cairo herself when I was trying to head out to the expedition site," Micah told him. "I'm very interested in what she may know. Or more specifically, what she knows that she didn't share at the time. She was the one who first sounded the alarm about the uprising. Everything was pure chaos when I was there, which I'm sure you remember, Wiley. But, yes, if you find her, I'd very much like to speak with her."

"We're on it from this end—with the Egyptian police, of course."

"Of course."

"We get the impression that they're perplexed about the situation. She's disappeared."

"Thanks for letting us know," Micah told him.

There were a few more exchanges, and then they ended the video call.

Egan looked thoughtfully at Micah. "To be honest," he said, "I'm not sure what you can learn from this woman—or what you could prove—this late in the game. Crews are still going through whatever evidence they could find at the museum after Vivian was attacked, but…"

"I know, sir," Micah said. "But it's only been a matter of days. And I'm pretty convinced that Vivian Richter's attack relates back to Henry's death. And if not, well, we still need to know who the hell would attempt to murder a woman with nicotine-soaked linen wrappings."

"Yes, and we *will* find the truth," Egan said with conviction. "I'll inform you of anything we learn through our people here and in Egypt, and through any chatter they pick up." He hesitated. "If they can't find this woman…"

"There's always the possibility that she's dead," Craig finished.

"Why kill an interpreter?" Egan mused.

"There's also the possibility that she's alive—and more of a player than we'd imagined," Micah said. "Or that very fact could account for her death. If that's what happened."

"When you talked to her, did you get the feeling that she was involved in any way?" Craig asked.

"She seemed harried, frightened and glad to be back in Cairo. But I was still trying to catch up with the Americans involved. Now I realize I should have given her more attention then. The entire situation was terrifying, so of course it seemed reasonable that she'd be upset. And I still don't see her with a motive of any kind to strangle Henry."

"You never know," Egan told him.

"Except we do know that she's definitely not in the States," Craig said. He suddenly began to feel his pocket, which was apparently vibrating. "Phone," he muttered. "Excuse me, two seconds. This may be important." He answered the call, taking a step back from Micah and Egan.

"She's not in this country that we know of, anyway," Micah said to Egan. He hesitated, speaking carefully. "I still don't think she killed Henry."

"But you think she might know who did?"

"I think she knows *something*," Micah said. "She's Joe Rosello's alibi for the time Jensen Morrow and Harley Frasier were away from the camp. What if she lied because he either cajoled her or bribed her?"

Egan nodded. "That's a possibility."

"You're talking about Joe Rosello?" Craig asked, putting away his phone.

"Yes," Micah said.

"That was Kieran. She's going to Times Square with Harley. And it's about Joe Rosello. The man's an actor, and he's in a zombie walk today. Not sure I actually get it, but Kieran knew about it because of her twin, Kevin. He's one of the performers hired on as an improvisational actor and guide for the walk."

"Sounds like a good time for us to get to Times Square and see just what he's up to," Micah said.

"Zombie walk?" Egan asked, shaking his head.

"They're all over the country now," Micah told him. "The power of television and mass media today. The popularity of certain television programs can create some strange circumstances."

"There's a show on TV about mummies?"

"Mummies, zombies, walking dead. Close enough, I think. Let's head on out," Micah said to Craig. "With your blessing, sir, of course," he added, addressing Egan.

"Go, sir, with righteousness!" Egan said. "And get the whacked-out son of a bitch, will you? Speaking of media—they're having a heyday with this. Mummies! As if we didn't have enough of the plain old walking, living, flesh-and-blood kind of criminals!"

A majority of the "zombies" there for the walk and to support the charity were dressed up.

They wore zombie makeup, tattered clothing and many looked as if they'd rolled in the dirt.

Luckily, not all the participants were dressed up, and since it was a charity walk, whatever one chose to wear was fine. Joining the walk cost ten dollars. The fee included a comedy "zombie" performance at the end, with the bleachers reserved for those who'd paid. Anyone could see the show, but since the entry fee went to charity—three of the major children's hospitals— virtually no one was going to mind paying.

"This would've been fun no matter what," Kieran told Harley, surveying the crowd. "A lot of the costumes on the walkers are really cool. Oh, there, at the sign-up tables. There's Kevin."

Kieran started walking ahead; Harley quickly followed.

Kevin Finnegan was an exceptionally good-looking man, tall, with great bone structure, a toned body and broad shoulders. He and Kieran were clearly related, but of course, they weren't just siblings—they were twins. Like Kieran, he had deep auburn hair and his eyes were a true blue.

Harley waited while Kieran greeted her brother with a hug and a kiss; she then greeted him, as well.

"I'm so glad you came out. I know how you feel about crowds in Times Square," Kevin told his sister.

"It's…well…" Kieran began.

"Ah. I'm being used," Kevin said, but his smile was affectionate. "What do you need? How can I help?"

"We signed up legitimately, don't you fear," Kieran said. "But do you know a Joe Rosello?"

"Not that I'm aware of."

"No? Oh, I guess you don't know everyone working here today," Harley said.

"Actually, I do."

"Oh! Well, supposedly, Joe's working."

"Maybe he works under a different name. SAG rules mean you can't use a name if someone else has it already. Or even if he's not SAG, he might be using a stage name," Kevin said.

"That's him! That's him right there!" Harley exclaimed.

"Oh, so that's your guy. His name is Robbie. At least when he's here it is. Nice guy, or so it seems."

Joe—or Robbie Rosello, as he was calling himself for the day—was standing over by one of the tables. As Kevin had been doing, he was posing with people who wanted their pictures taken with a zombie.

He was dressed in tatters. Not like a mummy, just in tatters. His skin was painted white and he had very effective makeup that darkened his eyes and made his cheeks sink in.

As Joe so often did, he was flirting.

"Yep, that's him!" Harley said again.

The girls with whom he'd been posing moved on, and Harley ran over to him. He turned to look at her and his eyes widened with surprise, alarm—and wariness.

"Harley!" he said. "Um, what are you doing here? You're a zombie fan?" He sounded skeptical.

"It's a good cause, right? You know, I was shocked to find out that you're an actor."

"Oh, well…" He smiled at her awkwardly. "I'm not really an actor, more of an 'I love the movies' kind of guy who likes to get work as an extra. I don't hide it, but I guess I don't talk about it at work. There are people who don't think you can be a serious academic if you…if you do things like take part in a zombie walk."

"That's silly."

"Yeah? Well, we both know the world can be full of silliness, some of it malicious."

She nodded. "I guess, but if this is something you love, you shouldn't have to be afraid that others won't approve."

He frowned. "I agree."

"I guess we have to work on convincing the rest of the world."

"The academic world, anyway. How did you even find out about this?"

"You remember Craig Frasier, my cousin? He's dating Kieran Finnegan. And her brother, Kevin, is an actor—"

"Kevin is a *serious* actor. He actually makes a living at it," Joe said. He grimaced. "I don't think I'd be able to do that, so I have to be a serious academic instead."

"By the way, you look great," she told him.

"Thank you."

"Is the costume yours? Do you have many…costumes?"

"Oh, no. No," he said firmly, apparently figuring out just where she was going with her question and why she was really there, "No! Emphatically no. I've never dressed up like a mummy." He hesitated. "I swear, I'd never have hurt Henry, and I did nothing to Vivian Richter. I swear!"

"Hey, Robbie! Zombie dance thing starting up," someone called.

"Excuse me, gotta go. Don't worry. I'll have thousands of witnesses for my every move today," he assured Harley.

"Have fun!" she said.

He gave her a thumbs-up and joined a number of other actors, Kevin Finnegan among them. Someone struck a chord on a guitar, and the group went into a shuffle dance, akin to the one in the music video for Michael Jackson's old "Thriller."

The song was very clever, and the words had to do with giving generously to fight disease.

And when it was over, Kevin—the head zombie, apparently—stepped out from the group and announced they'd be walking down Broadway. Volunteers with water were positioned along the route. The walk would end at the bleachers, where some of the entertainers would then be performing.

Harley turned and looked around until she finally saw Kieran. Kieran saw her at the same time and hurried toward her as a sea of people—some in zombie rags and makeup, some not—came between them. They were almost carried along by the crowd. Kieran shrugged and waved at her from a distance, then laughed as they were both pushed along.

Harley tried to thread her way through the would-be zombies.

Kieran did the same.

Now and then, they'd come across another kind of creature, something from Disney or perhaps one of

Jim Henson's characters from his movies or television shows.

Harley ran into some comic characters she didn't recognize. A man in a very large banana suit struggled to maneuver to the side.

He fell over.

She tried to reach him, but he was helped up by a group of grapes. Police were everywhere on the street and they also tried to help the banana; the grapes were just faster.

It was Times Square, after all.

And Times Square on an especially crazy day. It reminded her why she usually avoided the area. But a lot of the theaters were down here, too, and she did love going with Craig and Kieran to see plays when Kevin was in them—and even when he wasn't!

But today…

"Hey there!" Kieran called. She was walking parallel with Harley, a few feet to the left.

"Hey!" Harley called back, grinning.

But then she saw the mummy.

On a day like this, it was difficult to discern the differences between costumes; many were tattered white, and appeared to have been made from linen strips.

But this…

This was a mummy.

It was a mummy that looked exactly the way Vivian Richter had looked when she'd staggered into the midst of the gala. It might've been created by the same costume artist! Or would-be costume artist…

The thing was behind her, lurching along. Harley scanned the crowd. The mummy seemed to be walking alone.

And walking in a casual manner that brought it closer and closer to Harley.

"Kieran!" she screamed.

At first, her friend turned to her with a broad smile. Then she saw the mummy. And she began to stride aggressively over to Harley—with the mummy between them.

The mummy sensed pursuit and headed toward Kieran. But then, it headed back in Harley's direction with a purpose and a vengeance, no longer staggering.

"Come on, come on, I'm ready for you!" Harley thought. "Police! Police!" she cried.

And then the thing was upon her, placing a hand on her chest. It looked right at her, but she couldn't see its eyes. They were covered in the same linen gauze that stretched over the body, dirtied and rendered old, as if— mummy or zombie—the creature had long been dead.

The throng of people was impressive, particularly for a charity event.

Micah assumed many people were out just for the entertainment value and, of course, the fun of dressing up as a zombie.

But it made for a massive crowd—tens of thousands at the very least, and maybe many more considering the size of New York City.

"I see Kevin Finnegan," Craig said.

"Where?"

"Leading the zombie charge."

"You're sure that's Kevin?"

"Yes, and if so, Kieran is near him, and if she is…"

"Then Harley's near Kieran. Let's go!"

Wending their way through the horde of people

wasn't easy. Apparently, no one had thought to tell the regular performers who thronged Times Square daily in costume, charging for tourist pictures, that zombies would be ruling the day.

Maybe it didn't matter. As they hurried past the Times Square Marriott, Micah saw a zombie posing with a Disney figure and with one of the imitation "naked" cowboys who'd staked a claim on the street.

He kept up a brisk pace, saying "excuse me" almost every other second.

And then he saw Kevin Finnegan, laughing, talking, making announcements through a speaker and pointing to the bleachers ahead.

He also saw Joe Rosello dancing along with a group as he moved forward in costume —ragged jeans, ripped rock band T-shirt and heavily made-up face and body.

And there...

A mummy!

A mummy, standing in the street, touching Harley, touching her with wrapped hands that appeared to be wet, soaked in something.

"Stop now!" he shouted.

He barely avoided knocking over a teenager playing zombie-on-a-crutch. In a circuitous route, he cleared a number of teens. As carefully as he could without losing speed, he continued to press forward through and around people.

The mummy saw him—and turned to run.

He heard Harley shout. She was starting to run after the thing.

"No!" He caught up with her.

"We have to catch that mummy!" she said.

"No, no—get your shirt off!"

"What?"

"Your shirt. Get your shirt off."

"Here? In Times Square?"

Craig, gasping for breath, had reached them. "Get your shirt off! The hands—the mummy's hands were covered in something. Get it off *now*. Harley, damn it, there could be poison on your shirt. Get it off before…"

She cried out, all but ripping the shirt from her body. It fell to the ground.

There were creatures of all kinds gathering around them.

"Way cool!" a passing zombie said.

"Yeah," said another. "It's legal, you know. Men can go topless, and women can go topless! New York City, man. What a great place."

"Maybe she'll take off her bra!"

"Moron!" Harley breathed, swinging around.

"I've got the shirt," Craig said, slipping into gloves and reaching down.

"The mummy's probably shedding poison with every step," Micah said. "Cops. Get cops over here. Warn them there's a hazard…gloves, bags…"

He didn't need to talk; Craig knew what had to be done as well as he did. Micah had already begun moving, and as he did, he swore. The "mummy" was indeed shedding, leaving what was likely poisoned and hazardous material every few steps.

But the trail of wrappings at least gave him a direction to take, as clear as tracking any animal, human included, in a forested wilderness.

"Look!" a girl cried. "It was a mummy! A mummy!"

She'd picked up some of the shredded linen that had

been cast on the ground. Micah swore again, using his gloved hands to snatch it from her.

"Hey!" she protested.

"Get to a cop. Get to a doctor. That might be poisoned material," Micah said. A man quickly appeared at the child's side, holding her, and taking Micah more seriously than she did, apparently.

"Cop! Doctor!" Micah ordered.

"Yes, sir!" the man said, clutching his daughter.

Micah hurried on.

Cops were filling the area. Craig had gotten to Kevin Finnegan, and Kevin was announcing the problem, warning people not to touch the linen, to get to a cop, hospital, or doctor if they had.

Micah kept running. He saw more of the linen along the road. Swearing, he knew he'd have to stop and add it to the growing cache he stuffed into a large evidence bag as he hurried along.

The "mummy" had planned well, knowing that the police and FBI were fully aware that poison—using poisoned linen—was his or her talent.

And that they'd definitely be delayed in their pursuit, trying to keep others from becoming victims of possible illness or even death.

The last piece of linen was in front of an alley that led from Times Square down one of the side streets.

Micah swung around the corner, racing down the street. And then he stopped.

The street was filled with massive office buildings; there was also a massage place, a Chinese restaurant and somebody's bar and grill.

And there was no one on the street.

It was New York! Where was everyone?

But it was Sunday. Offices were closed. Whoever was getting a massage was already inside; any diners at the Chinese restaurant were already seated.

Micah hurried along the street. The mummy couldn't possibly have changed so quickly.

Or maybe it had. Maybe the linens had been shed completely and the mummy was just a normal person now, enjoying a delicious bowl of lo mein.

Micah moved on down the street.

Yeah, by now, the mummy might be just a "normal" person.

But Micah was sure it was going to be a normal person he knew. And he was determined to find that person. This time, he was chasing the damned mummy—person, whoever it was—to Jersey or Connecticut if he had to.

There! Up ahead.

The mummy was turning onto Fifth Avenue and heading north.

Micah started to run.

"Do you know who it was? Do you have any clue who it was?" Kieran asked Harley.

It had been a ridiculous, uncomfortable day. She was still half-naked, feeling embarrassed and exposed. Just because one *could* go topless according to NYC's equality laws, didn't mean she had any desire to do so! She was running through the crowd, Kieran keeping pace beside her, anxious to get to a car so she could go home and have a shower.

A taxi stopped for them when they made it over to Eighth Avenue. The driver grinned wolfishly at Harley, nodding when they gave him her address. A quick conversation with one of Craig's ME friends had assured them that Harley's going home for a shower would be fine; if the poison had touched only her clothing, there should be no problem, and of course, once the contaminated linen was analyzed, they'd know what they were looking at.

"We aren't even sure there *is* poison on the wrappings," Harley said.

"What do you want to bet?" Kieran asked her.

Harley didn't want to bet.

The mummy had taken her completely by surprise. She'd wanted to knock the thing in the head and rip the linen wrappings from it.

And instead...

It had touched her, and only Micah's arrival had kept her from contact with linen that was possibly doused in nicotine.

"How the hell is that damned mummy wearing poison and not dropping dead?" she demanded. The driver was staring back at her in his rearview mirror, even more interested than he'd been earlier. She leaned forward, ready to snap at him—and then didn't.

What the hell. She dropped back against the seat.

"Kieran, how is he or she doing it? All that poison?"

"Wearing something underneath the wrapping, I guess. We don't have anything analyzed yet, although I'm convinced that was actually an attempt on your life—or a warning for you to back off."

"Okay, so the mummy found me. But it looked as if the mummy was running through the crowd, touching anyone and everyone," Harley said.

"That was to stop the police or anyone in pursuit," Kieran told her.

"Hey!" Harley snapped. The taxi driver was grinning; he was about to take a roundabout route to her building. "No, go straight and then turn right!" she said.

"One-way street," the driver said in a singsong voice.

"And it's going the way we want it to!"

They reached their destination and Kieran paid the cabbie as they stepped out; Harley realized she was being rude.

"I'm sorry. Didn't mean to make you pay that!"

"Harley, that's the least of our concerns at the moment," Kieran said.

"They haven't called? Micah or Craig?"

"Harley, Micah was in hot pursuit and Craig was headed in to get those wrappings to the lab. It takes time. We're here. Listen, just smile at the clerk or security guy on duty," Kieran advised. "He's staring at you just like the taxi driver was. Now let's get up to your place."

Harley did manage a nice smile for the security guard on duty. He was staring at her, as Kieran had said, but at the last minute sent her a confused smile in return.

Upstairs, Harley told Kieran to make herself comfortable, and Kieran said she would. Harley showered.

And showered, nearly scrubbing herself raw in the process.

She emerged from the shower, wrapped in a robe, and hurried downstairs.

Kieran was on the phone. She turned to look at Harley.

"Good call on Micah's part. Yes, those wrappings were soaked in nicotine."

There was something odd about the way she was speaking.

"What is it?"

"Micah followed the mummy on foot—all the way up to Central Park and the museum."

"The New Museum of Antiquity?" Harley said.

"Yes. And he found a mummy…half-dead."

"Mummies *are* dead."

"No, I mean… I'm sorry, Harley. Arlo Hampton is probably going to die. He was found on the floor, stretched out in wrappings, right in front of the Temple of Ra."

Chapter 7

The same day Vivian Richter was released from the hospital, Arlo Hampton was rushed in, swiftly ripped out of torn swaths of mummy wrappings.

This whole thing was his fault, or so it appeared.

He was both the would-be killer—and his own victim, in the end.

At least, Harley thought, that was how it appeared. Or how it was *supposed* to appear.

It seemed evident that he'd dressed up as a mummy but carefully gloved his hands in plastic before soaking a number of loose and shredded strips of "decayed" linen in nicotine and then heading out to assault a "zombie" crowd. Afterward he'd returned to the museum, only to collapse there.

Perhaps he had started back in the Sahara. Perhaps his jealousy, his determination to rise in his field, had caused him to attack Henry Tomlinson back at the expedition prep tent. He must have attacked Vivian as a mummy. She'd blacked out and he had dressed her up and when she came to, he'd sent her, crazed, into the crowd, where she'd been saved.

Today...

No one really knew his intent. Had he just meant to poison a bunch of random "zombies"? Had he known, perhaps, that Joe Rosello was going to be among the actors? Had he thought Joe knew something and needed to be silenced?

He'd come up to Harley.

He had touched her with his poisoned linen rags.

But he couldn't have known Harley would be there; Harley hadn't even known that herself until the last minute. That seemed to make Joe the chosen target.

Unless, of course, Arlo Hampton had just wanted to indiscriminately poison people in the crowd. None of them could determine the truth as yet. And if Arlo died, they might never find out.

Arlo might be accused of killing Henry, or the attempted murder of Vivian—and intent to attack Joe Rosello and a number of innocent "zombies" in the crowd. But he'd calculated wrong; he hadn't taken the right care. He had not been immune to the poison he'd been trying to administer to others.

They knew this, because Craig gave them whatever information he could over the phone. He and Micah had managed to get to the museum quickly; in fact, Micah had reached it just minutes after everything happened. He'd pursued the mummy from Times Square!

Harley insisted that she and Kieran needed to get to the museum.

She didn't know why; she just knew the whole thing simply didn't feel right.

They got there fairly fast. Officers in uniform were maintaining crowd control—the entire museum had been closed down—but someone on duty recognized Kieran. Craig was summoned, and the two of them were let through with Craig leading the way past more officers, spectators, and a sea of media at the entry.

Arlo Hampton was no longer there, of course; he'd been rushed to the hospital. Photographers and crime scene technicians were still at work. Apparently, Arlo had been discovered by a pair of teenage girls who remained in a corner of the room, huddled together. They were still in shock. According to them, Arlo had grunted and tried to reach for them when they'd first found him, nearly giving them joint heart attacks. They'd now told their story a few times and were waiting for their parents.

Rydell and McGrady were there; it remained, after all, a joint investigation. They were with Craig and Micah, trying to create rational scenarios as to what might have happened.

Micah was looking at crime scene photos on his phone, photos snapped by the security guard first on the scene.

McGrady tried to stop Harley when she stepped forward to reach Micah.

"Ms. Frasier, I'm sorry, but you're in the way."

Micah immediately came to her defense. "She's got more degrees in criminology than the rest of us put together. She knew Arlo. She was stalked by him earlier and he tried to get to her at the zombie walk. Ms. Frasier may have something useful to say."

"What's there to say?" McGrady muttered. "He's probably going to die. We weren't there to get him to a hospital fast enough. Nicotine poisoning. Doc just said so—it's all over the wrappings. Jerk dressed up as a mummy for that damned zombie walk, and now he's dead by his own hand."

"It's not him," Harley said.

"What?" McGrady spun on her.

"That's not him—"

"Harley, it *is* Arlo Hampton," Craig interrupted, his tone firm as he frowned at her.

"Yes, Micah, I know Arlo's the one who was found here, but that's not the mummy who was at the zombie walk."

"Harley," Micah said slowly, "trust me. I've been running after him. Olympic-style running. I saw him when he turned north on Fifth. I followed this mummy from the zombie walk, and then I followed him down a bunch of streets, and I saw him go through the tunnel entrance to the museum. By the time I got through the maze down there and back up to the exhibit, those two teenagers were screaming." He was quiet for a minute. "Harley, it *had* to be him. We can't find any other mummies in the museum."

Harley blinked, looking at him.

"Yes, sorry, I know," Craig said, sounding aggravated and weary. "The museum's full of mummies. I mean living mummies. Living people dressed up as mummies. This place is crawling with security and we—"

"You're being an ass!"

He winced, and quickly apologized. "Yeah, sorry. I just don't see—"

"There are so many rooms and tunnels, and I'm telling you, this isn't the same mummy."

"What's different?" Craig asked her.

She didn't know! She couldn't tell. Judging by the photographs Craig and Micah had shown them, the wrappings appeared the same. True, the mummy walking through the crowd had been stripping off pieces of his wrapping, but that wasn't what bothered her, since Arlo's wrappings looked quite disheveled.

Somehow, this mummy—the mummy in the pictures, the Arlo Hampton mummy—was different. Not the wrappings so much, but…something.

"You think the cops are incompetent, Ms. Frasier?" McGrady turned his back on her.

Rydell shrugged apologetically.

"No, Detective, I think the cops are great. I've worked with lots of cops, including some of the ones here right now. Like I told you, I think they're great. You're not great. You've got a chip on your shoulder a mile wide."

"Harley," Micah said quietly.

"He's not just being patronizing and rude, he's jeopardizing an investigation!"

"Yes, that's true, but for the moment…"

"We're lead on this," Craig said.

"We need to start another search!" Micah announced, his voice booming.

"This is going to be reported," McGrady threatened.

"You bet," Micah promised him.

"Rydell, you saw it all."

"Yeah, I did," Rydell said.

Furious, McGrady stomped off. He seemed to be heading for the exit.

"Sorry," Harley murmured.

"No, you were in the right," Micah assured her. "Someone find me a blueprint of this place. Let's get on it. Every room, every display, every office. It's going to be a long day, folks. We're going to have to get down to the basement and below. Search everywhere."

A man in one of the crime scene jumpsuits approached Micah and Craig; they spoke for several minutes, and then a group of people in crime scene jumpsuits began to emerge from various corners of the exhibit. They were given instructions and dispersed, everyone going in a different direction.

"Micah?" Harley asked. "May I go to the museum lab? I'd like to see what's been going on there. I swear to you, I'm not sure how I know, but I'm convinced that the mummy who confronted me in the street didn't look the same as those pictures of Arlo. Maybe I can find something in the lab."

"I'll keep her company," Kieran volunteered.

"All right. I'll inform the crime scene people," Micah told them. "I'm going down below. Arlo was the one who showed us all the basement tunnels and entrances and exits." He watched Harley as he spoke. She wondered if he believed her; he'd stood with her against McGrady, who was being such a jerk, but she had to wonder...

Just how many mummies could there be running around?

Living mummies, rather than the dead ones.

Micah turned away and spoke with the crime scene people again. She noticed that Detective Rydell hadn't gone with his partner; he was awaiting a discussion with Craig and Micah.

"Come on through. We're going to be searching the offices," one of the crime scene women told Harley and Kieran. "Just follow us."

As they left the exhibit space behind and came into an employee hallway, Harley saw that Gordon Vincent, director of the museum, was arguing with the crime scene people. He looked at Harley with annoyance and then pointed at her. "This whole exhibit has turned into a disaster."

Harley looked back at him, startled. "Mr. Vincent, I'm sorry you feel that way. I don't think the exhibit can be blamed for what this person's doing. The artifacts that were discovered are amazing, sir, and law enforcement will get to the bottom of this."

Kieran stepped forward, offering Vincent a hand, "How do you do, sir? We haven't actually met. I'm Kieran Finnegan, a psychologist with the offices of Fuller and Mira. They're psychiatrists who spend a great deal of time working with law enforcement. From my field of study, I'd guess that—sad though it is—these horrible events won't hurt your museum. On the contrary— this will cause an influx of membership and tourism. People love mummies…and mysteries. You're receiving unbelievable media attention, and while these days may be hard to weather, I believe that in the end you'll find that the museum itself is in an excellent position, no matter how discouraging a comment that might be on humanity."

Vincent turned to Kieran, blinking. "Fine. It's all closed for the day. Make sure the powers that be within the FBI and NYPD let me know if I can or cannot open my museum in all or part tomorrow!"

He strode on by them.

Harley looked at Kieran and laughed. "I'm not even sure what you said myself!"

"It worked, though. I guess that's what matters."

"You were excellent."

"You can be more excellent in this situation. You're so involved. You need to really think about the people who are connected to the exhibit, and how and why they might be acting a certain way. You know all the players, Harley, and you have to think about every one of them."

"Well," Harley said, "I guess we can let Joe Rosello off the hook. I'm almost positive that he was the intended victim today. But then I happened to be there. And who knows what was really planned, since—"

"Harley, are you absolutely sure that Arlo Hampton wasn't the 'mummy' who came up to you at the zombie walk?"

"Kieran, I'm telling you, it wasn't him. And remember, Vivian Richter said a mummy came to her, and then, apparently, that mummy dressed her up as a mummy, too, in poisoned linen."

"I know," Kieran said. "But—"

"But that's the point, right? Vivian Richter was working in her office. A mummy came in and suddenly she's a mummy. Isn't it possible that the same thing happened today?"

"Of course," Kieran said. "But everyone's been searching…and they haven't found the stash of nicotine that's being used."

They reached the lab and walked through the outer entry; there were paper gowns and caps and booties to be worn inside the room.

"Really? Do we have to do all this?" Kieran muttered.

Harley laughed. "Yes! It helps prevent the spread of

anything, any bacteria, that might be on antique, long-buried objects from getting out into the world. And it keeps us from bringing in anything that might be harmful to very old stuff."

"Okay, makes sense," Kieran said grudgingly.

"What I really want to do is get to Arlo's desk over there. The small one. See?"

Kieran nodded and followed Harley's actions as she suited up, donned gloves and booties, and then headed into the actual lab.

"What bothers me about this is the lack of clear motive," Kieran said. "It should be obvious, right in front of our faces. These people are dedicated to their work. It means as much to them as anything else in their lives. Maybe more. Most of us live for our mate, spouse, and so on, first—or our children. The instinct to protect a child is strong, except when you're talking about a person who's truly mentally impaired. But in our type of science, in psychiatry and criminology, you come across people who are more devoted to their work than to family or friends."

"Yes, and we think someone was terribly jealous of Henry—which is why he was killed. Now it seems that someone is trying to kill Vivian and Arlo—who are also hardworking and respected members of the Egyptology community. But..."

"But what?"

"I know I keep saying this, but I don't believe that Arlo and the mummy on the street were the same person. I just don't believe it. And Arlo was the one to walk Micah and me all around this place the other day. Do you think...?"

"Think what?"

"There's another motive? There's something we're missing?"

"Of course. That's always possible."

"Love, hate, greed, jealousy. Vengeance," Harley murmured.

"Ah, vengeance. For what? And against whom?"

Harley made her way to the small aluminum desk in the far corner of the room. It was made so it could be constantly sterilized, but still allow for a notepad, pens, tablet, computer or whatever else the scientists and lab techs might need to accurately notate their work.

She opened the first drawer, which held a large plastic container of sanitary wipes.

She opened the second drawer. There was an unused notepad and a case of pencils.

There should've been a computer somewhere. A tablet. Even a voice recorder.

There was not.

Harley opened the third drawer. And there she saw, shoved against the back, a small, almost archaic, flip phone.

She pulled it out and studied it carefully. It had the look of a phone that might be bought at any convenience or drug store—pay as you go. She hit key after key; nothing on it denoted ownership. She went to contacts.

Her own number was there, along with the numbers of others who'd been on the expedition.

"Kieran," she said slowly.

"You found something?"

Harley looked up at her. "Maybe. I think I may just have found a way to reach our liaison, Yolanda, who hasn't been seen since the night of the party. And I think we might have a connection to our long-missing interpreter, Satima Mahmoud."

"In 1524, New York was called New Angoulême by the Italian explorer Giovanni da Verrazzano," Micah said to Craig as they traveled deep into the underbelly of the museum. "The first recorded exploration by the Dutch was in 1609. In 1664, English frigates arrived and demanded the surrender of the city. Peter Stuyvesant sent lawyers to arrange the capitulation—the Dutch and the English liked to go at it in those days. Well, come to think of it, over the years most European powers went after one another. Anyway, it was in 1665 that the city became New York under English rule."

"A lecture on New York history while we're looking for mummies—which happen to be a good bit older than the city," Craig said.

"True, but my point is that although it's not old in comparison with some cities in Africa, the Middle East, the Far East and Europe, New York *is* old. And while it all started downtown—Wall Street, Broad Street and so on—it's been many years since people came up to this area by subway. And down here in these tunnels, especially with so many routes now abandoned, it's just a jungle."

"Yep. And hey, love my city and all...but you just gave away the fact that you were some mean historian before you were a special agent."

"Actually, I'm complaining. This is like looking for a needle in a haystack," Micah said, and he sighed, leaning back against a wall to catch his breath.

He nearly fell backward.

"What the hell?"

"Hey!"

Craig made a grab for Micah's arm; Micah caught hold of him just in time to keep from plunging through a decayed section of wall.

They both half fell and half stumbled into the remains of an old subway tunnel.

The posters on the walls were peeling, but they were magnificent; they advertised Broadway shows opening in the 1930s. There were stairways to nowhere crafted of wrought iron and beautifully designed.

"There!" Micah said, gesturing with one hand at something extremely modern that marred the time-travel look of the place.

In a corner where plaster and paneling had decayed with time, there was a pile of insecticide containers.

At least fifty of them.

Enough poison to kill… God alone knew how many people.

"There has to be some evidence there, right? *Something?*" Harley asked anxiously.

She was seated at a corner table at Finnegan's, along with Micah, Craig and Kieran. Crime scene crews had gone into the offshoot of the abandoned subway station, and they were studying every piece of evidence—primarily the containers of insecticide—with every technique available to them to find out who had used them. Or at least where and when they'd been purchased.

No one had answered when they'd tried to reach Yolanda Akeem or Satima Mahmoud; Egan had people working the phones as well, trying to find a way to pin down the locations of the women's phones via the contact information.

Now it was a matter of waiting.

And it was still Sunday. Although it was late, they had friends in the kitchen, so they were able to enjoy Sunday's traditional roast.

"Here's the thing. We've known that Yolanda Akeem was here in New York. She was at the museum when everything happened with Vivian," Harley said. "And after they questioned her briefly, she left."

"She was visible on security footage," Micah reminded her.

"I think we definitely have a problem, and everyone's part of it—the museum and the Egyptian Department of Antiquities, as well as our government and their government," Craig said. "The truth was left to slide."

"Murder is ugly. No one wants a part of it," Micah murmured to Harley.

"Were any artifacts stolen?" Kieran asked.

"No. Not that I know of," Harley replied. "And what about the motives for any of this? Jealousy, as we already discussed? I keep thinking that a longing for glory seems obvious. Too obvious? The people who would've been jealous of Henry were Arlo and Vivian—and they were the ones who were attacked."

"And you don't think I was an intended victim?" Joe Rosello asked. "Rather than you?"

Harley looked up and smiled. Joe and Kevin had arrived together, all cleaned up and out of their zombie makeup.

Micah and Craig had risen; Kevin brought a couple of extra chairs to draw up to their table and then left telling Joe he was going to arrange for two more meals.

"You *were* an intended victim," Micah told Joe flatly. "Had to be. The culprit couldn't have known that Harley was going to be there. Harley didn't know it herself until she talked to Kieran and found out about the zombie walk and that *you'd* be there."

"But…we should be safe, shouldn't we? I heard Arlo was the culprit and that he's in the hospital—and they don't know if they can save him or not."

"It's true that Arlo is in the hospital. And many people believe he was the mummy and that he was guilty of trying to kill Vivian. She did, after all, say that a mummy had come to her."

"Was there time for the mummy to have reached the museum and attacked someone else to create a new mummy?" Kieran asked.

"You did say that you were right behind him, getting to the museum," Harley said.

"I'm afraid that yes, there was time. I followed the mummy, but I was still some distance away when I saw him go down to the basement area of the museum. Then, of course, I stumbled around down there myself for a while. They need to wall all of that off, because if they don't, they're going to lose some curious fifthgrader down there one day."

"I'm taking a leave from my job," Joe said. "I'm getting out of here tomorrow morning. When this is all over, I'll come back. I called the museum I'm working at and they understood."

"That might be your best move," Micah told him.

Joe let out a long sigh. "Thank God! I thought you were going to tell me I wasn't allowed to leave town."

"We'll need your contact information. However, you were in full sight of thousands of people most of the day. It would be very hard to prove you had any involvement," Craig said.

"Thank God," he muttered again.

Kevin Finnegan returned to the table. The talk shifted back and forth between the zombie walk and the situation at the museum.

Suddenly they all seemed to realize it had grown very late.

"I'm going home so I can get out of here in the morning," Joe said. "You all take care."

"We need to know where you'll be and how to reach you," Craig said.

"You bet. Just no sharing anything that's gone on," Joe said.

"No sharing," they all swore at once.

"I take it you're getting Harley home?" Craig asked Micah.

Kieran looked at Harley—who refused to look back at her.

She didn't know. *Was* he seeing her home? She'd thrown herself at him last night; maybe he'd changed his mind about her during the very long day.

"Yes, I'll make sure she gets home safely," Micah said. He managed to keep a straight face. Harley was surprised that he could.

Actually, she was surprised that she didn't flush. She just smiled sweetly at Kieran, who was obviously amused, intrigued and, Harley hoped, glad that she and Micah seemed to be getting on very well, indeed.

As he drove her home, there was so much to say; so much speculation in which they could indulge.

But they didn't talk at all.

The minute they reached Harley's place and closed the door to her apartment, they were in each other's arms. Micah impatiently shed his Glock first; Harley shrugged out of her jacket, grabbing for his shirt as she tore at her own buttons.

Micah drew the shirt over her head before she could get to the last of the buttons. She had her hands on his waistband and his belt buckle, while their lips merged in a deep and fiery kiss that was also sweet and breathless and filled with laughter.

There was a fair amount of awkwardness that went along with stripping so quickly, with wanting nothing more than to touch, to feel, to kiss…

Clothing wound up strewn all over the floor.

Harley hoped there was no one on the street as she raced past the windows and headed for the stairway.

Micah caught up with her. He swept her into his arms.

"Oh, no! You can't…they're winding stairs. We'll end up—"

"I can do it this way!" he assured her, tossing her over his shoulder.

And he could. He made it up the winding stairway. Dropped her naked on the bed and fell beside her. Still panting, he raised himself on one elbow.

Harley pushed him back down.

She rained kisses over his naked body, reaching all around, taking him into her mouth.

He lifted her up, pulled her to him, rolled with her, kissed and teased and took his kisses everywhere until she cried out. They kissed and laughed in the tangled sheets, and then they were locked together again and the laughter was gone. They were too breathless, too desperate…

This was new. So new. It had been a long time since

she'd chanced a relationship with anyone. It was wonderful because...

Because it was wonderful.

She knew with an indefinable certainty that it would always be good with him. They were so easy together. They could laugh, even do silly things, and those things somehow became erotic. She wanted to forget the world and curl up next to him forever, except that one could never really forget the world.

And, of course, that was it.

She could be with him—as if he were an oasis—and still talk about the burning sands and the desert around them. She could make love, hot and wickedly wet and exciting—and she could still tell him what she was thinking. They could share confidences and exchange opinions without any risk of betrayal.

She was in lust...and maybe falling in love.

"She knows something," Micah was saying. "I'm sure she does."

"She? Which she? Vivian, Belinda, Yolanda or Satima?" Harley asked. She propped herself up on an elbow to look down at him.

"Satima. I mean Satima," he said. "As for Yolanda, I think she just wants to keep her nose clean. She hates it that something connected to the Department of Antiquities has negative baggage attached to it. I'd swear she just doesn't want to get involved with the ugliness of it. Egan is working the diplomatic channel to get her to come and talk to us. As far as we can tell, she's still in the States. She may not have anything for us, but I'd still love to talk to her myself."

"McGrady could have turned her off American law enforcement forever and ever," Harley said.

"Sad thing is, he might have been a decent cop. You don't get to be a detective unless you come up through the ranks or know someone. He has no patience."

"And no ability with people," Harley put in.

Micah shrugged. "I want to talk to the missing girl, Satima, as well. And now we have a number for her that we didn't have before—thanks to you knowing where to dig. So to speak."

"Ah, yes…dig. The crime scene people would've found that phone. I don't know why Arlo had it where he did—or why he thought he needed a special phone."

"It's a chip phone, good around the world. Maybe that was the intent," Micah suggested. He sighed, bringing her closer. "I keep feeling we're looking at a giant puzzle and we should be able to see what it is, what the whole picture represents. Except there's one piece missing. If only we had that piece."

"We will have that piece," Harley said confidently. "You and Craig, the FBI, NYPD. You'll find that piece. It's like…"

Her voice trailed off.

"Like?"

"Well, you know my main role in the expedition was to find more clues as to what might have happened to Amenmose. He was murdered. He was buried hastily by someone who loved him. There are many suspects, of course. He was a threat to Ay, who was regent for Tut, and who did become pharaoh in his own right. He was also despised by Tut's sister and brother-in-law. But nothing I've found in any of the ancient stories or records suggests that one of those people killed him. He had a family, and servants, so I guess the suspects are endless. I feel the same way about that as you do—as

we both do—about our current case. Suspects everywhere, but it seems impossible to get the real motive
pinned down. Or to determine the whereabouts of each
suspect at the crucial times."

"Process of elimination," Micah said. "Joe Rosello.
People did see him all day long."

"Vivian Richter. She got out of the hospital late that
morning."

"I'd still like to find out if she was home the rest of
the day!"

"But…"

"Something might occur to her," Micah said.

"Everyone, including you, seems to believe that Arlo
Hampton is guilty. That he poisoned himself trying to
poison others."

"Hey, I keep an open mind! You say the mummy
who touched you on the street was someone different.
I believe you."

"We don't know where Jensen Morrow was today.
Or Belinda."

"Or—at this moment—Vivian or Ned Richter. Or
Roger Eastman. But we'll know soon."

"We will?"

He smiled at her. "Of course. Craig and I are just
cogs in a giant machine, a machine that doesn't stop.
Anyway, I agree with you. Something still isn't right.
First thing I want is a conversation with Satima Mahmoud. Then Ned and Vivian Richter. Then…"

"It's about motive," Harley said.

"Motive," he repeated.

He was done talking.

He pulled her back into his arms.

And she lost herself in the feel of him against her.

Chapter 8

Micah woke to the sound of his phone ringing—somewhere.

He remembered that he'd shed his clothing downstairs.

He leaped out of bed and hurried down the winding wrought iron staircase, glancing at the picture windows that looked out over the night, the city and Grace Church.

He sped across the room, thinking they had to remember to buy drapes—major drapes—before night fell again. Of course, that was being presumptuous, but...

He couldn't force his thoughts in any other direction.

His phone. He dived for his jacket and caught it on the eighth ring.

"Fox."

"Fox!" It was Richard Egan. "We have Yolanda Akeem down here. She's going to be returning to Egypt later this morning. She's with a friend of mine from the State Department. I suggest you get in quickly. I'll inform Frasier, too."

"Yes, sir!"

Micah turned off the phone and ran around finding the rest of his clothing. He tore up the stairs.

Harley was sleepily beginning to rise.

"What is it?" she asked anxiously. "It's not even seven," she murmured. "I guess that's not so early."

"I have to go. Now. They've got Yolanda down at the FBI office. She's leaving for Egypt, and she's with someone from the State Department."

"Go!"

He ran for the shower. She didn't follow him.

They both knew why that wouldn't be a good idea.

In a few minutes he was dressed and heading for the stairs. Harley had slipped into a robe to accompany him down. "We should've set coffee to brew last night," she murmured, opening the door so he could leave.

He paused to kiss her quickly on the lips.

"We weren't thinking about coffee. Personally, I'd forgo the coffee for what we did last night. I'll call you as soon as I know anything. You're not working today, are you?"

"No, nothing for Fillmore," Harley said. "Maybe I'll hang around and read for a while."

"Sounds good. Talk soon," he promised.

Then he was out the door. The office wasn't far, and once there, he could leave the car with a young agent in the street. No more than thirty minutes had passed since he'd answered his phone to Egan, but he couldn't help being a little afraid Yolanda might already have left.

She was returning home; this was his chance.

To his great relief, she was there. He learned from the receptionist that Egan was with her in the conference room. He hurried there—just in time to fall in step with Craig Frasier, who'd arrived, as well.

"Think she has anything?" Craig asked hopefully.

"Your guess is as good as mine." Micah shrugged. "But anything she does have might be worthwhile."

"Too true, when we keep stumbling in the dark. Literally. In the basement and below at the museum."

"Someone knows the museum—and knows it well."

They'd reached the conference room. When they entered, Egan and the handsomely dressed man who had accompanied Yolanda Akeem rose to meet them. Yolanda started to rise; they quickly urged her to remain seated.

"Gentlemen, Ms. Yolanda Akeem and Mr. Tom Duffy from the State Department," Egan said. "Special Agents Craig Frasier and Micah Fox."

Everyone sat then.

"Thank you for being here," Micah told Yolanda. "We know you don't have to speak with us. We're grateful that you're willing to do so."

Yolanda Akeem was an attractive woman, probably approaching fifty. Her eyes and skin were dark, a testament to a rich and diverse background. Her appearance was dignified, almost regal.

She nodded. "I would have spoken earlier, if I'd thought I had something of value to say," she said. She wrinkled her nose. "I spoke with that silly policeman when Vivian Richter was attacked. He wanted to know if I believed that mummies could come to life—if I thought that curses were real! They *are* real, of course, when we are cursed with foolish people!"

"We weren't in charge of the investigation then, Ms. Akeem," Egan said.

"Yes, I know. And I spoke with Special Agent Fox before, when we were both reeling from the loss of a dear friend." Yolanda Akeem looked over at Micah and smiled sadly. "So, so sad. So much trouble. Such a terrible time."

"Yes, a terrible time," Micah agreed.

Yolanda waved a hand in the air. "Everyone running and rushing—and Henry barely cold. And then, of course—the insurrection! Children mewling that they are not privileged enough. A mountain out of a molehill. But…safety first, always. Yes, it's a tough world and there are very real terrors and threats. But in this case…"

"Yes."

"My friend, Special Agent Fox, believes that something about this entire situation, and about the tentative conclusions we've managed to reach, isn't right," Craig said. "Frankly, we may be looking too hard at the wrong suspects."

Yolanda Akeem hesitated. "I wish I could say, 'No, you're wrong.' But, you see, there's a bad taste in my mouth, although I don't understand why. The expedition was going well, or at least I thought so. Henry had worked in my country many times before. We loved him. And his students…they were charming. I was happy to work with them, too. The people from Alchemy…well, I overheard them having arguments with each other over money now and then. How much was being spent, where they needed to save. Of course, it was funny because Mr. Richter was the on-site CEO for the company and he was watching pennies, while his wife… She's a true dreamer and scientist, I believe. Money meant nothing to her." She grinned. "Henry ignored them all. Arlo Hampton tried to remind everyone that *he* was the main Egyptologist for Alchemy. Still, despite the little spats, it all seemed to be going well enough. But then… Henry died."

"You were at the camp that night?"

"I was. Belinda was going to go into town with Harley and Jensen, but she's engaged, you know. They will marry soon, I hope. Video chatting with her fiancé was a highlight for both of them. Belinda used my equipment for her chats. I was doing paperwork, and she was with me."

Micah glanced at Craig. It seemed that they could definitely scratch Belinda off any list that had to do with Henry's death.

"But you saw Henry."

"I saw Henry. Just for a few minutes early in the evening. I also saw our young interpreter, Satima Mahmoud, with Mr. Rosello. Joe, yes, Joe Rosello."

Micah nodded. Joe was already off their list. He'd been on the zombie walk—and he'd been costumed as a zombie, not a mummy.

He couldn't believe he was even thinking that way!

Yolanda suddenly frowned. "Perhaps trouble was in the air. I heard Satima arguing with Joe. They didn't usually argue. They were beautiful people, you know? Both of them. But that night Satima was tired. She just wanted to go home. Joe kept saying that he wanted to finish the work. She said the work wouldn't go away, and she had family she had to see. So it was…a hot, troubled evening. Yes, hot in the desert, of course. But the Richter husband and wife were arguing, and Satima and Joe were arguing. Henry was busy with his new treasures. Arlo wanted a bigger role, and I think he saw Henry as a means to that end, but he knew he had to leave him at some time. He was testy… That evening I wanted nothing more to do with any of them. Satima was…almost nasty to me! If I'd hired her, I would have fired her right then and there. I speak many languages. My father was Egyptian, but my mother was Mexican and French. I can interpret nicely. I wish I'd been the one doing that job."

She looked at them all and released a long breath.

"I will admit that I wasn't crazy about Vivian Richter, but I'm sorry she was hurt. Arlo… I'm sorry he was hurt, too. After Henry's death, he got his own way with Alchemy and the exhibit, but he did not seem like a bad person. Did he do all this? Why? For position? For glory? They say that he is going to die, most likely. He was not found as quickly as Vivian."

"We don't know if he was guilty," Egan said. "Or if he was a victim."

Yolanda shook her head. "I'm sorry. I know nothing more. And I did not mean to be…unhelpful. You may feel free to call me with more questions if you wish. I am returning to Cairo, but I will be accessible to you, if I can be of any more help."

Everyone rose, bidding one another goodbye.

Then the man from the State Department and the Egyptian liaison were gone. Egan, Craig and Micah were left to look at one another.

"This is the first I've heard of everyone fighting," Micah said. "Even when I was in Cairo, it didn't come up. Of course, everything was chaos then."

"That could explain," Craig began, "why Ned Richter

wasn't sitting at his wife's side the entire time she was in the hospital. If they'd been fighting, I mean."

"And maybe he wasn't with her yesterday," Egan said. "Check into it. And also, we've got people hot on the trail of the interpreter, Satima Mahmoud. Let's hope they'll be able to find her. They work hard at keeping up good communications with the police, here and abroad."

"What about Arlo Hampton?" Micah asked. "Anything? He made it through the night?"

"He's alive, yes, hanging on. Unconscious," Egan said. "Doctors… Well, I'm used to speaking with medical examiners. Seems I understand them a lot better than the guys who treat the living. Anyway, Arlo Hampton's still alive but they're not sure about neurological impact."

"The guy could end up a vegetable," Craig said.

"He could pull through all the way. They had to put him in a medically induced coma. When they bring him out of that, we might learn something. Anyway, he's alive, but he's sure as hell not going to be working soon," Egan said.

"Let's trust that he makes it," Micah said quietly.

"I guess maybe we should try speaking with Ned Richter and Joe Rosello again," Craig said.

"Rosello came out squeaky clean," Egan reminded them.

"Yes, but I don't think our missing interpreter is so squeaky clean," Micah said.

"You really think this Egyptian woman—who isn't even in this country—is involved?" Egan asked, puzzled.

"Yes. But I haven't figured out how. She can't be found. I'm hoping that doesn't mean she's dead," Micah said.

"Joe wasn't playing a mummy yesterday. We know

that. But I agree with Micah," Craig said. "It'll be interesting as hell to find out what was going on between him and Satima Mahmoud."

"I'm so sorry. You sound terribly depressed," Harley told Jensen.

He'd called early, right around eight. Of course, by eight, half of New York was already bustling, but with no real plans, Harley had actually thought she'd be able to sleep in.

And simply enjoy the fact that she lay in sheets where they'd been together, where Micah's scent still lingered.

But she was glad to hear from Jensen; he was still trying to function, despite all else.

"Well, of course, I'm depressed," Jensen Morrow said over the phone. "Cops all over the place. It's necessary, I guess. Vivian came around fast—got better, survived!—but I understand Arlo's in bad shape. On the other hand, if Arlo did kill Henry and tried to kill Viv, he deserves whatever's happening to him."

"I don't think he did it, Jensen. He didn't commit any crimes yesterday, at any rate. I saw the mummy in the street, or *a* mummy in the street, and—"

She broke off. She suddenly knew what had been different about the mummy in the street and the pictures of Arlo Hampton as a mummy, passed out, almost dead, on the museum floor.

She wasn't sure it would be wise to share that information with anyone other than Micah, Craig and the police.

Jensen didn't seem to notice that she'd abruptly stopped speaking. "I'm here at work," he continued. "Let's see, Ned Richter is due in, and—you're not going to believe this!—Vivian Richter is coming with him. She's barely out of the hospital. She may be a bitch on wheels, but she's a trouper, I'll give her that. The woman loves her Egyptology! Needless to say, Arlo won't be here. And it's lonely without him. None of our buds are around. Belinda and Roger are busy with their own work. Talked to Joe—he left town this morning. He's scared. He thinks the mummy in the crowd was after him. And that might be true. Who knows? But if the mummy *was* Arlo, then none of us has anything to worry about. Right?"

The mummy in the street had not been Arlo Hampton. Arlo was tall. The mummy hadn't been very tall.

"Jensen, I don't think Arlo was guilty of anything."

"Some criminologist you are! You want to believe the best about everyone," Jensen muttered. "Are you going to come in and keep me company and help me ward off mummies?" he asked.

"I—I was going to spend some time with Craig's girlfriend."

"The lovely Kieran. So the two of you are going to dig deep into all our minds and figure out which one of us is the sicko? Whoever it is has to be crazy as a bat. I can see the defense in court. 'The bacteria made me do it!'"

Harley couldn't help smiling. "Defense attorneys. It's their job. But, yes, bacteria. It can affect the mind."

"Should I leave town?" Jensen asked her seriously. "Man, I love this place. I know I can come off as a jerk sometimes, but I love this city and this museum. I loved the expedition, too—until Henry was killed. But I can't let all our work fall apart, Harley. It meant too much to Henry. And it's too important for future generations."

"You're right," Harley agreed. "The cops—"

"Are idiots. Whoops, sorry. Maybe the Feds are better."

"Killers make mistakes—and they get caught," Harley said.

"And sometimes they don't."

"This time, they will."

"You haven't seen the half of it. The stuff here, Harley, it's ironic that it all started with a murder, isn't it? Amenmose, I mean. Maybe you can figure out who killed the guy. That was the major thing for you on our expedition, right?"

"Yep. I still find it incredibly interesting that he was killed, and yet he was rewarded with the kind of tomb that would allow him to move into the afterlife," Harley said.

"Come in today! I'll meet you at the doors. You'll be safe. Lots of cops around. I'll get you any piece of research material you want that I can find! I'll be like your apprentice!" Jensen said.

"Okay," Harley agreed. "I'll text you when I'm at the entrance."

She ended the call and glanced around the room, running her hands over the sheets. So much for luxuriating in memory.

She hurriedly showered and ran out, anxious to get to the subway and up to the museum.

Despite herself, she found that she kept scrutinizing the crowds of people who thronged around her. It was still morning rush hour. People were everywhere, on their way to work and school.

She was looking for a mummy, she realized.

That was ridiculous, she thought. And yesterday,

it didn't seem bizarre at all that there'd be a mummy around; a mummy fit right in with the zombies.

Rush hour on Monday. Not likely that a mummy would be running around. Then again, it was New York, and people might see a mummy and merely shrug.

No mummies appeared—and she had to admit she was grateful.

As she neared the museum, she texted Jensen. He texted back that he'd meet her at the entrance.

Jensen and an NYPD officer were at the door; Jensen explained who she was and Harley showed the officer her ID.

She was allowed to come in.

It felt strange to walk through the entry with Jensen when everything was so empty. He told her there were at least ten police officers in the building, along with what he believed were "fledgling" FBI agents—probably bored to tears, but assigned to watch over the museum. Jensen talked about the museum itself with great enthusiasm; he just couldn't resist. She already knew that the facility was devoted to ancient civilizations, from Mesopotamia to Rome to Greece and ancient Egypt and other societies. He explained that he considered it a homage to humanity creating civilization; there was even a wonderful new section on the development of humans, back to the hominidae or great apes speciating from the ancestors of the lesser apes. "When this is…when this is solved, when things are back to normal, when life at least *feels* normal, you really have to come and spend a day here, just touring around, checking out the exhibits. It's a phenomenal museum. And I'm so happy to be here, except now the rest of the scientists, curators, historians—and even the café and gift shop employees!—hate us."

"Oh, I doubt that."

"Nope. It's true."

"When life does get back to normal, they won't hate you. And, as we've noted before, I'll bet all the insanity's going to make the museum more popular than ever. It has a really wicked mystery story now," Harley reminded him.

"Well, anyway, let's head back. In one of the prep clean rooms, there are some papers Henry'd been working on. Plus, there are a number of mummies in the room—still in their coffins, for the most part, except for our 'screaming' mummy, the one we saw with Henry before he…died. Anyway, I have a meeting with the museum director in a few minutes."

"Gordon Vincent," Harley murmured.

Jensen nodded. He glanced her way and sighed. "Yeah. They don't know if Arlo's going to make it or not. If he does, I heard he's probably going to be arrested."

"He didn't do it," Harley said again.

"But—"

"I'm telling you. He was a victim. Like Vivian."

"Well, from your lips to God's ears, right? Anyway— and honestly, I wouldn't want something to come about this way—I believe I'm going to be promoted to curator director for the Amenmose exhibit."

"Oh. Wow," Harley murmured. "Congratulations. Well, I guess… I mean, I understand, no one would want things to work this way, but wasn't Arlo employed by Alchemy?"

"Yes, but he was being offered the permanent position here," Jensen said.

They walked by the temple and the exhibits that were usually open to the public, then went to the employee section of the museum and one of the rooms next to Arlo's lab.

"It's mainly artifacts," Jensen said. "But that desk has boxes of Henry's notes. No one could read his scribbled handwriting as well as you could. Maybe you'll find something. I'll come back as soon as the meeting's over and we can go to lunch. Not in the museum, I'm afraid, since everything is closed down today. But I'm sure we can think of someplace you'll like."

"How about the sandwich shop over on Sixth?" Harley suggested. "It's a five-minute walk."

He gave her a thumbs-up and left. She listened as the door clicked shut.

This room didn't require "clean" suits, but it was climate controlled. Harley assumed it would be taken for granted that anyone in the room would have complete respect for ancient sarcophagi, bodies and other artifacts.

For a moment, she just looked around.

Many things were still crated. There were just so many artifacts that they were switched in and out of the display. Some of the sarcophagi—the magnificent, beautifully designed and painted outer coffins—had been unpacked. They'd withstood time and climate well, since they were made of hardwood and precious metals.

Shelves on the wall held numerous canopic jars; others were heaped with jewelry. One shelf contained dozens of statuettes and, carefully set in a corner of the room, was a pile of chariot wheels, the body of a chariot and a set of harnesses.

Another shelf held several mummified cats.

Yet another held weapons, some of them simple, having belonged to rank-and-file soldiers. There were maces, shields, daggers, swords, knives and more. Some were inlaid with precious jewels and gold.

They were worth a small fortune.

But to the best of Harley's knowledge, nothing had ever disappeared from the museum.

The motive for murder wasn't for treasure. So it seemed, anyway. Then why...?

She shook her head. It was like a puzzle, as Micah had said—with one crucial missing piece. But if you could find all the pieces and put them together, a picture would emerge.

A picture from the past? Perhaps. And what might that have to do with the present? Probably nothing at all. But then again, sometimes just turning one's mind to a different puzzle helped solve the one that was more pressing.

Harley examined the many offerings in the room that would eventually be catalogued and join other treasures on the museum floor. Then she moved to the cheap aluminum desk—with the cheap aluminum chair in front of it—that was piled high with cardboard boxes of Henry Tomlinson's observations and recordings. They ranged from his calculations as to where they would find the tomb, to his reactions the day they discovered it. If she knew Henry, the boxes were also stuffed with research papers and anything else he'd found or received that complemented his own work.

Harley sat down and began to read.

Surely, museum staff had at least scanned them before this.

But maybe they hadn't read everything. Maybe they hadn't known Henry.

Maybe they hadn't been determined to catch a killer.

Ned and Vivian Richter had a house—a Victorian manor in Brooklyn, in the Williamsburg area, not far from Pratt Institute.

"Swanky," Craig murmured, ringing the bell.

"It is nice," Micah agreed. "When I was around here several years ago on that special assignment I worked with you, this area was still kind of sketchy. Lots of drugs and crime—and 'swanky' places like this were usually turned into frat houses or apartment buildings with dozens of closet-size apartments."

"This area has come up in the world—and someone's put real money into this house. But Richter's been a CEO on expeditions with Alchemy. I guess he's earned plenty of bonuses and more through the years," Craig said.

"I guess so."

Craig rang the bell again.

"What do you want to bet a maid's going to answer?" Micah asked.

"I wouldn't bet against you!" Craig replied.

"Nothing wrong with being rich," Micah said. "I'd love to try it one day."

They were right; the door was opened by a pretty young woman in a maid's outfit that would've done any movie set proud.

"May I help you?" she asked. She had a strong accent, possibly Slavic.

They showed their badges.

"We need to see Mr. and Mrs. Richter, please," Micah told her.

The woman pursed her lips. "You are aware, sir, that Mrs. Richter is just out of the hospital," she said.

"Yes, we are aware. We plan to be brief," Craig assured her.

She led them into a parlor that looked like a furniture showroom. Micah wondered if anyone had ever been in the room before.

But they were only there a minute or two before Vivian Richter made an appearance. "Gentlemen. What can I do for you? I'm about to head into the museum. With everything that's been going on... Well, I keep thinking that maybe someone's out to sabotage the exhibit. I keep going over our books, our notes—and, of course, our artifacts. I'm saying 'our.' They aren't ours, as I'm sure you realize. Everything we discovered will be returned to Egypt. We're not thieves anymore. There was a time, though... Did you know that during the Victorian era, mummies were so plentiful they were often used as kindling? That's shocking, isn't it?"

"I think I've heard that somewhere," Micah said.

"Well, anyway...how can I help you? Would you like to come into the museum with me?"

"Actually, we'd like to know where you were yesterday, once you got out of the hospital, and if you were with your husband all day. We'd like to speak with him, too."

"Ned's already gone to the museum. But in answer to your question, he was with me all day. He's a devoted husband."

"When did he leave?" Micah asked. "This morning, I mean."

"A little while ago, I believe," Vivian said.

"You *believe*? You didn't actually see him?" Craig asked.

"I spent yesterday and this morning sleeping, resting. I know when my husband's with me. I can feel his presence. Are either of you married? No? You see, after years of marriage, you don't need to *see*, gentlemen—you *feel*. You're both still young. Wait until you've been married for years. You'll understand what I'm talking about."

Vivian Richter was dressed in an attractive, business-like pantsuit; she looked very thin and a little flushed, but otherwise well.

"Agents, why exactly are you questioning me?" she said to them. "I'm a victim. And you can't possibly suspect Ned of any wrongdoing! The whole expedition rested on his shoulders. He wouldn't want anything to go wrong."

"Our apologies, but questioning is necessary, under the circumstances," Micah said.

"Part of the job," Craig added ruefully.

"Oh, please!" Vivian said. "Agent Fox, I heard that you saved my life! And you, Agent Frasier, have been hard at work on the case. I'm grateful to you both, although—due to my recent bout with near death—I haven't had much chance to socialize with law enforcement."

"Mrs. Richter, I can't take credit for saving your life. Anyone there would have dialed 911," Micah said. "We're just glad to see you looking so well."

"Yes! I thank God!" she said. "Great hospital staff,

wonderful EMTs… I'm a very lucky woman. I understand I was poisoned with insecticide but apparently, according to the doctors, there's been an upsurge in problems of that kind because of the liquid nicotine used in electronic cigarettes. They hit me with activated charcoal, and they monitored me for seizures. I was lucky, so lucky. I hear Arlo may not fare as well, that he was exposed to a heavier dose of poison and that he was unconscious when he was found. But I also heard that the police believe Arlo was guilty. That he might've been the 'mummy' who attacked me. Who meant to kill me!" she ended in a whisper. "Arlo and I… We worked well together. I thought so anyway. I wonder if he was worried because I'm married to Ned. Maybe he was worried that would put me in a better position for a raise at Alchemy. And I realize that some people are convinced that Henry was killed… I never knew what to think. I mean, we had to run! There was death coming at us from the desert!"

"Of course," Micah said sympathetically. "So, you believe we'll find Ned at the museum now?"

"Yes. He should be there working."

"But he didn't actually tell you he was going in. And you didn't actually see him," Craig said.

"No, as I was telling you…"

"Yes. You felt him. When's the last time you *saw* him?" Micah asked.

"I, uh… Yesterday's a bit of a blur for me. We left the hospital and then—"

"He came to the hospital to get you," Micah inserted.

"I told you! He's a loving and devoted husband," Vivian said. "Yes! He came to get me. I'm going to call your superiors, gentlemen, if you suggest once more that he's anything less than a wonderful man."

"You still didn't answer the question," Craig pointed out.

"All right! I don't know what time he left this morning. I know he was going to the museum. And he knew, of course—" She suddenly stopped speaking.

"Yes?" Micah prompted.

"I knew he was going into the museum, and he knew I was coming in later today. With everything that went on, and cops, technicians, crime scene people everywhere… I need to see to the integrity of our entire exhibit—especially in light of what happened to Arlo!"

"We'll see that you get there safely, Mrs. Richter," Craig offered. "We have a company car, so we can drop you off at the museum. However, considering what you've been through, I recommend you contact one of the policemen on duty there today. I think you should be under protection."

"I'll make a call," Micah said.

"It's not necessary to request protection," Vivian said. "Honestly, I'll be fine. Now I know to watch out for people coming near me."

"I'll make a call," Micah repeated firmly.

Vivian smiled. "Thank you. It's so lovely that you're watching out for me."

"We'll wait here until you're ready," Micah said.

"Well, then…thank you! Excuse me. I'll be right with you."

She left the room. "You'll take her in?" Micah asked Craig.

"You're going to speak with the housekeeper?"

"Yep."

"You think she's an illegal?"

"Yes. Okay, right now I'll call Egan and get him to talk to whoever's in charge of guarding the museum. They need to keep an eye on Vivian and get eyes on Ned Richter, too. Then I'll come back here and talk to the housekeeper. Find out the last time she saw Ned Richter."

"Okay. I'll get her to the museum," Craig said. He hesitated. "Richter. I just don't see him as a player in this game. He's in big with Alchemy, but he's not a fanatic Egyptologist."

"Maybe, this time around, jealousy isn't the motive," Micah said.

"Then what the hell is?" Craig murmured.

Vivian reappeared, a heavy bag over her shoulder. Craig politely took it for her, and they exited the house.

Micah opened the passenger door of the agency sedan for Vivian. She looked at him, obviously a little confused. "I don't mind riding in the back."

"Ah, but we'd rather have you ride up front with my partner. He'll enjoy your company," Micah said.

"You're not coming?"

"I have some things to do," Micah said vaguely. "Don't forget, Mrs. Richter—I'll get a cop assigned to you. Stay safe and take care of yourself."

When he started to close the car door, she stopped him. "Agent Fox, don't be suspicious of my husband. I know I'm repeating myself, but he's a very kind man. People love him and that's why he's good at his job. He'd never hurt me."

"Stay with an officer, Mrs. Richter," he said, and he managed to close the door.

He glanced back up at the house.

He thought he saw the drapes move and, as soon as the black agency sedan with Craig and Vivian Richter turned the corner, he went back up the walk to the door.

The housekeeper was afraid; he was certain of that. Her immigration status was probably not legal, as he and Craig had guessed.

She might try to hide.

But he wouldn't leave.

And he knew that—whether it was face-to-face or through the door—she would listen to him when he threatened her.

He hated threatening people, especially a young woman like this, working hard to get into the country.

But he had to know the truth.

Because someone else could die.

Standing there on the steps, waiting, Micah realized that he was afraid for more than just an elusive *someone*.

He was afraid for Harley. She'd been on that expedition, she'd been determined to voice her suspicions. Harley was poking her nose into everything.

And Harley Frasier was among those who might be targeted by a mummy. A living mummy armed with deadly poison.

Chapter 9

Harley lost track of time.

She'd known for years, ever since she was a teenager and saw Craig join the FBI, that she wanted to solve crimes. She hadn't wanted to run around the streets with a gun, although she'd been more than willing to partake in classes at a shooting range. What she loved was the puzzle part of crime-solving. She also loved the concept of profiling, and was extremely glad of her friendship with Kieran Finnegan and, through her, Dr. Fuller and Dr. Mira. They were giving and generous with their time, and they'd talked to her upon occasion about criminal profiling. She'd considered going through still more school and entering the field of profiling.

She'd been part of the Amenmose expedition because of her fascination with figuring out motives, clues, possibilities. The puzzle aspects of a crime.

Not that solving the murder of a mummy could help with a present-day case.

Still, solving what might be considered an *extremely* cold case was certainly a useful exercise.

That afternoon, in the room with the mummies and the artifacts and Henry Tomlinson's notes, she found herself even more fascinated with the crime— committed thousands of years ago—because, despite time and place, people were people.

She was familiar with Tutankhamen, but read more about him, including some material that was new to her. She read about Ay. There were numerous references to Amenmose, as well. He knew the stars; he could navigate by them. He knew the heavens and the earth.

And he knew about Ra, about the dishonor Tutankhamen's father had done the ancient gods.

She reviewed the facts about Tut and Akhenaten in Henry's notes and translations, as well as those prepared by other scholars. The discovery of Tutankhamen's tomb by Howard Carter in 1922 had opened their ancient lives to investigation, leading to years of speculating. Some of that speculation had proven to be true; Akhenaten had tried to create a monotheistic society, his one god being Ra, the sun god. When Tutankhamen came to the throne, his father's efforts had been completely erased. In fact, his father's reign had been erased from records, and his mummy had disappeared.

Among Henry's papers, Harley found a research document dated 2010, of which he was a coauthor. It was about the discovery, in a cache of royal mummies, of one who'd proven through DNA testing to be Akhenaten.

But in Tut's time, there must've been many people who still believed what Tut's father had believed. Perhaps there were people prepared to kill a man like Amenmose, a man so ready to help Tut and Ay obliterate his father. Or not. Most experts concluded that Ay had ordered the murder.

Then Harley came across the translation of a letter mentioning a woman named Skrit; more digging showed that she was Amenmose's wife.

Harley rose and walked around the room for a moment. Was one of the mummies there Skrit?

She saw nothing that would indicate such a thing.

Why wasn't the woman buried with him? Of course, the tomb had been a secret. Had she, his loving wife, planned it, planned the burial? Amenmose had been murdered, but he'd been given all the correct funeral rites such a man would have required.

Frustrated, Harley sat back down. She began to read and research again, referring not just to the notes they had, but looking up entries online made by scholars through the ages.

She stopped looking for Amenmose. She started looking for Skrit.

And what she found was truly fascinating.

Micah knocked again.

He knew the housekeeper was in the house.

He'd been there for nearly ten minutes, and she had yet to answer the door.

But he knew she was in there. And that she was hovering close to the door.

"I just have a few questions," he said loudly. "If you don't care to answer them…well, I can have some people from Immigration come down here in a few minutes. I can call Homeland Security, too."

The door finally opened. The pretty housekeeper stepped back. Her eyes were huge and wet with tears she was trying not to shed.

Micah felt like a real jerk. "I'm sorry," he told her. "I don't want to hurt you in any way. I just have to ask you a few questions. And I need you to answer me honestly."

She nodded, looking anxiously out at the street, then pulled him quickly inside.

"I am Valeria. Valeria Andreev. I don't want to go back, please. I want to be legal. Mr. Richter has said he will help me. He pays me well. He is a kind man."

"I don't want you to be sent back, either. You obviously want to be here, and you seem to know the language well."

"I want to be American."

"We can try to help you. But I need your help."

She nodded again, an earnest expression on her face.

"Did Mr. Richter go to the hospital to bring Mrs. Richter home yesterday?"

"Yes, that is true. It is not a lie."

"What time was that?"

"Close to noon."

"Okay, thank you. And then?"

"And then Mrs. Richter asked me for juice and some food, and told me that she would sleep, and she didn't want to be disturbed."

"And?"

"I did not see her again until this morning."

"Okay, thank you. And what about Mr. Richter? Did he stay with her? Talk to her, take care of her and make sure she was all right?"

Valeria looked stricken. She didn't want to tell the truth.

"I saw him… I saw him bring her home."

"He went into her room?"

"Yes."

"But he didn't stay there."

Valeria bit her lower lip and shook her head unhappily.

"I don't think so. I think…they argued. I think she was angry with him. I heard their voices, and then I heard nothing, and I thought…"

"Yes?"

"I thought I heard the door slam."

"Did you see when Mr. Richter left today?"

Valeria shook her head. "No… I… I saw him yesterday. I didn't see him at all today. But, of course, that means nothing. I do not sit here and stare at the door, you know. I don't mean to be a—what do you say?— wiseass. But I don't know."

Micah smiled. "It's okay. I don't think you're trying to be a wiseass. What you do know is this—Mr. and Mrs. Richter fought. They came home from the hospital yesterday at about noon. You saw them both go to her room. You haven't seen Mr. Richter since—and you saw Mrs. Richter for the first time today when you went to get her for my associate and me?"

Valeria nodded, wide-eyed.

Micah handed her one of his cards. "If you need help, call me."

Her eyes brightened and she held the card close to her chest.

Micah headed out to the street. He saw a taxi and grabbed it, pulling out his cell phone as he did.

They were nearing the bridge when he got through to Craig.

"The maid didn't actually see either of the Richters after about noon yesterday," he told Craig. "Until she brought her to the door this morning."

"Interesting," Craig said. "Because Ned Richter isn't at the museum. I talked to the officer in charge. No one's seen him since yesterday, sometime in the afternoon. In fact, right around the time Arlo Hampton was found."

Harley jumped up, determined to find Jensen. She was almost certain that she'd discovered the truth about Amenmose. She'd put well-known facts together with information from less well-known sources—and had come up with her theory.

She wondered if there was a way to prove what she believed she knew.

Not easy.

Because, of course, if the murderer was Ay or any other person with power, he or she wouldn't have performed the deed himself—or herself. He—or she—would have had lackeys.

But Harley was convinced her theory made sense. Perfect sense.

Amenmose had been killed. He'd been killed because he'd secretly been a far greater fan of Tutankhamen's father than he'd ever let on. Ay had probably known that Amenmose whispered in the boy king's ear. Amenmose had been skilled at playing the political game. He'd pretended to listen to every word that left Ay's mouth; he'd proclaimed himself a man of the future, not the past. But in his heart, he'd felt certain that Tut's father had been right. And because of that—because those closest to him had known and others might have suspected—anyone connected to him, related to him, or even just a friend or servant to him, might have been in danger.

She left the room and glanced quickly down the hall. There was no one to be seen; not a police officer, not an employee, no one.

"Jensen?"

No answer.

"Jensen, where the hell are you?" she wondered aloud.

She hurried down the hall, past the lab. No one there, either. Of course, Arlo was the person who usually worked in the lab. And Arlo...

She hadn't heard that he was dead. Maybe he was still clinging to life, even if his poisoning had been worse than Vivian's. She hoped so.

Because she just didn't believe that he was guilty.

"Jensen!"

Past the lab, she made for her friend's office and knocked. Once again, no answer. She tried the door and it opened easily, but Jensen wasn't inside.

"Damn you," she grumbled. "Bring me in—and then disappear!"

Harley closed the door and tried the offices of Vivian Richter, Ned Richter, Arlo—even the museum director, Gordon Vincent's. No one was in any of them.

As she stood there, she again heard the terrible screech of a cat.

Just as she had heard when she'd been looking at the cat mummy.

Nothing mysterious about that, she told herself. There was obviously a cat somewhere in the museum. She'd meant to ask someone. It had probably been a stray, and a museum employee, unable to stand the sight of the poor creature begging in the street, had brought it in. That person must have fed it and kept it hidden here somewhere.

Poor thing; it deserved better.

"Where are you?" she murmured aloud. "Little creature, where are you? Where's Jensen? Where's anyone?"

She went back into the hallway, listening for the cat.

She heard it meow. She thought the sound was coming from the walls—or from beneath her.

She guessed the cat was down in one of the old tunnels, maybe in a section of the abandoned subway.

Harley remembered the day she and Micah had been with Arlo, and she hurried to the stairway that led below.

It was dark, of course.

She had her flashlight—of course.

She turned it on and walked carefully down the steps, first to the basement, through rooms and rooms of storage, and then down another level.

To tunnels of nothing.

To darkness that led nowhere.

And then she heard it again. It wasn't a scream this time. It was a pathetic kind of mewling.

She hadn't even seen the cat yet, but she felt so bad for the little creature, which was obviously scared. It probably had no idea where it was, how to get out, how to find help or sustenance.

Maybe she could keep a cat. A cat would be a good companion.

She wondered if Micah liked cats.

She wondered if it mattered.

Harley knew she was definitely in lust and halfway

in love, but she'd told herself it *was just temporary*, that she expected nothing. He was living and working in Washington, DC, and he'd go back there. He'd given her no hint, nothing to suggest Harley should go back with him.

And yet she couldn't accept the fact that he might walk away. They'd met and joined forces over Henry. They got along extremely well, but they were both determined and stubborn, and she didn't intend to forget that she wanted to pursue her career.

Everything had begun just a few days ago, and already she couldn't imagine her life without him in it.

She gave a little scream, startled when the cat let out another mew. The sound was very close.

"Kitty, kitty, where are you?" she called.

The pathetic squeaking began again.

"Where are you? Come on, kitty, kitty, kitty. I'll help you!"

She came around a corner and almost fell into a niche in the wall. She tried to steady herself and realized she was leaning on an old maintenance door.

It creaked open on very rusty hinges.

She heard the cat cry again, really loudly this time. She'd found it!

"Hey, there you are," she said. "Come on, little one. I'll take you somewhere safe and warm and get you something to eat."

What if Micah Fox was allergic to kittens? She'd never asked him about pets.

She'd never asked him about anything. She'd just fallen into something crazy, she'd wanted him so desperately.

She shone her light around again, seeking the cat.

"Hey, sweet thing, I'm going to find you," Harley said out loud.

And then she froze as her light fell on the crying kitten.

And on so much more…

"Get in here. We've got Sanford Wiley, our man in Cairo, ready for a video chat in twenty minutes," Richard Egan told Micah. "He has some information."

"On Satima Mahmoud?" Micah asked.

"That's what I imagine," Egan replied.

Craig was doing the driving. He was a damned good driver, and as a New Yorker, he could maneuver the streets as few could.

Micah had a feeling that whatever Sanford Wiley had discovered, it was important to their case.

He put a call through to Harley, anxious to talk to her, to hear her voice.

She didn't answer.

Craig glanced over at him.

"She didn't say she was going out," Micah murmured. "Or, she might have said that she was going to be with Kieran."

"I wouldn't worry. Leave a message. If she's on the subway, she won't get it for a while."

"I'll bet she went to the museum. Jensen—that friend of hers—I think he keeps encouraging her to come in. I don't feel good about it, but I'm not sure why."

"At least Vivian Richter seemed fine. She seems to believe that Arlo tried to kill her and that he might've killed Henry Tomlinson."

"Yeah, well, I *don't* believe it, and I'm positive you don't, either. Also, I know damned well that Harley doesn't believe it. And Craig, what I've said before is true—Harley's had more classes of all kinds than we have. Yes, in a classroom. She doesn't have much practical experience, not really. But she's smart as a whip. If she says something is off, it is."

"I'll call Kieran. She'll track her down. How's that?"

"Thanks. Tell her we'll join the tracking party as soon as we're done with the video chat," Micah said.

"Will do."

"She's at work, though, isn't she?"

"She won't have a problem. Tell them it's an active case and the good doctors will be more than happy to send Kieran off—or get into it themselves!" Craig assured him. He spoke to the car phone; it dialed Kieran.

"Anything new?" she asked. "What's going on?"

"Can you find Harley?" Craig asked her.

"Sure. I know where she is."

"You do?"

"At the museum. I talked to her briefly when she was on her way there. Jensen asked her to come in. They're good friends, you know, and I think he's feeling pretty lost and alone in all this."

"Yeah, lost and alone," Micah murmured. "Can you get over there? I tried to reach her by phone. She didn't answer."

"I'll go right over," Kieran promised. "I'll find her, don't worry. And when I do, we'll give you a call."

Kieran said goodbye and hung up; Craig looked at Micah. "Feel better?"

"I wish I did."

"You don't like Jensen."

Micah shook his head. "But he was with Harley when Henry was killed, so…"

"Yep." Craig was quiet for a minute, and Micah knew what he was thinking.

"Two people could've been involved," he said quietly. "It's a question of which two. Do you think maybe Ned Richter? Would Richter actually have done that to his own wife?"

"They fight quite a bit, or so we've heard," Craig said. "Yolanda told us she heard them arguing, and the maid told you that they were fighting yesterday."

"Yes, but…wrapping someone in nicotine-soaked linen?"

"She was found immediately. So she survived," Craig said.

They reached the office. Leaving the car, they hurried through the ground-floor security check and up to Egan's office.

Egan was already engaged in the call with Sanford Wiley.

On the video screen, they could see that Wiley looked glum.

"Did you find her? Did you find Satima Mahmoud?" Micah asked.

"Yeah, we found her," Wiley said.

"But you didn't bring her in."

"She's dead," Wiley told them.

Micah had been standing. He sank into one of the chairs in the conference room. "Dead? Not…as a mummy?"

"As a mummy? No. Right now, they have some of her friends in custody. She was likely killed by a member of her 'group'—although exactly who that is, I don't know—or by an enemy of this group. That's just what we're being told. The situation's complicated, but from what we've gleaned so far, there was no real insurrection planned for the night Henry Tomlinson died. We know this because the Egyptian police are questioning someone they pulled in. Some kid who didn't want to spend his life in prison. He says they were contacted by Satima Mahmoud. She had money, a lot of money. She was willing to pay them to get a fake insurrection going. That's why it was such a pitiable show. No one really wanted to bear arms, go against anything—or get caught," Wiley explained.

"So we've been thinking in the right direction," Micah said. "It was all a diversion to keep the police or any other authorities from discovering what really happened to Henry Tomlinson."

"Yes, that's what we believe on this end," Wiley said. "Satima Mahmoud was found with a bullet in her back. We think it could've been fired by someone in a group with a different political view for the future—or, as I said, someone in her own group. Many people were arrested for taking part in the so-called uprising. Perhaps someone wanted revenge."

"Still hard to understand," Craig said. "The Amenmose find was worth a fortune."

"Yes, there were priceless objects. And, yes, they might have wanted them for their monetary value to support their cause, whatever that was. Thing is, the black market is hard to navigate these days. And if you're caught...not good. Cash—cold hard cash—is far better than even a priceless object. Someone gave Satima a lot of cold hard cash. At the moment, that's all I know. If we get anything else..."

"Thank you, Wiley," Micah said. "You've been a tremendous help. I'm sorry the woman is dead," he added.

Egan finished up with Wiley, and they cut off the chat.

"Cold hard cash? Someone with access to a lot of it?" Egan mused. "That's not your average grad student."

"There's Richter," Craig said. "Or…well, some grad students come from family money. That's how they manage to study forever and ever. We have background checks on everyone. I've skimmed all the files…"

"Morrow, Jensen Morrow. His father invented some kind of cleaning product. He's got money," Micah said. But it was true, too, that they'd just left the Richter house, which had to be worth millions.

Craig nodded. "Yeah. But to be fair, it *could* be Richter. He'd have the money. He was supposedly with his wife when everything was going on back in the Sahara. We know now that the two of them fight, although Vivian Richter swears that her husband is totally loving and good."

"But the maid said differently," Craig pointed out.

"The maid?" Egan asked.

Craig waved a hand in the air and said, "Sir, I think we may have to help that woman out when this is all over. She talked to Micah about Richter's whereabouts."

"Go and get Vivian Richter," Egan said. "Bring her in. I think it's time we had a conversation here in the office."

"On our way!" Micah said.

They hurried back to the street where the car was waiting.

As they drove, Micah tried Harley's number again.

"Still not answering," he muttered to Craig.

"We'll find her," Craig promised. "Don't forget," he said, "she's my cousin."

There was a grim set to Craig Frasier's mouth.

Micah was glad for it. That meant he wasn't alone;

they were going to find Harley, and they'd damned well find her fast—and she'd be all right.

It was ridiculous, it was horrible, and it was like something out of a horror movie by a master of the genre.

Harley had found the cat.

And the cat was sitting on the head of a man.

The man was dead. It was Richter. Ned Richter.

She couldn't scream.

The last thing she *should* do was scream!

In fact, she was worried about having her flashlight on. But the whiff of gases or decay, some ghastly smell, that was coming to her made Harley think the man she was staring at had been dead for some time, probably at least twenty-four hours.

He hadn't been wrapped in linen. He probably hadn't died from any kind of poisoning.

Ned had been stabbed through the heart with an Egyptian dagger. He was shoved up against a wall; he'd probably died right there, she surmised, studying the pool of blood that surrounded him. Blood that had grown sticky.

He'd been killed yesterday. Either just before Arlo had succumbed to the linen wrappings and their nicotine, or just after.

If Arlo had tried to kill Ned Richter... Wait, that made no sense. Why stab Ned with an ancient Egyptian dagger, and then dress up in linen wrappings himself?

And who the hell had that been on the street, the person shorter than Arlo who'd approached her, touched her with the poison?

"Harley? Harley, where are you?"

Jensen?

Jensen was calling her now.

Sure, Jensen was taller than the figure who'd come up to her. But what if he was working with someone? What if he'd gone with her that night in the desert just to throw suspicion off himself? He hadn't killed Henry Tomlinson; that would've been impossible. But he might have been in on it.

She forced herself to stay silent.

But to her great distress, the kitten took that moment to mew desperately for help once again—apparently deciding that help wasn't going to come from Harley.

"Kitty! Aw, here, kitty, kitty!" Jensen said. "Who the hell would be keeping a cat down here?" he asked himself.

He was coming in her direction.

He didn't sound like a killer.

To make matters even worse, Harley's phone began to ring.

It was on vibrate, but even vibrate sounded shockingly loud to her!

She saw that it was Micah, and that he'd called several times. The calls hadn't gone through. Suddenly, now—now!—they were.

She backed as close as she could against the wall. She almost let out an involuntary scream; she'd backed into the corpse. She was stepping in the sticky blood.

"Micah!" she whispered.

He was talking as she answered. She didn't think he'd hear her, and she didn't think he had any idea that she wasn't in a good situation.

"Harley, you're at the museum, right? Kieran's coming there to get you. Leave. Leave with her. Wiley, the agent in Cairo told us Satima Mahmoud's body was found. She was killed either by a rival political group or by her own friends, they don't really know. But here's what's important—there was no insurrection. It was staged to cover up Henry's murder. The killer could be Ned Richter or possibly Jensen Morrow," Micah said. "You need to get out of there—"

"It's not Ned Richter," she said in a hoarse whisper.

"How do you know?"

"I'm looking at him. He's dead. Dagger to the heart," Harley said.

"Where are you?"

"Subbasement, I think. Near the old subway station."

"What are you doing down there, Harley? Never mind, never mind. We're on our way. You need to get out!"

"Yes, but—"

"Get the hell out of there now! It could be Jensen. Get out, Harley!"

"I can't!" she whispered.

"Why not?"

"Jensen is down here, coming right at me."

Chapter 10

The were a number of hallways and tunnels, entrances and exits down here.

Harley knew that because Arlo had shown her and Micah around the basement and subbasement levels. She had to think; she had to remember everything they'd learned that day. She needed to...

Find a way out.

The kitten was continuing to cry. He had jumped off the body of Ned Richter and was coming to Harley at last, trying to wrap around her ankles.

Harley swept up the kitten.

Poor little thing was sticky with blood; so was she.

Ned Richter's blood. Ned hadn't done any of this. He was innocent—and he was dead. It was almost as if they'd all been victims of a pharaoh's curse.

"Hey, kitty, kitty! Where are you?" Jensen called.

"Harley? Damn it. Where are you, girl? Why haven't the police gotten these damned tunnels closed yet?" he muttered to himself. "Harley? Hey, anybody down here?"

He was coming closer and closer.

A weapon. She needed a weapon!

There was a dead man right next to her. A dead man with a dagger protruding from his chest.

She carefully put down the kitten and crept toward Ned to get the dagger.

It wouldn't move! It was stuck deep in his chest, as if the man's body, his flesh and blood and bone, refused to give up what had brought about its demise!

She would've sworn out loud except that Jensen was coming closer and closer.

Micah and Craig were on their way. They'd be here soon. Kieran was up in the museum somewhere, and it was crawling with police. Kieran wouldn't wait long when she couldn't find Harley; she'd insist that the police start searching the place, tearing it apart.

"Harley?"

Jensen couldn't be more than twenty or twenty-five feet from her.

"Jensen Morrow! Stop right where you are!" a male voice thundered.

Harley knew the voice—it was McGrady. Detective McGrady. He'd followed Jensen down here. She hadn't even seen him, hadn't known he was at the museum.

Harley switched off her penlight.

The darkness seemed overwhelming, except…

She could see Jensen. He had his own light. "McGrady, what the hell is the matter with you? I'm trying to find Harley. You can help me. Harley, where are you and what the hell… Jeez! What's that smell? Is it cat poop? If so, it's the worst damn cat poop I've ever smelled."

He was talking about cat poop. He didn't know he was smelling a dead man. But if he'd killed Ned Richter, he would know.

"Stop, Morrow, or I'll shoot you, you murdering bastard!" McGrady called out.

"What?" Jensen demanded, obviously thrown. "I stopped! I'm right here."

Harley straightened in the dark, letting out a breath. McGrady was here. He was a cop. He had a gun.

But Jensen wasn't guilty. He was just looking for her. Looking for a cat. She believed it with her whole heart.

Harley held her breath for a minute, afraid to speak, to cry out—to warn Jensen and the cop—and afraid not to.

She had solved one mystery that afternoon. The mystery of Amenmose's death. His wife, Skrit, had ordered him killed. She had hired the assassins. She hadn't hated him—well, maybe she had. But despite wanting him dead, she hadn't wanted him deprived of an afterlife. She'd seen to it that he'd died; she had done so to protect herself and their children from the growing power of Ay. She'd been no threat to Ay's position, but her husband had. Still, she hadn't denied him their form of heaven.

And now...

"Harley!" Jensen called, sounding desperate.

She stepped into the darkness of the hall, ready to call his name.

But just as she did, she saw a dark figure streak out from behind Jensen, coming straight at him.

"Jensen! Watch out!"

Harley screamed the warning just in time. He spun

around, avoiding a lethal blow from Vivian Richter, who was wielding a jewel-encrusted pike. But Vivian was quick to double back, hitting him hard on the head with the end of her weapon.

Jensen went down. And as he did, his light went out.

"What the hell?" McGrady roared. "Mrs. Richter, are you all right? Are you all right?"

Something flew through the tunnel—heading directly for the cop. Harley cried out his name. "McGrady! Get down!" she shrieked.

She couldn't see what happened next.

Jensen's light was gone; McGrady's was, too.

Harley and Vivian Richter were both suddenly left in absolute, subterranean darkness.

Craig and Micah arrived at the museum just in time to find Kieran telling a policeman that she was going down to the basement, with or without him, but if he valued his employment, he would be accompanying her.

The policeman was telling her that an officer had already gone down, following Jensen Morrow.

"Detective McGrady is down there. He said there's no good reason for any of those science people to be running around in the basement."

Micah didn't wait; he had to get down to the subterranean levels.

Craig went to explain to the officer that they were FBI and to get Kieran, from where she had been speaking with the cop.

Micah ran, ran hard. He reached the stairs Arlo Hampton had so recently shown him. He stumbled down them, afraid to use his penlight.

When he got to the bottom, he paused.

He began to move slowly, feeling his way.

Then he smelled death.

Yes, as Harley had told him, Ned Richter was down here. And he was dead.

Had Jensen Morrow killed him?

"Help! Oh, my God, help me!"

He heard the cry. It came from ahead, down the long hallway before him. It was coming, he thought, from the abandoned subway section where they'd found the stash of insecticide. The nicotine poison.

The voice belonged to Vivian Richter.

"I'm coming!" he called. "Are you okay? Are you in distress?"

"No...he's going to kill me. Agent Fox? It's Jensen. He's going to kill me. He and Arlo...they killed Henry. The two of them. They tried to kill me. Jensen tried to kill Arlo because he had to make it look like Arlo had worked alone... Oh, my God! He killed my husband. Jensen killed Ned, my poor Ned!"

"Where are you?" Micah asked.

He was moving very slowly and very carefully, determined not to give away his position. But as he spoke, he ran into something with his foot.

Something hard—and soft at the same time.

He stooped down, his heart in his throat. A body.

Harley?

It wasn't Harley. He quickly realized it was a man.

Ned Richter? Jensen Morrow?

It couldn't be Ned Richter; he wouldn't be warm.

He wouldn't be...breathing.

"So that's it!" he said loudly, checking for Jensen's pulse. It was weak, but it was there. The man would need help, though, and fast.

"Vivian, where are you? You poor woman, attacked… Thank God Arlo was still so new at it. He ended up killing himself, but you're all right, barely touched! And Ned—killed by Jensen! Where are you? Let me help."

They were both playing a game, pretending they believed what the other claimed as truth.

Harley. Where the hell was Harley? Was the woman holding her somewhere? Was she down on the ground, dying…bleeding?

He heard a scream of rage.

Light suddenly filled the dank, dark space.

And he saw Vivian. She was bursting out of the old subway tunnel, a lantern in one hand, a dagger held high in the other.

She was coming right at him.

He stepped out of the way; she would catapult into the wall.

But she didn't.

Because there was another cry of rage that tore through the darkness and death and decay of the tunnel.

It was Harley. And she'd found a weapon of her own—an old paving brick. She flew at Vivian, encountering her before Vivian could close in on Micah.

Both women went flying down to the floor. Vivian's lantern rolled away as they fell, casting light and shadow everywhere.

Micah reached down, catching Vivian's arm, grasping it hard.

Vivian screamed and released the antique dagger from the painful pressure he'd placed on her arm. He kicked it far from her.

Footsteps pounded down the length of the tunnel hall. Craig was there, Kieran right behind him.

Micah walked away from Vivian and drew Harley to her feet and into his arms. He held her; he wanted to hold her forever in the strange darkness and shadows, keep her from the horrors.

But of course, he couldn't.

Time meant everything just now.

"We need an ambulance for Jensen," he said. "And…"

"McGrady's here, too. I don't know how badly he's hurt. He's here somewhere!"

"Here! Here I am!"

They saw a form stumble toward them. And as it did, the tunnel blazed with light. Police officers, all carrying lights, came surging toward them.

"It was her!" McGrady said, swallowing hard, shaking his head. "Her! The woman poisoned herself to throw off any suspicion. She killed Henry, and she killed her husband. Yeah?"

Craig had Vivian Richter up by then. She was in handcuffs—and spitting mad. "I shouldn't have had to kill the bastard! Don't you get it? That mealymouthed little snake, Arlo Hampton—he was supposed to kill Ned. I did away with Henry Tomlinson, and Arlo was supposed to kill Ned. He said he couldn't do it! But I got him…oh yeah, I got both of them!"

"Who the hell would have suspected this!" McGrady said.

Micah looked at Harley, and his eyes darkened with concern.

"There's blood on you!" he murmured.

"Not mine," Harley said.

"Thank God." Micah looked toward McGrady. "Then we're ready for the next step."

Harley smiled and nodded.

"McGrady, go ahead, do the honors. Bring Mrs. Richter in. We'll handle things down here. We'll get the medical examiner and the techs for Mr. Richter," Micah said.

"And an ambulance for Jensen. She got him pretty good," Harley said.

"Why don't you and Kieran go to the hospital with him?" Micah suggested.

"Yeah. Yeah."

They stared at each other for another long moment.

Then Harley turned away, bending down to Jensen. The EMTs arrived, followed by the medical examiner and the crime scene people.

And the night went on.

Light continued to blaze through the tunnels and the abandoned subway station as day turned to night, as the medical examiner came, as the body of Ned Richter was taken at last to the morgue.

Micah and Craig worked the tie-up in the tunnels. Long hours, a lot of waiting, a lot of speculating and figuring.

Meanwhile, Vivian had been questioned at the station—and confessed to everything, despite her attorney's cautions.

"The whole thing sounds like Hitchcock," Micah told Craig. "In a sick and twisted way. *Strangers on a Train*, except they weren't strangers. Vivian Richter was working with Arlo Hampton. Arlo wanted Henry's place as lead of the expedition. And Vivian was willing to kill

Henry. It was an easy trade, or so it seemed. She'd kill Henry and Arlo would kill Ned. And, of course, she was willing to pay so that Satima Mahmoud would get her political group of disenfranchised students to fake an insurgency to cover up the murder. But as I said, in return for Henry being killed, Arlo was supposed to kill Ned. He screwed up. Vivian was afraid that Joe Rosello might figure out that Satima Mahmoud had been paid, so she decided she should poison him, which was why she showed up at the parade. And it was how Harley knew it wasn't the same mummy. Vivian is nowhere near as tall as Arlo. But Arlo didn't follow through on his part of the bargain. And Vivian lost control. When she saw Harley, I guess she wanted to do her in. But she hated Arlo for leaving her in the lurch. She was ready to kill Ned without blinking—and poison Arlo."

"Yeah, so all that 'beloved husband' stuff was just an act. For our benefit," Craig muttered.

"In Vivian's mind, her husband never gave her the respect she deserved. She was bitter, says he constantly claimed that she only had a job because of him. I guess she grew to hate him. If Arlo had played his part properly, he would've been the big cheese and she would've held the second position. But Arlo failed her, so she poisoned him. Otherwise, what was he going to do? Blame her."

"So if Arlo does make it, he'll be under arrest. Conspiracy to commit murder—even if he chickened out on it," Craig said.

"Yeah," Micah agreed. "But…"

"But?"

"I'm glad that Jensen Morrow and the other grad

students have been proven innocent. They're Harley's friends. For her, I'm happy."

"Yep. I'm going topside for a while. I'll try to find out about Jensen's condition," Craig told Micah. "I'll let you know."

Micah nodded. He hoped Jensen Morrow was going to be okay.

He was, Craig reported a short time later, upon returning to the tunnels. Jensen had a concussion, and they'd watch him at the hospital for a few days. After that, he'd be as good as new, according to the doctors.

Finally, just as dawn was breaking, they finished in the tunnels.

He and Craig left.

Craig didn't ask where he wanted to go. He dropped him off at Harley's.

"I should've called her, I guess," Micah said.

"She'll be waiting for you," Craig told him.

And she was.

The night security guard waved him in. He had no idea how Harley knew exactly when he'd reach her door, but somehow she did.

The door opened, and she hurried into his arms.

He held her tight. She was bathed and sweet and fresh, and the scent of her hair was intoxicating; he kissed her, a long and lovely kiss, then pulled away.

"The tunnels," he said with a shudder.

And the blood of a dead man and the rot of millennia, he might have said.

He didn't need to.

She drew him in and up the stairs, to the bedroom, where he tossed his gun and holster on the table, and undressed quickly with her help. In minutes, she got into the shower behind him, forgetting to shed whatever silky thing she was wearing.

The water was hot and wonderful. Sensual, erotic and yet comforting.

He wasn't sure when they left the shower; he wasn't sure when she shed the wet silky thing. He knew they were still damp when they fell onto her bed. The room was in shadows, dawn was breaking with a spectacular light, and nothing seemed to matter except that they were together, touching each other.

They licked, teased, breathed each other.

Made love.

And made love again.

And then they slept for hours and hours and finally awoke.

Just for good measure, they made love yet again.

Later, when another day was almost gone, Micah looked through the great windows at the beauty of the church beyond.

"We're going to get married there," he said.

And then, of course, he remembered that they'd really only known each other for less than a week.

"One day," he added. "Somewhere along the line."

"What a proposal," she said lightly. "So romantic!" But she smiled. "One day... Yes, I like it. I like it very much!"

As she replied, he suddenly heard a mewling sound. He looked at her with surprise.

"Oh!" she murmured.

She hurried away and returned with a little ball of gray fluff in her arms.

"Um, we have a kitten. I hope that's okay?"

He laughed. "How did you...?"

"I found him in the tunnel. With... Ned's body. I think he helped us, really. He...he needs a home."

"So where has the little guy been?"

"I guess he went into hiding while we were all down there."

"And then?"

"He followed me up to the ground floor, and one of the officers took him for me until I got back from seeing Jensen at the hospital," she said. "I was thinking of calling him Lucky."

"Lucky it is," he said, and he took her—and the ball of fluff—back into his arms.

Lucky.

Yes.

Epilogue

"I was part of it all—and I still don't get it," Jensen said, shaking his head. "Okay, back to the beginning. Vivian Richter and Arlo Hampton made some kind of devil's bargain. She'd kill Henry. He'd kill Ned. And no one would suspect either of them because it wouldn't make sense. They wouldn't be guilty of the same crime. But Micah wasn't going to give up and they both knew he was coming to the opening of the exhibit. So she poisoned herself to throw off any possible suspicion?"

"Something like that," Harley said. She'd just finished up the last of the work she'd told Jensen she would do. With Arlo and Vivian gone, he'd fallen behind with the exhibit. She'd also been eager to finish what she'd written about the murder of Amenmose. Everything would be on record at the museum, but it was a museum specializing in the ancient world—and her job here had been to explain what had happened to Amenmose and how it had all fit in with that world.

For Henry.

Arlo was still in the hospital. He'd regained consciousness, but the poison had swept away a great deal of his mind.

He had no idea he was guilty of conspiracy. Sadly, he wasn't even sure who he was anymore, or what he'd done.

Vivian's attorney was still telling her to shut up. She, too, however, had apparently had some kind of mental breakdown, because she wouldn't stop talking to the press. She was going to go for an affirmative defense and claim that she'd been horribly abused by her husband and that he'd made her say things that weren't true. She also insisted that Henry Tomlinson had killed himself and that she'd long been a victim of chauvinism and abuse at the hands of both men.

"It's crazy. All crazy, huh?" Jensen asked her. "And you know what's even crazier? That horrible woman killed Henry and her husband, she tried to kill you and me and that cop—and I still love being at the museum."

"It's a good museum. Henry was a very special man, and loving the museum just honors him," Harley said.

"Hmm. And what about that cop? He was a jerk, and…well, you know, he came by to apologize to me."

"McGrady," Harley said. "Yep. He apologized to me, too. And thanked me for saving his life. He told me he's going to be a good cop—and that it'll be because of me! I sure hope that's true."

"You can find out, I guess."

Harley smiled. "Not for a while," she said softly. "For right now—"

She stopped talking and got up; she saw that Micah and Craig had come into Finnegan's. She waved, so the two of them could see her.

"Still don't see why you have to go to Washington," Jensen said.

Harley flashed him a smile. "Because I'm in love," she told him.

"Yeah, yeah. And okay, he's decent. And I'm happy for you both."

"Funny, he says you're decent, too. And he's happy we're friends."

By then, Micah had come to the table. He greeted her with a kiss and Jensen with a handshake.

Craig reached the table next, and then Kieran arrived from her day job. Kevin came over, then Kieran's youngest brother, Danny, and her older brother, Declan, joined them. Micah and Harley were surrounded by friends and family, and they were toasted. It was something of a goodbye party.

They might come back to New York eventually; a transfer was always possible for Micah. But Harley wanted to train with the FBI academy and work toward joining a profiling team.

Washington was best for both of them right now. Harley wasn't giving up her uncle's apartment; they'd be up visiting often enough.

Everyone talked; everyone had a great time.

Joe, Roger and Belinda came later—with Belinda being the happiest of the bunch. Her fiancé was back from his deployment overseas and their wedding was coming up.

"Will there be any kind of Egyptian motif?" Joe asked Belinda, smiling.

"No!"

"What about you guys?" Jensen asked Harley.

"No! Grace Church, and you're all invited. We'll let you know when."

"No zombies, mummies, or any form of ancient lore?" Joe asked.

"No!" Harley and Micah said together, the word emphatic.

They celebrated awhile longer. Then it was time to split up, and they hugged and kissed each other on the cheek and promised to stay in touch.

The most difficult thing for Harley was to say goodbye to Kieran and Craig, but they wouldn't be far away and they'd all go back and forth often.

"I know you don't have a firm date for the wedding yet, but what are you thinking?" Kieran asked Harley.

"We have no solid plans yet. We just know where," she said. "What about you two?"

Kieran laughed. "We have no solid plans, either. Not yet. All we know is that we *will* have a wedding, and oh, yes! The reception will be here!"

Micah caught Harley's hand. "We have a lot of dating to do," he told Kieran and Craig. "And apparently my proposal was lacking. I'm going to work on a better one. I'll fill you in on how that goes. We might take a honeymoon before we actually do the marriage thing. I want to make sure Harley knows we have some great history down Virginia way, too. It's not ancient, but it's pretty cool. I've got a friend who's working a dig in

Jamestown. We can visit him for a while. And meanwhile, we'll date…"

They left. They went to spend their last night in the apartment with the great windows and the beautiful loft that they'd have for a while.

"Yes, we need to date…" Micah said.

Harley whispered in his ear.

He smiled. "Oh yeah. That, too. Lots and lots of that!"

The moon shone through the windows.

They hurried up the curving wrought iron stairway.

Tonight was an ending and a beginning.

And a beautiful night, made for love and for loving.

* * * * *

FATAL REUNION

Jessica R. Patch

To my husband, Tim, for loving me like Christ loves the church. I can't imagine doing life without you; and as you know, I have an immense imagination.

The Lord's love never ends; His mercies never stop.
They are new every morning;
Lord, Your loyalty is great.
—*Lamentations* 3:22–23

Chapter 1

"Tell me she's still alive." Piper Kennedy gripped Harmony's hand as they rushed down the halls of Baptist Memorial East. The drive from Jackson, Mississippi, to Memphis had been eternal. The thought of losing her grandmother sickened Piper. *Not Mama Jean.* "This is all my fault."

"It's not your fault. I knew you'd think that. Eventually, you're going to have to stop looking over your shoulder. It's over." Harmony wrapped an arm around Piper as they made their way to the ICU. She'd always been a good friend even when they were up to trouble.

But Piper wasn't so sure things were over. Chaz Michaels hadn't been found, and hadn't turned up, since that last job they did ten years ago, the day after he'd threatened to kill her if she walked away. Her plans to escape that life had backfired, and the person she'd loved most had been caught in the cross fire. Piper had been waiting—and watching—every day for Chaz's payback. Looked as though it might have come tonight.

"And yes, she's alive. I think they'd at least tell me if things went wrong in surgery, family or not."

Piper's insides did a gold-medal-worthy gymnastic routine. She should've never left Memphis and Mama Jean. Too many regrets. Too much pain.

They turned left down the hall toward the ICU; a wave of antiseptic burned Piper's nose. "What could Mama Jean have worth stealing?"

Harmony grunted. "I think that boarder of hers may have had something valuable...or drugs."

Piper frowned. She loved Mama Jean, but she never thought taking in boarders was smart. Guess Mama Jean thought if she couldn't help her own daughter, she might as well try someone else.

"Maybe. When Mama Jean's pastor called, he said the guy had been murdered. Looked like a burglary gone wrong." The irony that she'd been robbed didn't fall short of Piper's attention. "I'm just thankful Mama Jean's life was spared. Maybe they thought she *was* dead." Piper shivered.

They reached the nurse's station. "I'm Piper Kennedy. Here to see Jean Kennedy. I'm her granddaughter."

"She's just out of surgery. Have a seat. Coffee in that room to your right. We'll call you when you can see her." The nurse smiled and returned to her charts.

"I'll get us some coffee. You sit tight." Harmony handed her a magazine. "She's strong."

"Harm, you don't think... I mean...we..."

Harmony gave a confident shake of her head. "Not a chance. We've been out of that sick world a long time.

We don't owe or have any money. My bank account will testify to that." She chuckled. "This is in no way connected to us."

"But what if Chaz is—"

"He's not. End of story." Harmony headed for the coffee room while Piper flipped open the magazine, then chucked it on the table beside the chair. She wrenched her canvas jacket around her. April in Memphis was chilly, and the hospital kept the rooms cold.

A few families huddled together. A man with dark hair and a black leather jacket nosed through a golf magazine. Piper had no family to lean on while she waited. No one but Harmony.

"Piper Kennedy?"

Piper raised her head. "That's me."

A nurse motioned for her. "You can see her now." She led Piper through the halls. "She's asleep. Surgery went well."

Doctors shuffled in and out of patient rooms. Monitors beeped, and with every step, Piper's chest constricted. "Can you tell me what happened?"

"I don't know details of the circumstances that led to her injuries, but she received a gash on the back of her head. Her arm is broken in two places, and the femur is fractured."

Piper's eyes burned. Who would harm an innocent old woman? People she used to call friends. Bile rose in her throat. The nurse opened the door and Piper froze.

Her gaze flitted past Mama Jean to the man standing over her bed. Time had put a few crinkles around his blue eyes. Piper wasn't close enough to see the flecks of green, but memory told her they'd be there. His hair was a little shorter now and a shade darker with a touch of gray at his temples. Too young to have gray but it worked for him. Piper's stomach somersaulted, and she forced herself to breathe. Did he still despise her? Think about her?

The suffering in Luke Ransom's narrowed eyes—from that last night ten years ago—mirrored hers. He straightened his broad shoulders. Large and in charge. As always. Piper switched her attention to Mama Jean, lying feeble in the hospital bed. She shuffled closer and held her limp, wrinkled hand.

Piper should have moved her out of the old East Memphis neighborhood a long time ago. She'd let Mama Jean down. A fresh streak of shame flamed over her. Like a branding iron to her bones.

Luke stepped back and remained silent. Was he assessing Piper or simply giving her a moment to take in the sight before her? If history was any indicator, he was doing both. Always was considerate.

After kissing Mama Jean's hand and swallowing back the burning lump, she faced him. A flash of something flickered in his eyes, but Piper couldn't be sure what it was. She fought the urge to take his hand for comfort, as she'd done so many times before.

"What are you doing in here?" Piper needed to control this conversation and hope it didn't lead to the past.

"I wanted to make sure she was okay. When she wakes, I'll have questions." He cleared his throat. "I have a few questions for you."

"What could you possibly want to ask me? I just got here." Piper had no answers but a slew of her own questions.

Luke's throat bobbed, and he swung his gaze across

Mama Jean's face. He'd always been fond of her, and Mama Jean had always adored him.

"Did you know Christopher Baxter?"

Piper shook her head. "Should I?"

"I don't know. That's why I'm asking." His jaw twitched. Was this as uncomfortable for him as it was for her?

She never thought she'd see him again and especially not the second she blew into town. "I never met him. I haven't been home in…" Dropping her head, Piper focused on the starched white sheet covering Mama Jean's body. "Since—"

"Fine." The word was clipped. "Take a look." Luke held out a photo of a young man, early twenties. Curly brown hair. "Familiar?"

"No," she rasped. "How did he die?"

"Blunt force trauma to the back of the head. Much like Mama— like your grandmother's injury. Several bruises indicate he fought back."

Piper compelled herself to stare Luke in the eye. He didn't have the clean-shaven look anymore, or maybe he simply hadn't shaved. The stubble covered the dimple on his chin. "What do you think they were after?"

Luke shrugged. "I don't know. I don't investigate thefts anymore. I'm here about Christopher's murder. Homicide."

Piper nodded once. Guess they'd both abandoned anything to do with theft. "What do you know about him?"

"I know he has a background in armed robbery and that he's been in rehab twice. But the pastor from Jean's church says he's been clean for the last eighteen months.

I also know it's easy to be deceived, so I won't believe it until I see the tox screen."

The barb made a direct hit on its intended mark. Piper's heart. "Will they let me into her house?"

Luke's eyes softened, then steeled again. "I'll see what I can do. Where are you staying in case I need to contact you?"

Oh, he was going to love this. "I'm staying with Harmony Fells. I can get you the address."

A puff of air escaped his nose. He shook his head.

"We've changed. And I have nowhere else to go." Piper had cut ties with everyone else she'd been involved with, and Mama Jean's house was a crime scene.

"The address?"

Piper rattled it off.

"Nice neighborhood. How does she afford that?" Luke scribbled the address on a notepad. The accusing tone in his voice rang loud and clear.

Piper bristled. "She works for an insurance company, and she has her Realtor's license. The house was a foreclosure. But I'm pretty sure that has nothing to do with your investigation, and from here on out, I'm only answering questions that pertain to my grandmother's case."

Piper caught the corner of Luke's mouth twitch north, but then he grew serious. "Fair enough. I think your grandma was an innocent bystander. This Baxter guy may have invited trouble. But if not, would there be anything you can think of that might have led to her place being trashed?"

Piper had stewed over that same question during the drive. Was God punishing her for her past? Not that she didn't deserve it, but Mama Jean was the sweetest woman on the planet, and she loved God, so why would He allow this to happen to *her*?

"I don't know. She lives on a fixed income. Doesn't even have a computer or a cell phone. I can't imagine someone thinking she had anything of value. It must have something to do with Christopher Baxter." Mama Jean had blinders when it came to wounded souls. When she was stabilized, they'd have a talk about that, but until then Piper wasn't going to sit by and let some low-life get away with hurting her grandmother. And while Christopher Baxter might have been a thug himself, no one deserved to be murdered. She had every intention of finding out who had done this and why.

"The detective in the theft unit told me the basement had been meticulously disarranged. Even a few holes in the walls. Whoever did this was hunting for something, Piper." He eyed her until she fidgeted. "If they didn't find what they were after, they could come back."

And if it was connected to Piper's previous mistakes, they would. Invisible icy claws scraped down her spine. Was Luke trying to terrify her? It was working.

"If it was something they wanted from Christopher Baxter, they got it. Otherwise, they'd need him alive." Piper adjusted Mama Jean's covers and ran her hands over her bony fingers jutting from the cast.

She needed to be alone. She'd barely had time to process being back in Memphis. The fact that Luke Ransom was a foot away was too much to bear. Instead of trusting her all those years ago, he'd believed the worst about her. She'd never got over that pain.

"You may be right. I just hope whatever is going on doesn't implicate you." Regret and a hint of accusation laced his voice.

"I would never do anything to hurt Mama Jean, and you know that if you know nothing else." Piper had half a mind to throttle him right here in the room. To insinuate Piper had anything to do with this—would ever intentionally put Mama Jean at risk… She rubbed her temples, a migraine trying to break through.

"Getting one of your headaches?"

The familiarity between them pushed against her chest. Piper had a sick feeling this was the first of many headaches to come. What if this did have something to do with her former messed-up life?

Luke might as well have been hit with an atomic bomb. The minute Piper had stepped into the room, he'd imploded. Lost his breath. And hated himself for it. She might have lied about loving him once, but Mama Jean was her world. The one person she refused to disappoint, though if Mama Jean ever found out about Piper's infractions, it'd send her to her grave. But maybe not. Mama Jean was a strong woman.

Strong like the one standing before him now. Hazel eyes that bordered brown. She didn't hold the hard edge anymore, but Piper Kennedy radiated tough. And no doubt she was even fiercer than when he'd loved her a decade ago, considering the martial-arts path she'd traveled after leaving Memphis. Despising himself every time, he'd checked up on her throughout the span of ten years.

Piper dropped her hand from her temple and clutched her purse to her side. "Sometimes. When I'm stressed."

"The theft unit will probably want to ask you some questions, as well."

"Why? Because you told them about my past?" Her voice invited a challenge.

Luke wouldn't share her past with a soul. Never had. For her sake and his. He'd put his career in jeopardy over Piper once, and now he was up for a promotion to sergeant. No way would he risk that. "No. Because you're family. But since you're bringing it up, you should know if this has anything to do with that, it'll come out. They'll look hard at you."

Her face blanched, and she white-knuckled her purse. "I'm clean."

"I'm just saying." She didn't have an ally in Luke anymore. Not since that night ten years ago when she gave him false information about a burglary, sending him on a wild-goose chase. While they were waiting to bust Chaz—at the wrong location—the real burglary went down and south quick. A woman almost died. And Piper had been right there in the thick of it. Betraying him for a criminal like Michaels.

So why did he want to take her at her word now? Because he wanted to believe the best about her. Always had. He prayed she wasn't entangled in this.

"I have my own business. My own home. You can dig all you want—you won't find anything."

That was what he was banking on. Luke was aware Piper owned a karate dojo in Jackson. That she'd competed in international championships. And won. She'd gone from scrappy to stealth. Beneath the still-raw pangs of betrayal, he hated to admit he was proud of her in that area. Unfortunately, just because her nose seemed clean didn't mean it was. He refused to let tender feelings for Piper—though unwanted—cloud his judgment on this case and ruin his shot to move up.

"*They*, Piper, not me. But if his murder leads me back to you, I can't let it go. Not this time." He brushed past her and out the door. If Piper had connections to this burglary, and ultimately Christopher Baxter's death, he wouldn't be played. Luke had wised up since his rookie days undercover with the theft unit. A pretty face wasn't always an innocent face.

Piper had proved that.

The moment he'd laid eyes on her, when she was eighteen and he was only twenty-one, a fierce need to protect her gripped him. But he'd always been a protector—a fixer, like Granddad—whether it was a stray cat, a broken bird or a hungry dog. Piper had been broken, wounded—a stray—when they met inside that pool hall. Turned out the one thing Luke should have protected, he'd left vulnerable.

His heart.

Eric Hale, Luke's partner, stood with a cup of coffee in his hand. "You were in there awhile. Did she wake up?"

Eric had given Luke a few minutes to see Mama Jean. The woman had always cared about him. He'd checked in on her over the years, and she'd promised never to tell Piper. Looked as if she'd kept up her end of the bargain.

"No. Her granddaughter showed up. I asked her a few questions." Eric had no idea about his connection to Piper, and until he could figure out what to say about her, he'd like to leave it that way.

"She offer anything useful?" Eric finished his coffee, trashed it, then fell into step with Luke as he zipped up his black leather jacket.

"Useful? No."

"You believe her?"

That was the question. Could he trust her again? Time would tell. "Let's throw the flashlight on Baxter's history and see if it lands on her. I'm not ruling her out."

Eric chuckled. "You really are a hardnose."

He had Piper to thank for that.

"Must want that sergeant's promotion bad, huh?"

Luke had worked tirelessly to be where he was. Paid penance every day for his prior mistakes. He wanted this promotion. Needed it. Piper wasn't going to get in the way this time, but his gut screamed everything about this case would track back to her. And it terrified him because the instinct to defend and shelter her had resurfaced the second she'd marched into Mama Jean's room. It'd been difficult to keep a tough exterior, but then, he had plenty of old hurts to fuel him.

Luke would do his duty to serve and protect and nothing more. He wouldn't allow Piper to rob him of his heart again. No getting tangled up with emotions. But as he resolved the issue, a sliver of doubt wiggled like a splinter in his chest.

"Did I see who I thought I saw?" Harmony asked as she and Piper breezed through the glass entrance doors. The wind picked up Harmony's shiny blond hair, blowing it in her face.

"I think I should stay the night in the waiting room," Piper said, ignoring the question.

"Mama Jean is gonna be out cold all night. You need some rest. Come back early. Fresh."

Harm was right. But there was no way Piper was going to sleep well. Her nerves tingled on edge already, but something else wafted in on the night's current.

She paused and scanned the parking lot. Only a few lit posts dotted the area. The hairs on the back of her neck stood at attention.

"What's the matter with you, Pipe?" Harmony paused and followed Piper's gaze. "You looking for Luke?"

Piper put her arm out to block Harmony. "Something's off."

"What do you mean? What did he say to you? Was something stolen?" She removed Piper's arm from across her middle.

"He's working homicide now. Investigating Christopher Baxter's murder."

Harmony rifled through her purse and plucked her keys. "He know anything?"

"I don't know." Piper swallowed; a knot swelled in her abdomen. "I guess I'm just freaking out."

"So what *did* he say?"

Slowly, Piper started toward her car, Harmony at her side. "Not much, and I doubt he'd offer any additional information. He thinks I'm involved. Of course."

"That's ridiculous and he knows it." She pointed across the lot. "I'm over there. See you at the house."

"Okay. Be careful." Piper watched as Harmony hurried to her car, unlocked the doors and climbed in. When she safely drove away, Piper strode toward her own car. Could Chaz have reemerged and hurt Mama Jean? He was that evil.

Piper pressed the fob on her key ring to unlock the doors to her car. She rounded the hood to the driver's door.

A shadow leaped from the side of the car, throwing Piper off guard, her bag falling to the ground.

Something heavy struck her thigh, sending a blinding pain up her side, clear to her teeth. She stumbled backward, tripping over the concrete parking bumper, and landed on her backside.

The attacker, dressed in a dark hoodie, mask and gloves, lunged forward. She jumped to her feet, landing a front kick to his chest.

Grunting, he faltered and dropped his weapon.

The tire iron clattered against the asphalt.

Piper gasped. Same weapon used to assault Ellen Strosbergen—the woman nearly killed in that last burglary Piper had been a part of a decade ago.

Her assailant hunkered down and came at her full force, but she dodged and kicked him into the side of the car. He bounced off the back door with a thud, leaving a dent, then grabbed the tire iron and hightailed it through a line of parked cars.

Where was the parking security?

Piper gave chase, weaving through the vehicles. A dark van squealed into the lot, and the shadowy figure hurtled in before speeding away. She rubbed her thigh and fisted her hands to control the shaking. Hobbling back to her car, she scrambled in and locked the doors, heart beating out of her chest.

What to do? Find Luke? She peeled out of the lot. Would he even believe her? No. He wouldn't. She was on her own.

Luke ducked under the crime-scene tape and slipped a pair of blue bootees over his shoes while studying the mechanic shop. Eric did the same. So much for getting a solid night's sleep. Crime never rested, and he wouldn't have been able to anyway. Piper was back and mixed up in this somehow. A train sounded in the distance. Horns blared and tires squealed over Poplar Avenue, piercing through the chilled night.

A uniform filled him and Eric in on the scene at hand. "Girlfriend said he didn't come to bed. Found the vic in the bay. His face is pretty mangled."

Luke followed the officer into the bay, the smell of oil and exhaust wrinkling his nose. A Caucasian male, early thirties, lay in a pool of blood, a stained tire iron beside him. That would definitely rough up a face. Brought back memories of poor Ellen Strosbergen.

It might have been used to bloody the vic's face. But from what Luke could tell, it wasn't the cause of death. The man's head was lying at an odd angle.

"Neck broke?" Eric asked.

"Pretty sure. I'm interested to know which came first, the bludgeoning to the face and head or the snapped neck. Medical examiner on his way?" Luke browsed the area. Two cars raised on jacks, a few tires lying around. Tools in disarray, but not due to someone tossing the place—just seemed business as usual. A few greasy rags dotted the grimy concrete floor.

"Yeah. Crime-scene unit, too," the officer said.

"Name?"

"Tyson Baroni. Thirty-four. Owns the shop. We called his next of kin. Has a brother that lives in Arlington."

Tyson Baroni. He was hardly recognizable. Luke's stomach soured, and he chomped on the inside of his lip. Squatting, he carefully retrieved Baroni's wallet. A card fell out.

He read the name scrawled across the middle.

God, why now? I'm finally getting beyond it after all this time.

"Whose card is that, Ransom?" Eric asked.

"Piper Kennedy's. Business card for her dojo in Jackson."

"The granddaughter from the hospital?" Eric's eyes held questions.

"Yep." Piper claimed she wasn't involved, that she was clean. "I want to talk to the coroner and the girlfriend. Rule her out." He reached into his jacket pocket and popped two antacids. With skilled martial-arts training, Piper was more than capable of snapping a neck. Was the girlfriend? Dread churned like a frosty tornado.

"What do you think she had in common with him?" Eric stared at the body, squinting.

Everything. "Ten years ago, Baroni ran with Chaz Michaels. A low-life dirtbag who got his jollies burglarizing the elderly who lived in wealthy neighborhoods. He was the wheels."

"You think he had something to do with the robbery-homicide earlier? How does that link with the granddaughter?"

Luke stretched his neck from one side to the other. "Piper Kennedy was Chaz Michaels's girlfriend for a while." And much more. "She and Baroni were friends."

Eric stroked his thumb across his lower lip. "So, you like Baroni for the robbery and think the Kennedy chick retaliated for knocking her grandmother around?"

Possibly. Whoever was in Mama Jean's basement had a mission. The question was: Did they accomplish it? Did they find what they were after? And if not, what next?

"Let's interview the girlfriend, then pay Piper a visit when sun's up and ask." Luke had hoped he wouldn't have to see Piper again—at least not under these circumstances. Where she was concerned, he had a hard time discerning truth.

God, give me the strength to see clearly.

Chapter 2

"It has to be Chaz. A tire iron? Interesting choice of weapon." Piper gnawed her thumbnail. Had she made the right decision not calling Luke or the police in general? Her thigh throbbed.

Harmony laid a hand on Piper's shoulder. "No way. Why now? It makes no sense."

"He's come to get even. He has to believe I knew Luke was undercover the whole time." Which she hadn't. By the time she found out, she was already in love with Luke. "He blames me for Sly getting caught and going to prison for assaulting Ellen Strosbergen. Or he thinks I took something from the house."

"Did you?"

"What do you think?" Piper paced the kitchen floor. "I should call the police."

Harmony sighed. "You said yourself Luke suspects you. Will he believe your story?"

"Probably not." She had no one to blame but herself for that. She had no concrete evidence that she had even been attacked. Luke might accuse her of making the whole thing up to throw suspicion off her. Call her a liar. Again.

No way was it random. Not after the attack with a *tire iron*.

Harmony took Piper's cold cup of tea to the sink and dumped it. "Maybe you should come with me to the Realtors' conference. Get out of Dodge."

"And leave Mama Jean? No way. I have to find out who this is." With or without Luke's help. Piper rubbed her chilled arm. "Because if Mama Jean saw the attacker, he might come back to finish off what he started. Could be why he came after me tonight—he might think she told me who it was." Confusion twisted in her chest.

Harmony sank in a kitchen chair. "What are you going to do?"

"I don't know. But for tonight, I think it's best if I sleep in your master bedroom. You'll be safer upstairs. If he comes back, I want to be downstairs where I can hear."

"You're scaring me, Pipe."

"I'm trying to protect you." Piper was scared, too. And she had no idea what to do, but maybe by morning she'd have a clue. It was after midnight now.

Harmony grabbed Piper's hand. "I'll go upstairs. But I don't suspect either of us will be sleeping."

There was truth to that. Piper followed Harmony to the master bedroom. "Why do you need this house? It's huge."

Harmony switched on the light. "It's my way of hoping for a family."

A dream they both shared. But Piper had relation-ship paralysis. The few men she'd dated, she'd measured against Luke. Every single one came up short.

Hairs prickled the back of Piper's neck again, as if a presence was in the house. Or outside. Watching. She switched off the light.

"Hey—!"

"Shhh." Piper peeked out the window that overlooked the backyard and beyond into the woods. "Where does that lead?"

"A creek and then I don't know. I've never taken a jaunt." Harmony closed the blinds and then flipped on the lamp. "I think we're safe. And if we aren't, I'm counting on you being able to take down a grown man."

Piper could. But that didn't mean she wasn't fright-ened.

Harmony left the room, and Piper hurried and un-packed then threw on a ratty pair of gray sweats and a Shotokan T-shirt with the tiger emblem on the front pocket. She'd been studying Shotokan karate since she was eighteen. Since Luke kicked her out of his life with one word. *Run.*

At twenty-nine, she'd worked hard and made it to the position of Shihan-Dai—fourth-degree black belt. She was still working toward professor of the art. But no amount of martial arts could fight off the past that seemed to be colliding with her present, choking her.

Piper slid into bed at 12:52 a.m. and stared at the clock until her eyes grew too heavy to hold open.

A creak pulled her from sleep.

Her eyes shot open as a cloth smothered her face.

A sickly sweet smell and taste filled her nose and mouth. She reached for the bulky hand and broke free.

She gulped fresh air, but her head spun, and nausea swept over her.

He came at her again.

Couldn't. Think. Clearly.

Piper punched him in the sternum, cutting off his air supply, and bounded out of bed, but whatever she'd inhaled had weakened her. Grabbing the lamp, she chucked it at him. It crashed into the wall behind the headboard. Barreling forward, the attacker tackled her to the floor near the bathroom. She reached up and grabbed his mask, pulling it from his face.

Not Chaz.

Drawing her knee up, she made contact with his groin, garnering a wail from him and giving her time to wiggle free.

Her head was still fuzzy and pounding, but she scrambled for the door. Needed a weapon. Her phone.

"Piper!" Harmony yelled.

The assailant turned toward the sound of Harmony's voice and bolted. Piper raced across the bedroom, but she was off balance, shaky.

A door slammed.

Harmony stood midway on the stairs, a bat in hand. "What's happening?"

Piper ran to the back door and turned the locks, panting. "It wasn't Chaz."

"Who wasn't Chaz?"

"A man. Here. I saw his face." Piper's pulse hammered, dizziness flaring. "He put something over my mouth." The rag. She rushed to the bedroom and retrieved it.

Harmony stood at the threshold. "What is it?"

"I don't know. Some kind of drug. Glad I wasn't

sound asleep." Piper bent at the waist, her mouth watering. "Get me a plastic bag for this. I'm gonna be sick." She scurried to the bathroom.

Harmony returned with the bag as Piper flushed the toilet. She dropped the rag inside the gallon-sized Ziploc.

Piper leaned against the wall, eyes burning. It wasn't Chaz. But whoever came after her at the hospital wasn't working alone. Someone drove the van. "Chaz could have sent someone to kidnap me." He could be outside right now, waiting. Her stomach churned.

"Kidnap! Why?" Harmony paced the bathroom floor.

"Why else drug me?"

"If it was the same guy from the hospital, maybe he wised up and knew he couldn't take you without evening the playing field." She froze. "I can't believe I just said that."

Piper rinsed her mouth, her vision clearing and nausea subsiding. A few seconds longer and she'd have been out cold. "No. You're right."

"I'm not going to that conference, Piper. I can't leave you."

Piper's temple throbbed. "Now more than ever, you need to. It's the only way to keep you safe."

Harmony's eyes pooled with tears. "What about you? Will you go to the police now?"

Piper wasn't sure. But one thing was clear. Whoever was after her wasn't going to stop.

Piper sat on Harmony's bed as she scrambled around in a frenzy trying to pack. It was almost 6:00 a.m. "I have to call Luke. He may not believe me, but…"

"I understand." Harmony rifled through drawers, tossing random things in the suitcase. "You sure you don't want me to stay?"

Piper folded what she'd dumped inside. "I'm sure."

Harmony dug in a top drawer, undergarments falling out. "I don't even know what I packed. I can't think straight. This is a bad idea." Her hands shook as she clawed through the items.

Piper placed her hand over Harmony's. She had to be strong for her. "Let me. What do you need?"

"A scarf. I don't even know. Black. Gray. Who cares?" Harmony collapsed on her bed, hands over her face. "I can't go to a conference and concentrate when I know bad stuff is going down here."

Piper calmly combed through the scarves and undergarments. "I'll feel better knowing you're out of this mess." She paused. Wait. Something caught her eye, buried under the scarves. "Harmony, this is the guy! The guy in the house!"

Harmony's face paled, and she grabbed the photos. "Are…are you sure?" She stared at them. "I should've burned these."

"I'm positive. Who is this? Why are you in a photo with him?"

Harmony's lip quivered, and then her eyes widened. "Oh no."

"What?" Piper demanded.

"That's Boone. Pipe, he must have mistaken you for me last night. You were in *my* bed."

"But why?" Piper shook her head. Seemed too coincidental with the earlier attack.

Closing her eyes, Harmony groaned. "I dated him for, like, two seconds. Found out he was trouble, and I broke it off. Until now, he's only called a few times and shown up at work. He was probably trying to scare me quiet, as if I'd ever rat him out."

"Do you hear yourself? Guys don't drug their ex-girlfriends to scare them. And rat him out for what?" What in the world was going on here? "We definitely have to call the police."

Harmony shook her head. "No cops. Not about this."

"Why?" Piper stared her down. "What did he do?"

"He robbed a convenience store six months ago, and I was with him." She squeezed her eyes closed and shuddered. "I had no clue he was going to do it. I was in the car, but if I go to the cops with that story—with my past—they'll never believe I wasn't intentionally in on it. And you can be sure Boone won't only come after me—again—he'll falsely incriminate me. I can't. You can't."

Another headache was forming. Harmony had *never* attracted a nice guy.

Neither had Piper. Until Luke.

"He's dangerous, Harm. This wasn't some scare tactic to shut you up."

"I'm sorry." Harmony hugged her. "Give me to Monday to figure it out. I'm scared with our history and Luke pointed on us like a bloodhound. Please, Piper, don't do anything for now. I mean, if you wanna call about what happened to you at the hospital, fine. But nothing about Boone. I just…can't."

Piper understood the fear. The confusion. "Go to Vegas, and on Monday when you get back, we gotta talk seriously about this guy."

"I'm so stupid!" Harmony wiped tears with the back of her hand. "Come with me."

"Mama Jean needs me. And I can't run." She helped carry Harmony's luggage outside and lobbed it in the backseat. "In fact, I'm heading that way after you leave."

Harmony slid into the driver's seat. "How did he get in?"

"I don't know. We know some tricks, so he probably does, too." When Harmony left, Piper would check entry points.

"Text and let me know how she's doing. You sure I shouldn't stay?"

"Go."

"It's gonna be okay. It has to be, right?"

"Don't worry." Easier said than done. Could she really keep this from the police? Would her conscience let her?

Harmony drove off, and Piper searched, finding scuffs and splintered wood on the back door, which told the tale.

If nothing else, Harmony was getting a security system installed ASAP. If the ex was involved in burglaries and robberies, he could have ties to Chaz. They could be working together. A nagging feeling that her past had returned with a vengeance plagued her.

The doorbell rang.

Piper peeked through the hole. Great. Luke and the guy she saw at the hospital with dark hair and a leather jacket. Her throat tightened as she opened the door. "Is it Mama Jean?"

"No," Luke reassured her. For a moment his features softened with his voice, but then he hardened his jaw.

Piper eyed him. "So what's going on?" Did someone witness the attack at the hospital and tell him?

"Can we come in?" Luke didn't wait to be welcomed and stepped inside.

"Sure." Swinging her arm out, Piper motioned for the other detective to enter. "Do you want coffee?"

"Since when do you drink coffee?" Luke asked, and he flinched when his partner gave him a quizzical expression. Didn't seem as though he'd let the other detective in on their connection to each other. Couldn't blame him.

"Do you want any or not?" Patience wasn't a virtue, and Luke had made it clear last night there was nothing but a case between them. So why make with the pleasantries?

"I'd like a cup." His partner extended his hand. "Detective Hale."

Piper shook his hand and sized him up. About two inches shorter than Luke, putting him at six-one. Lush, pitch-black hair, kind brown eyes. Easy smile.

"Piper Kennedy." She grabbed a mug from the cabinet and started pouring Detective Hale a cup. "Luke? I mean, Detective Ransom?"

Luke shook his head, and she looked at Detective Hale. "Cream? Sugar?"

"Black, thanks."

She handed him his cup and sat at the table. "Any news on Christopher Baxter? He have anything to do with the break-in?"

Luke glanced at his partner. "This is about a new case. Tyson Baroni was murdered." Luke scrutinized her as if waiting for her to admit guilt.

"How?"

Luke cracked his knuckles. "ME says his neck was broken. Right after someone mangled him with a tire iron. You know anyone who could do that? Snap a man's neck?"

A tire iron. Piper's stomach nose-dived, but the accusation flared hot.

She inched out of her chair, narrowing her eyes. She knew he'd never believe her. "Get out."

"I'm just asking a question. Why so defensive?"

Eric put his cup on the table and studied them.

"You're not asking me a question. You're implying. Could I snap a man's neck?" She placed her hands on the table and leaned forward. "Yes," she hissed. "Would I ever? No."

Did he really believe she could kill someone?

"When is the last time you saw Tyson Baroni?" Eric interrupted their standoff and Piper slowly turned her head in his direction.

"I haven't seen or talked to Tyson in a decade." Why would she?

Disappointment filtered through Luke's eyes and he sighed. "Then why did he have your business card in his pocket, and why were your prints on it?"

The air deflated from Piper's lungs. How did Tyson get her business card? "He's never been to the dojo, at least not that I've noticed. And I haven't seen him here. I came straight to the hospital, and I need to be there now or I'm going to miss visiting hours."

Luke tightened his lips, his eyes impassive. No trust in them whatsoever. Could she expect him to trust her after the lies she'd told years ago? Lies to protect him, but he'd never once come to that conclusion. Still smarted.

"I am sorry about that, Miss Kennedy," Detective

Hale said. "But you can see this presents a problem. Straighten out the confusion for us."

"I can't!" Piper threw her hands in the air. "I'm as confused as you." The past was back. Blaring everywhere she turned. This couldn't be a coincidence, but how would anyone know she was in town? Seemed as though she'd been here just long enough to be framed for murder and attacked twice. The reality pushed her to her seat.

"Piper?" Luke laid a hand on her shoulder. "What is it?" The warmth seeped into her bones. She'd missed his touch. His comfort. His strength.

"Nothing. It's…nothing." If only that were true.

"Where were you last night after you left the hospital?" Detective Hale asked.

Luke folded his arms over his chest. She buckled under his intense gaze.

"I didn't kill Tyson. I don't even know where he lives."

"He lived in a small apartment attached to his shop in Midtown. And that's where we found him." Luke drew his notepad out. "If you would just tell us the truth, it would help."

The truth? Harmony was going to go ballistic, but Piper had no choice. They could believe her or not. "Fine. The truth is…"

Luke scooted his chair closer to hers, his knees touching Piper's.

"The truth is…?" Luke leaned down, forcing her to make eye contact.

"Something happened in the hospital parking lot. And then…here."

Luke's face grew taut—the protective expression she'd seen hundreds of times. "What happened, Piper?"

She squeezed her eyes shut, doubted he'd believe her, but told him everything.

"What!" Luke bulleted to the back door and studied the scuffs. Would he think she put them there herself? "Why didn't you call me?" He turned on her, grabbed her shoulders, eyes brimming with emotion she hoped was concern and care. "You could have been killed!"

"I didn't have your number."

"You could have asked for me at the precinct. I would have come. Immediately."

Piper wanted to collapse in his arms and cry. But she didn't.

Detective Hale stood. "Can I have a look at that rag?"

Piper wiggled free of Luke's gentle but firm grasp and retrieved the bag and photo from Harmony's room. To know he still cared whether she lived or died meant everything. She handed Detective Hale the bag. He opened it and took a whiff.

"Chloroform, maybe. Or antifreeze."

She handed Luke the photo of Boone and Harmony. "This is the guy."

He kneaded the back of his neck. "You should have called 9-1-1, Piper. I need to talk to Harmony."

"You can call, but you'll get voice mail. Her flight already left." She gave him her number.

"*Why* didn't you call 9-1-1?" Luke studied the photo.

Piper almost laughed. "You already think I had something to do with this. I'm on my own." She clenched her teeth. "Just like I've always been."

Luke's eyes flashed with torment. "I believe *this*. And I would never want to see you harmed. Ever." He pointed to the back door and raised the photo. "I need this guy's last name."

"I don't know it."

Luke laid his hand on her shoulder again. "I don't know what his motives were. Mistook you for Harmony. Trying to take you out to get to her. To take you both." He shrugged. "But the guy at the hospital... I don't think it was this Boone character. Why go after you there?"

Good question. "Two isolated events? Maybe Chaz is back, and he and Boone are in cahoots?" She had no clue which it was, but her gut said Chaz was in the thick of it.

"It's possible, and that brings us back to Mama Jean's basement and what was hiding down there."

He still thought she had something to do with this, if even indirectly. Luke rubbed his stubbly chin. "Don't go back to Jackson, Piper. We're not done, and you aren't safe here. Can you stay somewhere else?"

Piper folded her arms across her chest. "I'm not going anywhere. And by that I mean Memphis or this house."

Luke worked his jaw. "I don't like you here alone."

"I don't care what you like or don't like. I'm still standing." No one would protect her like she could protect herself. And she didn't want Luke protecting her— much. It hurt.

Luke pinched the bridge of his nose, nostrils flaring. "You are so stinking stubborn."

"I'm not leaving." She jutted out her chin.

"Let me drive you to the hospital."

"No." She wasn't going to rely on Luke. She couldn't.

Looking at Detective Hale, Luke shook his head. "I don't know what to do with her."

Detective Hale scratched his head. "We could kick you out and call this a crime scene, as it is, and force you to leave."

"I like that idea," Luke said.

"Get real. Boone's prints are probably all over this place. They dated. You're both being jerks."

"Technically, we're doing our jobs." Eric smirked. "But okay."

Luke frowned, and they seemed to carry on a silent conversation.

Detective Hale left them at the door. Luke turned to her, his voice quiet. "Baroni had your card. Somehow you're connected. And I hate leaving you alone."

"You left me on my own ten years ago. Now shouldn't be any different." Piper dared him to respond.

Luke opened his mouth to say something else, then clammed up. A wave of grief splashed across his face. "You're right about prints. Doesn't mean I won't have them come out anyway. You're out of the house, at least for a while today. Call if you need to." He handed her his card then phoned the crime unit. "I'll wait outside until they get here. But you're free to go see Mama Jean."

His protectiveness sent a skitter into her pulse. Luke closed the door behind him and she beelined it to her cell to call Braxton, one of her karate instructors.

He answered on the second ring. "Hey, Piper. How's your grandma?"

"Stable." She snatched her car keys. "Hey, quick question. Did anyone by the name of Tyson Baroni come into the dojo recently? About five foot ten, a ginger with freckles."

"Doesn't sound familiar."

"If I send a picture, could you tell me if you'd seen him?" She snagged a banana and hurried to the front door.

"Probably. Is everything okay?" Concern laced Braxton's voice.

"Yeah. Just checking on something. Thanks." She hung up and stepped onto the stoop. Luke and Detective Hale were in the driveway staring at her car along with two other officers.

"What's going on?" Piper asked and slowed her pace.

They split as if drawing open a curtain, revealing center stage. Piper's car had been keyed and the tires slashed.

Piper thrust back her head and inwardly groaned. "I'm gonna need a lift after all."

Luke opened the back door to their Dodge Durango and Piper slid inside. She seemed calm and collected for a woman who'd been victimized, twice. Hearing that someone had put his hands on her, hurt her, sent a wave of hysteria into his bones, then infuriated him. Had Chaz come out of hiding? If so, he must have a solid reason. One that Piper refused to cough up.

His gruff questioning had got him nowhere. In fact, it had made things worse. He couldn't help it. Old bitter feelings had risen along with the impulse to protect and make sure she was cared for. And she wouldn't leave the house. He couldn't bring her to his. Frustration knotted his neck muscles.

"I'm sorry about your car, Piper. I can have someone tow and fix it for a decent price." Offering her an olive branch was all he knew to do without getting too close.

Surprise flittered in her eyes. "Thanks, Luke."

"I didn't even notice it driving up." He'd been a walking disaster, stewing and hoping she wasn't directly linked.

Eric had a million questions, but surely he'd figure out what Luke already knew. Piper wasn't going to cooperate if she didn't want to.

"Hopefully, we'll get Chaz's prints off that door."

"Doubt it," Piper said, and they hit the interstate, the car charged with deafening silence. What was he supposed to do? Make small talk?

"How's the dojo?" Guess he was.

"Growing. I'm thinking about leasing a building for a second location. Closer to Madison." She picked at her fingernails and fisted her hands. A knee bobbed. He'd made her uncomfortable. Or maybe she was anxious to get to Mama Jean. Probably both. She was too stubborn to be scared. What could he do to make her leave Harmony's house?

Her sweet jasmine scent wafted through the car, reminding him of times when he'd held her close, danced with her at the pool hall, kissed her good-night.

"Do you have a picture of Tyson?"

Luke frowned. "Why?"

"I want to send it to Braxton—he's a sensei in my dojo. See if Tyson came by at some point. I called him after you stepped outside. He says no one matching that description visited, but after ten years, who knows how much Tyson has changed. Not that I wouldn't recognize you a mile away, but I see some differences."

Luke glanced back. "Me, too." Softer face. More athletic build. Her hair was still all one length but longer.

The dimple that rested under her left eye on her cheek-bone seemed deeper.

"I don't have any gray." She smirked.

He touched his temples. "They say it's a sign of wisdom."

Detective Hale snorted. "Not in your case."

"I don't know. I think compared to, say, a decade ago, I've wised up some. How about you, Piper?" He didn't mean to be antagonistic, but the teasing and friendliness was harder than he'd anticipated.

"I have."

"So, tell me about your dojo," Detective Hale said as he eased onto I-240. "You been in competitions?"

"Not as often as I used to. I run a program for troubled teenagers. Martial arts changed my life. Gave me the confidence and strength I needed."

"I've found, in my life, God has been my source of confidence and strength. But hey, good for you." Detective Hale glanced in the rearview mirror and smiled. "I think discipline is smart for unruly teenagers, and it gets them off the street."

Luke didn't say anything. God was part of his life, too, and right now Luke was curious to know what the Almighty was up to. He called and had the precinct send a photo of Tyson Baroni. "Give me your number, Piper. I'll send this over."

She gave it to him and then texted the photo to her friend at the dojo.

A few minutes later, Piper sighed. "Braxton doesn't recognize him."

"Then how did he get your business card?"

Piper shook her head. "I wish I knew. I guess he

could have come in and taken one from the desk without anyone seeing."

"Your prints are on them."

"Well, yeah. I have to touch them to put them in the card holder." She pinched her lips as if she were holding something back she'd like to say.

"Not all of them." Luke threw her a pointed look. "And why would he drive all the way to Jackson just to get your business card?"

"Your guess is as good as mine." She rubbed her temple again and gawked at the passing traffic.

Eric pulled up to the doors at the hospital. "I hope your grandma is feeling better."

"Thanks. I can catch a cab home or something."

Luke opened his door and stepped out. "I'll walk you in."

"Again, I can take care of myself."

"I believe you." He ignored the hostility and escorted her inside. "Piper, Eric doesn't know about our previous relationship. He's going to ask, though. I'll tell him the bare essentials."

"That we loved each other once?" Behind her eyes, a storm brewed. Like the one gathering in him.

At one time he had loved her. Bought a ring and everything. But she'd ruined it when she chose a criminal over him, when she'd lied to him and put him between a rock and hard place, when she'd destroyed everything they'd meant to each other with her blatant deceit. He thought he'd got over it, but the crushing sensation he was experiencing proved the opposite. "*We?* You mean *me*. I loved *you* once. I'm not sure what to call what you did." His tone blasted more heat than he'd intended.

She lowered her head. "I need to see about Mama

Jean." She brushed past him. He ought to chase her down and apologize, but he stood firm as she practically trampled a nurse to get away.

He met the questioning eyes of Eric when he slumped into the passenger seat. "Okay, so we knew each other."

Eric continued to stare.

"What?"

"Nothing. I'm just gonna do that thing I do."

Luke buckled his seat belt. "You mean where you eyeball a person of interest until they shift under your scrutiny and cough up information?"

"Yep." He drilled Luke with intensity.

"Not gonna work on me." Luke stared back. "Fine. I was twenty-one when I met her. She was eighteen. We had a thing." He swallowed hard.

Eric broke eye contact and cheesed. "I'm a Jedi."

"No." Luke laughed. "I don't have time for a staring contest. We have a homicide to investigate."

"A thing. I'd say you had more than a thing. I saw the way you looked at her. The way she didn't look at you." He slowed at the stoplight. "She beat you up and bruise your ego?"

Something like that. Exactly that. Luke flipped open his notepad.

"Your silence says so much." Eric chuckled. "For the record, she doesn't seem like the kind of woman to be messed up in something like this."

Luke grunted. "Let's take the evidence to the lab, and then we need to get some more information on this Boone person. I'm interested to see what kind of winner he is."

"I'm more interested in what the killer wanted out

of some sweet old lady's house. I'm not convinced the guy staying there didn't bring in trouble of his own."

Piper might not be directly related to Christopher Baxter's and Tyson Baroni's murders, but she was in the middle of it somehow.

"What are you thinking?" Eric asked.

"Just running down scenarios in my head." Trying to untwist the knot in his gut.

"You think Piper offed Christopher Baxter and Baroni?"

Luke stared at the car ahead of them. "No. But based on Piper's entanglement with Chaz Michaels and his crew, I think she might have hidden something that he or someone wants. Baxter and Mama Jean got in the way. And maybe Tyson Baroni."

"Mama Jean?" Eric smirked. "Like I said, more than a thing if you're calling Jean Kennedy *Mama Jean.*"

Luke expelled a heavy breath. "Okay, it was more than a thing. But it's squashed. She's nothing more than a person of interest in our homicide investigation."

"Okay."

Silence permeated the atmosphere.

"I'm a Jedi."

Luke frowned. "I wish you were a Jedi. It's gonna take that kind of force to get Piper to back down or at the very least stay somewhere safer." Didn't matter why or how she was connected—the fact remained she was in serious danger.

And Luke had no intention of letting a single thing happen to her.

Chapter 3

Mama Jean had been moved from ICU to her own room now that she was stabilized. Piper had sat by her bedside as she slept. A few times she woke, but was disoriented and didn't realize Piper was near. She'd left to have a bite of lunch in the cafeteria, read a few boring magazines, then called to check in with Braxton. Classes were running smoothly.

Opening the door to Mama Jean's room, Piper pasted on a happy face. "You're awake." She strolled to her bedside.

Mama Jean pushed a cup of Jell-O away and gave a thin-lipped smile. "Am I dreaming, dear one?"

Piper planted a kiss on Mama Jean's wobbly cheek. "No, ma'am. I came as soon as I heard. How are you feeling?"

"Like I fell and hit my head, broke my arm in two

places and broke my leg." Her voice sounded garbled. "The police were here a spell ago."

Had Luke swung back by while she was in the cafeteria? "And?"

"I told them what I remembered. It happened so fast." Mama Jean's hand shook underneath Piper's. "I was asleep, but a commotion in the basement, where Christopher stays—stayed—woke me." Tears flushed her gray eyes and dripped down the wrinkly cracks on her face. "Poor child. He was doing so well."

Now wasn't the right time to reiterate Mama Jean shouldn't be taking in strays. Piper had been a stray, too. Nothing but an unwanted burden not worth the effort it took Mom to love her. But Mama Jean had done her best.

Piper clamped down on the rising ache inside. "I'm so sorry this happened. Did you see who it was?" Piper held her breath, hoping it wasn't someone from old times. Guilt seeped into every vein and overloaded her brain. She bit down on her lip.

"No. Just a dark blur. I got up thinking Christopher had the TV up too loud. I came downstairs and saw him struggling with a man— I tried to run back up but…he grabbed me and I hit my head on the stairs when I fell. The next thing I know, I'm here."

Piper pressed Mama Jean's hand to her cheek and willed herself to pull it together. "I'm sorry," she whispered through a choked-up voice. For not being everything she should have, for getting mixed up with Chaz and for her stupidity during her teenage years.

"Dear one, you have nothing to be sorry for. This wasn't your fault."

If Mama Jean only knew. She had more than her

share to be sorry for, and she was. Piper had asked God over and over to forgive her. But she wasn't certain that He had. How could He?

Piper would make up for her mistakes and find who did this. She'd start with Christopher Baxter. "Did Christopher ever have any friends over? A girlfriend?"

"A friend of his came by a few times. Nice young man. Big."

Mama Jean thought a smile and a polite voice that used "Ma'am" and "Sir" constituted nice. "You remember his name?"

Mama Jean tilted her head. "Ron— No, Rick— No… Riff?"

Blood drained from Piper's head. Riff wasn't a person. Riff was a place. One Piper knew well. "You sure that wasn't a place they talked about playing pool in?" Riff's was the woodwork that roaches crawled out from. Didn't look as though things had changed in a decade.

"Maybe. I think his name was… I don't know. But Riff sounds right."

It was a start. She may not know the friend's name, but if someone recognized Christopher, they most likely would have a clue about whom he hung with.

"Have you spoken with a doctor yet?"

"He says I'll need physical therapy but doesn't see why I won't make a full recovery. I'm optimistic." She patted Piper's cheek. "Look at you. A vision."

Piper squeezed Mama Jean's hand. "If I'd have been here, I would have pulverized him. Protected you." Anger spiked through her blood, splashing over the guilt. Adrenaline raced. She had to find whoever had done this. No matter what the cost.

"You and the karate chops." Mama Jean chuckled. "God protected me."

"Your injuries state differently." Piper gave her a pointed look.

Compassion filled Mama Jean's eyes. "I'm alive. You have a lot to learn about the good Lord. I'm glad you're here. I've missed you."

God could have spared her. But Mama Jean was right. She was alive, strong and a fighter. "I'm going to grab some water. Can I get you anything?"

"You being here is enough."

If she could find who'd done this and bring him to justice, without getting killed in the process, then it would be almost enough. "Rest. I'll be back."

She closed the door, and leaning against the wall was Luke. "What now?" Piper gritted her teeth and strode down the hall to the drink machines.

Luke ambled along beside her. "I have a few more questions. And a cab is expensive."

Piper sighed. "I'm planning on staying the night, so don't bother with the offer to drive me home." She shoved her dollar into the machine, punching the button for bottled water with more force than necessary. "I was hoping you were here to bring me answers, not questions. Mama Jean is so weak and pale." Anger brewed fresh. "I'm gonna get whoever did this. So while you run me down, I'll actually be finding who hurt my grandmother." She snagged her bottle of water and challenged him with a glare.

His nostrils flared. She'd struck a nerve. "First off, going vigilante isn't smart and will only cause more problems. Secondly, did you know Boone Wiley— that's his last name—has a rap sheet and has done time?

Armed robbery, larceny, and I saw my old partner in the theft division. He says he's suspected of being involved in a hit on a jewelry store nine months ago. But they don't have sufficient evidence."

The cool water did nothing for Piper's parched throat. Theft. "Why would I know that? I told you, I'd never seen him before he attacked me, and that he was trouble."

Luke raked his hands through his thick hair, a habit when he was frustrated. Piper always found it endearing. She focused on his face instead. Mistake. Squared, strong jaw, well-sculpted cheek and jaw bones. The green stood out in his eyes today. Must be the chambray shirt with green flecks. Full lips pursed. "Don't you think it's odd that this guy is dating Harmony?"

"Was. Not is. And Harmony's only downfall is her attraction to the wrong kind of men." Piper could relate. Things would be so different now if she'd never met Chaz Michaels.

"I think all of you are connected. It'd be easier if you'd come clean."

Piper waited for the two additional words: *for once.* They were getting nowhere going down this road. And whoever had hurt Mama Jean and killed Christopher Baxter could be long gone by now.

"Did you run down that boarder—Christopher Baxter?"

"No ties to Boone, if that's what you mean. We're looking into it. Running the drug angle in case he had a stash hidden. If he did, his killer found it because we sent dogs in. Nothing."

"But you'd rather focus on me. A dead end." In more ways than one.

Luke sighed. "I decided to talk to Harmony after all.

I'd rather do it face-to-face, but I can't wait until Monday evening. She's not answering."

"I don't answer numbers I don't know." Piper ought to call her, too. How mad was she going to be hearing Piper hadn't followed her wishes and told the police about Boone after all? "I've got to get back and see to Mama Jean." Piper headed toward Mama Jean's room. Luke stayed with her.

"Is she going to be okay?" he asked. Concern touched his voice.

"Yeah. Needs therapy. Probably have to stay in an assisted-living center while going through it. In the meantime, I'm going to try and talk her into moving into an apartment or something in a better neighborhood. Or maybe I can rope her into coming back to Jackson with me. I should have done that long ago."

Luke shoved his hands in his jeans pockets and stopped outside Mama Jean's room. "You—you doing okay in Jackson? Making a good life?"

The hesitation in his voice melted her. Her throat tightened. "Yeah. I've got a nice house with an extra bedroom for Mama Jean—if she'll move. It's a quiet life. Until now."

Luke looked as if he wanted to ask something else, but he scuffed the toe of his shoe against the tiled floor. "Good. That's…good." He avoided eye contact, nodded and scratched the back of his head. "I'll keep you posted. Be careful, Piper. You might be strong, but you're not invincible."

Piper stared at his back as he traipsed down the corridor, her insides exploding. No, she wasn't invincible and everything told her to run, to hide. Chaz Michaels terrified her. Always had. But she couldn't sit by while

Mama Jean's attacker ran scot-free, especially since it might be Piper's fault. She entered the hospital room. Sterile. Lifeless. A lot like the way Piper felt.

Was her life good? On the surface, yes. But inside, Piper was never settled or at rest. Longing for a family of her own dogged her as the aging clock ticked by. Competing internationally had been a brief stint of contentment, keeping her focused and occupied, but when those karate competitions were over, Piper came home to an empty house with no one to love and no one to love her back.

"I thought I heard a man's voice," Mama Jean said as Piper neared her bed.

Should she tell her about Luke? He was going to ask her some questions anyway. Why hadn't he done it just now? If Piper didn't know any better, she'd think she'd run him off with something she'd said. But what?

"I was talking with Luke Ransom. He's working Christopher's case. He was here yesterday, actually. Checked in on you. He'll want to ask you a few questions about the incident."

"He's a wonderful man. I always hoped you two would get married. I know how much you loved him."

Piper wasn't sure anyone could know how much she'd loved Luke. How much she still did. Even if she'd tried not to. It wouldn't take. "So, what's on TV?" Thinking of all she'd lost ached too much, and she needed Mama Jean engaged in a show. Piper had no choice but to hunt down the scumbag who had hurt her. Starting by sifting through the crowd at Riff's.

Luke sat in his car gripping the steering wheel but going nowhere. He'd come to the hospital on his dinner break with every intent to talk with Mama Jean about the incident.

Then Piper went and talked about her good life— a life without him—and Luke wanted nothing more than to bolt.

Before he'd left the precinct, he'd received some information on Boone Wiley, sending Luke's mind and heart into a game of tug-of-war, flustering him. His heart said Piper was innocent and would never do anything that might put Mama Jean in danger, while his mind continued to replay the night he'd shown up at Ellen Strosbergen's house ten years ago.

Luke and his old partner, Kerr Robbins, had been staking out that bogus address Piper had given them. In the end, she'd been loyal to a criminal, and Luke had carried the guilt from the events that escalated that night. He still struggled with how it ended. How Piper flushed what they had down the toilet.

Maybe he should have never got in too deep with her in the first place. But the moment he'd walked—undercover—into that smoke-infested low-life pool hall on Beale Street, she'd captured him. Not with her beauty, though she was beautiful, but with her downcast expression. As if the world had chewed her up and spit her out, leaving her alone and hopeless. As if she needed fixing.

Turned out to be her eighteenth birthday. And where had she been? Alone, sitting at a booth.

Luke pawed his face and rested his head on the seat, forcing the memories down. He tried Harmony's number and got voice mail again. So what now? His phone rang. Not Harmony.

Eric.

"Hey, bro."

"I talked to one of my CIs downtown. Says he knows Baxter but he hasn't been down for a fix in a long time. Hung out at Riff's. Easy place to score. But he found Jesus at that shelter off Front Street. So it's looking like our vic is clean. Not saying he didn't have some money stashed away, but I think we need to turn direction and roll down Piper Kennedy's street."

Luke had a contact at Riff's, too. The very place he'd met Piper.

"I put in a call to Baroni's brother. Haven't heard from him."

The coroner had confirmed the blunt force trauma to the back of his head had probably knocked him for a loop, but it was the swift crack of the neck that had done him in. Not from a fall but a perfectly executed break.

Luke had asked if it were possible for a woman about five foot three to have done that to a man six feet tall. Unfortunately, the coroner let him know if the man had dropped to his knees from the blow, it would have been easy.

Another nail in Piper's coffin, but the theory wasn't enough to arrest her. And quite frankly, he couldn't make himself believe it.

"Luke, you hear me?"

"What? No. Sorry."

Eric sighed. "You need to get focused, man. I said no prints on the tire iron. I was hoping there would be, not that I want the Kennedy woman to be guilty, but since her prints are on file…"

No, this wasn't going to be a slam dunk.

"I'll meet you back at the precinct, and let's see if we can dig anything else up on Boone Wiley. Maybe we can directly connect him to one of the old crew members. And let's turn over a few rocks, see if any of Christopher Baxter's friends are lurking underneath."

Luke bought two coffees and met Eric at the precinct. Luke handed Eric his caffeine jolt and collapsed into his office chair.

"I need more information about that night back when you worked theft, man."

Luke tapped a pen on his desk calendar. "At the time, we suspected Chaz Michaels was running a crew who burglarized the elderly in wealthy neighborhoods. In and out. No injuries. No fatalities. I'd just come on board the Crimes Against Property Bureau. A little younger than Chaz and his crew but a prime candidate for the undercover work. Get in, snoop around, see if I could get close to them."

Eric raised an eyebrow and paused middrink. "Piper Kennedy was your in."

Luke nodded. It hadn't started out that way, though. He'd simply taken a seat in the booth with her. Had no idea she even knew Chaz. Never dreamed she'd been in a romantic relationship with him. But the door was open. And he went through it.

"Do we know where this Chaz Michaels is?" Eric set his cup on the desk, pulled a Twizzler from his coat pocket and went to work on his computer.

"I've already searched the system. It's like he vanished after Ellen Strosbergen was brutally beaten. They arrested Sylvester 'Sly' Watson and he's doing time at Riverbend."

Eric played drums with his fingers on his desk. "Did he beat the woman?"

"Prints on the tire iron says he did. He never ratted out a single other person."

Eric gave a side nod. "That's devotion. Gang-like."

"They were, in a sense." Luke opened a drawer and found a roll of antacids.

"And Harmony Fells was wrapped up in this group?" Luke nodded.

"She's squeaky-clean now. A few stains on her juvie record." Eric finished his coffee and shot the cup into the can a couple of feet away. "Score!"

"Couldn't place her, Tyson Baroni or Chaz Michaels at the scene that night." But he could place Piper. She'd been two blocks from the Strosbergen home, running like Carl Lewis in the hundred-meter sprint.

"I know you and she had a thing—"

"It won't affect my job." He'd make sure of it. Never. Again.

"I was going to say that even though you had a thing with her, we ought to take a little look-see into her Jackson life. See if she's as innocent as she says." He stood and clutched his jacket. "Get some rest tonight."

"You got a date?"

Eric wiggled his eyebrows. "Wouldn't you like to know."

"It's why I asked." Luke chuckled. "And you answered my question. You don't."

"When I can find a woman who won't freak every time I holster a gun to my shoulder, I'll be set. Call if something pops."

Hopefully, when something did, Piper's name wouldn't be anywhere near it. The churning in his gut said otherwise.

Beale Street hadn't changed much in a decade. Neon lights lit up the murky sky. Ashy clouds slithered around the full moon. Not a star in sight. Piper flipped the collar of her black canvas jacket around her ears. The wind was colder and stronger coming off the Mississippi River. Shards of glass and trash littered the sidewalks. Horses clip-clopped down the street eagerly waiting for couples who wanted a romantic ride in lit-up carriages. Quite the contradiction.

Blues music drifted from clubs, restaurants and bars. Saturday night. Throngs of people packed into the buildings. Riff's turned a blind eye and welcomed anyone who at least looked sixteen, mostly riffraff. Piper had been coming and going since she was fifteen.

The neon pink sign blared over the aged brick building. Two large windows revealed patrons enveloped in cigarette smoke and pale lighting. She stood out front, inhaling the tangy scent of BBQ and char-grilled burgers. Liquor permeated Beale Street on Friday and Saturday nights. Wasn't even May yet. Memphis in May would draw huge crowds.

She could stand here with a million regrets or go in and try to dig up some information on Christopher Baxter.

A chill swept up her spine. That being-watched feeling coated her skin. No time to second-guess the idea. It was now or never.

Chapter 4

Piper marched through the doors, cigarette smoke burning her nostrils. The smell of pungent sweat, stale beer and peanuts sent a wave of nausea through her. How could she have ever called this her stomping ground? A few leering eyes roamed her, but she maneuvered through the mob. Pool balls clacked together. Laughter and the thump of bass mixed with a tenor voice crooning an old Bonnie Raitt song.

Everyone seemed young. Not that Piper was old, but she'd aged before her time in many ways. Made a lot of shoddy decisions, thinking she was all grown-up. She ached to go back to age ten, when Mama Jean had sent her to church camp and she had walked to the altar to ask Jesus into her life. On the following Friday evening, Mama Jean had come and watched her be baptized. That moment had felt like warmth cocooning her. A safe place. She hadn't wanted to come up out of the water.

What happened in those next years? How had she fallen so hard so fast? Mama Jean would say, "Dear one, you spend more time with those friends than the friend that sticks closer than a brother." Piper didn't understand exactly what she meant, other than she was talking about Jesus. Mama Jean always talked about Jesus.

She slipped her coat off and hitched herself up onto a high-top chair. A greasy menu was laid out for her to skim. Her stomach protested the thought of food. Behind the bar, cooks in white shirts and hats slung hash.

An eruption of laughter and applause exploded near the pool-hall section. Piper checked out the crowd. No one she recognized. Did she expect anyone to still linger here?

"Well, look who else the cat dragged in."

Piper turned her head and smiled. "Jazz." The big burly guy, skin the color of espresso beans, now in his fifties, wrapped her in a bear hug. His physical strength overpowered her as much as the scent of grease and onions. "How ya been?"

"Holding my own, Pipes." Jazz had managed this place for as long as Piper could remember. A fairly decent guy—never tried to take advantage of her. "What brings you back here?"

"You wouldn't know a guy named Christopher Baxter, would you?" Hope and a prayer—that God probably wouldn't hear—floated from her mind. Something Jazz had said a minute ago hit her. "Wait, what do you mean 'who else'? You said 'look who else the cat dragged in.'" Piper's hands turned clammy. "Who else is here?"

"Your boy from way back. Came in about five minutes ago."

Chaz? Piper might pass out. "Which boy?"

"Luke."

He must have a lead. "He say anything?"

Jazz shrugged. "Just came in, shook my hand like old times."

Luke had been undercover once. Was he trying to stay that way?

"So Christopher Baxter. You know him? Who he ran with?"

Jazz clucked. "That fat cat, Derone, and him were tight till Baxter found the Lord over on Riverside. They call Derone 'Wheels' 'cause that tricked-out Caddy he be drivin'."

"Is Derone here?"

"Was fifteen minutes ago."

Now for one more question. "Have you seen Chaz around?"

"Not in years. Saw Tyson a few times, but he didn't go in the back. Not after Sly went to prison." Jazz removed his toothpick and pecked Piper on the cheek. "Don't go gettin' in any mess."

"Me?"

"Mmm-hmm." He gave her a knowing look and strutted behind the counter. Piper snagged her coat and pushed through couples dancing, playing pool and darts, past the bathrooms that flanked the narrow hallway to double doors leading to the real action. Anyone jonesing for trouble gravitated back here. Cops showed up, easy exit. The dull metal door opened to an alley that connected with an Italian restaurant.

Piper opened the door to a massive room, sectioned off by wooden half walls with cedar beams towering to the ceiling. Smoky. Crimson shades hung over dim lights above red vinyl booths that lined the walls. Several games of pool and darts were going on. Black-topped tables with matching scuffed chairs splotched the right side area.

No sign of Luke yet.

"You look lost." An athletic-built man with shaggy black hair and intense blue eyes sidled up to her. "Are you?" His voice was warm-paraffin kind of smooth, and in the old days Piper would have already swooned. And been sorely burned. This guy was wildfire.

"I'm looking for Derone."

"You his girl? Because I'm not seein' it." He flashed a grin. Definitely not a meth head with those Colgate-white chops. Dimples creased his scruffy cheeks.

"I need to find him." She scanned the crowd around the pool tables.

"If I tell you where he is, will you have a drink with me?" His spicy cologne was enticing.

"I don't drink."

"Not even water?" He chuckled. "Tell you what. I produce Derone, and you have a drink of water with me. Just water."

Never gonna happen. Nobody back here was up to anything honorable. No matter how incredible they smelled or appeared. "I'm not thirsty."

He gave a quick nod. "I can live with that answer. My name's Holt. Holt Renard. I'd remember if I saw you before. First time here?"

Piper peered over his shoulder. "Which one's Derone?"

He sighed and jerked his thumb over his shoulder. "Last booth on the right. Nice girl like you don't need to be tangling with Wheels."

Piper pitched a lukewarm shrug. "I'm not known

around here as a nice girl." And shame painted her skin red.

She charged toward the booth. A beast of a man with a tattooed bald head swung around the corner with a pool stick in hand and a leering eye.

"You looking for a good time?" he rasped.

Would this never end? Piper glared up at him. "If a good time is named Derone."

"Derone." He laughed. "Derone can't show you a good time. But I can."

Losing her patience wasn't smart. But the ape loomed over her, and getting in her personal space was a mistake. "You need to seriously consider stepping aside."

"Feisty, aren't ya. I like it."

He had no idea just how feisty Piper could be.

"And if I don't?"

Piper didn't encourage fighting, especially picking one, but she had a mission, and the longer this goon messed with her, the chances of finding Derone slipped away. "I don't have time for this. Move."

She started to step around him, but he clasped her shoulder, digging his fingers into her flesh.

Mistake.

Piper laid an elbow into the giant's sternum with a quick jab. He fought for a lungful of air, but she'd knocked the breath out of him, sending him into a panicked state. Taking the small open window of opportunity, she grabbed his hand, twisted around, faced him and landed a double-front kick to his rib cage, toppling him over the pool table.

"You said you liked feisty." Piper ignored the stares, hoots and applause and targeted on the last booth to the right. Where was Luke? Had he already found who he was searching for? Had it been a bust?

"Was that necessary?" Luke appeared from a crowd near the darts area, a twinkle in his eye. He led them to a quieter corner away from the humiliated man seething over getting beat up by a woman and where they could have a more private conversation.

"He was in my personal space and wasn't going to let up. And if you came by to see if I was hanging around my old place for fun and giggles, you're wrong."

Luke fiddled with a blue chalk square lying on a high-top table. "I had no idea you were here. But I'm not surprised after you so sweetly told me you planned to track down the person behind Mama Jean's assault and probably yours."

"And I meant it."

"And I still believe you." He lifted his eyebrows. "So, your plan is to go all Bruce Lee on everyone until you get answers?"

"If that's what it takes." Did he have to be so attractive with his grin, one side lifting higher than the other? "What have you found out?"

"I was just starting a conversation when you pulled your stunt. Baxter frequented here at one time and ran with a guy named—"

"Derone. I know. Got that from Jazz." Piper tried not to inhale his scent or be hypnotized by the gravel in his voice.

"How would *you* know to find Derone here?"

"Mama Jean mentioned Riff's. I also know the kind of people who frequent this joint. It doesn't take a detective's shield to make that dog hunt." Piper propped her hands on her hips. "Excuse me while I find him."

She forced a tough exterior, hoping Luke wouldn't bring up her lack of invincibility. She *was* only one person. But she was the only one she could depend on. *Keep the brave front, Piper. Do what you have to do. Find out who's behind this.*

"How about we find him together?"

Luke rubbed his chest. Feelings he didn't want to experience seeped to the surface, ignoring his attempts to keep them behind the wall he'd built. Piper lived in Jackson now and was happy, according to her. A good quiet life. No room for him. Not that he wanted her to make room.

She needed to stop digging into things on her own.

"Piper, you should go home." It hit him. "Wait a minute… How did you get here? Your car isn't going to be ready until Monday."

Piper glared. "I took a cab from the hospital. I'm not helpless. And I'm not leaving until I have answers."

No. Piper wasn't helpless, but sniffing around might get her killed. Karate was an excellent defense, but it wouldn't stop a bullet. "Please don't make me arrest you for obstructing justice." Throwing her in a cell would keep her safe.

Piper invaded his personal space, pinning him with a glare; the smell of jasmine messed with his head. "I'll tell you what—if you think you can get a pair of cuffs on me, I'll let you haul me in."

The dare in her eyes only furthered his attraction. Piper wasn't going to let anyone, including him, run all over her. This wasn't the same woman from ten years ago. She was stronger, more determined and unstoppable. A wave of admiration and respect swelled within him.

Better to work with her than against her. Having her near would be smart, to keep an eye on her and to protect her. But when it came to his heart, it might be the dumbest move in history.

"Fine. You can stay."

"Can?" She shot another lethal glare.

He glanced around the crowd, making sure Bald Guy hadn't decided to go another round with Piper. Looked long gone. "That came out wrong. Let's put our heads together." Last time they'd put their heads together, they'd been kissing. His sight trailed to her soft lips.

"How are we supposed to do that when I'm a suspect to you?" Piper rolled her shoulders around. He could relate to the tension.

Her eyes widened and she shot her hands up. Luke turned to see a man who should be playing linebacker for the Chicago Bears slide from the booth and head for the restroom area.

"Derone!" Piper shoved past Luke. Derone sized Piper up and bolted.

"Wait!" Piper took off after him as he thrust open the exit door and burst into the alley.

"You wait!" Was she crazy? Luke blew after her, but she was so much smaller it'd been easier for her to maneuver through the crowd.

Piper was halfway down the alley by the time Luke ran out the back door.

Derone obviously thought she was a cop. No wonder, the way she came in owning the place. Piper never did understand subtle. Luke sped up, gaining on Piper, who was dogging Derone. He whipped right, hauling it past a gathering of spectators and ignoring the foul remarks and name-calling.

Derone was about twenty feet ahead and Piper was gaining. Man, she was fast.

Derone shot down a side street. Luke pumped his legs harder. The cold air burned his lungs. The guy might have a gun. He had to get to Piper. Or to Derone first.

"Freeze! Police!" Piper screamed.

No. She. Did. Not.

Derone slowed down, craned his neck in Piper's direction. He was gonna run again. It was all over his face. Around he turned and disappeared into a blues nightclub.

Luke nearly caught up with Piper. "Have you gone mad?" he shouted toward her. "He could have shot you."

Piper's glassy eyes barely registered his presence. She didn't even slow. She was after one thing and one thing only. She entered the club and Luke followed. "He's going to get away. He's my only link to Christopher Baxter." She shoved her way through the masses, leaving Luke, and sprinted for the side door Derone blasted out.

Luke burst through the tangled web of people separating them and worked his way to the door just in time to see a dark blue van screech to a halt at the end of the alley.

Piper flew down the backstreet, unaware. Derone came out of nowhere and coldcocked her, knocking her off balance.

"Stop! Police!" Luke pulled his gun.

Derone ignored him and barreled into the crowd, disappearing.

Bigger problem. The van door slid open and a man in a mask jumped out, heading for Piper. A band of drunks came out of a club on the other side, blocking his view. No! His chest squeezed. "Move!" he shouted, and they screamed and scattered.

The man in the van had a hood over Piper's head, dragging her inside.

"Stop! Police!"

Luke ran for the van. Piper was halfway inside.

Aiming for a tire, he pulled the trigger and dashed toward the end of the alley. Piper's foot blocked the door from closing, and then she slid it all the way open.

She tumbled out and the van squealed down the street. Luke hadn't even got a plate number.

But Piper was safe.

She tossed the hood and sat square in the middle of the alley, hair disheveled, a bruise already forming on her left cheek, shaking like a wet kitten.

"Piper," he whispered and ran his fingers across her cheek. He'd almost lost her.

She blinked several times. "He got away." She clutched the side of her face and bent over her knees. "Same van…at the hospital."

Luke put his arm around her and caressed her shoulder. "We'll find him. I'm more worried about you."

Piper stood and rubbed her cheek. "I should have been paying attention. I didn't even notice the van. Not when it opened. Nothing."

Luke hugged her closer as he led her down the alley. "Let's get you back to Riff's. Get something to slow that swelling down, Speedy Gonzales. You need a doctor." But he already knew she wouldn't go.

Piper's face scrunched and she kicked a can next to the door. "I'm better than that."

"You got out of that van. That's pretty good." Relief washed over him.

Inside Riff's, Luke guided Piper to a booth. "Don't do anything while I'm getting you some ice. You might have a concussion."

"I've been hit harder than this." Her face softened, and she smiled. "But thank you. Getting that shot off gave me a smidge of time."

Luke's heart was pretty much toast. "I'll be back."

When he returned, Piper's head leaned against the seat, eyes closed. He stole a few seconds to simply watch her. Her bravery had dissolved, her face was pale and her hands trembled. As if she knew he was staring, she opened her eyes and caught him. Heat crept up his neck and he held up the ice. "I bring gifts."

Piper brushed her fingers against his when she accepted it and flinched. Had she felt the connection, too?

Pressing the pack to her face, she groaned. "Now what?"

"Any idea who that was? Did you see any faces?"

"No. Everything happened so fast. I can only think of one person who wants to hurt me." Her bottom lip trembled and she sucked it inside her mouth. "Do you think Derone was working with whoever was in the van?"

"I don't think so. He had no idea we'd look here for him. And he didn't get into the van. But he might be indirectly connected since he knew Christopher Baxter." Did Piper realize the biggest concern yet? Someone was tailing her.

Luke needed more information on Derone Johnson. On that van. Chances were whoever was driving it prob-

ably didn't hang out here, but Piper was in danger. He'd
bark up any tree no matter how high. The undercover
DEA agent throwing darts with some roughnecks might
have information. But how to extract it without blowing his cover?

"I can get us some answers, and I promise not to
keep them from you, but I need you to hang tight and
not interfere."

Piper studied his face. She'd trusted him once—or
had she? If she'd trusted him, why give him that bogus
address?

"What are you gonna do?" Lowering the ice, she
peered up at him.

"Trust me. I mean it, Piper. Don't interfere. No matter what. Not even a 'Freeze. Police.'"

"Caught that, did you? I figured it was worth a shot."

"Mmm-hmm." He touched the bruise forming on
her cheek. "Stay put."

"Fine."

Her mouth said "fine." Her face said no such thing.
He released a frustrated breath and pulled his shield,
then strode toward the undercover agent. "Holt Renard,
I'd like to ask you a few questions."

He clenched his teeth just before Holt's fist made impact. Pain sprinted into Luke's head like a camera flash.
If Holt was going easy, he'd hate to see a real punch to
the face from this guy, and Luke knew punches. He'd
boxed in college.

Luke seized him by the arm, twisted him around
and cuffed him. "I'm so glad you did that," he hissed in
his ear and prodded him through the crowd. He caught
Piper's curious gaze as he pushed his way toward the
front of Riff's.

Was she buying this? Would she stay in the booth?

Luke led Holt to a small parking lot, crammed him into the back of his Durango and jumped in the driver's side.

"You got something against me, McKnight?" Luke rubbed his jaw, then uncuffed him.

"Keeping it real." Holt sniffed. "What's so important you'd risk my cover?"

"Derone Johnson. And a blue van. But they probably aren't directly related."

The passenger door opened, and Piper climbed into the seat.

"I told you to stay put," Luke growled.

"Hey, it's Mr. Miyagi." Holt grinned and concentrated on her bruise. "Wow, that's gonna look bad in the morning. Told you not to go chasing down Wheels."

Piper lasered in on him then Luke. "What is going on?"

Luke sighed. "Do you ever listen?"

"No."

"What unit you with, Miyagi?" Holt's eyes and polished tone oozed flirtation. He was known as a wild card and a ladies' man. Luke didn't like it being practiced on Piper. Not. One. Iota.

"I'm not a cop. But you are, aren't you?" She didn't seem mesmerized by Holt. "And don't call me Miyagi."

"Do I look like a cop?" Another movie-star grin.

Luke raked his hands over his face. "Enough." Piper hadn't followed orders, and now Holt's cover was about to be blown, at least to her. "He's undercover as Holt Renard, and you can't say a word. Not to anyone." He could taste his promotion slipping away.

"Give me a break. I can keep a secret."

"Ain't that the truth," Luke shot back with more venom than he meant. He was frustrated and feeling guilty for not protecting Piper better. No wonder she doubted his efforts.

Piper's face colored with anguish and she turned to Holt. "Derone Johnson. Where can we find him? I lost him over on Front Street."

"Why you chasing him when you aren't a cop?"

"I have my reasons."

"Will you have that drink with me?" Holt arched an eyebrow and shrugged when Piper didn't answer. "That wasn't me pretending. But I admit I *was* trying to steer you clear of the back room. Now you know why."

"I can hold my own," Piper said with smugness.

"I saw that."

"What drink?" Luke demanded as his ire rose. Green sludge spewed from his gut clear up to his eyes. Enough with Holt's advances. Luke explained everything that had transpired. "So?"

Holt's stare lingered on Piper, then turned to Luke. "Derone runs a smooth drug operation. Much like the Black Mafia Family out of Atlanta. I've been trying to take him down for the last fifteen months." He glanced at Piper. "You mind stepping out of the vehicle?"

Little late for that.

"You mind me going inside and telling everyone who you really are?" Defiance flared in her eyes. Piper might back down if it concerned only her, but Mama Jean had been injured. Damage was done anyway. And here he was once again letting protocol slip because of this woman. He had to get a grip and fast. Luke wasn't going to jeopardize his career or the promotion.

"Fine." Holt rubbed his wrists where the cuffs had

cut in. "I can't say that I know the Baxter dude all that well. But if he's mixed up with Derone, it's drug related. Derone stays in the Hickory Hill area sometimes. No permanent residence. Got people to hide him if necessary."

Could all this have to do with drugs? "Name Tyson Baroni ring a bell?"

Holt nodded. "Yeah, but he wasn't into drugs. Boosted cars and chopped them up in his shop over in Midtown. Probably done some car work for Derone, but I've never seen them together."

So a connection between them was possible. But that didn't answer the question of why Piper's business card was on Tyson or why she was attacked in the hospital parking lot. Was this Boone character working for one of these guys?

Piper shifted in her seat. "Derone must've thought I was police. He ran. Question is, was he guilty of the drugs or hurting my grandmother...or both?"

"Well, you did come in with some serious swagger. Sure you don't want that glass of water?"

"Still not thirsty. Thanks."

Holt shrugged. "Your loss. Ransom, drop me in the parking lot by the Orpheum. I can't go back in Riff's tonight."

Luke drove Holt to the theater happily. His hand ached to return the punch. "If you see Derone or a van that fits the description, call me."

"Will do." Holt hopped out and leaned back in. "Ice that jaw, dude." He gave one last tenacious look at Piper, winked and hauled it to the parking lot.

Luke grimaced. "Why did he offer you a drink?"

Piper rolled her eyes. "Maybe I looked parched. Or he's hospitable."

"If you weren't hunting down Derone, would you have had one?"

Piper scowled. "What does it matter to you?"

Luke's irritation tightened his already-coiled shoulders. "It doesn't." It shouldn't. But the thought of Piper sharing a drink, even just water, with Holt drove him crazy. He cleared his throat. "Now what?"

"Now I'm going to call Harmony." She dug out her phone, made the call and a few seconds later hung up. She chewed her thumbnail. "I'm worried."

"Maybe she lost her phone." Doubtful, seeing the fear in her eyes... He had to try to act optimistic.

Piper poked her lips out and cocked her head. "And couldn't even call from the hotel?"

"Which hotel? Call and see if they'll ring her room."

She lightly rapped her hand on her forehead a few times. "I can't remember the name, but the information is at Harmony's."

"Guess you won't need a cab after all."

He parked in Harmony's drive and followed Piper inside. She flipped on the kitchen light and snagged the hotel information. "The Bellagio. I should have remembered that."

Luke slunk in a chair at the kitchen table while Piper made the call.

"Yes, could you ring Harmony Fells's room, please?" Piper's face turned ashen. "I see. Are you sure?"

She laid the phone on the counter, a haggard expression on her face. "Luke...she never checked in."

Chapter 5

Turning left onto Walnut Grove, Piper spied the Starbucks where she was meeting Luke. Neutral location. A place they'd never visited together. Going back to Riff's the other night had brought a wealth of memories. Had Luke felt them, too?

Days had ticked by. The hurry-up-and-wait game was growing excruciating. Every second Harmony's chances for survival faded away and the probability of another attack on Piper grew. Sleep was as nonexistent as the leads Piper and Luke tracked down. Some of the animosity dissipated between them after Piper discovered Harmony had gone missing. Luke had put on a pot of coffee and worked with her, not against her. It only deepened the ache.

Harmony never boarded her flight from the Memphis airport, but her car was in the paid parking garage.

Monday, after Luke had dropped Piper off at the mechanic to pick up her own vehicle, he'd had the crime-scene unit out to print and send fibers to the lab before taking Harmony's car to the police impound lot.

Piper had forced Harmony to go, thinking she'd be safer. Now she was missing. Guilt devoured her inside out like a swarm of locusts. She should have let Harmony stay and maybe Piper could have protected her better. Luke said the video footage had her in the parking garage, but after that—nothing. Maybe Chaz was coming after everyone left from the old crew. Tyson. Harmony. Piper. Sly was in prison. Couldn't get to him. That was the only explanation she could muster.

Piper's attention webbed in a million directions.

At least Mama Jean was secure in the new facility, with a lush garden. She'd love that. It hadn't taken much to settle her in. After the deed was done, Luke and Detective Hale had returned and questioned Mama Jean.

Piper had perched by her side, barely listening. Compassion lightened Luke's gravelly voice. He'd kept his eyes trained on Mama Jean, not letting a single word fall to the ground. If only he'd listened to Piper in that way instead of commanding her to leave him that night he'd caught her running from the Strosbergen home. If he hadn't assumed the worst about her.

His patience with Mama Jean as she'd struggled to recollect information settled like sunshine into Piper's wintry bones. One of the attributes Piper admired most about him, something she had little of herself.

She spotted Luke at the door and he opened it for her. Smells of freshly baked vanilla scones, blueberry muffins and the delicious scent of caffeine welcomed her along with Luke's smile.

"You find it easily?"

"I did." After placing and receiving their orders, Luke led Piper outside to a wrought-iron table with two chairs and a green-and-white-striped umbrella to shade them from the sun. April was almost turning into May and the temps had begun to rise.

"Please tell me you have some good news." Piper plucked her green stopper from the cup and sipped on her white-chocolate mocha.

"I wish I could. I talked with Harmony's managers at the Realtor and insurance agency. They assumed she was in Vegas."

"I don't understand. Was no one else going to that conference?"

"One. Tom Deluka. Left two days earlier to make it a mini vacation with his family. It's a big conference. He never noticed Harmony's absence."

Piper's coffee unsettled her stomach. "This is my fault. I made her leave, thinking she would be safe. But..."

Luke tilted forward, hesitating to speak, forcing Piper to look him in the eyes. "You are not to blame. Understand?"

She gave a weak nod. "Are you any closer to finding Boone or Derone Johnson?"

"I have a BOLO—a be on the lookout—out on them both. We'll find her, Piper."

Luke's hand covered hers—masculine, slightly rough, warm. Would he use his thumb and stroke her knuckles like he used to?

No. He jerked his hand away and into his hair as a muscle in his cheek twitched.

Sliding her hand into her lap, Piper willed the familiar sting of rejection away. "I hope when we do, she's alive."

Luke licked his bottom lip. "There's something else, Piper. Boone Wilcy has more of a connection to Harmony than you realize."

Luke had discovered the convenience-store robbery. Information Piper should have confided, but kept quiet to spare Harmony the humiliation. Luke would be furious, trust her even less, wonder what else she was withholding. "I know."

"You do?" Faint lines in his forehead deepened.

"Harmony told me. But she didn't know until it was too late. I didn't think it was relevant." Until now.

Luke squinted and cocked his head. "You didn't think Boone and Sly Watson sharing a cell for a period of time was relevant?"

Piper's world spun. "What?" Sly Watson—Chaz's old buddy—who had been in prison for almost killing Ellen Strosbergen during that last job, had shared a prison cell with Boone Wiley? "No. I didn't know that."

Luke's face relaxed. "Then what are you talking about?"

Piper needed Luke's trust. To stop whoever was behind these attacks and to bring closure to the past that had careened into her present. And because the agony had never subsided from that night. Piper carried the dull ache every day.

She explained about the armed robbery and Harmony breaking things off immediately.

Luke rubbed his chin. "They're all tied together. They have to be. The attacks on you prove Boone isn't just a jealous boyfriend scorned."

Piper's chest tightened. "I'm thinking the same thing."

Luke tented his fingers on the table. "I'm going to start digging again into Ellen Strosbergen's attack." He waited a beat, searched her eyes. "If there's anything you need to tell me…now is the time. I don't want any surprises. Any *more* surprises."

"You won't get any." Her phone rang. She grabbed it from her purse. Braxton. "I need to take this."

She answered.

"I'm glad I got ahold of you, Piper." Braxton's voice sounded rushed and slightly panicked. "You in Memphis?"

"Yes." Something was wrong. Piper glanced at Luke, his features turned to granite.

A whoosh of air filled the line.

"What's the matter?" Piper asked.

"Someone broke into your house. The police came by looking for you. Said your neighbor called them. I gave them your cell. They left, like, five minutes ago."

Piper's stomach dropped. "You're kidding me." What did they think she had?

"Wish I was."

She finished the conversation and hung up. "I can't believe this."

"What happened?"

Her phone rang again. Jackson number. "Piper Kennedy," she said. The police. After giving them the information they requested, she hung up. "I guess you got the gist of it."

Luke snagged their empty cups and tossed them in the trash. "Piper, I want to believe in your innocence. But every time I start to, something happens, and it makes me think you aren't being completely honest. Again."

Piper refused to cry, but she could crumble right here. Was that all he saw? Her dishonesty? Hadn't she been crushed just as much with what he'd done? More like what he hadn't done. He hadn't given her the benefit of the doubt. Hadn't even asked questions. Hadn't thought she might be trying to protect him the only way she knew how. "I have to go home. I'm sure paperwork is involved, cleanup and insurance stuff to deal with."

"Okay. Let's think. You say you don't know anything. If you had to guess, what would they be after? Why now?" The plea in his voice wasn't lost on her.

Piper racked her brain. "I wish I knew."

"I don't want you going to Jackson alone. Can you wait until tomorrow? I could go with you after my shift. Make sure everything's taken care of."

Piper fell in line with him as they walked to their cars. Go with her? He couldn't even touch her hand without shrinking away. How would he survive a whole weekend? "Who do you think has been taking care of things for me the last ten years? Me."

Trust went both ways, and when it came to her heart, Piper couldn't risk Luke with it again. But every day was a struggle. Could she survive a weekend with him? "I can handle it alone." She had to.

Luke rubbed his forehead. "You think you can, but you can't."

"So you're calling me weak?" She ground her teeth. "Maybe once, but not anymore."

"Not physically, but, Piper, we're all weak. We only have so much strength in ourselves." Jamming his fingers in his hair, he raked through it, leaving it disheveled. "Think about it, okay?"

Luke had a point. Each disaster wore her thinner

from the inside out. Having some support when she stepped foot into her home would be reassuring, especially someone on good terms with God. Piper slid into her seat and turned the ignition. But Luke? Even now, she wanted to smooth down his tousled hair and inhale his fresh clean scent. She might be allowing him to protect her physically, but emotionally she was cracking.

"I… I don't know."

"If it's as big a mess as Mama Jean's, you'll need another hand." He wiggled his fingers. "I have two of them."

She let a smirk slip. "Luke… I—"

"I'll get a hotel room. No worries about sleeping arrangements."

Sleeping arrangements had nothing to do with it. It was how she felt when they were awake. Tapping the steering wheel, she batted the idea back and forth. It *would* be lonely. And if he got a call about Harmony, Piper would be right there with him.

"If…if you really don't mind, I guess I can wait another day. The police have most of my information. Just need a few signatures on reports."

Luke's shoulders relaxed, and he laid a firm but gentle hand on her forearm. Part of her wanted to cave and lean into him, draw from his strength. But for how long? What would she do when she went back to Jackson permanently? There was no point getting used to depending on him this way.

Piper could rely on only one person. Herself.

She gave a half smile and fixated on the steering wheel. Luke was nothing but a helping hand and a pipeline for information on the case. That was all it could be.

Luke's hand slipped from her arm. "Good. Whatever you need done, I'll fix. Promise."

"I don't want to even think about it right now." She'd already done so much work on the house.

Luke clutched the hood and leaned into the car, stopped her and held her gaze. "Just because our history isn't one for the movies doesn't mean I don't care about you or that I won't pray for you, because I will. I am."

Piper clamped down on her bottom lip to hide the quivering. Luke had always seemed to stay strong by standing on his faith. But then, Luke was a good guy. He didn't have Piper's shaky past attached like a looming shadow everywhere he walked.

"Thank you," she managed.

"We'll leave first thing Saturday morning. In the meantime, don't go hunting down Boone alone. I couldn't— Just don't go all Crouching Tiger, okay?" The corner of his mouth turned up, but his eyes held a swirl of emotion. What was he going to say? He couldn't what?

Might be better if she never knew the end of that sentence.

"Hey, man, you look like the baked potato I ate earlier," Eric quipped.

Luke wrinkled his nose. "Starchy?"

"Overcooked. You sleeping?" Eric sat at his desk—across from Luke—gnawing on a strawberry Twizzler. Weird vice.

Luke squeezed an orange tension ball in his fist and released, then repeated. He'd been living off coffee and oatmeal cream pies. Tomorrow, he and Piper were driving to Jackson to reassemble her house and hopefully unearth a few clues that might give them another space to move on the board.

At the moment, they couldn't find Boone Wiley or Derone Johnson. They'd done a search on blue vans, but without a plate number it was a joke.

"Is the case bothering you or the fact that you still care about her?"

It was both. Eating him alive. He touched her and a memory materialized. Smelled her shampoo, a longing filled his gut. Didn't matter how hard he worked to bury it, protective instincts had surfaced, and Piper consumed every spare second that cropped up in his mind. Torturing himself, he wondered what their life might have been like. They'd be married. Have children. A stabbing sensation filtered from his heart into his ribs, needling each one.

"I want to find something that I can work with. Let's go to Riverbend and have a chat with Sly Watson."

Eric chucked his empty Twizzlers bag in the trash. "He never once gave up any of the others who worked the Strosbergen home with him. Why would he talk now? Especially if he's in on it."

"What if Sly is behind it all?" He might not be able to search on the outside, but Boone could be his hands and feet. "Sly might have even told Boone about Harmony, and Boone pretended to be into her to get information. Piper said Harmony's downfall was picking crummy men to date."

Rolling his cuffs, Eric nodded. "I guess we can give it a shot. I can do that thing I do."

"Jedi mind trick?"

"Yeah, that one."

"Maybe I should go alone." Luke chuckled. "But

first I wanna talk to Kerr in the theft unit again." If his gut was right, the past was back. And that was why he needed to run it down with Kerr.

"The old partner?"

"The one and only."

"I hope he has some answers. You're looking enervated."

Luke arched an eyebrow. "Enervated?"

Eric lifted a flip pad off his desk. "It's my smart word for the day. Getting it in when I can. It means not having any physical strength."

"I know what it means."

Laughing, Eric shook the licorice stick at him. "No, you don't."

Okay, he didn't. "You worried about my health?" Luke teased.

"I'm worried if someone shoots at us, you won't have the strength to raise a gun to save my behind."

Luke slapped Eric's back and headed to the theft division, to meet with Kerr. Time hadn't robbed him of his physique or the same crew cut from his military days.

"Hey, hey, my man." Kerr gave him the guy hug, shaking his hand and pulling him in while clapping his back a couple of times with the other. "What brings you down here twice in one week?"

"Still working on that case that might connect to Chaz Michaels and his ring."

Kerr inhaled and shook his head. "I wish we would've found that scum." He motioned Luke to have a seat. "Or did you? Dead? Alive?"

Luke crossed his foot over his knee. He filled Kerr in on everything that had transpired since they'd last talked. "Something went down that night. Maybe money was lifted. Whatever it was, it's enough to trash homes, hurt innocents and murder people." Luke leaned forward, elbows on his knees. "What do you think?"

"I think that Piper Kennedy has you loopy again. And you're searching for any way possible to pin this on someone other than her." Kerr pointed to him. "I'm not saying she killed anyone, but she's withholding information and possibly hiding something...like a large chunk of change. How did she pay for her dojo?"

Tension thumped in Luke's temples and at the base of his neck. "She took out a business loan. Had a few thousand to put down, but that could have come from her grandmother."

"Did you ask the grandma?"

"No." He was afraid she'd say she hadn't given Piper any money. "But I will." He had no choice. "She promises she's innocent."

"So does everyone who's guilty. She gave us a false address, and while we were staking out the wrong home, she took part in a robbery across town that almost ended Ellen Strosbergen's life."

Luke had been humiliated. New to the job. Handfed false info. The jokes had never ended, some of them raunchy and cruel.

"I mean, allegedly took part. I never actually saw who I was chasing down. Chaz. Tyson. Doesn't matter now." Kerr shook his head. "I hate we lost that one."

Luke's fault.

Piper had never admitted to being inside the house. Either way, she'd lied to save Chaz Michaels. Said she was leaving that life behind for Luke. Chaz was gone, and Luke had a ring with no finger to place it on.

"If I can think of anything, I'll call you. But, Luke,

wise up. I said it then and I'll say it now. You didn't work her. She worked you. Don't think for a second she won't do it again."

Luke nodded but couldn't form a word. Kerr might be right, but deep in his marrow, he couldn't believe it. *God, can I trust her? I'm scared.*

"You pull the old case files?"

"Yeah," Luke rasped. "Over a week ago. I've been mowing through them. So far I haven't picked up on anything new. But I'll keep digging." If Piper had lied to him and was immersed in this, he wouldn't tell her to run; he'd have to arrest her.

"I hear you're up for a promotion. Congratulations."

Luke grinned. He'd worked tirelessly making arrests, closing cases. Right now he was teetering on the edge. Piper was already breaking down his defenses. She knew about Holt's undercover work, for crying out loud. "Thanks." He shook Kerr's hand.

"Don't need a case that links to theft to visit an old friend."

"You're right." Luke left and called Eric to let him know he was on his way. Time to see what Sly Watson had to say. Chances were he'd give him squat, but he had to try. Anything to bring closure to the past and solve the present homicides.

Inside the precinct, Luke met Eric by the elevator.

"What's going on?"

"Remember when you wanted to see if Sly would shank Boone by coughing up some information? Yeah... tables got turned. Sly Watson got *himself* shanked. He's in surgery. But they say he'll make it."

"You think it has anything to do with our case?"

"It's fishy. But Riverbend is out at least until Monday."

Eric looked behind Luke's shoulder, eyes wide. Luke turned. Piper stepped off the elevator. "Piper, what's wrong? What are you doing here? I thought you were at the rehab center with Mama Jean."

"I was. I thought I'd come by and see if you have anything new." She rubbed her hands together. Fidgety. Instinct said wrap her in his arms, calm her and reassure her things would be okay. But that would be a lie. And dragging her close wouldn't be smart.

He checked his watch. "You eaten anything?" A couple of hours to keep her mind off things wouldn't kill them, and he didn't have to embrace her to eat a meal. Plus, if she was with him, he wouldn't worry about something happening to her. "I'm running on fumes."

Eric cleared his throat. "Yeah, well, I'm fully tanked. That came out wrong, but you know what I mean. I'll man the fort here and call if anything's progressed."

Piper nodded. "I guess I could eat. And I'm..." She blinked several times, as if trying to hold back tears. Luke had rarely seen Piper cry. She was on the edge but didn't want to admit it. And he couldn't blame her. They were turning up dead ends and Chaz was like a shadow. Luke was anxious, too.

"We'll get something other than hospital or rehab-center food," Luke said.

"Hey, the hospital has great food. Sometimes I go just for lunch." Eric blinked at Luke with innocent eyes. "What? It's true."

Luke shook his head and led Piper into the elevator. "What sounds good?"

"I'm not the one who's on fumes. You tell me."

Once, they'd loved to eat fried chicken at Gus's.

Would that bring up too many memories? Hitting a neutral location might be the best option.

"We could go to Gus's. I'm due." Piper's lips turned up in a sheepish grin. "But if you want something else, I can eat anything."

Luke's throat turned to sandpaper. "No…no, that sounds perfect."

Chapter 6

The radio filtered a classic-rock station inside Piper's car. Outside, the Saturday morning was clear. The sky shone robin's-egg blue, and it appeared God had painted the clouds with a spray can of whipped cream. God. Was He just a powerful being in the sky, bringing each day and watching over the world? Mama Jean talked as if they knew each other on a one-on-one basis. Talked every day. Of course, what wrong had Mama Jean ever done? Naturally, she and God were friends.

Luke drew his long legs up and then pushed them out again.

"You want to stop and walk a minute?"

"Nah. We're almost there now. Unless you want to."

"I'm fine." Piper kept her eyes on the road as Luke shifted in the passenger seat.

Comfortable silence enveloped the interior. Last

night at Gus's they'd forged through the awkwardness over spicy fried chicken, mashed potatoes with savory brown gravy, sliced white bread and sweet tea. They'd taken measured steps to dance around their prior relationship and why it had ended. Instead, they'd talked about Luke's preference for the homicide unit over theft, Mama Jean and her recovery and Piper's martial-arts competitions, including the last one in Bangkok.

Getting over the hump made the drive south to Jackson bearable, but a minuscule ripple of tension lay under the surface of their words and now their silence.

Piper turned left at the light and entered an older neighborhood with large oaks sheltering the seventies-style homes. From the corner of her eye, she caught Luke studying his surroundings.

"It reminds me of Mama Jean," she said. "The older homes. When I left… I missed her so much that when I could afford a place, I chose a fixer-upper." She missed Luke terribly, too, but that wasn't going to air from her mouth. "I've done a lot of work, but it's not finished yet."

Luke shifted in the tan leather seat, his eyes revealing the compassion she'd loved about him. "I never meant for you to leave Mama Jean. I—"

"That's my house on the right with the carport." Piper couldn't go back to that time. Not now. Maybe not ever. She'd buried the memories. Those words. That pain. She'd poured it out with every punch, every kick and every kata.

Luke stroked the stubble around his cheeks and chin. "I like it." A frail tone filtered his words.

"I dread going in." She swallowed hard and sighed. "That's Ms. Wells. She's the one who called the police."

Piper pointed to the older woman with rollers in her hair, shuffling over. Piper and Luke stepped out of the car, and Piper popped the trunk. "Hi, Ms. Wells. Thank you so much for calling the police. Sorry for the drama."

The woman's steps were slow, but her mind was sharp and her green eyes flashed bright and clear. "Honey, I'm so glad you were gone when this happened. I took Tootsie for her morning walk, checked your mail, and when I walked in the kitchen I nearly had me a come-apart."

"You don't know how relieved I am that he was gone before you went inside." Piper cleared her throat as Ms. Wells eyed Luke. "Detective Luke Ransom, meet Ms. Frances Wells."

Luke shared a welcoming smile with her neighbor and shook her hand. "Very nice to meet you."

"Likewise. Glad Piper has a nice strong man by her side. But I can call Bubba to come if you like? It's a real mess." Ms. Wells had been trying to smash Piper and her grandson together for a year. Bubba was a decent guy, but he just didn't do it for her.

"I think we can manage."

"You need anything, anything at'tall, you holler."

"Yes, ma'am." Time to face the heap. "Well, come on. I'll give you the two-cent tour." Forcing a grin, Piper ambled toward the side door that led into the kitchen. She opened the screen door, then unlocked the wooden one.

"Piper, it's okay to be emotional." Luke rested a gentle hand on her shoulder. She shifted it off. No time to sink underneath it and fall apart.

Inside, it smelled of mulberry from the potpourri she'd burned before going to Memphis, but the wreckage sent pinpricks behind her eyes. A mountain rose in her throat. "This was the kitchen."

Dishes had been swiped from the new oak cabinets she'd installed and painted white. Shards of glass dotted the laminate hardwood flooring. With a shaky breath, she maneuvered through the mess and into the dining area that opened from the kitchen. Just a table with four chairs. Untouched.

Sliding glass doors opened into a small fenced-in backyard. The stick she kept in the sliding door track to keep intruders out lay near the baseboards. "I can't believe I forgot to shove that joker in the track. Cops said that's how he entered."

"I'm sure the call about Mama Jean had you shook up. Not thinking straight."

Piper flexed her fingers. "Doesn't matter. If a person wants in a house, they're getting in."

Luke's eyebrows rose, but instead of throwing words in her face and reminding her that she ought to know that better than anyone, he probed the house like a detective. Or was he once again giving her some space to process? Probably both.

Staring into her modest living room, Piper's shoulders slumped. The couch, matching oversize chair and ottoman lay upside down, gutted like pigs. Outside the picture windows, Ms. Wells walked her Yorkie-poo, Tootsie.

"Piper? You holdin' up?" Luke's husky tone reached her ears, but she couldn't utter a syllable.

No. No, she was not.

This was her home.

Violated.

She crept down the hall to her left. Pictures of sunrises, sunsets and rolling hills were crooked. Straight ahead, the medicine cabinet hung off the wall in the bathroom, and the linen closet had been eviscerated. Towels, washrags and blankets littered the green-and-yellow linoleum. Choking back sobs, she knelt and clutched a fluffy pink rag.

"I haven't gotten around to remodeling this room."

Luke trailed behind, a foot of space between them. "Piper," he whispered. That one word revealed his deepest empathy and impotence to fix it.

She refused to face him. Refused to fall headlong into him. Her feelings contradicted each other. She wanted his strength and at the same time she didn't.

The guest bedroom to the right was as trashed as her home office.

"It's surreal." All those home owners years ago. This was exactly how they'd felt walking into their sanctuary, their safe place. Beloved keepsakes. Hard-earned valuables. Gone. Nothing but ruination left in the wake of what Piper's old friends had done—of what Piper had done.

This had to be a divine reckoning. Punishment. More than ever, remorse filled her.

God, I deserve this and so much more. Can You ever forgive me? I can't.

Scenes of broken hearts weeping—not so much over what was stolen but the frightening feelings that accompanied a burglary. All because of Piper's mistakes.

Her chin quivered as she slid down the wall onto the floor, drawing her knees up against her chest. "Guess I had this coming," she choked out. She pressed her lips together, holding back sobs. "I—I need a minute alone, Luke." Tears pooled and she widened her eyes to contain them.

Wordlessly, he left the room and the door closed with a quiet click.

Luke leaned against the wall. Every hiccup and sob scraped across his heart. How could he fix someone who pushed him away? Piper was about to break, but he didn't want to pick up pieces. He wanted to keep them from shattering. His hands jittered to reach out. To do something. To bust open the door and gather her up whether she liked it or not.

Did he want in? Did he want to be more than a detective trying to solve a case?

He was here, wasn't he?

But Piper would never let him, and it wouldn't be wise. He needed a level head because he was certain of a couple of things: Piper didn't murder anyone. But someone wanted him to think so. But who? And why? If she did have something, by now surely she'd have admitted it. What else could they do? The thought slicked his throat like tar.

Luke drove his hands through his hair and gripped. *God, I am so confused. Please give me some discernment. Should I believe her completely? I want to, but I'm scared she'll destroy me again. Leave me with mud all over my face.*

Piper might not want his help, but the house begged for it, and he was a detective. Time to do what he did best. Investigate. He'd need to call the local police and see if any prints were lifted or evidence collected.

He hustled outside, grabbed his duffel bag from the car and worked his hands into the latex gloves, then snagged a few plastic evidence bags. He made the call to the local police department and spoke with the lead detective.

Prints had been taken but no results yet. Backed up. Same in Memphis. Too many crimes and not enough hands on deck to move quickly. Ms. Wells smiled as she walked her ball of fluff into the yard. Luke went back inside and combed the kitchen, moving from room to room.

Nothing odd leaped out.

The office door creaked and Piper appeared in the hall, red-rimmed eyes and pink nose. She brushed past him, trying to hide her vulnerability, her brokenness, but it was there. Running water whooshed from the bathroom sink. Piper blew her nose and came out as if nothing had happened.

How long could she go like this?

"You find anything?"

"No. I called the Jackson police. Reports aren't in yet." He pointed down the hall. "I'm going to take a look in the backyard."

"I'll come. What do you hope to find?"

"A sign with the name of who did this on it would be great." Luke grinned and a light, wispy laugh escaped her lips. So much better than tears. "We'll figure this out."

"I hope Harmony's safe."

Luke had a sick feeling, but he needed to stay positive for Piper's sake.

Outside, the maple leaves swayed. Fresh and green. Spring in the air. Tulips bloomed in a flower bed stretching across the front of the house. They rounded the side. The fence gate was open. "Do you normally keep that locked?"

"Yes."

Luke inspected. "Someone cut it. Probably came at night."

"They obviously knew I was gone."

Luke grunted as he stalked across the spongy lawn. "I think it wouldn't matter. Mama Jean and Christopher Baxter were home." He stepped onto the deck. "This new?" Smelled like fresh wood.

"I like to sit outside. The previous owners let the deck rot."

Yep, she was making a good life. Settling in. Remodeling. Building a deck. She even had a charcoal grill.

"Luke?" His name came out in a hushed tone.

He turned. She was closer than he'd expected. Her jasmine scent working its way into his senses. "Yeah."

"You know I didn't kill Tyson, right?" Piper's desperate plea for him to believe her and the fear on her face plunged into his heart. They both knew it looked grim for her. Against his better judgment, Luke caressed her velvety cheek.

"I know. We need to find out who did. Smoke Boone out of his hole and go see Sly when he's released from recovery."

Piper's nose scrunched, her brow creased. "Recovery?"

"I'm going to Riverbend on Monday to pay Sly a visit. He might be using Boone to do his dirty work on the outside. But someone shanked him on the basketball court before I could go last week."

"I'm going, too, then. I could play him to get the

information we need in exchange for what he's looking for."

Play him.

Piper was a pro at that. Another stabbing slice opened up ancient wounds. He gritted his teeth. Where was the peace? Why the bitterness? "I'd like to know what it is he's after."

"So would I."

"We'll go together, then." Letting Piper out of his sight wasn't an option. When she was living here in Jackson, he at least had known she'd been safe. If someone tried to wipe her off the planet—he wasn't sure he'd ever get over that.

Piper went inside and Luke followed. "Guess I need to get to steppin' because this place won't clean itself." Grabbing a broom, she began sweeping up the broken glass. She ran the broom under the cabinets, dropped it and squatted. "This isn't mine."

Luke hovered over her. "Don't touch it." He yanked an evidence bag from his pocket and picked up the nearly empty cigarette box from the floor. Camel brand. Must have fallen from the intruder's pocket. "Hope we get prints from this." Finally a break. About time.

Piper stood. "Doesn't mean it'll lead us to whoever's behind all this."

No, that would be too easy. A cigarette pack wasn't going to solve this case. And whoever was after her or trying to set her up—or both—wasn't going to stop until he had what he wanted. They'd come after her again.

A chill slithered down Luke's spine.

Piper wasn't home free yet.

Chapter 7

An entire box of trash bags later, Luke plopped onto Piper's gliding rocker. His back ached and his stomach growled. He checked his watch. After nine o'clock. Piper came through the dining room in worn jeans and a faded, thin black T-shirt, her hair in a sloppy ponytail. A few smudges of dirt splotched her cheeks and chin.

"Do you know what time it is?" she asked and sat in the dining chair. They'd hauled the slashed couch cushions outside and piled them under the carport.

"Feels like midnight. You hungry?"

"Starving. I have a frozen pizza. Probably tastes like cardboard, but at this point I might even eat that." She grinned and started to rise.

"I'll do it. You haven't rested once. Chill a few." Luke stood, his knee cracking. Wasn't getting any younger.

He grinned at the magnet on her refrigerator. It read:

Keep Calm and Kick On. Chuckling, he opened the freezer and pulled out a meat lover's. He slid it in the oven and turned it on. Preheating was a suggestion, right?

He brought her a bottle of water but stopped when it hit him she was actually resting. Eyes closed, lashes fanning her high cheekbones. Her neck bobbed when she swallowed. "Why are you staring at me?" she mumbled. "I can feel it."

"I was debating whether to give you this water or let you doze." Never mind—he was enjoying the view.

"I wasn't asleep." She opened her eyes and reached for the bottle. "I was thinking."

"Great. Thinking is good," he teased and sat next to her.

Piper shook her head and waved off his comment. "Sly Watson was stabbed in prison. You think that it's coincidence? I mean with it happening now."

Luke didn't believe in coincidences. Especially when it came to criminal activity. "Probably not. But if he's behind the whole thing, it wouldn't make any sense."

"Unless Boone found what he was looking for and paid someone to take care of business for him." She drank half the water.

Easy silence permeated the air along with baking cheese and crust. Luke rolled scenarios through his head. "Hopefully we'll know something Monday. If Sly was working with Boone and Boone double-crossed him, he may have heaps to say."

They sat quietly until the oven timer beeped, and Piper threw her hand up. "I got it. If I sit too long I'll pass out." She went into the kitchen and Luke followed. She slid the pizza onto the cardboard and placed it on the counter. Golden-brown edges and bubbly cheese. Pepperonis held little pools of grease, sausage and beef peppered in between. Luke's mouth watered. He must be famished when a frozen pizza sent his taste buds into overdrive.

Piper sliced the pizza and nabbed a couple of paper plates from the pantry. Carrying their plates to the dining area, they took their time eating. Finally, Luke spoke. "If you still want to toss the cushions in the Dumpster at the dojo, we should do it tonight. You don't want critters taking up homestead in them."

"Still afraid of skunks?"

"Of getting sprayed by them? Yes. The animal itself…maybe." He winked.

Nodding, Piper plucked a string of cheese that had attached to her chin and hung loose. "Rain's in the forecast anyway. You can see the dojo if you want, when we get there."

Luke nodded and brought the rest of the pizza to the table, snagging two more slices. "I'd like to." To see Piper's new life. The one with no room for him. Not that it mattered.

"Tell me about this promotion you mentioned." Piper helped herself to another slice.

"You know Granddad was a lieutenant. I think he'd be proud of me following in his footsteps."

"And your dad?"

"He's never gotten over the fact I chose law enforcement over politics. But I think if I made it further up, I could do a lot for the city. Serving in a…"

"More honest capacity." Piper chuckled.

Luke and his father got along, but he thought service meant from behind a desk. Granddad always said Luke was more like him than Dad ever was. Dad wasn't corrupt, but he wasn't beyond reproach, either. "Exactly."

"Sergeant Ransom." She wadded her napkin and laid it on her empty plate. "Nice ring to it. Planning to climb the ranks to commander?"

"Higher I climb, more I can do for the city." If he didn't mess up this latest case. He'd left the theft unit after the mayhem with Piper for fear he might come across her in another investigation, and he couldn't be sure he wouldn't let her go again. And now?

He couldn't answer it honestly. He shoved his plate away.

"I think your granddad would be very proud of you." Piper stood and collected his plate. "Let me put on a jacket and we can take those cushions. I think they'll fit in the trunk and backseat." She trudged down the hall and came back with a black zip-up hoodie.

After loading the cushions, they sped off to the dojo. Ten minutes later, they pulled into a small lot with a few potholes. A fairly decent-sized brick building with two glass front doors that read Kennedy Martial Arts came into view. Luke stared, not sure what he was feeling.

Piper unlocked the door and held it open. "Come on in." Luke entered the dark lobby area, the smell of lemon and bleach coming in full contact with his senses. Piper flipped on the light switch. A high counter with a register and credit-card machine sat on the left. A few black plastic chairs with metal legs lined the right wall, and a large window opened into a darkened room.

Behind the counter was another large window into another room. Above that, two ornate swords hung, crisscrossing each other. "You sword fight?"

"Some. Braxton is the master. He's a military man,

so anything to do with knives, guns, swords, fighting...
you name it, he can do it. But those are mine." Piper
flipped the light on to the room on the right. "Karate
in here. Sparring in the other room or it can be used
for practices and a second class that Braxton teaches."

She'd mentioned him before. "So, how do you know
him?"

"Braxton?" She slipped off her shoes and pointed
to Luke's. He toed off his shoes. "He's actually from
Memphis. I met him at a tournament in Birmingham.
He was looking for a job and I needed someone."

"And he moved here from Memphis? For a job?"

"Why is that odd?"

It wasn't. Just burning jealousy. He shrugged and
followed Piper into the karate room. She bowed at the
edge of the mat.

"Do I have to bow?"

Piper laughed. "Habit. Only if you were a student."
Luke stepped onto the light blue mat. In the corner, several red punching bags on stands bordered the single
wall that wasn't mirrored. Gold trophies and medals
lined the shelving edging the walls. Photos of Piper,
and a few men and women, engaged in competition
hung in glass cases; in some of the photos Piper wore
a proud smile.

"My office is down the hall by the bathrooms and
then the storage room is across from them." Piper
hauled a punching bag to the center of the floor. "Wanna
go a round?"

"With the bag or you?" Her cheeks flushed. Hadn't
seen that in a while. Luke could hold his own, especially if it involved boxing. He'd been doing that for
years, but if Piper started her Bruce Lee moves, she

could do some serious damage. And he'd like to keep all his organs intact. "Why martial arts, Piper?" Luke jabbed a punching bag.

"Got a job when I moved here at a Piggly Wiggly. Cashier. Met a guy who was into it. So I thought, why not?" An unreadable expression crossed her face.

What wasn't she telling him? Luke stopped punching. "Piper, why?"

Piper nailed the punching bag with a roundhouse kick. Having Luke beside her all day, in her house, helping clean, sharing a meal—this was what her life could have been like if she hadn't messed up so badly. If Luke had forgiven her and not turned her away. If he'd trusted her. He'd been having a hard time believing her. Maybe if she shared some truth, he'd consider her more of an ally now.

"I was tired of being afraid and weak." She shrugged as if it was no big deal, but Chaz was a scary man and Sly even more cutthroat. Chaz's threats had been lethal. If she left the crew or turned on them in any way, he'd kill her. Kill Luke. Kill Mama Jean.

And she'd believed it.

But this time, she hadn't been weak or unable to defend herself. And she was going to fight tooth and nail to protect everyone she loved. Even if it meant going up against Chaz. She shuddered. Double punch, side thrust kick to the bag. "You know it doesn't take a big person to do a lot of damage. I've seen men less than one foot away from an opponent barely draw back and send an assailant across the room."

Luke leaned on his bag, his biceps flexing underneath the cottony fabric of his V-neck T-shirt. "Piper, why were you afraid? I told you I'd keep you safe."

For how long? Besides, when the chips were down, Luke had stamped her a criminal and sent her packing. "I needed to learn how to keep myself safe."

"Didn't you trust me?" He closed the distance between them, clutched her wrist and brushed his thumb like a feather across the sensitive area. She could flip him on the floor. If she wanted. His touch revved her pulse almost as much as the tenderness glistening in his eyes, but the confusion and unasked questions that swirled behind them kept her from gravitating closer.

"Yes," she whispered. Once. But her actions hadn't been about trust or mistrust. Piper did what a nineteen-year-old girl who had been under the thumb of two insatiable animals for five years thought was best. She'd been protecting Luke, and he'd never once come to that conclusion. Searing pain flashed hot from her stomach into her neck. "I don't want to talk about this."

Luke released her wrist and sighed. "So teach me some moves, then."

Piper shook her head. "You have your own moves. Just a tour of the place."

"Come on. Show me the Piper I see in all these photos." The green flecks in his eyes seemed to grow greener, which was impossible.

Piper studied him. Then, in a blink, she came in with a slice to the side of his neck but withholding force. Luke's eyes grew the size of half-dollars, and he stepped back. "I didn't see that coming."

Piper grinned. "You weren't supposed to. That's a knife-hand strike." She held out her hand. "Keep your index finger straight and bend your last three fingers.

You want to strike with this part." She ran a finger down the side of her hand. "Go for the carotid artery. It shoots blood into the brain, making an attacker dizzy. Gives you a chance to make another move or run."

She modeled it for him again. He was taller than her, but with a step and expertise she could land it easily.

"That's crazy."

"It works." She chuckled. "Grab my shoulder."

Luke hesitated.

Piper wiggled her eyebrows. "Scared?"

"Honestly? Little bit." No need to use a knife-hand strike at her. His lopsided grin dizzied her plenty.

"Shoulder. Grab it."

Luke faced her and clasped her shoulder. She used the knife-hand strike, just missing his groin. Then she rammed the same arm—elbow up—into his chin, swinging with her right hand, giving him another knife-hand strike to the side of his neck. Again, withholding force.

"You move like lightning. And thanks for not making contact. I'd like to live pain-free the rest of the night if possible."

Piper folded her hands in a prayer-like gesture and bowed. "I can take care of myself."

"Still won't stop a bullet." Luke frowned. "Overconfidence could ruin you."

Piper didn't need a lecture, and overconfidence had nothing to do with it. It was called survival.

"What if I came in from behind?" Luke darted around her and sank into her personal space, his chest pressing against her back, his body heat seeping into her shirt. His right arm slid around her neck, gently putting her into a headlock. Masculine cologne and fabric softener tickled her ribs. She swallowed and grabbed his forearm, corded with muscle. Could she save herself from him?

"I'd… I'd grab your arm like this." She clutched his arm, tucked her chin into the crook of his elbow, but had a hard time moving quickly. The feel of his skin brought back so many memories of cuddling over a movie or holding hands through the park.

"And?" he whispered, lowering his head. The hint of cinnamon escaping his lips toyed with her senses.

"And then I'd extend my legs." As if she were about to do a jumping jack, she widened her legs, pulling her weight forward to throw him off balance. Dropping on one knee, she brought her head straight down to the mat. When she almost made a connection, she twisted to the left, which caused her body to dip and turn, sending him over the top of her and onto the mat.

Luke looked up, grinned and froze.

What happened?

A glint dangling from her neck caught her eye.

Oh.

"You…you still have that? Still wear that?" Luke sat straight up and fiddled with the silver infinity symbol, dangling on a silver chain.

A gift from Luke. Forever. That was how long they were supposed to be together.

He was too near. With his hand only inches from the tender hollow area on her neck, she jerked back and tucked the necklace into her shirt.

"I like it." She shrugged. What was she supposed to say? *I've clung to this knowing it could never be. Every time I touch this necklace I think about you. By the way, I wear it every day.*

She extended her hand. "Come on. I'll show you my office."

Luke accepted her hand and brushed off his jeans. "I seriously think you could beat me up."

"Ain't no *thinkin'* about it."

"Unless I sucker punched you. TKO immediately."

Piper elbowed his ribs. "Which you would never do."

"No, Piper." He paused in the hallway. "I would never hurt you."

She licked her dry lips. But he had. Worse than any sucker punch.

Without responding to his statement, she hurried down the hall. She switched on the light. "Yeah, this is my office."

Luke's arm brushed her shoulder.

"It's nothing special. Well, that's not true. This whole place has been my sanctuary. My hope for the future and my safe haven." It meant everything. "Mama Jean gave me the funds to put down on it. I felt guilty taking it. It was like she was rewarding me, but if she ever knew who I really was—*had* been—"

"She'd have given it to you anyway. Mama Jean is forgiving. Like God."

Piper trailed her finger along her dusty faux wood desktop. "I don't think God's so forgiving. Look at where I am. The middle of a murder investigation, somebody's scapegoat. My own house was demolished. And someone wants me six feet under!"

Luke's brow gathered, making a deep crease. "You think God's doing this to you because He's not forgiven you?"

"If I believed in Karma, I'd say it's coming around to bite me in the behind." Piper wasn't sure what to believe. The God she'd learned about as a child was loving, kind and fair. These circumstances would be fair. She deserved to have done to her what she'd done to others. Wasn't that the Golden Rule or something?

"Piper, God isn't wreaking punishment on you because He's mad at you." Luke placed his hands on her shoulders, leaned down and looked her squarely in the eyes. "I can't say I know why God allows these kinds of things to happen—I see them every day—but it isn't to be vindictive."

Luke was too much in her personal space. Piper needed air. Lots of air. She inhaled and exhaled. "I don't know. Let's—"

His head snapped to attention. "Did you hear that?"

Piper craned her neck, listened. She was too focused on him. "No, but the building is old. Could be pipes or something."

"Maybe."

Piper took another deep breath and hairs spiked on her neck. "Luke, do you smell that?"

Wary eyes made contact with hers. "Yeah. Smoke. Stay here. Close the door."

"I can—"

"Take care of yourself. I know. Stay put anyway." He shoved her farther into the office and closed the door behind him.

It was probably nothing.

Piper clutched the knob. Twisted. No. She'd stay put. Offer him another olive branch—if she did as he requested, he might trust her. But could she trust him again fully?

She tapped her hand on her thigh. How long was she supposed to wait?

The smoke alarm shrilled.
No. Not her safe haven.
The smoke grew more pronounced.
Where was Luke?

Chapter 8

Piper paced her office, gnawing her thumbnail. When was it legitimately time to come out and find Luke? Trust or no trust, what if he was hurt? Or worse.

"Luke!" she screamed. "Are you out there?" This was ridiculous. She opened the door; a fog of smoke choked her. Practically blind, she dropped to her knees, then army crawled down the hallway, coughing, sweating. No flames in this direction.

"Luke!" He wouldn't leave her. But he didn't answer, either.

Cracking and popping like wood kindling resonated. She pulled her shirt over her nose and stood, groping the wall until it opened into the martial-arts room. Everything was engulfed in flames.

No! Piper's stomach turned. She needed to move fast, but her feet were cemented to the floor. The lobby area was blocked by flames. She'd have to maneuver around the back hall to the sparring room.

She hacked, smoke filling her lungs, the burn intense. Feeling along the warm walls, she turned the corner. "Luke," she rasped and dropped to her knees.

Need oxygen. Where was the fire department? How much time had elapsed? Piper sputtered and tried to keep her mouth and nose covered. Her eyes burned.

Gotta find Luke.

She stumbled into the sparring room, where smoke hung like heavy drapes. Her head spun. Tired. So tired. "Luke!" The taste of burning wood filled her mouth, coating her tongue with soot and punching her gag reflex.

She groped the air and recoiled when her hand connected with flesh.

"Piper!"

Luke. He coughed and grabbed her, pulling her along. "Can't get out the front. It's in flames."

"Back door. Quick."

Flames would be licking up every solid inch of her dojo. They danced across the ceiling, taunting them.

They were going to die. Right here in Piper's sanctuary.

"I think I found the door." Luke thrust forward. Must be ramming his shoulder against it. "I can't open it."

The blaze came with roars. Cracking. Splitting. Hissing. Ready to consume her. This was punishment. God was taking it all. And had Mama Jean not loved Him so, He might have taken her away from Piper, too.

"I—I can't—" Luke continued battering the door. Piper helped him. Together they pushed, but it was steel. "I've got to get you out of here, Piper."

Window!

"The storage area. Has a window. Not very big… but…enough." Could they make it in time?

Luke gripped her hand and urged her forward. "Stay down, nose to the carpet. I'm going to get you out of here, Piper. I promise."

Her throat ached and burned, as if poison ivy had infected it.

"I—I don't know which way," Luke said.

Scorching heat surrounded them. Sweat slicked down her back. With little strength, Piper felt along the wall and yanked Luke to the left, the commercial carpeting scratching against her skin.

Snap. Like twigs breaking.

Roar. Hiss. New bursts of flames shot from the walls.

Luke mumbled. Sounded like prayers. She hoped God listened to Luke.

"Where's the window?" Blinding, inky smoke had smothered this room, too; not a sliver of moonlight gave the location of the window. Piper was disoriented.

So sleepy.

Something shook her shoulders. No, not something. Luke.

"Piper!" A ripping noise then pressure on her wrist. Was he tying his shirt to her? Ringing pierced her ears.

Dragging. Luke was dragging her.

"God, help us!" he hollered, and she squinted, eyes watering. The fire had found them. Inhaling the door.

Coming right for her.

The clinking of glass shattering drew her attention away from the clawing flames. Luke untied the bond tethering her to him and lifted her. "Piper, you can fit through the window."

Was that sirens in the distance?

"Luke…"

"Be careful—there's glass." He heaved her up to the window, and the cool night air fanned her scorched face. She tried to inhale oxygen, but her lungs burned. "Go, Piper!"

Wait.

You *can fit through the window*?

Luke couldn't? No! She wasn't going to let him take her punishment. "I'm not leaving you."

"Piper," he urged through coughing and wheezing. "I'll be right behind you."

"You promise?" Her stomach roiled, but she wouldn't move an inch farther.

"Right behind."

That wasn't a promise.

"Piper, if you ever loved me, even for one minute, please go!"

She propelled herself out the window, a burning sensation sliced down her side and she toppled to the ground.

An arm wrapped around her and yanked her up.

"I'm fine." Piper snapped off the oxygen mask, flicked the finger probe from her index finger and glanced around the curtained hospital room. "Where's the man who was in the dojo with me?"

A nurse reapplied her mask. "He's here, as well. And he's going to be fine. But if you keep taking this off, you might not be." She gave her the same look Mama Jean had when she meant business.

Luke was going to be okay. He'd risked his life for her. Her side burned. She peered at her seven stitches

and winced. Glass had done a number on her while she
burrowed out the window. Why couldn't they open it?

"The police are outside waiting to talk with you."

Had Luke already spoken to them?

"You're one blessed woman, you know that?"

Piper frowned. "I don't know if I'd use me and the
word *blessed* together." They'd barely escaped with
their lives and her dojo was gone. Sure, insurance might
cover it when they proved she hadn't burned it down for
the cash, but she'd think the stitches and almost dying
would contribute to the fact she hadn't.

A doctor stepped inside. "X-rays are clear, Miss Kennedy. No damage to your lungs. You need a couple more
hours of oxygen, and then you'll be free to go."

Piper thrust her head on the pillow, wincing again
at her tender side. She pulled her mask down. "I want
to see Luke. And I'm going to keep yanking this off
until I do."

The nurse sighed. "Fine." She set her up with a rolling oxygen tank and led her to Luke's curtained room in
the ER. He was wearing an oxygen mask with a finger
probe monitoring his levels, too. Soot stained his face,
and sweat had left greasy lines down his scruffy cheeks.

Piper stood by his bed and touched his filthy hand.
His other one was bandaged. Probably cuts from breaking the window.

Who'd done this to them? Chaz definitely would
have, and then stood in the distance watching as everything Piper could claim as her own literally went
up in smoke. Boone might have, too, if he was working with Sly Watson—or all three working together.

Piper gave herself the small pleasure of running her
hands through Luke's hair. Tiny flecks of premature

gray flickered. This man was more than beautiful—he was brave and willing to put her first. Was it his duty to protect as a law enforcer or did he have feelings for her? Either way, she was thankful.

His eyes fluttered open and blinked a few times. A smile formed under his oxygen mask, and he removed the mask. "You're okay."

"Thanks to you." Piper touched his bandaged hand. "Cuts?"

He nodded. "I'll live."

"I should knife-hand strike you for that stunt." A tear threatened to roll down her cheek. "The police are here."

He nodded again. "Have a nurse send them in."

Piper moved to go, but Luke grasped her hand and squeezed. He didn't say anything, but his eyes warmed, and Piper didn't have to wonder anymore. Not just duty. He cared.

Was that enough?

The hospital had released them late last night, and Luke sat in Piper's rocking chair running the past few hours around in his head. He'd filled in the Jackson detectives on the events leading up to the fire, but he'd kept the cigarette box they'd found in Piper's kitchen. His connections at the Memphis TBI, Tennessee Bureau of Investigation, might be able to put a rush on the prints.

His chest still pounded. *Thank You, God, for protecting and getting us out.*

Luke was sure it had been over for him inside that dojo, but he couldn't let Piper die. Stubborn woman wasn't going to leave him. The thought moved and terrified him at the same time.

The fire department had fought their way in and rescued him.

The detectives had confirmed what the uniformed officers had said at the scene. Someone had nailed the window shut and started the fire at exit points.

Whoever set the fire wasn't trying to scare or abduct Piper for information. They wanted her dead—and Luke, too. Or maybe he was collateral damage. Either way, whoever was behind all this must have found what they wanted. Why else try to kill Piper now?

"You want a glass of water?" Piper held one out as he glided in her rocker. "I'm going to ride over to the dojo." She rubbed her temples. Another one of her headaches. "I can't talk to the insurance company until tomorrow. Are you sure you don't mind staying at a hotel one more night?"

He'd never used his hotel room. Instead, he'd kept watch from Piper's car. Only when the sun rose had he gone back to his room for a quick shower.

"No. It's fine. I can go with you if you want, but it's late." Luke gulped down his water.

Piper collapsed on the coffee table. "I can do it alone."

Luke sighed. "I know you can. But you don't have to. Piper, it's okay to need a shoulder to lean on."

Her lip trembled. "Everything good in my life is gone. Not that I can't find a new location, but that'll take time. I'll lose some of my students. Braxton and Kelly are out of jobs, and I can't afford to pay them even a partial salary while waiting to relocate. I feel like I've brought everyone into my chaos."

"That fire wasn't your fault. Some sicko made a choice. God made a way for us to escape. Took us through the fire without getting burned. And not metaphorically."

Piper lifted one shoulder. "Maybe He saved us because of you. Either way, I'm thankful to be alive."

Luke wished she'd see that this wasn't continued punishment. "Why go to the dojo? To sulk over ashes? What will that accomplish, Piper?"

"You're right. I can't stand over a pile of ashes and wonder what if. I have to buck up, go back to Memphis and find Boone Wiley and hope it'll lead to Chaz. Right after we talk to Sly. Any news on Harmony?"

Luke had called Eric an hour ago. "No, but Eric has put feelers out with other divisions. If anyone fitting her description hits, we'll know."

"Every other body has turned up. Makes me think she's alive." She set her glass down and rubbed her hands together. "I have to believe she is."

"We can hope and pray."

Piper stood. "You should go get some real sleep. I know you pulled an all-nighter in my car last night."

Luke smirked. Nothing got by her. "I don't like leaving you here alone. Why don't you get a hotel room? Same floor as me. That way I won't worry. My treat."

Piper shook her head. "What he wanted wasn't here."

"That fire wasn't about scaring us, Piper. He attempted murder. He failed. He's going to try again. So I'd like you as close to me as I can get you." How close could he draw her without her overtaking his heart? How close was safe?

Her cheeks reddened. "Fine. I'll pack a bag. But I can pay for my own room. After that fiasco, I should pay for yours." She stomped down the hall.

Another thing bothered him. Piper hadn't raised the

question yet, but it was only a matter of time. How had the killer known they were in Jackson and at her dojo?

She was still being followed. And not by a van. Luke had been watching for that.

Chapter 9

"Hey, Mama Jean. How you feeling?" Piper and Luke entered her room. Piper brought a vase of tulips she'd picked from her yard. "We went by and did some work at your house early this morning."

"They're beautiful, dear one. It's nice to see you, Luke. Thank you for helping out so much."

Luke patted her hand. "Nice to see you doing better, and I don't mind at all. I'm going to go for a coffee. Anyone want anything?"

"No, thank you," Mama Jean said. Piper shook her head and Luke left them alone in the room. "Sit the flowers where I can easily see them." Mama Jean's color had come back, and her hair was combed. Needed set. Piper arranged the vase on Mama Jean's rolling cart.

Since Jackson, Luke hadn't left her side regardless of how many times she told him she was fine. He saw right through the lies. She wasn't fine, but she was trying to be. Pulling up the proverbial bootstraps and all that jazz.

Having him close brought her a measure of comfort but also misery. He was a walking billboard displaying her mistakes. Did he see her the same way? If so, he never brought it up, but occasionally she'd catch frustration on his face, regret in his eyes. Asking was off the table. She didn't want to know. Only, she kind of did.

Yesterday, she'd spent most of the morning talking with the insurance company, calling students. Braxton and Kelly had taken it hard but were willing to do whatever was necessary. All her trophies. Her photos. Medals. Everything that gave her an identity or proved her capability had gone up in smoke.

"You look like your world just crumbled. What is it?" Mama Jean asked.

She'd have to tell Mama Jean at some point—might as well be now. "My dojo burned down this past weekend." Didn't have to tell her she was in it when it happened.

Mama Jean looked to the ceiling and tsked. "I'm so sorry. What happened?"

Piper sank into a chair by Mama Jean's bedside. "It went up in flames. Every part of me went up in flames." She sniveled and buried her head on Mama Jean's bed. Wrinkled fingers brushed through her hair, soothing. "Mama Jean, I've done a lot of bad things…things I can't change. I don't think God can forgive me."

"Oh, honey, God isn't vengeful. He's merciful. And I know you did some alarming things growing up. I'd wake in the night, and the good Lord would press me to pray for ya. Because He loves you."

Piper wiped the tears with the back of her hand.

"You're everything to me, and I'm a disappointment to you."

Mama Jean kissed her damp hand. "You are not. You were just a child trying to find her way. And you got wrapped up with some hoodlums. But look at you now."

Yeah, just look at her. "I think it's my fault that you got hurt and Christopher died."

Mama Jean's eyes turned watery, and she firmed her grip on Piper's hand. "Now you listen to me, young lady. Did you force that brute into my home? Did you make him shove me down? Did you make him take Christopher's life?"

"No, but—"

"But nothing. Consequences come with each choice we make. But *we* make the choices. And that man chose to do what he did. You had no control and aren't to blame."

It just seemed as if everything was falling apart.

"I love you, Mama Jean."

"I love you, too."

Piper hurried to wipe her tears when the door opened. Luke stepped in with his coffee. "Okay if I come in?"

Mama Jean's eyes brightened. "Anytime a handsome man wants to keep me company, I won't stop him."

Piper lightly swatted her hand. "Mama Jean!"

"Admit it. He's even more handsome now than when he was a boy."

Piper's cheeks heated. No one could hold a candle to Luke back in the day, but Luke Ransom in this day? His presence sucked the air from her lungs.

"Well, are you gonna gawk or are you gonna answer your grandmother? Go ahead...admit it." A mischievous grin inched north; his eyes twinkled.

"I plead the fifth, and as a man of the law, you have to oblige me that."

Luke narrowed his eyes in a playful manner. "Hmm…" He shifted to Mama Jean. "Is there anything I can get for you? Bring you something from a bakery? A book?"

That was Luke. Always had a rough time seeing someone suffer. Once when Piper had the flu, he'd brought her chicken noodle soup—from a can—but it had been the sweetest gesture. Piper hadn't been able to buy a can of chicken noodle soup since.

"I'm right as rain. But you look like a man on a mission. And I'm a little sleepy. Think I'll rest a spell if you don't mind."

Mama Jean's way of allowing them to leave and not feel guilty. "I'm going out of town for a few hours but should be back by evening," Piper said to Mama Jean. "You have my cell number, so call if you need me, or Brenda Ann said you could call her."

Mama Jean's next-door neighbor took good care of her, and that gave Piper some relief. Who knew what would've happened to Mama Jean if Brenda Ann hadn't picked up that phone and called the police during the robbery. A shudder rippled through Piper.

"Go on and have fun." Mama Jean blew them a kiss, and they slipped out the door.

Visiting Sly Watson wasn't going to be fun. Unlike Chaz, Sly had never pretended to be anything more than what he was—a sociopath. Inky sharklike eyes matched the color of his slicked-back hair. His leers had been like a wolf licking his chops.

Neither were men you lightly walked away from—if you tried to walk away at all. Seeing him wasn't something Piper wanted to do, but lives were at stake, including her own.

Outside in the hallway, Luke took her hand. "You okay?"

If she made it out alive she would be. "Just thinking about how much work is left after the dent we made at Mama Jean's this morning. She was a pack rat to begin with and now... I dread going back in. If I had the money, I'd pay someone to come haul it off. Plus, I'm filthy." She eyed Luke. He had a few smudges on his shirt but that was it. "Hmm, looks like one of us must have worked harder than the other."

"Maybe just one of us is messier than the other." Nudging her ribs, he grinned.

Piper chuckled, and they breezed down the rehab corridors to the parking lot.

Luke grabbed the keys from his pocket and opened her door. She climbed in and fastened her seat belt. "If Sly won't spill, how are we going to find Harmony? We're all she's got."

"Let's cross that bridge when we get there." Luke's words sounded firm, but beneath them Piper caught the uncertainty. "You know, I can wait in the car while you clean up if you want."

If she wanted? No, more like he wanted. He'd become her own personal superglue.

Piper laid a gentle hand on his forearm. "I'll be fine. I'll make sure and lock all the doors when I get inside. You can even watch to be sure." She wasn't denying the fact that she was in danger—that any moment whoever was after her could strike. The idea sent a frigid shiver into her bones. But the brave front needed to stand tall.

Luke hesitated, glanced at her neck. Yes, the necklace was hanging there close to her heart. "Okay. And I'm going to take you up on watching as you lock the door." He opened his mouth as if to say something then clamped it shut a few moments before speaking again. "You thought any more about what your Realtor said?"

"A little. I think I'm going to lean toward leasing. I can resume classes sooner. I think that's important if I want to retain students." Now she wasn't sure she could do a second dojo in Madison, but possibly. If the insurance paid up and she leased in Jackson.

Luke's cheek twitched. "Good. That's…good."

Didn't sound as if he thought it was good. He parked in Harmony's drive, and Piper stepped out of the car. "I'll see you in a little over an hour."

"Or less. I'll be here."

He'd said that before. That he'd always be here for her. If Luke still had feelings, if they came out into the open, could Piper reconnect? Could he?

The qualm in her stomach said no.

After a quick shower, Luke headed back to Harmony's. His nerves had rattled the entire time he was away from Piper. For safety's sake and for other reasons.

Like the necklace and what it had represented.

Forever.

Love he'd once given to her without hesitation.

Now there were too many hesitations. Already, she had plans in the works for a new facility and her eye on a second one in Madison.

Who was Luke kidding, anyway?

Even if Piper wanted to give it another shot, he was scared he'd wonder if she was telling the truth, that he might not be able to trust her again completely. Two big factors to make a relationship successful.

Not to mention, the random surges of bitterness he felt at times. It slid over him like gooey tar. He despised it. Wanted cleansed from it.

"Lord, I've asked forgiveness for my actions. And I've asked You to help me forgive her. I thought I had. But these feelings… They creep up and make me think I haven't forgiven her at all."

Later, he'd sit in his recliner and search for truth in the scriptures, truth that would lead to peace and rest.

Piper opened the front door, her hair spilling over her shoulders. She wore a green T-shirt under a short denim jacket. Not just anyone wore denim well. Piper did. She must have been watching for him. After locking the door, she met him at his personal vehicle. An almost brand-spanking-new two-door black Chevy Impala.

"Nice ride," Piper said and slid into the passenger seat.

Luke patted the dashboard. "I think so. Remember that old Nova I drove when we were—" He stopped short.

"Yeah," she whispered. "Was that your real car or for your undercover persona?" Piper fiddled with the radio. Some habits never died.

"Undercover. Too bad I couldn't keep it." How many times had he kissed her in that car? Held her hand. Went for long Sunday drives talking about the future. He'd fallen for her. Hard. Over a birthday brownie. Clenching his jaw, he held back the emotion.

Luke rolled to a stop at the sign. "Why did Harmony pick a big house in the country? I know I asked before, and you said it was a foreclosure. Just seems lonely."

The car on his left took a turn early.

"It's hope that she'll have a family someday." Piper rested her head on the headrest and rubbed her side. "And it was a steal." She cringed. "Bad choice of words. She got a good deal."

"Stitches acting up?" He glanced over and noticed a dark SUV a few feet behind.

"Not too bad. I have a high tolerance to pain." She flinched.

"Yeah, I see that." He slid another glance in the rear-view mirror as he turned left. The SUV stopped at the sign. Probably nothing. "So what about you?"

"What about me?" she asked.

"Do you think about family?" Was he a glutton for punishment? "Anyone…special in Jackson? Maybe that Braxton guy."

Piper snorted. "Yes. No. Definitely no."

A gush of relief relaxed him. The SUV picking up speed wiped it away. Luke hung a right down a back road instead of continuing on the main highway. Nothing out here but land for miles.

Keep going. Don't make this turn.

If the SUV turned, there would be no doubt he was following them, and the car wasn't being inconspicuous. Might turn ugly. Better for it to happen on secluded roads than innocent people injured on the main highway.

"Luke, you made a wrong turn."

Luke gripped the wheel. The SUV turned. Not good. Whoever had followed them to Jackson had kept to their blind spot. This guy wasn't even trying. Luke made out a man, dark baseball cap pulled low. Large aviator glasses covered his face.

Piper shifted. "I know that look. What's wrong?"

She started to crane her neck to peek behind, but he gripped her knee.

"Don't turn around. Keep your eyes on the road. We may have an issue." Luke accelerated, and the SUV picked up speed.

Luke made another right. Nothing but fields on the left and woods on the right. The SUV kept up and increased speed. Luke slammed on the gas, kicking up dust.

"Boone?" Piper's voice had raised a pitch.

"I don't know." Luke concentrated on driving. He was up to about eighty-five.

The car lurched forward as the SUV made contact, shaking them like rag dolls.

Piper shrieked.

Luke increased the speed to ninety. Any faster and the orange line on the speedometer would tick. One wrong turn at this speed and he'd kill them both.

The SUV slammed into their bumper again. Piper grabbed her neck. The seat belt had sliced into her skin. A fine red line formed. He had to do something.

He swerved left then right, fishtailing to keep the SUV off their behind. "Piper, get my phone and find Eric's name. Call and tell him where we are."

"I don't know where we are!" She fumbled for the phone as the SUV edged up on them again.

Slamming right, the SUV crunched into the driver's side. Luke gripped the wheel for control, and Piper dropped the phone. She bent to retrieve it and the SUV smacked into them again. Piper's head hit the dash with a frightening thud, and she fell back into the seat and moaned.

Time to get proactive. Luke made a sharp left and rammed the SUV, sending it fishtailing onto loose gravel at the shoulder of the road, giving Luke time to gain a few feet in distance.

"Piper? Talk to me. You okay? Can you get the phone?"

"Yeah." She snatched the phone and scrolled with trembling fingers. Luke turned left again. Hopefully, it was one big circle and he'd come out where he started. He could give Eric directions to the main road.

"Eric! It's Piper. Someone is trying to run us off the road. We're somewhere near Harmony's. Okay. Yeah… okay." She hung up. "He can track your phone and is on his way."

That would only get them within the vicinity of a cell phone tower.

Another slam to the back of their car pitched them forward. The smell of rubber and oil assaulted Luke's nose. His clammy hands clung to the wheel, and he zigzagged at about eighty.

Riding on his bumper, the SUV crashed into them again. Luke's back sliced with spasms that shot into his neck and head. He kept his jaw clamped for fear of biting off his tongue.

As it made another go, Luke steered to the right and slammed on his brakes, hoping to throw the SUV ahead and put Luke in the rear. He could get plates. But whoever was driving must be a NASCAR professional; he slowed as well and rocketed into the driver's side. The window shattered, and the sound of metal crunching rang in Luke's ears.

"No!" Piper shouted and ducked. But it was too late.

The car tipped and rolled.

Piper screamed.

Burning, sharp misery. Every bone in Luke's body

felt disjointed. His ears hummed. His head throbbed. Something warm slicked down his cheek.

The car landed upright, rocking and jarring them.

Where was the SUV? A dizzy spell disoriented Luke's senses.

Piper!

He turned his head, no major difficulty, and it was still attached to his neck. "Pip!"

She groaned and gripped the side of her head. "I am *sick* of this guy!"

Luke chuckled. Then it turned into a deep belly laugh. Delirium. Had to be. He laughed and groaned at the same time.

"What?" Fire flared from Piper's eyes. "I am sick of being the victim. I'm sick of being chased. I'm sick of being hurt, and if it kills me I'm going to find whoever did this and destroy them! I mean it!"

Luke laughed harder until his stomach hurt, or maybe it was the seat belt cutting into his gut.

"Stop laughing! It's not funny."

He held up his thumb and index finger and pinched them about an inch apart. "It's a little funny." Okay, none of it was funny, but sometimes the body had to have a release. Laughing must be his.

"We gotta get out of here. He could come back to make sure we're dead. Besides, I think it's obvious you have a concussion." Piper undid her seat belt and leaned over him, wincing when she hit a speck of glass. She sucked her finger and turned his chin toward her. Eyes went wide. "Oh, Luke."

Her face hovered inches from his, enough to see the brown-and-green mix of her eyes, to see her long lashes and the faint sheen of gloss on her unpainted lips. "You're beautiful, you know that?"

Her tender smile lit up his insides.

"Your head's bleeding. A lot." The mint from her breath tantalized him. "Are you okay? Tell me the truth."

"Are *you* okay?" he whispered.

"Yeah."

"Then I'm fine. I'm more than fine."

She rested her forehead on his and inhaled sharply. "Are we gonna make it out of this?"

Did she mean out of the killer's path or the feelings they were having? Like an elephant in the room. Stronger than ever. Settling deep into his marrow, and if he had to guess, hers, too.

Her nose pressed against his. He swallowed hard. "We're gonna make it."

Inching back, she peered into his eyes. "Promise?"

"Promise." He cupped her neck and brought her to his lips, claiming them. Pouring his promise into her, his oath to keep her safe or to die trying. His heart might end up a mangled mess, and his body might end up haggard, but he would see to it that she made it out alive.

When he broke the kiss, she whispered, "I believe you."

"Piper?"

"Yeah."

"You smell that?"

Gasoline infiltrated the interior.

She sniffed, and her face paled. "Can you move? We gotta get out of here. Now!"

Luke tried to undo his seat belt. "It's stuck." He grappled and jerked. A pop then a hiss sounded. Flames shot out from under the crunched hood.

"Luke!"

Chapter 10

Piper grabbed Luke's seat belt, her hands uncontrollably trembling. They didn't have much time. "There's got to be…a…way." She grunted as she tugged and shook it.

"Check the glove box. I keep a knife in there."

"Now you tell me?" She flipped open the glove box and rifled through the maps, insurance, title papers… and knife. Flicking it open, she sliced the belt in two places, freeing Luke.

"Get out, Piper. I'll be right behind you."

"Been there done that," she growled. Luke's side of the car was crunched. She pulled the door handle. No. No. No. "We have another issue. My door is stuck." Fire fanned the hood of the car. She turned toward the trunk. Glass everywhere. "We gotta go out the back. Get away from the flames."

"Go first."

She narrowed her eyes. "You better be right behind me. Can you move?"

"Yep—go!"

The smell of gasoline and exhaust waved over her face, the heat burning her skin. She scrambled into the backseat. Luke followed. Piper glanced at his leg. Blood seeped through his jeans.

"We're going out the back dash window."

"I can help."

"Not with that leg." Piper couldn't be sure how bad the wound was.

Wrapping her arms around the passenger seat from behind her, she leaned back, pressing all of her upper body against the seat. She raised and kicked with both feet, everything she had.

Nothing. She growled and thrust again. "Anything in here to smack it with?"

The fire hissed. They didn't have time to dig around. Where was Eric?

Piper kicked repeatedly.

Luke shook his head and groaned. He reached behind them and opened the console. "Cover your ears." He aimed and fired his gun into the glass, sending the bullet through the middle; the glass spider-webbed.

"My right leg is fine. On three."

Gunpowder and smoke singed her nostrils, and her ears rang. Piper glanced at him. He'd just kissed her. They had to make it out alive. She had to know what that meant. "One…two…three…"

They kicked the glass together, sending it to the ground. "You go first," Luke hollered. Piper tucked her hands into her denim jacket to help protect her skin from possible cuts.

Adrenaline rushed through her veins. She didn't feel a thing scrambling out the back and as she rolled off the trunk to the ground. She lay on her back, gasping for air, her chest heaving.

Luke tumbled onto the ground next to her, then clambered to get up. "Run!" He jerked Piper up. She broke into a run, Luke keeping pace. His left leg had a slight limp, but it didn't slow him down.

The chilly air whipped across Piper's face, blowing her hair behind her as her feet nearly came out from under her. Her eyes watered from the biting wind.

A roaring from the vehicle sounded. Luke tackled her to the ground, protecting her from the explosion.

Like the sound of fireworks magnified a million times, cracks and booms split the atmosphere. Dirt and debris rained down on them, Luke receiving the brunt. Another blast shot out. More debris pelted them.

Luke's body weight lifted from hers, and she looked behind at the raging ball of fire that used to be Luke's car. She tilted her head and peered into his eyes. Dirt and blood caked his face.

"You okay, Piper?" Piper. Earlier, he'd called her his old nickname. Pip.

"I am so *sick* of fire!" Now that they had once again survived, a blazing surge of anger devoured her.

Luke rested his head on hers, a soft chuckle escaping his lips. "Me, too." He stood, grimacing, then shifted his weight to his right foot. Taking her hand, he helped her up. Other than serious stiffness and a few cuts, she was okay. She searched the bottom of each of her shoes, picking the glass out. Then they staggered to the road.

In the distance, a dark SUV rolled down the street.

"Give me your gun." Piper smacked Luke's chest. "I'm so done with this joker."

Luke snorted. "I hope you're kidding. I'd hate to have to arrest you after this."

"I'm just gonna shoot out his tires, then beat the ever-lovin' daylights out of him."

Wrapping a strong arm around her shoulders, he dragged her close to his side. "No need. It's Eric."

The driver's-side window rolled down, and Eric, sporting an impish grin, raised his eyebrow and skimmed their beaten appearance. He nodded his head in the direction of the blazing vehicle. "You know, you could've just shot a flare or sent up the bat signal. Don't think it was really necessary to blow up your car. I'd have found you eventually."

Luke shook his head, opened the back passenger door and helped Piper inside. Then he limped around the Durango and eased into the front.

Eric pulled off the shoulder of the road. "So…hospital or bust, right?"

Piper ground her teeth together. "I am so *sick* of hospitals."

Trying not to jerk when the doctor sutured yet another couple of places where glass had split her open, Piper focused on the curtain, barely hearing the doctor babble on about how to care for them. Minor injuries. A few lacerations but mostly abrasions. She grunted her answers. Where was Luke? How bad was his leg?

This was completely out of control. Why would anyone—Chaz… Boone… Sly—want her dead? She had nothing.

"Miss Kennedy, you're all set. I prescribed you some

Percocet for the pain and stiffness. You're a blessed woman. Not everyone makes it out of a rolling vehicle and an explosion."

Blessed.

Didn't feel blessed, but she was alive, and Luke was alive.

God, if You did that...if You saved us again, thank You. I didn't deserve it, but thank You. And...

Piper spent most of her prayers begging for forgiveness. But maybe...maybe she was feeling brave, especially if God had shown her some mercy.

...and could You please help us find whoever this is and show us why this is happening? If...if it's not punishment for my mistakes—which You know how sorry I am, how I've never stolen a single thing in ten years, and made up for all that I did wrong by helping other troubled teens—then please let us find Harmony, and keep us safe.

A bit of breathing room opened in her soul. Piper took the scripts the doctor handed her and shoved her filthy clothes onto her body. A shower. She craved one. Exhaustion swept over her, but sleep would have to wait.

Opening the curtain, she stepped out of the triage area in the ER and searched for Luke. Now that he wasn't half out of his mind and on the brink of death, would he regret that kiss? Would he even remember sharing it with her? Piper touched her lips. Something about it was even better than when they were younger. Piper couldn't quite place her finger on it, but she wouldn't forget it. May never get another.

In the moment, it'd felt right. Like coming home. But home was in Jackson. She'd made a decent life there. The teenagers in her class needed her to champion them, to teach them to overcome their fears and take control of their lives. They trusted and relied on her. She'd become a mother figure to them.

Every time Mom had shown up at Mama Jean's, Piper shook with excitement, believing this time she'd take her away someplace clean and safe. No more drugs. No more house-hopping, no more forgetting to buy groceries. Piper wouldn't fear the men Mom brought home, their leering eyes on a child.

But that never happened. Piper had ached for love and attention, and while Mama Jean gave it, Piper wanted her mother's love. A father's love. She had no idea who had fathered her. Mom probably never had, either.

By the time she was twelve, when Mom overdosed, Piper had come to terms with the fact that she'd been nothing more than a mistake. A burden.

Then she met Chaz at fourteen.

Piper balled her fists and sank into the waiting-room chair. Luke would appear eventually. She bobbed her knee and bit her thumbnail, a habit she'd never been able to break—to master.

A mother rocked a baby with glassy eyes and feverish cheeks, placing light kisses across his forehead and humming to lull him. He closed sleepy eyes and snuggled closer.

Piper bit back tears.

Would she be a good mom? For a while she'd become everything she despised, ignoring Mama Jean's pleas to do right. To let the Lord be her source of joy. To let Him fill all of Piper's empty places. Piper didn't have empty places—she was one walking black hole.

Even with karate, a void consumed her.

Luke stepped into the waiting area and she stood. A square bandage covered the skin above his left temple and he limped. Piper rushed to him. "How d'you feel? Do you have a concussion?"

"I have a major headache, and I have a few stitches on my left leg, but nothing I won't recover from. You?"

Piper explained her injuries. "I'm going to look like Frankenstein if they put another stitch in me."

Luke caressed her cheek. "Doubtful."

Eric wound around the corner with a few cups of coffee. "Healing juice. Who's in?"

Piper chuckled. The man was a riot, but she hadn't missed the concern in his eyes when he'd shown up on the road, and he'd stayed at the hospital waiting. Jokes seemed like his defense mechanism.

Anger. Anger was hers. She'd spent so long too weak to stand up or fight, cowering like a scared rabbit. No more. She had the power to fight back. But the wounds on her body were wearing her down. What happened when she physically couldn't fight?

"...for the Lord your God is He who goes with you, to fight for you against your enemies, to save you."

Where had that verse come from? It'd been ages since she'd read a Bible or gone to church, but Mama Jean said that when the time was right, God would always help those who needed to hear His voice. He'd bring back a truth they'd heard or read at one time.

Was God speaking to her? Why would He want to fight for her? She'd abandoned Him long ago. Betrayed Him with her sins. Even Luke couldn't get over her sins. How could a holy God?

Piper used her coffee to force down the mounting lump in her throat. "Now what?"

"Now you get some rest. We're useless when we're exhausted, beat up and fuzzy in the head. We need to focus. Regroup and start fresh. And to be honest, I need a shower."

"You really do," Eric said and sipped his coffee. He clasped Luke's shoulder, and they spoke with only their eyes. Yeah, Eric cared. Just bad with emotions.

Piper related.

"I'll head back to the office and handle reports. The files from Strosbergen's case are still on your desk. Get a few z's and we can start digging again," Eric said.

"What about Sly? Don't we need to see him?" Piper cupped her hands around the hot coffee cup, enjoying the warmth seeping into her skin.

Luke clicked his teeth together. "Yes, but it'll have to wait a few days. If he's the one behind this, he might think we're dead. Let's take advantage and rest up. Plus, I'm going to have a mountain of paperwork."

Piper sighed. "I doubt Harmony's resting. We could ferret out Boone's haunts. He could be holding Harmony there."

"We've already visited several and the location of his last known job. Construction site. No go." Eric plunked his coffee in the trash can by the glassed automatic door. "Even stirred up a few friends he ran with. Say they haven't seen him in a while."

"Fine, I'll sleep, but only for a few hours, and then I'm back at it. With or without you."

Luke pinched the bridge of his nose. "You give me an ulcer when you talk like that."

"Take stock in the Rolaids Company, then. I'm not playing around."

"Thus the ulcer." Luke motioned Piper out the doors.

Four hours. That was all the time she was giving Luke. Because they were running out of it.

Luke turned onto Harmony's street. "You feeling it yet?"

Piper nodded. "Pretty stiff and frazzled."

Luke laced his fingers between hers. "Which is why you need to get some shut-eye."

Piper studied their intertwined fingers. "What is this?" She lifted their hands. "That kiss back there? What—what is going on?"

Luke wished he could be 100 percent sure.

"Did we get caught up in an intense moment? I'm confused." Piper slipped her fingers from his hands. "I don't… We can't… Things won't ever be the same between us, Luke." Her voice caught in her throat.

Luke fought a rush of emotions. No, they couldn't get back to what they'd had before the lies and deceit wedged between them. But that didn't mean he didn't want her as much or more than he had back then. "Just answer me this…" He had to know. He'd been fighting the thoughts for ten years. "Did you do it because on some level you loved him?"

Piper's mouth dropped open. "Of all the reasons why I did what I did, *this* one sticks with you?"

"What else was I supposed to think?" Anger simmered on the tip of his tongue.

Piper shook her head. "I told you I loved you. Obviously, you never believed it." She jumped out of the car, slammed the door and stalked to the front door.

Luke sprang from his seat and limped after her. "Wait. You can't just run away." What other conclusions were there? Piper's actions had spoken volumes.

She hadn't trusted his promise to protect her, to keep her safe if she ran from Chaz. Or she simply hadn't loved him enough to leave.

Piper jerked around, fierceness in her eyes. "Oh no? It's what you told me to do that night. 'Run, Piper. Run and don't look back.' Isn't that what you said? Well, you can't one minute tell me to run and the next tell me not to. I'm so *done* with this day." She jammed the key into the lock.

A frenzy bombarded his body. She was rejecting him. Again. "Talk to me, Piper!"

"You should've talked to me then!"

"I was angry!"

"Well, now *I'm* angry. So go away. Sit in your car and try to protect me, go home or go investigate, but get away from me!" She burst through the door and for the second time slammed it in his face.

Try to protect me. Try. What did she think he'd been doing then? Doing *now*? Not trying. Doing!

Luke glared at the barrier between them.

He could bang on it, beat it down, kick it in, but Piper wouldn't listen to him. Wouldn't give him a chance to explain. Explain what? She'd sent Luke and Kerr on a wild-goose chase so Chaz could once again get away with taking things that didn't belong to him. And a woman had almost died. He stomped to the Durango and slid inside.

Piper's question blared in his mind. *What's going on here?*

Luke punched the steering wheel and peeled out of her driveway.

Nothing. They'd messed things up too badly.

Too much time had lapsed.

Chapter 11

Two days had brought rigidness to Luke's body, and his leg relentlessly burned around his stitches. But not nearly as intense as his chest burned or as rigid as his interactions with Piper had been. Leaving her alone with a killer on the loose wasn't going to happen. She might not think he could protect her, but she was wrong. He could, and he was going to keep on keeping on whether she liked it or not.

At the moment, it felt like not. At least she wasn't yelling at him to go away. Before she went to bed, Piper had brought him a cup of coffee while he watched her house from the road. Staying the night inside wasn't appropriate, and the nearness was insufferable at times.

Speaking of… Piper moseyed out the front door, slim jeans fitting just right, a billowy shirt with long, flappy sleeves. She wore anything well. Luke clambered out of the car. "Evening."

Piper heaved a sigh. "I'm calling a truce. I can't handle this arctic wave between us. I think we should let the past stay where it belongs."

Luke licked his bottom lip. "But it's not where it belongs, Piper. It's right in front of us, hanging in the here and now. We should deal with it."

Piper's shirt fluttered on the night breeze, her loose hair following suit. She rubbed her forearms. "I'm not ready to deal with it. I want to stop these monsters and go back to my life in Jackson."

The words caved into his chest like a wrecking ball. She was saying *he* needed to stay in the past. Massaging his brow, he exhaled. "Fine. Truce."

Piper's shoulders relaxed, and for the first time in two days she smiled. Half a smile, but it was better than nothing.

"I'm leaving in about ten minutes. A friend is going to—"

"Babysit me?"

Luke choked back a smart remark. "I got some information from the undercover DEA agent at Riff's—"

"Holt McKnight?"

Luke pinched his lips. Why did that man's name rolling off Piper's tongue send a green streak through him? "I see you remember him."

"What's that mean?"

"Nothin'."

Piper snorted. "Fine. Information?"

"I'm heading to West Memphis. Southland Park."

"The dog races?" Piper scrunched her nose. "We can find Boone at the tracks?"

"McKnight says Boone has a bookie there. Which

reminds me—I need to call Eric to meet me." He pulled out his phone.

"Us. Meet us."

"No. Not us. This is police business, Piper."

"Fine, but if I just happen to feel like watching greyhounds grace the tracks, don't be surprised to see me."

Luke should have taken stock in Rolaids. Better to have eyes on her than let her go rogue. "Fine." He scrolled to Eric's name. "And wipe the smug smile off your face. You didn't win. I'm going with the lesser of two evils." Besides, she was ridiculously cute with it plastered across her face.

Eric answered. "I'll take a double pepperoni and a two liter of Coke. The real thing. No diet."

Luke grinned. "How about dog racing instead?"

"Ah. Information. So what does my egomaniac friend have to say about Boone?"

"You are talking about McKnight, right?" Eric knew Holt from the Academy days.

"Yes. You're just a maniac. Is our little ninja playing nice today?"

"I'm with her now."

"So she is. Or...do you need me to call an ambulance for you?" He chuckled. "Okay, dog races. Southland Park? Why?"

"Boone's a gambling man. We could find him, or maybe Smoky the bookie has some info."

"I'm sorry—did you just say 'Smoky the bookie'? What are we? In a Marlon Brando film?"

Luke grunted. "He even wears a fedora and has a gold tooth."

"Count me in. I love dogs and fedoras."

"Meet you there in forty-five minutes."

* * *

Luke threw the Durango in Park and texted Eric. Piper waited impatiently. Every second that leaked by was a second longer Harmony was gone and Piper was a sitting duck.

"He's already inside. Keep your eyes open for Boone, too. Just in case." Luke grabbed his phone and scrolled through the camera roll. "This is Willis Fitzgerald, aka Smoky."

Piper studied the face. Smooth skin, bushy eyebrows. Beady eyes and a big gold tooth. "Okay, got it."

"Let's do this, then."

They exited the Durango and made their way inside. Gambling machines dinged as patrons dropped quarters hoping for a line of cherries. Coins clinked into metal slots, and laughter hung in the air almost as thick as the cigarette smoke.

Eric waved and lightly punched Piper's arm. "How you feeling?"

"Sore." Inside out.

"Should we sweep the gambling hall or go to Winner's Edge?" Eric asked.

"The kind of gambling he does probably wouldn't go on in that room. Race just started. Let's search the Main Mezzanine first." Luke stalked past the poker and blackjack tables, straight through the slot-machine area lining the wall and to the section with theater-style and free table seating. Piper and Eric trailed along.

The smell of greyhound and dwindling paychecks hung in the air. Luke stood over the brass railing scanning the small wooden tables with red tops and private televisions keeping up with the race. The wall of windows opened to greyhounds sprinting around an oval track.

Eric strolled through the tables.

"Where's he going? Dinner?"

Luke grinned. "He's taking the south end. Lot of tables to cover."

"Should I go that way?" She pointed to the far end. They could cut Smoky off, make sure he didn't slip from their grasp.

"Are you a police officer? Screaming 'Freeze! Police!' doesn't make you official."

She sighed. "It slowed him down, didn't it?"

Luke grunted and kept his focus on the faces. Piper spotted a black leather fedora. Short, portly man. "I see him."

He better have some answers.

They weaved in and out through the clusters of gamblers. "Stay with me."

Piper and Luke neared Smoky. He raised his head, held Luke's eye contact, then glanced behind him. Farther in the distance, Eric was coming his way.

"He's gonna pull a greyhound," Piper whispered.

"Yep," Luke muttered.

Smoky and the big dude with him lit out of the corner and rushed through the tables, knocking over a trash can and zipping from the Main Mezzanine. Piper hurdled the can and made like a cheetah.

Luke growled something between his teeth, but Piper didn't have time to listen.

He edged up beside her. "I've got this, Piper!"

"Yeah, I see that." She blew past him and made a sharp right.

Smoky had lost the fedora but kept running. He jerked right, the other guy left, and blasted through the doors into the casino. Piper stayed on Smoky's tail, bobbing between casino-goers, Luke right behind her.

"Yell it or I will, Luke!" This guy wasn't going to get away.

Luke hollered, "Freeze! Police!"

Smoky darted around one cocktail waitress and smashed into another; a round tray of drinks clattered to the floor before she did.

They were going to lose him unless she cut the jerk off. Piper zipped left.

"I said stop!" Luke growled. A collision overpowered the dinging of slot machines. Piper glanced back. The big guy had come out of nowhere and belted Luke in the chin. Luke returned the punch and tackled him.

Should she help him? Smoky would get away. Luke was a big boy. She had to take down Smoky. An elderly man shuffled across the floor with a pile of chips, and Piper nearly careened into him.

Smoky appeared at the end of a nickel-slot-machine row, a grin on his face as he looked back at Luke cuffing the big guy. *You just wish you were home free, Willis Fitzgerald.*

Piper erupted from the side and tackled Smoky to the floor, his head nailing the carpet with a thud. She pressed his cheek into the floor. He deserved the carpet burn.

An older woman squealed and onlookers surrounded her like a SWAT team.

Luke split the crowd and stared down at her, the big guy in front of him with a scowl on his face.

Piper wasn't sure if Luke was appalled or amazed. Either way, this punk was hers. She craned her neck at Luke. "Don't worry. I didn't put him under arrest for ya."

"Well, it's the little things that bring me pleasure."

"Get off me!" Smoky's foul words bounced off Piper as if she wore an invisible shield.

"Shut up!" she countered.

"This is po-lice brutality."

Eric jogged up, took in the sight on the floor and cocked his head, a mischievous grin quirking. "I don't even know why we come to work." He removed his cuffs from his belt and held up his shield.

Most of the crowd scattered. Folks in this place didn't want to get too nosy about police business.

Eric held out the cuffs to Piper. "You wanna do the honors?"

Luke dropped his jaw. "Are you serious?"

"Nah." Eric chuckled. "Smoky, you have the right to run from a girl. You have the right to be pummeled by a girl." He hauled him up and leaned toward Piper and whispered, "No offense on the whole girl thing."

"None taken." She frowned. She'd yet to figure out Eric Hale.

"Smoky, you even have the right to holler 'police brutality.' Had a police officer shoved you to the ground and smashed your face into the carpet."

Luke shot Piper a glare.

She didn't have the decency to blush for going overboard.

"You also have the right to tell us what you know about Boone Wiley."

Smoky shrugged out of Eric's grasp and brushed his hands on his jeans. "I don't know no Boone Wiley."

Luke shot forward, venom in his eyes. "You do, and if you don't tell us what we want—"

"We'll sic *her* on you again," Eric interjected and pointed at Piper.

Luke rolled his eyes. "I'll haul your boy here in and take a closer look at your activity today. How would you like that?"

Smoky shifted his sight to Piper. *Yeah, I dare you to even try it.*

"You'll let him go?"

Luke worked his jaw. Under normal circumstances, she guessed he wouldn't.

"Against my better judgment."

Smoky nodded at his giant friend. "Whatcha wanna know?"

Wise decision.

Luke uncuffed the guy. He rubbed his wrists, mumbled a few choice words and disappeared. "When was the last time you saw Boone?"

Smoky squared his shoulders. Probably trying to get back the dignity Piper had yanked from him. "He was here two weeks ago. Owes me six large, so when you find him tell him he better pay up."

Strong motive to hunt down something valuable. Maybe Sly told him about something he thought Piper or Harmony had taken in the past. She looked at Luke. His eyes said he was thinking the same thing.

"How often does he come to the track?" Luke cracked his middle knuckle and studied Smoky's face as he answered.

"Depends on how much he owes. Right now he better not show until he has my money. You feel me?"

"I'd rather not." Luke sniffed. "He come in here alone or with friends? A girl?"

Smoky jutted his lips forward. "Mostly alone. But I seen him stroll in a time or two with a big dude. Drove a pimped-out Cadillac."

"Derone Johnson," Piper said.

Luke nodded. "You know where he lives?"

"I ain't his mama."

Luke raised his eyebrows at Eric. Eric handed Smoky his card. "You see or hear anything else, call us. We'll make sure he knows you want your money."

Smoky glared at Piper. "You really not the po-po?"

"No."

He rubbed his back and grumbled, "A'ight, man. We done here?"

"For now."

Smoky was a dead end, but they had a few more trails to sniff down.

Piper kneaded the back of her neck as Luke and Eric chatted over dinner. The sun had already dipped below the horizon, leaving the night windy and starless.

After the chase at Southland Park, Luke had dropped her at the rehab center to visit with Mama Jean while he and Eric tracked a few leads on Derone.

Piper's stomach had growled like an angry bear, but as Luke and Eric brought up Ellen Strosbergen, her appetite had gone to pot.

A server brought another round of sweet tea and made googly eyes at Luke. Another emotion rumbled in her stomach. Luke wasn't hers. No right for jealousy over an overflirtatious server.

"We could at least try to talk to Strosbergen," Eric

said. "Maybe something went missing that wasn't reported."

Piper's face heated. Luke's eyes were on her. She pushed a baby tomato around her giant sirloin strip salad.

"You weren't there, Eric. When Kerr and I interviewed her, she'd already forgotten about the attack. Couldn't even figure out why she was in the hospital. But hey, she did remember her great-aunt Lily was a lovely quilter." Luke paused as if Piper had something to offer.

She didn't. "When I said I didn't know anything about what happened in that house that night, I meant it. I'd tell you if I knew."

Luke shoved his plate away, ignored her and looked at Eric. "Even if she could remember, her mind's fragile. And nothing she said would hold up in court."

"Then let's talk to the great-grandson. His report was given."

"He lived with Strosbergen. Came up clean as a whistle, and his alibi checked out. And the great-granddaughter was out of the country at the time. She was just as clean."

"Okay," Eric said and wiped his mouth, "they didn't steal anything and can't be connected to anyone who did. That doesn't mean that something wasn't taken they didn't report. People hide things all the time. What if the old lady had valuables they didn't even know about? Maybe over the years, she mentioned it to them, and they thought she was talking out of her head."

Piper cleared her throat. "Anything is worth a shot. Ask them."

"That's that, then." Luke paid the check, and they slid from their booth.

Eric left a generous tip. "I'm going home to get some sleep. Start fresh tomorrow."

"See you then." Luke stood on the curb as Eric headed for his car. "Piper, I need to run home, change and grab a few things before tonight. You mind coming by the house?"

"You mean before you sleep in your car all night? How can you start fresh when you have a crick in your neck? I'll be fine." She kept saying that. He kept ignoring her, because it wasn't true. But she'd fake it until it was.

"I'll feel better. So running by my house? That okay?"

No. She didn't want to see where he lived. Didn't want the memory of it—of wondering if they could have made a home together. "Yeah, sure."

Luke opened the car door for her, then rounded the Durango and eased into the driver's side. "Running like that earlier tortured my leg."

"I resemble that remark. Only my side and neck." She yawned and closed her eyes. When she opened them again, they were turning into a fairly new subdivision.

A park with a yellow slide came into view near a wooded area. A place children could play while moms and dads chatted. Piper should have said no.

Luke stayed as silent as the neighborhood.

"How long have you lived here?"

"About five years." He pulled into the drive and rested his finger on the garage-door-opener button. "You…you want to come in?"

Did she? Yeah. But she wasn't going to. While everything about her neighborhood was old, this home and community was all new. As if he didn't want to be reminded of anything old—in the past. Of her.

"I'll wait. I'm tired."

Luke touched Piper's hand, then drew away. "Okay. But I'd feel better if you were inside, where it's safe."

"Your garage isn't safe?"

"Guess I just want you close."

Why couldn't he have said that years ago? Luke shut the door, and Piper closed her eyes, then opened them when the hairs on her neck sprang up. A chill ran down her arms.

Something didn't feel right.

Chapter 12

Entering the mudroom, Luke removed his holster and laid it on a table with his badge. He stepped into the kitchen.

What in the world?

It was torn apart. He turned to go for his gun when a hulking man in a ski mask and black hoodie came from nowhere, shoving him into the fridge.

Luke lost his balance but regained it quickly, wounds throbbing. He collared the attacker by the shoulders, putting distance between him and Luke's gun, calling like a beacon from the mudroom table.

The man elbowed Luke's nose. Warm blood dripped into his mouth. The taste of iron coated his tongue. Luke yanked his hoodie and caused the intruder to stumble backward. He turned and swung at Luke.

Luke ducked and rammed his shoulder into the assailant's gut, sending him into the breakfast area and over a kitchen chair. The man grunted and jumped up, darting through the living room.

Luke hurled himself on top of him and wrestled with the ski mask. The man punched him in the wounded leg. A blinding pain ran up his side into his skull.

The creep lunged forward, but Luke remembered the trick Piper had taught him. He thrust the side of his hand toward the man's carotid artery, making impact. He shook his head and Luke jumped on top of him, grunting and panting. "You are under—"

Something sharp sliced the top of his arm. He drew back. A serrated knife glinted.

Luke held his hands out, bracing himself for another attack. He watched the man's eyes but kept the blade in his sight. The intruder swung the blade like a grizzly bear slicing at prey. Luke bounced back.

A brass bookend sat on the table next to him. He grabbed it, and as the attacker lunged again, he railed his arm with it, sending the knife skittering across the hardwood floor.

"Luke. I changed my mind. Maybe we do need to…" Piper's voice trailed off.

"Get out, Piper!"

The attacker made like a linebacker and smashed into Luke, knocking him onto the love seat. Piper came at the attacker full force, nailing him in the gut.

Luke dived, knocking him to the floor, but he caught Luke on his already-sore jaw. Luke connected a jab to the ribs. Hoped he cracked a few.

Piper moved in, but the intruder must have caught her coming. He pivoted and rocketed into her with his full weight, sending her sprawling over the coffee table.

Her feet flipped over her head, and she fell into Luke's bookcase, several novels toppling onto her.

No!

The attacker reared back to pound her face.

Luke ignored the exhaustion and pain, channeling the fury at seeing Piper lying deathly still in a heap of books. He rushed him from the side, grabbing his fist.

Throw the cop out the door; this was personal. This was Piper. A guttural cry rose from his throat, and he threw the scum across the room into the wooden stair railing.

Grabbing on to the banister, the man stood and drew back, but Luke landed a left hook and a solid right uppercut. He toppled over at the edge of the stairs. "You think hurting women makes you a man." Luke stalked toward him, ready to yank off the mask and pulverize some flesh.

He brought his fist down, but Boone, Chaz, whoever, rolled to the side and scrambled to his feet, fleeing for the back door. Luke ripped through the living room but froze when Piper moaned again. She might need an ambulance. He growled and balled a fist. Next time. He so hoped for a next time. This wasn't finished.

Luke hurried to Piper, dropped to his knees and cradled her head in his lap. "Piper, talk to me. Anything broken?" He brushed her cheek with his fingers. He could have lost her.

"He's getting away," she groaned.

"You're more important. You need a doctor?"

"Why not? Pretty sure I've met my deductible in the last week." She rubbed the back of her head. "I'm kidding. About going, not about my deductible. Help me sit up." Her face scrunched in pain as Luke lifted her up and against the couch for support. "I'm sorry. I thought I had him."

"Don't be sorry." He embraced her with his good arm and laid his head on top of hers. "That scared me half to death." His heart raced.

Luke held his wounded arm close to his chest, sweat and blood trickling down his neck. Piper scooted away and clasped his arm. "Let me see." She gently rolled the cuff up and slurped air through her teeth. "I'm so *sick* of bleeding."

Luke breathed a laugh, wiped the corner of her mouth where a dot of blood had pooled and held his finger up. "Me, too."

"You need stitches?"

"No. I need to call Eric. Do a check and see what that animal stole, if anything."

"Why would anyone believe you had anything?"

He didn't, but he'd been involved with Piper. That was enough. "I don't know."

After he called Eric, Piper bandaged his arm, and then he did a quick sweep. The kitchen cabinets had been opened and a few dishes shattered. His drawers in the bedroom were pilfered through as well as the cabinets in all three of his bathrooms. The two guest rooms and the entertainment center had been nosed around in.

Compared to Mama Jean's place and Piper's, this was nothing thirty minutes wouldn't fix. Why not be as thorough? Probably because Luke interrupted him. But something churned in his gut. He was missing something. Question was: What?

Piper's head pounded even after the ibuprofen Luke gave her should have kicked in. She'd checked her face in the mirror. A split lip and a bump on the back of her head and probably a few bruises on her lower back, but other than that she was sunny-side up.

Luke leaned against the granite counter, an ice pack on his jaw. Piper studied his house. Nice. Family-sized. Another ache formed. She glanced over at him. He grinned and licked the corner of his lip.

"This wasn't exactly how I wanted to have you over."

Piper sipped on a bottle of water. "Not the way I wanted to come."

"It doesn't have the charm of your mature neighborhood and homey place, but I think it could be...homey. With the right touch."

Piper swallowed. Was he implying something? Did he mean her touch? Impossible. "Do I get a ten-cent tour?"

"You mean two-cent? Isn't that what you said about your house?" Amusement flickered in his eyes.

"My house is a two-cent. This is definitely ten." Not large like Harmony's home, but an easy 2,000 square feet, and she'd know thanks to her former life. Another lump swelled in her throat.

"Come on, then."

After touring the living area and a peek into the master bedroom and bath, they went upstairs and he showed her the two bedrooms—one he used as an office—the bathroom and game room. "I have some unfinished attic space. Maybe one day I'll finish it." His gaze held hers, and his voice softened. "Maybe put in an exercise room of some sort."

Was that another implication?

Piper's mouth turned to dried wood, and she slipped by him. "Let's go back downstairs and talk."

"Thought you were all talked out."

"I changed my mind. I kinda wish I hadn't."

He chuckled. "Coffee?"

"Coffee's good." Piper sat on the sofa in the hearth room, staring at the bricked fireplace. A wall of windows opened into a decent-sized backyard. "So you used the knife-hand strike. Technically, I saved your bacon again."

Luke tossed her a pointed look. "I shouldn't have told you that. Don't go getting all cocky." He closed the distance between them and handed her a cup.

She sipped it. Perfect. Cream and a pinch of sugar. Of course he'd remember. "I want you to know why I lost my cool the other day."

"Okay." He set his mug on the table next to the overstuffed chair and leaned forward with his elbows on his knees, giving her his undivided attention. Blue-green eyes melted her.

"You told me that first day in the hospital with Mama Jean that you didn't know what to call what I did to you back then. I'll tell you what to call it."

Luke's nostrils flared. Was he holding back emotion or was he angry? Still peering into her eyes. Still relaxed with his elbows on his knees. Emotion. This was going to be rough. Because once she shared the truth, that was it. Closure to their past.

Too much between the lines to make a go of it again.

"What would you call it?" he whispered.

"Love." Her eyes pooled with moisture. "I wanted out. So bad. I hated lying to you. I was afraid you'd leave me if you knew I was involved."

"But I didn't." He took her hand and kissed it, making things more difficult. "When you finally came clean and told me you knew they were running burglaries, I didn't leave you."

"In the end, you did. You saw me, called me a liar and then you told me to leave…to run."

He opened his mouth to speak, but she held her hand up. She had to get this out while she felt brave. "When you told me you were an undercover cop and that you loved me, after I told you the truth about my involvement… I tried. For a minute, I thought everything you said could be true. But I was wrong. And so were you."

Luke furrowed his brow and shook his head.

"I told Chaz I wanted out. That I was done." She closed her eyes, feeling Chaz's meaty paws grip her neck, squeezing until it burned.

You don't get to make that decision. If you leave, I'll kill you. Right after I slit your grandma's throat and put a bullet through what's-his-face's head. You leave when I tell you that you can. I let you have him as a play toy to occupy your time. But when I say it's over, it's over."

Sly had come in on that scene, and the tip of his blade pierced her skin. He'd accused Luke of being a cop. Piper had lied, kept Luke's cover. If they'd found out, Luke would have been dead for sure, right along with Piper and Mama Jean. There was no way out.

"He threatened you."

She nodded.

"You could have come to me. I'd have protected you." Luke gripped her hands. "You just had to believe."

"I was nineteen. All I'd known for five years was Chaz Michaels and Sly Watson and their world. I knew what they were capable of."

"Why the bogus address, Piper? I could have busted them. You could have testified at any time."

"Oh, yeah. And seal my death sentence? Go into witness protection if it came to that…without you." She bit the inside of her lip. "They suspected you. Thought I was your informant." Which was true, in a sense. "Told me you were using me, but I held fast, Luke. I didn't snitch. And not because of what he did."

Luke's eyes flashed hot. "What did he do to you?"

Piper shook her head. Didn't matter now. "It's over. But I knew if you showed up at that house, he'd kill us. Wouldn't matter that you were a cop. And I couldn't be the reason you lost your life. All I did was make trouble for you. Even now…"

Luke knelt before her, framed her face with his hands. "I wish you would have told me all of this that night."

Piper rested her hands over his. "Why should I have had to? Why didn't you know in your heart that I'd done it for a good reason? To protect you for once. Why did you say *run* when all I wanted to hear was *stay, I love you* and *I forgive you*?"

Luke's shoulders sagged and devastation flooded his eyes. "Pip—"

Piper's phone rang. Rehab center. This late? "I have to take this. It's Mama Jean's rehab center." She answered.

"Miss Kennedy, this is Angela at Baptist Rehab Center. Your grandmother spiked a high fever. The doctor's been in."

Luke's phone rang and he answered while Piper continued listening to the nurse.

"She has a urinary tract infection, but with the elderly comes additional side effects. She's having some confusion, which is normal, but I thought you'd want to know. We gave her a sedative and an antibiotic. To-morrow, she ought to be feeling better."

"I'm on my way."

"Oh, you don't have to do that, hon. I just wanted you to know."

"What time? Did he say?" Luke asked. A grim line slid across his forehead. Whom was he talking to?

"I'll be there in twenty minutes." Piper hung up and waited for Luke to end his call. She explained Mama Jean's situation.

"Okay. I'll take you over there."

"Who was that on the phone?" Piper said as they climbed inside the Durango and backed out of the garage.

"Turns out Holt McKnight talked with a guy over darts at Riff's, and Boone's name came up in a con-versation about Derone. They both stay in apartments close to the Mississippi line. Off Highway 51 and Ches-ter Drive."

"He could have Harmony there. We have to go now." But Mama Jean needed her, too. "Or you need to go now."

Luke rested his hand on her knee. "Holt's guys are doing a drug bust tonight. Finally taking down Derone. If Eric and I go snooping, we could scare them off. Ruin everything he's worked for."

Piper frowned. "But what if Harmony's there? What if she's hurt? Another day is too long."

"We need a game plan—"

"Easy. We go in there, your guns blazing and my feet ready to wipe the floor with that piece of work."

"I was thinking more along the lines of something with a level head. If Boone is in there, and we go all guns blazing and feet stomping, he might kill Harmony if..."

Piper rubbed her temple. "If she's not dead already. Okay. It's like no end is in sight."

"Everything has an ending."

Unfortunately. Not all of them happy. "Luke, Harmony is my best friend. How long are you going to have to wait?"

"Maybe first thing in the morning. I don't know. Mc-Knight's gotta have all the key players in place. I'll call you as soon as it's done." He pulled under the lit awning at the rehab center. "Piper." He hooked her chin, forcing her to make eye contact. "We're not done talking, okay?" He caressed her cheek, smiled until she hurt inside.

She nodded.

"I'll make sure you get home in the morning. Bring you breakfast." This seemed like more than doing his duty to protect and serve.

She slipped from the Durango, turned when she made it inside and waved, knowing he'd be watching until she was safe.

He waved and zoomed away. To form a game plan with Eric. Guns blazing might get Harmony killed. But waiting until daylight might, too.

Mama Jean had been sleeping soundly for the past hour. The nurse said she'd be out all night and Piper could go home and not to worry.

Piper held Mama Jean's hand, kissed it. Somewhere out there Luke was forming a game plan, and Harmony was slipping away.

Harmony had been her only friend. After Piper left Memphis, she'd lost all contact with her. With everyone, including Mama Jean for a short time. But when Piper turned twenty-one, Harmony had called on her birthday. They'd both left their sordid teenage years behind for better things. But Harmony had made a connection. Not even Luke had.

Losing Harmony would be like losing a sister—if Piper hadn't already lost her. No. She couldn't think like that. Piper could only hope that Harmony was doing whatever it took to survive. They were, after all, survivors.

The gnawing and anxiety climbed her like a cat running up a tree. She bobbed her knee, tapped her foot, chewed her nail.

One peek. The cops might ruin a drug bust, but a nobody like Piper could easily get in and out of an apartment complex, and she had the skills to slink around in the dark, to find Boone's apartment. Wasn't proud of the skills. No choice. Harmony had no other family.

She called a cab and stood outside until it arrived. Once it dropped her off at Harmony's, she changed into dark clothes and whipped out of the driveway at light speed.

Hitting the interstate, she kept to the speed limit until she exited at State Line Road. Chester Apartments were the only ones in the area. Now to find Boone's. She couldn't call the apartment manager and ask. He or she might tip off Boone.

God, please forgive me. This time it's for a good cause. And keep me safe if You don't mind... I'm scared, but I can't do nothing.

Piper drove through the complex. Single-floor apartments lined two sides of a street that opened into an elderly, run-down neighborhood. She parked near one of the houses.

The half-moon was enough light to see, but easy to blend in with the shadows. Piper glanced up. Yep. A pair of shoes hung from the telephone wires. Sign that within the vicinity was an easy score for drugs.

I'm coming, Harmony. Just hang on.

Trees over the apartment rustled. Cars from Highway 51 whooshed. Cackling came from three apartments. She just needed to find Boone's apartment, to look. Wasn't as if she was going inside. Not unless Harmony was in danger. Luke would kill her. And she was working to build trust between them. Not sure why when she was going back to Jackson and he was staying here.

Reaching the first four doors of the first unit, she ducked behind a bush and cocked an ear. A kid cried. A TV blared. A woman's voice chattered as if on the phone.

She crept around to the other side and strained to hear. Silence. She edged up under a window, swept the area, then inched up, trying to see in between raggedy plastic miniblinds. Too dark, but a light from the hall was on. She noted the number on the door.

Slipping from apartment to apartment, she'd noted six possibilities. One with a dog barking inside.

"Hey, bro, where you been?" A big guy with cliff-sized shoulders stood about two apartments down. Another wiry guy sat on the stoop, smoke billowing in the air. Maybe cigarettes, maybe not. But the wind would blow the aroma, and she'd know in a minute.

"Kendra's." He laughed.

Wiry guy laughed with him. "You want somes of this?"

The shoulders. So wide. "No, man, I'm straight." He held up a paper sack. Probably a nice big bottle of Colt 45 inside. "Hey, check it." He got inside the car and neon lights spun around the wheels.

Tricked-out Caddy. Wheels. Derone! She so owed him a punch in the face.

No sign of Boone.

How much time until the drug bust? She had to move quickly. Piper slipped around the building to make her way down the opposite side. About the fourth complex someone stepped out of the shadows, and she backed into the brick.

"Hey," wiry guy hollered.

Busted. Piper stepped out, hands up. He might have a gun on him. "Hey, no harm. Just looking for Boone." She dropped one hand and rubbed her nose back and forth, sniffing. "I… I'm needing him real bad."

Wiry guy hooted. "I'm sure you do."

She sniffed again and twitched. If he thought she was a tweaker, he could be useful. Most pushers like Derone and this guy didn't sell meth. Pot. Cocaine. Ecstasy. Boone? Yeah, he'd sell meth. Just as long as Derone didn't wander over. He might recognize her.

"Whatchoo into, girl?"

She twitched and clawed at her arms and face. "I need… I just need Boone."

Wiry guy took a drag of his smoke and laughed at her again. "I know whatchoo after. Boone ain't been around a few days. But he stay over there sometime." He pointed to the apartment with the dog. "If he ain't around, you come back over here and I can hook you up."

"Yeah. Yeah. I'll do that." She scratched relentlessly and kept her face hidden. He'd know she was lying if he saw smooth flesh not destroyed by the effects of methamphetamine.

Apartment with the dog.

Fantastic.

Time to get clever. Piper stumbled across the street to Boone's apartment complex. She turned back. Wiry guy was gone.

She listened at the door. Nothing. Not even a bark. Maybe Harmony wasn't here. Piper slipped around back and crouched under the open window, all ears. Quiet. The wind picked up, blowing bent metal miniblinds. From a dim light in the hall, Piper had the chance to look inside the bedroom.

A pop sounded and she jumped and turned. Someone's car must have backfired. The street was silent.

But she couldn't shake the feeling that eyes were on her. Watching. Waiting. As if knowing her next move before she did. Adrenaline raced, but she kept her breathing deep, even but inaudible.

No sign of Harmony. Or Boone.

One more peek then she'd get out of here.

A gust of wind gave her the chance to steal another glimpse.

Piper's heart vaulted into her throat.

A hand lay in a pool of something dark.

Blood.

What choice did she have? Harmony might be dead. Or she might barely be hanging on. What if she needed CPR?

God, please forgive me!

With a forceful shove, the screen gave way, but she caught it before it clattered to the ground, bringing in the dog. Wouldn't it be nice if it was a Yorkie-poo like Ms. Wells's dog, Tootsie? Piper laid the window screen by the bushes and hoisted herself up and into the window.

Lifeless eyes gaped back at Piper.

Chapter 13

Boone.

Who would have killed him? Piper slid in the pool of blood and caught herself, then surveyed the sparse room. For a thief, Boone hadn't been living high on the hog. The smell of death nearly wiped Piper off her feet. She covered her nose with her hoodie sleeve.

Where was the dog?

A low growl answered her question. Outside the door. She could open and chance it, or she could stay inside with Boone Wiley's dead body. Harmony might be wounded in another room. No time.

She had to call Luke. Once she did a quick sweep, she would. Every second counted. What if Harmony was lying on the floor bleeding out? Panic trilled from her stomach to her head, whooshing blood into her temples.

Something glinted under the moonlight. Was that…?

Blood leached across the floor, spattering the windows.

She squatted and covered her mouth with her hand to keep from screaming.

No.

Piper didn't need to pick up the Japanese sword to know it was hers. She had two of them hanging over the counter at her dojo. Her burned-down dojo. The killer must have lifted it before he lit them up. But why if he was going to kill her? Why would he need it? Why kill Boone with it? Plan B for the killer? That made no sense, and Piper didn't have time to whirl it around in her head. She had a dog to deal with.

Jitters rose in her throat.

The growling continued.

Luke was going to have a serious coronary. Piper reached for her phone.

Every second counted.

A fresh wave of panic hit her. What if he didn't believe in her innocence?

She tucked it back into her hoodie pocket.

Using her sleeve as a glove, she opened the closet. She didn't need added prints on the stack of evidence against her.

Growls turned to menacing barks.

Inside the closet, she snatched a blanket lying on the top shelf.

Standing next to the door, she counted to ten. Grabbed the doorknob with her hoodie and swung it open.

When the giant Doberman bounded inside, she hurled the blanket over its head, sprinted out the bedroom door and slammed it.

With a spiked pulse and blood beating in her ears, she headed down the frayed carpeted hallway. "Harmony?"

No answer.

She toed open the second bedroom. Nothing but a faux wood computer desk and an old desktop computer. Next came the half bath and then she checked the cramped kitchen and living room. Harmony was nowhere to be seen. Piper pulled her phone and with shaking hands scrolled for Luke's name. He might not believe her. He might be livid. But he needed to know. Now.

A commotion sounded outside the apartment. Blue lights flashed.

Guns fired.

Yelling.

Holt's drug bust.

Boone's front door splintered from the wall with a crashing thud and Piper shrieked.

"Hands up where I can see them! Now!"

Piper raised her hands, phone in one. A light blinded her eyes.

"Piper?"

"Luke, I can explain."

Eric followed him inside, lowering his gun. Luke continued to train his on Piper's torso.

"Luke, I was about to call you. I found Boone. He's in the bedroom. Dead."

"I'll check it out," Eric said.

"I wouldn't. I shut a Doberman in there."

"Big black scary one?" Eric asked.

Luke continued to flash the light in her face. "I can't see!" she screamed.

"'Cause that dog just tore into an officer's leg out there." Eric stalked down the hall. Must have jumped out the window.

Luke holstered his gun and shook his head. Same stunned look on his face. Just like ten years ago.

"I was scared, Luke. I wasn't going to break in. But I saw a hand."

"Don't talk to me." He started down the hall then twisted around. "Don't you dare leave this apartment, either."

Piper followed him into Boone's bedroom. "Luke, please."

"Be quiet!" he hollered, turning his back on her. Again.

Eric switched on the lamp. "Unless Boone was in cahoots with a ninja, or was a ninja, or really gets into Halloween, this doesn't look good for you, Kung Fu Piper."

Luke scanned the sword, the open window then the blood on the floor, tracking it to her feet. "Now is not the time to break out the funny, Hale." The muscles in his cheeks jerked and he eyed Piper, disbelief distorting his features. "I can't... I don't..." He pawed his face and pursed his lips.

"I was going out of my mind! You wanted to wait until morning."

"Yet I'm here right now. Do you have any idea what you've done? How did you even find this place?" Every word flung from his mouth with vehemence.

"You take down another one of Derone's guys?" Eric asked.

"I pretended to be a tweaker."

"You're great at pretending, aren't you?" Luke snapped.

Piper flinched, but she had that coming.

"Luke, get some air. I'll take it from here." Eric pointed at the door.

Luke stood firm.

Piper stepped toward Luke. She had to make him understand. "I didn't kill him. I never even meant to come inside. You have to believe me. I—"

"I don't have to believe a word you say. What am I supposed to do with this, Piper? I am up for a *promotion*!" He stormed past her, his shoulder knocking her off balance.

Eric puffed his cheeks and blew out a sigh. "I can think of easier methods to kill someone than ram a sword through his gut."

"I didn't kill him."

"I wouldn't think you'd be dumb enough to use your own sword to murder Boone—at least two days ago, if my hunch is right—then come back on a night you know cops are going to be swarming, only to break and enter, then track blood all through the house, leaving your footprints and blood on the soles of your Chucks. Which, by the way, are pretty cool."

Piper relaxed.

"Unless you're clever enough to know we'd never believe something so ludicrous, and therefore, that's exactly what you did."

She stiffened. "I did no such thing."

Eric stared her down, then waved his hand. "Nah, I didn't think so. Not that I don't think you're clever. No offense to your brainpower."

"Luke thinks I did this." He'd always come to the worst conclusions regarding her. Didn't forgive her then. No way he'd forgive her now.

God, I'm so sorry. I've made things worse than ever. I just wanted to help. And I'm willing to accept the consequences of my actions. Please don't be mad at me anymore.

Eric squatted by the body, yanked latex gloves from his pocket and snapped them on. "No, he doesn't." He reached into his pocket again and slipped paper boo-tees over his shoes. Turning the overhead light on, he checked the closet.

"He does, however, think you went behind his back, could have gotten yourself killed, put yourself further into this investigation since you were found with the dead body and the weapon. Which undoubtedly be-longs to you. As well as compromise a crime scene, let a rabid dog out to mangle a MPD officer's leg and maybe commit a felony. But you might be able to get out of that one." He went into the bathroom. "Not to mention you've put him in a precarious situation. He's going to have to make a choice. Let you walk or cuff and arrest you. Ever arrested someone you love, Piper?"

Sounded as if Eric might have. Piper's heart sank to her feet. Her legs felt like anchors holding her to the floor; she could barely pick them up and move forward. She was in a pile of mess. And Luke might be able to help her, but he wouldn't. He'd told her that first thing in Mama Jean's hospital room.

"I'm going to prison. And after everything I've done throughout my life, I deserve it."

Eric turned, and something about the way he eyed her sent a ripple of fear inside and yet drew her at the same time. Pity? Respect? Confused, she broke eye contact.

"You do deserve it, Piper. I know you did it to save a friend. But when you break the law, punishment is prison. But I'll tell you what I'll do. I'll give you some-thing you don't deserve. Freedom."

Freedom? "Why…? But what about…?"

"It's called mercy. We'll question you at the station, but I don't have to bring you in bound. You can come willing to cooperate with the promise from here on out, you won't break the law again. Can you promise me?"

Piper's throat constricted. "Why would you do that?"

"You figure it out. Go home, Piper. We'll be by in the morning."

"I don't know what to say." No one had ever done that… Luke. Luke had let her go free. But it hadn't felt like mercy. More like banishment. Was God showing her mercy? Was that what Eric was trying to tell her?

Yes. He had to be.

"Say 'thank you.' And go. I'll deal with Papa Bear."

Piper paused for a moment, then left the bedroom and slipped out the front door. Luke was nowhere in sight. She wasn't sure she could fix this, but she wanted to. She raced down the road to her car and jumped inside.

"God, thank You. For this mercy. I'm…grateful."

This was a new experience. While she didn't fully understand it and felt unworthy, she was grateful. So grateful. She started the engine and cried all the way to Harmony's.

"You did what?" Luke threw his hands in the air and paced outside Boone Wiley's apartment while CSU processed the scene and the coroner took the body.

"I didn't cover up what she's done. I just didn't arrest her. Tomorrow morning, first thing, we'll pick her up and bring her in. She's going to fully cooperate." Eric stared him down—the Jedi look.

Luke was beside himself. Couldn't think straight. Couldn't focus on the case at hand. His emotions were tangled. Just the way he'd promised himself they wouldn't be. "I have to recuse myself. I can't do this."

"Yes, you can. I need the best homicide detective at my side with this one, and it's you. That's why you're going to get this promotion."

"I don't know anymore."

"You've done nothing to compromise this case." Eric's immovable glint showed he wasn't going to back down. "I'm being serious right now. She broke the law, but we put her feelings aside and put a civilian on hold for a drug bust, and you and I both know Derone will walk. His gang will take the blame, and they won't be able to pin anything on him. And Harmony is gone. Whoever killed Boone either made off with her, or she was already dead."

Luke should have fought harder, pressed Holt to let him come in and search. Didn't make what Piper did right, but he understood the overwhelming need to save and protect. He felt it every day concerning Piper. But she'd known better. Didn't even consider the danger. She could have died, and Luke wouldn't be able to go on if she had. That ribbed him more than the possibility of losing his promotion.

What if he'd walked in and she'd been next to Boone, dead? His heart wrenched.

God, I love her. I'd give my life for her. I don't know how to make her see that she doesn't have to always be the hero. She has nothing to prove. I don't know how to fix her. Help me fix her.

"I can't interview her."

Eric clasped his shoulder. "I'll get Forbes to do it. He's honest. We'll fill him in. She's being framed. But there's enough circumstantial evidence mounting to build a case against her. Which we don't want to do."

"It has to be Chaz. She betrayed him, too. And he's never gotten over it." If they didn't find him soon, they might be pressed to arrest Piper for the murders. Luke couldn't breathe.

"Well, whoever tried to roast you and Piper like a Polynesian pig lifted the sword. This murder links him with the fire. Not sure about Baxter and Baroni. Deaths are different. Could be Chaz, could be Boone. Could be both. And I'm going to take a stab—no need to pardon the pun, I meant it—and say that whoever stole the sword and set the dojo on fire also tried to run you off the road."

Luke agreed. But why try to frame her if someone was trying to kill her? Were two separate things going on? "Nothing more we can do here."

Tomorrow he'd pull into Harmony's drive and bring the woman he loved—whom he'd always loved—into the interrogation room. He couldn't stop the chain of events about to unfold. He could only hope he'd have time to find the real killer.

As furious as he was, and deeply hurt, Luke couldn't let Piper possibly go down over circumstantial evidence.

After dropping Eric at his car, he rolled down the windows, letting the cold air blow against his face.

Luke replayed the kiss he and Piper had shared in his car. Tried to sort through what he was feeling. Not a single part of him didn't love her. There was nothing he wouldn't do for her, but no matter how hard he tried, he was inadequate.

He drove into his garage and marched into his bedroom, grabbing his Bible. He needed some peace. Needed to search for direction and answers.

With every day that Piper was close to him, he was reminded of how much he'd missed her. Missed her laughter. Her feistiness. Missed trying to mend her broken wings so she'd fly.

She'd come back to Memphis still wounded. How long could she pretend she wasn't? Instead of dealing with problems, she'd ignored them.

He heals the brokenhearted and binds up their wounds.

The scripture from the Psalm breathed into his soul, stinging him before smoothing over into a gentle tide of peace. Luke wasn't God, but he'd been trying to be Piper's Fixer for years. He'd exhausted himself to no avail and been left with nothing to show for his efforts but repeated failure.

Piper needed healing. And when Luke couldn't do it, she'd tried it herself. With karate.

Karate had become her source of strength instead of Luke.

Instead of God.

And it had been reduced to ashes.

Luke held the Bible to his chest. Truth settled over him, instructing him to be obedient, which warred with what he wanted. The temptation to mend her was beyond powerful. The solution overwhelmingly painful. Could he do what needed to be done?

Luke loved her too much to let her stay broken. But did he love her enough to do what God required of him?

God asked Abraham to lay Isaac on the altar and sacrifice him. Abraham had the knife raised when God intervened.

Luke hadn't been able to lay Piper down even though miles had separated them.

A thousand shards of glassy pain stabbed all through his rib cage, slicing into his gut and rushing to his brain. He forced down the singeing Mount Everest building in his throat, squeezed back the stinging in his eyes.

This was the right thing.

And God would mend him.

Over time. If he could do this. If he could give Piper up to God. Could he do this?

Luke's night had been full of tossing, turning and praying for the strength to let Piper go. He'd never give up hope that she'd find her wings and fly, and he'd always protect her. Fight for her. But he couldn't be her sole protector—the only shoulder she leaned on for support and strength.

He rang her doorbell and jammed a hand in his pocket to keep it from trembling. Piper opened the door, eyes bleary and red-rimmed. Compassion overrode his resolve, but he held his hand back from touching her.

"Figured you'd send Detective Hale," she said and motioned for him to come in. He stayed cemented to the stoop.

She inhaled sharply. "I'm so sorry. I never meant to hurt you. To put myself in a sticky situation. You have to believe that, Luke."

He tightened his jaw, holding back the emotion. He needed to do it. To cut the ties. But her fragile appearance and the panicked expression in her eyes had him backing down. He'd give her until after the interrogation, when the timing was better.

"We should go," he murmured. She silently followed

him to the Durango and remained silent as they neared the police station. "Piper, Detective Forbes is going to interview you today. Don't offer anything but direct answers to direct questions." Changing the subject might ease some of the biting strain hovering between them.

"So you do think I did it?"

"I know you didn't." No way was Piper a cold-blooded killer. "What I'm most worried about is now that Boone's been murdered with your sword, someone else is out there and behind it. Someone who wants to either kill you or frame you or both. I'm not making sense out of the back-and-forth."

Piper's hand trembled, and she bit down on her bottom lip. "There's only one person left."

Luke had been trying his best to hunt down Chaz, but it was as if he'd vanished. No money trail. Nothing.

"Chaz."

Luke nodded. "I think it's evident."

"He could have taken the sword before he tried to incinerate us. If he could slip in like he did, taking it was no problem. It hung above—"

"The counter. I saw it, saw both of them."

"We have to find him." Piper dug a tissue from her purse and wiped her nose. "I don't understand. For a minute I thought God might be merciful, that maybe He wasn't punishing me. But now, every time I turn around something worse happens."

"Piper, God never lets us go. He hasn't given up on you—if that's what you think." She needed to believe that, especially when Luke did what he was going to have to do. Maybe he should have already done it. But it hurt too much. What if God never let him have her back?

Piper squirmed in her seat, looked out the window

and dabbed her eyes with the crumpled tissue. "Let's just get through this interview, okay?"

"Okay," he whispered.

"I'm probably going to prison. I broke into Boone's home and I'm not a cop. Plus, my sword is what killed him. My business card was on Tyson's body. They may think I hurt Harmony, too."

"It doesn't look great. And anyone who saw a bloody hand would break in to try and save someone. Mitigating circumstances." The fact it was *her* sword made it a different story. But Forbes was unbiased. He needed to come to the same conclusion Luke had. Piper was being framed.

Luke pulled into the precinct.

"I really am sorry."

"I know." He wished it could go somewhere with them. Maybe someday it could. Wasn't as if he'd ever be able to love anyone else, but gazing into her watery eyes...he was losing resolve by the second. Time to change the subject again. His nerves were shot. "Direct answers only. Keep your cool."

Eric met them inside. Luke kept his hand on Piper's lower back, reassuring her things would be okay.

He wasn't sure he could do this. Sending her in like a criminal, then having to explain why he couldn't be with her when he desperately wanted to be.

Lord, give me strength. Give her strength.

"Piper, do you want a lawyer? That'd be smart."

Piper raised her chin, and with a straight face and stony eyes she stared dead into his. "I have nothing to hide. Not from last night or that night at Ellen Strosbergen's. I don't need a lawyer."

He led her into the interrogation room. Detective

Forbes scooted a chair out for Piper. "Just want to ask you a few questions, Miss Kennedy."

"Okay."

Luke paused at the door, gave her one more look and entered the adjacent room to watch.

Piper sat in front of Forbes, a cool exterior, but not defensive. Her posture was poised, but not stiff, hands resting in her lap.

Eric leaned on the wall. "So this has got to be a little awkward."

"You don't know the half of it." Luke scratched the back of his head. "She's clean. I just don't know what he'll say about her going through the window."

"He's not assigned this case, Luke. He's simply asking some questions, so if anything comes up later, in regards to her relationship with you, it's an unbiased interview."

Luke was biased. Riding so many hills of emotions he couldn't sit across from her and be objective. "Why didn't you do it, then?"

"You're my partner and my friend. Makes me biased." He smirked. "And the ninja's grown on me. She made a bad decision for the right reason."

Luke needed to talk about something else. Shoptalk. "How does a man vanish for ten years without a peep?"

Eric pushed off the wall and stood beside Luke, watching as Piper answered questions about Christopher Baxter, Tyson Baroni and Boone Wiley. "I don't know. He made off with something valuable and turned it into cash—if it wasn't cash—and disappeared."

Luke rubbed his chin. "Who knows? Maybe he's been living it up in Costa Rica."

"Does anyone really live it up in Costa Rica? Monte Carlo. The Caymans…but I don't know about Costa Rica."

A small laugh pushed through Luke's tension. Exactly what Eric had meant to accomplish. Humor was his way of relaxing a somber situation. Wasn't always appropriate, like last night, but Luke could stand to relax or he'd end up with a migraine.

Forbes pointed to the sword in the evidence bag. "Can you identify this, Miss Kennedy? Does this belong to you?"

Piper glanced at the sword. "I can't say whether it's mine or not. I have one like it. I can, however, identify it for you. It's a tachi koshirae. To be precise, it's an Ito Maki tachi."

"Sounds like an organic potato chip to me." Eric pressed his stomach. "Maybe I'm just hungry."

Luke sped to the door. "She should've gotten a lawyer."

"Calm down. She's doing fine."

"It was made in the koto era, worn by higher-ranking samurai." Piper kept cool and collected.

Luke was going out of his mind.

"You know a lot about Japanese swords," Forbes said.

"I do."

"Can you tell me how this ended up in Boone Wiley's gut?" Forbes leaned forward, wiped a layer of sweat from his forehead.

"I can't."

"Can't or won't?" Forbes's tone turned steely.

Luke raked a hand through his hair. "He's about to get belligerent with her."

Eric arched a dark eyebrow. "*Pretty* sure she can

handle it. She's not your typical damsel in distress, if you haven't noticed."

No, she wasn't.

"You know, not every guy has it made like you. Your job…doesn't scare her. She just bucks up and fights alongside you." Eric's tone carried an air of loneliness and longing, but they weren't about to have a heart-to-heart. Any minute—

"Or saves your keister." He chuckled.

There it was—turning serious into flippant.

"I'm secure enough in my manhood to accept that."

Forbes shoved his chair and leaned back, crossing an ankle over his knee. "So you think the person responsible stole the sword before he set your dojo on fire?"

Piper's expression shifted. The calm before the storm. Not good.

Eric pointed toward her. "Uh-oh. I've seen that look before. Right before she—"

Stretching across the table, Piper narrowed her eyes, heat blazing from them. "Maybe before or after he nailed the storage-room window shut. Definitely before he poured gasoline all over my front office and set my livelihood—everything I've worked for, everything I am—on fire. And it had to be before my lungs filled with smoke and I nearly died. Right before one of your own detectives saved my life and almost lost his own. Yeah, that's exactly what I'm saying happened, Detective Forbes. Either arrest me or send me walking. I am so done with this interview."

"I was gonna say right before she put you in your place at Harmony Fells's home. Looked just like that." Eric brushed his hands together. "Well, now that that's over, let's go get the real killer, shall we?"

"Absolutely." Luke's gaze lingered on Piper as she glared at Forbes.

Everything she is.

That wasn't true. She was more than a building. More than her job.

God, help her to see that. Somehow. Some way.

Chapter 14

Piper had endured the interrogation, trying to keep her focus on the questions and not on what Luke was thinking. Standing on her doorstep earlier, Luke had pain etched across his face and what looked like anger. He'd tossed out a few words and instructions, and then he remained quiet while he white-knuckled the steering wheel.

After the interrogation, he'd barely spoken other than to tell her she'd done a great job, even though she'd lost her temper toward the end. Twice, he'd turned down the radio and acted as if he were going to have a conversation, but after a few frustrated sighs, he didn't. And Piper didn't push. She was too afraid to hear what he had to say. And yet she wanted to know what was on his mind.

Looked as if it was going to be awkward silence and tension from here on out, though.

Piper trudged down the rehab corridors where Luke had left her, alone. Dazed.

Any second her insides were going to combust. Mama Jean. Right now, she needed her grandma.

Entering her room, Piper relaxed at the sight of Mama Jean. "You feeling okay? No more confusion?"

"I'm feeling better. You look worse for wear, though."

Piper touched her cheek. Couldn't hide the physical injuries, but Piper had a sneaky feeling Mama Jean wasn't even looking at the bumps and bruises. She'd had to tell her about the car accident. The circumstances surrounding it, not so much.

"If you'd shown up twenty minutes ago, you'd have missed me. Therapy. I'm getting stronger every day."

Piper wished she could say the same. "Good. You hungry? Want a drink or anything?"

"No. Come sit with me." She patted the back of the chair next to the bed. "Tell me why you're carrying the weight of the world."

Piper dropped in the chair. "Harm's still missing. I'm… I'm scared." There—she'd admitted it. Finally. Out loud. She was scared. Terrified.

"You should pray for her."

Piper licked her dry lips. "I… I have. I just don't know if God pays attention to my prayers. I wouldn't blame Him."

Mama Jean held Piper's hand. "Seems to me it's not God you have a problem with. It's you."

"Me?" Piper snorted. "What does that even mean?" Mama Jean also had a penchant for riddles.

"What do you think it means?" Her bright eyes shone even brighter, and she smiled.

"If I knew I wouldn't have asked."

"Well, I do believe I'll let you and God sort through that together." Accent of a true Southern belle and the evasiveness of a criminal.

"Wouldn't He have to talk to me first?" She thought He might be, but then it rained hail down on her. Even Luke wasn't talking to her.

"You telling me you haven't heard Him speakin' to ya, child? Feeling a bubbling sensation deep inside? Hearing things you know you'd never tell yourself, like thoughts talkin' a storm inside your heart?" She peered into Piper's eyes.

"Maybe. A scripture from the Bible popped into my head. Don't know where from, but I know I've heard it somewhere or read it before. Maybe at church camp or in church." When she used to go to church with Mama Jean.

"He's talking. Drop those crusty walls and listen. He's a good God, Piper. You can trust Him with your heart."

The few times she'd given her heart, someone broke it.

The day she asked Jesus into her life and was baptized came back. Had she even given God a shot after that?

Something tightened in her chest. No.

She'd been too afraid she'd ruin it. Disappoint Him. Terrified He'd hurt her. Like her mother.

In the end, she had disappointed Him. God had every right to be hurt and angry at her. He had every right to leave her. To turn her away if she came crawling back.

"Mama Jean, you always make my heart break a little...but I keep comin' back. I don't know. I feel bad and you come to mind. Then I see you and..."

"You won't always have me to run to. You need to be runnin' to someone who can do more than give you some sound advice. Someone who can heal you in places you hurt."

Piper hurt all over.

"Healing won't come without a little heart breakin' and pain." Mama Jean wiped her watery eyes. "Just speaking what I've learned over the years spending time with my Lord."

"Did you ever get angry when He didn't fix Mom? I… I did."

"Of course I did." Mama Jean's chest rose when she inhaled. "Let Him know it, too. It hurt, knowing my baby girl couldn't kick the habit. Knowing she died in a crack house. Nobody with her. No chance to say good-bye." Tears filled her eyes. "Like I said, takes some pain to get the healin', and I wanted to feel better. But she chose which kind of fix she wanted. I can't blame the good Lord for the choice my baby made."

Piper pressed Mama Jean's hand to her cheek. "I wanna feel better." Anything was better than loneliness and fear, hiding behind a facade of independence and strength. How long could she pretend? The dojo—karate—it was everything to her. And God took it. Consumed it in flames.

You shall have no other gods before Me.

Piper jerked up as the scripture struck her heart.

Mama Jean chuckled. "Keep listening. I see He's talking, dear one. Listen…and obey."

Martial arts. Had it become her god? "I will, Mama Jean." She kissed her cheek. "I'm gonna take a walk around the garden. You wanna come?"

"You go. I'll be praying."

Piper closed the door behind her and strolled into the garden, the fountain bubbling. Sun shining bright. Warm wind on her skin.

God, have...have You let me go?

He has never let you down, never looked the other way when you were being kicked around. He has never wandered off to do His own thing; He has been right there, listening.

But had Piper been listening?

Monday morning had come with a glorious sunrise—streaks of magenta, baby pink and violet. April showers brought May flowers. Harmony's tulips had sprouted like hope for a colorful future. A day like this should be used for lying on a quilt at a park, jogging at the track or sipping lemonade in a hammock.

Not barreling down the interstate with Luke to see Sly Watson at Riverbend penitentiary.

Piper fidgeted with the emerald ring Mama Jean had given her on her eighteenth birthday, thinking about the past few days.

She hadn't been arrested. Detective Forbes had come to the same conclusion as Luke and Detective Hale. Piper was being framed and Forbes called what Piper did mitigating circumstances and let her go.

Mercy.

Luke had cracked the window and his hair blew like reeds in the wind. Ray-Ban sunglasses shielded his eyes. To keep Piper from noticing how many times he glanced in his rearview mirror? A tick in his cheek proved he was as tense as Piper. Every car was a potential threat.

Luke still wore the haggard and twisted expression

of an inner struggle. But whatever it was, he wouldn't confide. He was business as usual. Friendly but distant.

He turned the radio down. "Prints came back on the cigarette box. But now that Boone's dead, it only established he was in your house. No way to find out why. Nothing on his body, not even a phone."

Piper twisted her ring around. "I feel like we can't get any traction." Not on the case. Not in their might-be relationship.

"I know. Hopefully, today will give us some. I'm fairly certain Sly now knows we lived through that wreck."

If Sly had even been behind the attack.

"How was Mama Jean this morning?"

"Better. Praying about the move."

"To Jackson?"

"To anywhere." The house was too much for Mama Jean to keep up with. Piper and Luke had tackled it again Sunday afternoon after she'd accompanied him to church. After betraying his trust, she couldn't turn his offer down, and he seemed desperate in his asking. As if something important was riding on her answer. And she wanted to go. Felt as though she needed it.

That hour and a half unsettled her in a peaceful kind of way. One verse stood out most. Not sure exactly which chapter or verse, or word for word, but it was in the second book of Corinthians.

Anyone who belongs to Christ has become a new person. The old life is gone and a new life has begun.

As she listened to the pastor, a picture had formed inside her head.

Her house. The fixer-upper. Tons of potential. When she'd first laid eyes on it, it was nothing but an old waste of space. Hideous wallpaper and filthy carpeting. But Piper had closed her eyes to really see. With the right skill, the house could be a beautiful home.

The intense work of scraping off the wallpaper and ripping up the carpet had been worth it in the end. The smell was even different. Fresh. New.

"Hey, Luke?"

He shut off the radio. "Yeah?"

"Never mind." She'd talk about it with Mama Jean later.

"Too late—you snagged my interest and I know you've had something heavy on your mind. You're doing that thing. Fidgeting with the ring Mama Jean gave you when you turned eighteen. Which, if I remember right, you've got another birthday coming in two weeks. It's on a Saturday this year."

Piper's heart fluttered and crashed. Just because he remembered her birthday didn't mean he'd celebrate it with her—this time. But maybe. A sliver of hope bubbled in her chest.

"Yep. The big 3-0."

Piper glanced at her ring. Mama Jean had given it to her the morning of her birthday, and that evening she'd hung out at Riff's. Chaz, Sly and Tyson had come in, but no one had remembered she'd turned eighteen. Harmony had made date plans, and Piper pushed her to go.

Piper had been drinking a Cherry Coke and humming to Maroon 5's "She Will Be Loved." Could have been her life. Broken smile. Broken girl.

Piper had raised her head and a man with broad shoulders and eyes so beautiful and mesmerizing strutted in. An honest face. A strong face with explicit features and the straightest teeth Piper had ever seen. *Good* was stamped across his forehead.

"Do you remember that night?" Piper asked.

Luke aired a laugh through his nose. "I remember every second like a captured snapshot in my head."

He'd asked if the seat across from her was taken. Piper was shocked. Why would someone like him want to sit with her? Luke had noticed her ring right off and asked about it. When he found out it was her birthday, he'd asked if she'd made a birthday wish yet. Mama Jean had baked a chocolate cake, no candle. No wishes.

"Me, too," Piper murmured.

Luke ordered a brownie since Jazz didn't have cake. And he didn't have candles. Luke improvised.

"I still have that lighter. Might even have some juice left in it." He turned to her and grinned, so achingly soft she nearly cried. There had to be hope for them.

"Birthday girls deserve a wish." Luke pulled a BIC lighter out of his pocket, held it over the brownie and sparked a flame. Not just in the lighter, but in Piper and between them. Best moment of her life.

She'd never made a wish over birthday candles before. Never made a wish. Didn't believe in them, but something about Luke had tugged deep within her. Made her feel as though she was worth a wish. Piper had leaned over and blew out the lighter's flame.

"You never told me your wish."

It almost came true.

Luke glanced at her again. "Not gonna tell me now either, are you?"

Piper struggled for a smile. "Nope."

"One day you will. What's on your mind?"

Piper rubbed her forearm. "I was thinking about

what your pastor said. About being new and old things passing away."

His eyes lit up. "What about it?"

"I think maybe I skipped the remodeling process." Piper bunted a shrug.

Belong to Christ.

Did she belong? At ten, she believed it. But then everything spiraled out of control.

"Remodeling…" Luke frowned. "I'm not tracking with you, Pip."

Pip. His pet word. Hadn't used it since they almost died. Since he kissed her. Would he ever do it again?

"Nothing. Just thinking."

"Okay." His tone was light, compassionate. "Think all you want."

A dark sedan sidled up beside them. Luke gripped the wheel, and Piper held her breath, but it zoomed on ahead and she released it. "I was unsure there for a second."

Luke laughed. "You and me both. Scared me. You know, because it's okay to be scared. Doesn't mean you can't be strong at the same time."

Piper rubbed the princess-cut emerald. "I'm getting that."

He glanced at her then the road. What was that expression? Hope? "You ready for this?"

"Sly?" Ready or not. "I want to find Harmony, clear my name, stop whoever wants me dead or framed—or both—and get on with life."

"In Jackson?"

Where else? Luke hadn't asked her to stay. Not last time. Not now. "Yeah."

Luke's nostrils flared, and his Adam's apple bobbed in his throat.

Piper concentrated on the penitentiary coming into view on her right. "What if he doesn't talk?"

"Then we move on. Pray that God will open up an avenue that will bring some truth into the chaos called our lives." Luke exited the ramp. "It's going to be all right."

That was what Harmony had hoped before she didn't make it home.

Riverbend Maximum Security Institution was scrawled in black letters across a stone half wall. Piper's stomach turned. Luke gave the guard his badge, and they waited a few moments, then passed through the gate.

Inside, the smell was bleach, sweat and the typical scent that came with cafeteria food. They passed through the checkpoint, where Luke had to leave behind his gun. They were led into a visiting area. A room sat empty with tables and chairs scattered across the scuffed tile floor.

A guard stood post at a door that would open and reveal Sly Watson. What had ten years and prison done to the man? "Does he get parole?"

"Not anytime soon." He must have felt her trepidation. Lifting her chin to him, he spoke airily. "You don't need to worry."

Luke didn't live in Jackson. Couldn't keep watch over her as he'd been doing while she stayed in Memphis. She managed a wan smile and straightened her shoulders.

"He'll come out in cuffs and shackles. You'll be safe."

"I dare him to come across the table at me."

Luke raised an eyebrow. "For a second it slipped my mind you can take care of yourself—in most situations."

"I know. I know. Won't stop a bullet."

The door opened and Piper's heart froze. Blood drained from her face but she held her head high, kept her shoulders back and ground her teeth. No fear. Not anymore.

Sly Watson had a head full of black hair that matched his inky eyes. A thick beard and mustache masked most of his face. He lasered in on Piper and formed a slow grin. Then he eyed Luke and laughed but took a seat across from them.

He smelled like strong laundry soap. He ignored Luke and fixed his shark eyes on Piper. A new tattoo ran up his neck behind his ear. "You finally start to miss me, Pippy?"

Piper bristled as he held out the name he used for her. Somehow it made her feel dirty. Luke sat stone-like. This was her moment—to finally show she'd overcome Sly and his intimidating tactics that forced her to cower.

"Miss you? Not quite. *Sylvester.*" Her turn to toss out a name. Sly refused to let anyone call him that.

His cheek popped. She'd hit a nerve. Good.

Luke laid a gentle hand on her knee, then released it. Piper caught his drift. Provoking Sly wouldn't garner answers.

"I heard someone shoved a blade in your gut." Piper worked to hold back the anger from ten years. It was everything she could do not to come across the table and show him just how strong she was. How powerful she could be—could wipe that smug, detestable grin off his leathery-skinned face.

His eyes slanted. Again, she'd hit a nerve. "Can't hold me down."

"The cuffs and shackles suggest differently." Piper batted her eyes. Take that.

Luke squeezed her knee again. Okay. That was the last remark.

"You know who shanked you?" Luke asked. "Would it have anything to do with Chaz Michaels?"

Sly grinned. "Ain't seen that mug in ten years."

"Since you nearly murdered Ellen Strosbergen."

Luke's harsh tone didn't seem to matter to Sly. Cocking his head, he sniffed and raised a shoulder.

"If you think your injuries had anything to do with Chaz Michaels or Boone Wiley, we need to know. We could keep it from happening again," Luke urged.

Sly shook his head and leaned over the table. Piper begged him to bring it. "You can't stop nothing in this place. Nothing."

"What can you tell us about that night at Strosbergen's?"

"Been so long. I forget."

Luke's lips tightened. He'd been right. They weren't going to get anything from Sly for no other reason than spite itself. "If the shiv in your gut has to do with Chaz, he won't quit until you're dead. Think about that."

Sly ran his tongue across his teeth and peered over their heads. "Chaz had a half sister lived down in Georgia somewhere. Adrianna. They got along okay. Her old man did a few jobs with Chaz. Nothing serious. He might have hooked up with them after I got pinched."

It was something. Which meant he might be more afraid than he was letting on. Luke folded his hands on the table. "So you do think Chaz put a hit out on you?"

Sly shrugged. "I got enemies inside and out. Can't say. Could've."

"Why?"

"Why not?"

The smugness had to go. He was half tempted to let Piper provoke him enough to get him to strike at her. Then Luke would love to watch her turn him to dust. But that would only further remind her that she needed no one but herself. Although, the conversation in the car proved God was doing something in her heart, had her thinking. Did he have to let her go? Like Abraham with Isaac?

His gut said he did and he'd yet to obey God, which pinched his heart. After the interrogation, he had no excuse. In fact, when Piper had agreed to come to church, he thought maybe he wouldn't have to at all. He switched gears and focused on the task at hand.

"Did Chaz say anything else to you? About that night. What did you see when you got inside Ellen's house?" *That's right—the woman has a name. She is a person. Not some wild animal to tear into with a tire iron.*

Sly slid his sight over to Piper. "You tell him."

"I wasn't inside."

"You went around back like you were supposed to."

"No. I didn't." Piper glowered.

Sly cackled. "Maybe he blames you for getting us caught. You ran off to this pig." He pointed at Luke. "Maybe Chaz knows you ratted us out to a cop, and he's been biding his time, just waiting to do what he said he'd do all along." He ran his finger across his throat and licked his upper lip.

"Let him come, then. I'm not afraid anymore." She

leaned forward. "And I'm not afraid of you either, you sick, twisted sleazebag."

"We're done here." Had to be. One or the other was going to make the first move. Luke stood and nodded to the guard to lead Sly away. As he neared the door he turned back to Piper. "He's coming for ya, Pippy. Better hide." His shifty eyes glinted as he focused on Luke. "You, too, pig."

Piper sprinted for Sly, but Luke fisted the back of her jacket, yanking her against him. The door shut and Piper turned into him. Luke continued to hold her in an embrace. "You and that temper."

Piper sighed. "Ten years ago, I'd have been angry but done nothing. I wanted him to know I'm not afraid, but walking in here…a little shaky. I'm glad I didn't have to do it alone. That you had my back."

His pinched heart twisted. She was still looking to him. And though he knew it wasn't right, he still wanted her to. She needed to know that when all was said and done, God had her back. She was never truly alone. He brushed a strand of hair from her face.

"What I did that night, not leaving him when I wanted to, giving you a false address… It was for nothing. Sly thinks I snitched. Chaz probably does, too, wherever he is." She shivered.

"He's out there and we'll get him, starting with the half sister. He'll make a mistake." He led her to the checkpoint. "And you faced your past and won."

She peered up, her lips begging for another kiss. He fought it. Instead, he ran a thumb across her cheek.

"You didn't cower, and he knew it."

Piper scuffled to the car. "What if we hit a dead end with Chaz's half sister?"

Luke unlocked the car doors. "We figure out a way to draw him out."

The car ride felt like an eternity. When he walked her to the door, the weight on his chest was insufferable. Piper motioned him inside, and he forced himself to go. Forced himself to do the one thing he hoped he might not have to after all.

But he couldn't mend her. Couldn't be her source. Each day grew harder. It had to be now.

"I know things are rocky since what I did, Luke. We need to talk about that night at Boone's. We haven't. It's killing me. I need you to say something. Anything."

He could think of only one thing. "Piper, I love you."

That was unexpected. Speechless, Piper gawked. Waited.

Luke's jaw pulsed near his ears. "But I can't be with you. I should have told you the morning of the interrogation, but…"

She really had blown it with going behind his back. Throat sizzling, she ground her teeth. But the past few days hadn't been so bad. They'd been to church and worked on Mama Jean's home. They'd shared a fond memory of meeting, and it seemed as though the feelings were still there, even stronger. The way he'd stroked her cheek at the prison… That hadn't felt like a goodbye touch.

"I shouldn't have gone. I know that."

Luke's eyes brimmed with emotion and he shook his head. "It's not because I think you're guilty of any of this. You know I don't. Not because you bring trouble to me. That's not true. Remember when you said that?"

Piper managed a nod. This man she'd always loved—who loved her—was destroying her. Again.

"It's not even because your faith is shaky. Or that I don't fully trust you, even though you went behind my back. Again. Do you know how much that hurt?"

"Luke—"

"I tried to move on after that night. I left the theft unit out of fear I'd have to face you in this exact situation you've been in." His voice cracked. "I'm not doing this because of what happened at Boone's. It's just… that's when I knew I had to. I've been struggling for the last few days."

"I don't understand," she whispered.

Luke lifted his head and blinked several times, inhaled. "I can't be with you, because I want to *fix* you. Every day. I want to try and be someone to you I can't be."

Piper *was* broken. Luke's words had ripped the scab off, and infection seeped into every inch of her. Blistering, brutal pain.

"You know, maybe we could have worked out something with you in Jackson and me in Memphis. I don't know. That was a hurdle all on its own, but this…" He swept his hand between them. "This is so much bigger, and if I don't walk away now, I'll ruin you. I'll ruin me. And you'll stay broken. In the end, all you'll feel for me is resentment. I'd die inside having to see that every day."

Piper slunk onto the couch. Her hands trembled and her insides quaked. What could she say?

He knelt in front of her. His touch like a million needles. "But I need to say something. I thought I'd made peace with how things went down between us, about the betrayal, the lies. Since you've been back, though, I feel unsettled and angry at times. It's been confusing me."

Piper wiped a warm string of tears from her cheeks.

"I've been carrying guilt over what happened to Ellen Strosbergen. I didn't even know it. I'd gotten used to the weight on my shoulders. Like people with chronic pain. Freedom from it feels like something might be wrong because they don't know what it's like to be well. Last night, I felt that weight and I asked God to lift it off me. I made peace."

Piper dropped her head. "I never wanted anyone to get hurt. I'm sorry."

Luke framed her face, peered into her eyes and tenderly smiled. "I know you are." He placed his forehead on hers, their breath mingling, reminding her of their earlier kiss. And how she'd never have another one. She clamped down on the inside of her bottom lip.

Luke pulled back. "It was when I did that—made peace—I realized why I felt unsettled and moments of bitterness."

"Why?"

Luke inhaled. "Took me a while, Piper, but I forgave you for that night. I should have called to tell you. Felt God nudging me to. Even got in the car once to come. But I couldn't. Call it pride. Fear. Whatever you want. No obedience, no peace. I ignored it until you showed up. Can't ignore what's staring dead in your face. Not for lack of trying, though."

He forgave her. "I did betray you. I did lie to you. Whether to protect you or not, I should have been truthful. You have every right to be mad."

"I need to say it, Pip." He gazed into her eyes, his turned red-rimmed. "I forgive you and I'm sorry that

I told you to leave, that my anger and hurt seeing you there dictated my behavior. I'm sorry for not coming to you. I don't know where we'd be if I had. We can't look back. But that's not even the point."

Piper's dam burst and she fell into him, draping her arms around his neck, sobbing. Luke held her like a vise; she didn't think she could breathe and didn't care. Could they have been together if he'd come to Jackson years ago?

He pulled away and sniffed. "I forgive you." Conviction flooded his voice. "And I need to ask you to forgive me."

Did she forgive him? Yes. So much easier than forgiving herself. She couldn't bring herself to do that. "I forgive you."

"Thank you, Pip." His husky voice sounded strangled. This was excruciating for her. How much more excruciating was it for him?

"But you love me."

"I love you." He brushed tears from her cheeks.

"But you can't be with me?"

Luke bit his bottom lip and slowly shook his head. "I'm sorry about how I acted at Boone's and these last few days. Leaving you hanging and wondering what I was thinking and feeling. I need to tell you that, too."

"I made a mistake going. But I was going to call you. Had my phone out. Regardless. I won't do anything like that again."

"I believe you."

But it wouldn't change anything between them. She loved him, too. But she couldn't return the words. Wished he'd never uttered them. It would only make things rougher for him to do what he felt was right. And for once she was going to make sure she didn't further contribute to his misery.

When this was over, if she was still breathing, she'd leave. Take Mama Jean with her, never come back.

Because Piper didn't know how long it would take to stop being broken. But she wanted to get better.

Not for Luke.

For herself.

Chapter 15

The week had whizzed by in a blur. Too quiet. Unnerving. Luke remained loyal to protect Piper or to see that someone was, but it killed him having to create a painful distance between them. To see accusing abandonment in her eyes every time she looked at him. But he'd done the right thing. Too bad the right thing didn't always feel good. Or right.

He glanced over at her, sitting mutely as they headed to the rehab center for her morning visit with Mama Jean. The next safest place if she wasn't with him. Luke had interviews to conduct and Piper couldn't come. She hadn't even asked, which slayed him further. It was out of character for her not to press.

"You're quiet," he said, not knowing what to say but needing to say something.

"Wrestling with stuff on my mind."

Him, too. Like how he was going to survive not having Piper in his life now that he was used to seeing her every day again. He'd kidded himself thinking he'd got over her. "I'll only be gone a few hours." He pulled under the awning at the rehab center and slid his sunglasses onto his nose. "Don't leave until I get back."

"Is there going to be a uniformed officer out there standing guard?"

"Does it matter?" She could easily evade them or take them down if she truly wanted.

Piper half grinned. "No. I've been good as gold this past week, and you know it."

He dipped his chin. "I do. And I appreciate your attempts to...behave." He chuckled. "I know how agonizing it is for you."

"Sure you don't wanna say hi to Mama Jean? She's sweet on you, you know?"

He grinned and sighed at the moment of easy banter. "I'm meeting with Ellen Strosbergen's great-granddaughter later this afternoon. If for some reason I get tied up, Eric says he'll swing by and take you home. To Harmony's. You know what I mean." Home would never be here. Probably never be with him.

"I know. Do you think she'll remember something new?"

"Doubtful, but I'm willing to backtrack or chase rabbits. Anything at this point." Luke raised his sunglasses back over his eyes. "Give Mama Jean a hug for me."

"I will." Piper made brief eye contact with him, her eyes watery. "Thanks for the ride. I know it's not easy being near me when you don't want to."

Her words salted his gaping wounds. "Piper—"

She bounded out and stalked inside.

Chasing her down and clarifying how much he did

want to be near her would only complicate things more. He took a deep breath and exhaled. Why couldn't things be easier?

Piper trudged through the foyer and down the hall to Mama Jean's room.

"Well, lookie there. You made it just in time for lunch." Mama Jean lifted the lid of her lunch tray. In a wheelchair by the window, she looked shiny and well.

"It's ten. You mean brunch?" Piper grinned.

"It's chicken and dressing. Lunch. Where's our handsome man?"

"Work. Can't be with me 24/7." Couldn't be with her at all. But he made sure someone was protecting her at all times, whether a friend he'd enlisted or a patrol car. As if Memphis city police had nothing better to do than sit outside a rehab center while Piper ate Jell-O and played Scrabble with Mama Jean.

Piper opened the nightstand drawer and took out the crossword puzzle book. Mama Jean was adept at doing one-armed things. "Does this really stimulate your mind, like they—whoever they are—say?"

"Not nearly as much as the good book."

"The Bible?"

"There's lots of good books, but you slap a *the* in front of it, and you know that's what I'm talking about." Mama Jean winked.

"I've been thinking this week."

"Nice to hear, dear one."

Her color was coming back along with her witty tongue, and she wore lipstick today…and… "Has Kathy Mae come by to set your hair?"

"Yesterday. Now, you been thinkin'?"

"About what you said. Me not having a problem with God but having one with myself." Piper wiped her clammy hands on her jeans. "I think maybe… I've been punishing myself or thinking every bad thing that happens is God punishing me. I keep asking Him to forgive me. But it's really me who hasn't forgiven me. I try to do good things. Help my neighbors. Run a program for troubled teens. I even give money to charities but… I never feel like I can do enough to erase my mistakes."

Mama Jean reached over with her well hand and laid it on Piper's knee. "Forgiveness isn't earned. If God can forgive you, you need to let it go and forgive yourself. Why do you think He died for you, Piper? 'Cause I can tell ya, it wasn't so you can mope around pitying yourself and stay beat down by regrets. Move on."

She'd been moping and beat down for sure.

"Jesus loves you. So much He died for you while you were missin' the mark, girlie. He ain't waitin' around for you to get all good before He loves you."

That would never happen. Piper would never be good enough. "What about…what about after? I did everything bad after I made a commitment to Him. I was ten, and I knew what I was doing, but I messed up most after that."

"You become who you spend time with."

Piper had become a new creation, then never did anything to clean out the old. Never spent time letting God remodel her. She'd let Chaz lure her away. Couldn't blame him anymore, though. She'd made that choice.

"Piper, have you asked forgiveness?"

"I just said I did! All the time."

"Then trust Him at his Word. He's faithful to forgive and fix us up, inside out." Mama Jean gave her the don't-argue-with-me look. "Remember that song I used to sing you when you were little? Every night before bed."

She closed her eyes, and the words floated into Piper's mind.

Jesus loves me, this I know...the Bible tells me so... they are weak...but He is strong...the Bible tells me so...

Luke had said everyone was weak and needed God's strength. She may have physical strength down pat. But it couldn't make her inside strong. And relying on Luke wouldn't do it, either.

Mama Jean handed her the worn leather Bible and pointed to the verse in First John that told her God would forgive her. She read it. Over and over. God loved her even though He knew she'd betray him.

Jesus loves me...for the Bible tells me so...

Yet He died for her to be forgiven.

What a price to pay for her betrayal.

A tear slid down her cheek.

"Dear one, I love you so much."

Piper closed the good book and laid it back in Mama Jean's lap. "I love you, too. How do you feel about going to church on Sunday? I think we could find a way to get you in and out of the car without too much trouble."

"Now, that's music to this old lady's ears."

The clear blue sky had disappeared as the day wore on. The temperature dropped, and heavy, dappled clouds rolled like a frightening slide show. Severe thunderstorms had been predicted for this evening until midmorning. Normally, Piper enjoyed a storm, but something disturbing grated against her spine.

Luke apparently got tied up. His interview with Judith Strosbergen had been pushed back, and she lived an hour away. Piper hoped he didn't have to drive when the storm turned terrible. Eric had picked her up from Mama Jean's. The conversation had been light, impersonal but easygoing. Twice he'd offered her a Twizzler. Twice she'd turned him down.

"Are you trying to quit smoking or something?" Piper pointed to the candy hanging from his mouth.

"No, I just enjoy licorice. I mean, you can't beat flavored plastic."

Piper snorted, eyed the Twizzler, then took one. "I don't get it."

Eric raised his eyebrows. "It's not a candy you have to understand."

Dare she ask what was? She swallowed the one-and-only bite she was taking and handed it off to him. "What's your story?"

"Why do I have to have a story?" Grinning, he rounded the curve as an SUV flew by.

Piper braced herself. When it didn't turn around and come back, she released a pent-up breath. "I'm so sick of dark SUVs."

"I'm so sick of those juicer infomercials. They play over and over. I'm sorry—I'm not adding kale to my diet in any form or fashion."

Piper laughed. But he'd eat flavored plastic. "I missed those."

"You don't stay up late enough, then." He slowed at Harmony's drive and turned in. "Did Luke tell you we got zip from Chaz's half sister? Says she hasn't seen him in over ten years."

A drop of rain splatted on the windshield, and then

another. The skies opened up and belched a spray of rain. "Are you going to sit outside in this?"

"No. I'm going to sit inside the car." He winked. "Till Luke gets here." The wipers raced across the windshield to knock the rain away. Wasn't doing the greatest job. Thunder smashed into the atmosphere and a slash of blinding lightning streaked in front of them.

Piper started. "You sure you don't want to come in?"

"Nah. I'm okay. Besides, I need to make a phone call. My sister's birthday would've been today, and I haven't had a chance to call home or go by there."

Past tense. Piper squeezed Eric's forearm. "I'm sorry. How old would she have been?"

"Twenty-seven." His smile was tight-lipped.

"How did she die?"

Eric stretched over Piper and grabbed an umbrella from under her seat. "You might want this."

Okay, that topic was off-limits. She shouldn't have asked. "I'm sorry. That was rude."

"Nah. It's a perfectly normal question. But I don't want to talk about it."

She declined the umbrella. "I'm fine but thanks, and thanks for babysitting. I'll bring you coffee later." She opened the door. The rain sounded as if it were applauding her exit from the car. She shrieked as it drenched her clothing and slithered like cold stabs down her neck and back. Puddles had already formed on the driveway. With each step, water seeped into her shoes and splattered on her jeans.

She reached the stoop, fumbled for the keys and unlocked the door. Another crack of thunder reverberated in her chest. Another slash of lightning knifed the sky.

Hurrying inside, Piper kicked off her shoes and

locked the door behind her. Rushing up the stairs, she shed her clothes, threw them in her room and jumped into a hot shower to warm up.

After dressing and slipping into her moccasin house shoes, she came downstairs with a novel she'd found in Harmony's guest room. A romance. Just what Piper needed—a book that would make her wish she and Luke could have made it.

Maybe they could. Eventually.

She nestled on the couch. The power flickered.

Great. Where did Harmony keep the flashlights and candles?

Rain pounded the windows, and flashes of lightning formed bizarre-shaped shadows on the living-room furniture and floor. Was Eric okay? Piper tiptoed to the front windows to check on him.

The car was gone.

Where did he go? A tingling sensation crept up her back. Why would he leave? And not tell her? Her phone was upstairs. She took them two at a time and snatched her phone off the bed.

The lights flickered again.

A missed call from Luke. Maybe he needed Eric on a case and was letting her know. She returned his call.

One ring.

Two.

He answered. "Piper!"

"Hey. Did you call the dog off? He's not outside my house."

"Lis… I tried to call…you…g…back…don't…"

"You're cutting out, Luke. Say it again." Piper pressed her hand over her free ear, hoping to hear better.

"I…don't…stay… Cha…"

"Don't stay where? Or don't go anywhere and stay? I can't hear you clearly." *Cha*... "Chaz?" Her heart leaped into her throat. "Did you find him? Luke. Luke? Luke!"

A beeping sounded. His call had dropped. She tried again. Voice mail.

Another sputter of power. Running into the guest bathroom, Piper scored a scented candle. Vanilla. Now to find matches. She plundered the cabinets in the kitchen and found a box. Piper lit the candle and set it on the counter, just in case. The flickering flame danced across the dark ceiling.

The lamp in the living room went out and the hum of the refrigerator stopped.

No power.

Had Luke told her not to leave, that he'd found Chaz? Or not to stay in the house because of Chaz?

She tried him again. Voice mail.

A clanging on the back door startled her and she shrieked. Her pulse hammered in her throat.

Someone stood at the back door.

Chapter 16

Piper tripped across the rug and stumbled to the back door. Standing with hands against the glass, Harmony looked like a drowned rat. Nails chipped, hair matted and dirt running like streams of mascara down her cheeks.

Harmony. Harmony! Piper fumbled with the lock, then swung the door open. "Harmony! It's you! It's really you." Piper yanked her inside, hugging her tightly. "We've been sick. Where were you? How did you get here? Did Boone have you? Are you okay?"

Harmony clung to Piper's neck. "He…he…"

Piper pulled back and brushed unkempt clumps of blond hair from Harmony's face. "Sit down. Come sit down. Let's go slowly." Harmony's hands trembled. "You need some warm clothes. Take those off but don't do anything with them. We might need them for evidence or something."

This was surreal. Piper couldn't stand there staring in shock. She needed dry clothes. Darting to Harmony's room, Piper dug through her drawers and found a T-shirt and yoga pants and undergarments. In the kitchen, Harmony hadn't made a move to take off her clothing. She must be in shock.

"Come on, Harm. Let's get you warm and dry." And fed. Who knew if that monster, Boone, fed her? "Where've you been?" She helped her into the half bath off the kitchen and out of her clothes into clean ones.

"Harm, look at me," Piper said and tipped Harmony's chin toward her. "Where have you been?"

Harmony shook her head. "I'm not sure. I was on my way to the conference. I parked... Then someone covered my face and drugged me... I screamed but then... black. I woke up." She shivered, and Piper helped her onto the couch. She slipped a quilt from the chair and covered her up.

A crack of thunder rattled the windows as the wind howled. Storm was getting worse by the second. No TV. No power.

"I need to call Luke. Try to, anyway. I think the storm is messing with the cell towers or he's somewhere with pitiful reception."

"Boone."

"Boone? He did this to you?"

Harmony's eyes widened, and her lip trembled. "I woke up and he had me bound. It was dirty. Smelled like...sweat and...and tires."

A mechanic shop? Tyson's, maybe? "Why?"

Harmony wiped her eyes. "He demanded that I tell him where they were. And I kept asking, 'Where what is?' but he kept demanding."

Piper settled next to her. "Did he tell you what it was he wanted?"

Harmony nodded. "Jewelry. Said I had a fortune. Sly told him about that lady's house. That millions of dollars' worth of jewels were taken. But I swore I didn't have them! I never even saw them."

Piper drew her into a hug and stroked her wet hair. "Shhh...it's okay now."

"Piper, I did something terrible."

"What?" Piper sat on the edge of the couch as Harmony jumped up and wore a path in the living-room carpet.

"I was so afraid... I thought if he believed I didn't have them, he'd kill me. He would have. He's dangerous. So dangerous. I'm so stupid."

"You're safe now, and that's all that matters. You made a bad choice about dating him. But you fixed it. You can't punish yourself for it."

Piper ate her own words. She had made bad choices. Asked forgiveness, but never moved on as though she'd been forgiven. Still blamed herself. But she wasn't blaming herself anymore. And neither was Harmony.

"Piper, that's not what I'm talking about. I told Boone you had the jewels."

Piper sprang from the couch. "Me? I don't have any jewels." But if Harmony hadn't given up a name, Boone would have killed her. "I get it." She gripped Harmony's shoulders. "I forgive you. You did what you thought was right in the moment. It's okay."

"It's not okay!" Harmony shook her head like a rabid dog with a piece of meat. "He's going to come after you. He'll kill you to get them." Too late, but no point making Harmony feel any worse.

"Boone is dead, Harmony."

She froze. "What?"

Another boom of thunder. Wind whipped the tree branches across the window and roof like claws. Piper looked up. Sounded as if it might cave at any moment. "He's dead. I found him at his apartment. Someone stabbed him with one of my Japanese swords. Tried to frame me."

"Chaz." Harmony squeezed Piper's hands. "It must have been Chaz. That's who I saw, heard."

Piper's heart rate spiked. "When did you see and hear Chaz?" Luke mentioned Chaz—or what might have been Chaz—on the call. She snagged her cell off the counter. Two percent left of charge.

"Who are you calling?"

"I'm going to try Luke." Piper dialed. Voice mail again. What if something happened to him? What if Chaz got to him? "Tell me what happened. Slowly."

"I only saw Boone, at first. I thought he was ticked over the breakup and was trying to scare me, but then he asked about the jewels. Necklaces, bracelets, rings and a few diamonds. I thought he was high or something, but then he said that Sly told him about the jewels and one of us had them. They were in prison together. That night, in my bed, I don't know if he mistook you for me or not. I think Boone used me as a mark. He never even cared about me. Just wanted to see if I had the goods."

At least Piper wasn't in the dark about what it was Chaz wanted anymore. How did he fit in with Boone, though? And where was Luke? Where was Eric?

"Well, you don't. And neither do I. Tyson probably didn't either since he ended up dead." But Harmony had lived. Escaped somehow, or she might be dead, too.

"How do you know you saw Chaz with Boone? Are they working together? Is Sly in on it, too?"

"I don't know. I heard arguing, and I saw a guy. Then I didn't see Boone again for a few days. I got the ropes undone and I ran… I just ran."

"Something doesn't make sense." Piper frowned. If the guy Harmony heard arguing with Boone killed him, why did he let Harmony live? Not that she wasn't happy, but the dots weren't connecting.

A bolt of lightning nearly burst through the window, and thunder rumbled too close for comfort.

Another banging sent Piper reeling. Someone was at the front door.

"Don't answer it, Piper! We have to get out of here before Chaz finds us. We gotta run and run far."

"I'm not running anymore, Harmony." Piper strode toward the front door. "It's time we all face this and end it." She peeped through the hole and relaxed.

Finally.

Piper opened the door to a drenched Luke. "You don't know how great it is to see you."

Luke grabbed her and drew her into his arms. "I was beside myself when I called Eric and couldn't get him. You're not safe, Piper. And Harmony—"

"Is right here. She got away. Boone kidnapped her for jewels. And Chaz is in on it. She thinks she saw him."

Luke's hair matted to his forehead, and water ran down his cheeks and dripped from his coat onto the foyer. It was the panic in his eyes that scared her. "What's wrong?"

"Get behind me."

Luke drew his gun and stormed into the living room and kitchen area.

"What are you doing?" Piper stepped in front of him, blocking his aim directed right at Harmony.

"Why are you aiming that at me?" Harmony squealed.

"Game's up."

"What game?" Piper looked from Luke, a somber expression on his face, to Harmony, wide-eyed with fear.

"I don't know what he's talking about, Piper. I've been bound in some rotten, forsaken hole for I don't even know how long."

Piper glanced at her wrists and ankles. No bruising. No marks.

"Get. Behind. Me."

Piper could stay put or trust Luke. She shifted to his side.

"Piper?" Harmony's shoulders sagged. "What can I say?"

"How about the truth?" Luke asked. "I talked with Judith Strosbergen. Had the most interesting conversation."

Harmony's face paled, and she dropped her mouth. What had Harm done? Was she in on this?

"We got chatting about her great-grandmother. Judith was beside herself when she found out that about ten million in jewels had been lifted the night Ellen was beaten half to death. At first, they didn't realize it. Said Grandma put the jewels in a safe-deposit box."

"What does that have to do with me?"

Piper'd like to know, too.

"But Ellen had dementia and happened to remove those jewels for fear someone would steal them. I suppose the irony hasn't gone unnoticed."

"Luke, I didn't know Ellen Strosbergen had any jewels." Piper gaped at Harmony. She stood like a statue. Gun aimed on her.

Wind howled and thunder continued to roll.

"I believe you, Pip. You've been played, and I'm sorry."

"That's not true. Don't listen to him, Piper. Who couldn't let you go? Me. I called you on your birthday. If Mama Jean hadn't been hurt or that boarder killed, you think he'd have rekindled things with you? No."

Piper flexed her hands. But the murder had brought Luke and Piper back together. "Luke, are you sure about what you're saying?"

"In the initial report, the jewels hadn't been included. Apparently, after discovering them missing from the safe-deposit box, the grandchildren tore the house apart. Ellen had a habit of hiding things. Misplacing them and then forgetting."

Harmony's eyes turned cold. What had she done? How far had she gone?

"So they reported it after. I'd already left the unit or I'd have been clued in. But the jewels were never found. Cost the family millions because Ellen had never insured them. Fast-forward ten years to Ellen's great-granddaughter, Judith, receiving a beautiful set for her anniversary and not wanting to repeat the same mistake as her dear grandmother. So she made sure her valuables were insured. Piper, would you like to know the name of the insurance company who insured Judith's valuables?"

"No." Harm would never hurt or betray Piper. "That's not true, is it?" Could she have done all this for some jewels?

"Yes, it's true," Luke said and turned to Harmony. "When you overheard Judith's story, you realized jewels were stolen that night and you went straight to Sly, didn't you? Did you offer to give him a cut when he got out on parole?"

"No."

Piper's throat constricted. This wasn't happening.

"Sly gave you Boone, his old cell mate. Easy to seduce to get what you wanted, wasn't he? You both used him like a dog. When hurting Mama Jean didn't work, you had him try and scare Pip outside the hospital. But she was too strong. So the next time, he tried to knock her out. He'd known she was in your bed. Because you told him. Then he came at her again in the alley at Riff's. He trashed all our homes. Looking for the jewels."

Piper studied Harmony and her heart twisted. She'd faked it. "You knew I'd insist on you going to the conference. You knew I'd find that photo of you and Boone in that drawer. You banked on me taking care of you, like I always have. You set me up so you could set up Boone." Her best friend had turned on her. For money.

Harmony's shoulders slumped. The game was up and she knew it. "It wasn't supposed to go like this. Mama Jean shouldn't have been hurt."

Blood drained from Piper's face. "Why would you think Mama Jean would have the jewels? She's in therapy! She could have died." The betrayal rubbed raw across her heart, like broken glass. "And Christopher Baxter was an innocent casualty."

"He wasn't supposed to die. It was only supposed to be a burglary because I knew you'd come home for her. I knew if you felt she was threatened, you'd do anything to keep her safe. You'd never tell me if you had them, but you'd give them up for Mama Jean. Boone did his own thing when he got there."

Did Piper believe that? Boone was dead. Harmony wasn't. "Why would you think I had the jewels?"

"You bought that building."

"Which you burned up!" Anger surged into Piper's veins. "You tried to burn us to the ground. You had Boone run us off the road! We almost died. And you tried to frame me for murdering Tyson and Boone!"

"No! That had to be Chaz! I told you I heard arguing that night Boone died. It's the truth. Chaz must have known about the jewels, too, or maybe Sly made a deal with him to double-cross me."

Luke pulled cuffs from his belt. "You're under arrest for the murder of Boone Wiley, Tyson Baroni and Christopher Baxter, and that's just a start."

"I didn't kill Boone! And Boone killed Christopher Baxter and Tyson Baroni."

"Why?" Piper clutched the sides of her head. "I don't understand."

"Things got out of hand! I couldn't control him like I thought I could."

"People died, Harmony, and you let it happen. You set it up."

"I didn't kill anyone. I only tried for the jewels. I'm broke. I'm going to lose this home."

Piper stepped toward her, fists at her sides to keep from punching her. "You faked being kidnapped for weeks. Weeks, I have been on the edge of my sanity. You had to have given Boone my business card to plant on Tyson, to implicate me. How else would he have got it? And you were going to let him kidnap and torture me for answers I didn't have!"

Harmony's face turned crimson. "No." She hung her head. "I only wanted to scare you and I needed you to think…"

"That you were kidnapped. So when you found the jewels, you could get rid of Boone and we'd believe he'd done it all alone. Even Sly would be dead and unable to talk. Did you put that hit out on him?"

"I wasn't going to kill anyone. But Chaz is out there now, Piper. He probably wanted Sly dead. He wants us all dead."

"Why would Chaz burn my dojo down to find jewels?"

"He wouldn't." Luke's sharp tone caused Harmony to shiver. "He was trying to kill us then *and* when he ran us off the road. Explain that."

Harmony cried. "I can't. I don't know what he's doing. I was at Boone's place. Hiding out. Waiting for you to give Boone the jewels so I could steal them… not kill him."

But he'd be a liability, turn on her. No way Harmony could let him live, but Piper wanted to give her the benefit of the doubt.

"Boone wouldn't take the fall," Luke said. "He'd bring you down with him."

Piper and Luke were on the same page, and by the look on Harmony's guilty face, she knew it, too.

Piper rubbed her temples. The headache was coming on strong. "What happened at Boone's?"

"I was in the bathroom. I heard yelling, like someone saying 'open up' or something. I turned off the shower and heard the commotion. I threw on my clothes and crawled out the bathroom window. I didn't see Boone's murder, but later that night when I came back, he was dead."

"And you left him. With the sword."

"I didn't know that was your sword and I panicked. Didn't know what to do. I didn't know about the car going off the road, the burning or Luke's place. That wasn't me. I'm pretty sure it wasn't Boone. It has to be Chaz! And that's why we have to run. Or we're all gonna be dead!"

"Did you see anything else? Anything?"

"In the parking lot at Boone's, I thought I might have seen—"

Like a needle scratching across a record turning things into slow motion, Piper saw it…a red dot beaming from the windows, straight to Harmony's head.

No time to holler. Piper rushed Harmony.

Luke screamed for her to stop and leaped toward Piper.

Glass shattered.

Piper fell in a heap.

Luke's voice boomed through the noise. "Piiii-per!"

Luke's heart shot into his throat, and he pulled his gun and reached for his phone. Not there! He'd left it in the car rushing in to make sure Piper was safe.

One second Harmony was a target for what looked to be a perfect head shot, and then Piper tackled her, shoving her to the floor.

"Piper, where's your phone?"

"Counter."

Luke reached for it. "It's dead!"

Blood seeped across the kitchen tile. Another shot slammed into the counter.

"We have to get out of here, now!" Luke hollered.

Piper crouched over Harmony.

Luke glanced at Harmony. "I can't tell how bad it is, but we're ripe for taking here with all the windows."

"Harmony? Can you move?" Piper tapped her face.

"I— My shoulder." She shifted. "I think I can move." Wincing, she sat upright.

"Stay low," Piper said.

"Outside. It's our best chance." Someone was coming straight for them and would expect them to huddle in a corner of the house and wait or bolt out the front door for the car—which was where his phone was. It was too dangerous to go out that way. They needed an advantage. The storm and woods would help camouflage them, and they could get to a neighbor's house and a phone.

Luke pushed Piper toward Harmony's bedroom. "We'll go out Harmony's window and make a straight shot into the woods." If the shooter stayed outside, he wouldn't expect them to take an injured person out a window. About twenty feet of mostly unsheltered ground before the woods opened up, and the lightning wasn't working in their favor, but it was the best idea he had.

God, help us into the woods. Hold off the lightning. Keep us hidden in Your safe hands.

Harmony clasped her left hand over her right shoulder as Piper linked her arm in Harmony's and ushered her forward. Luke brought up the rear. If anyone was going to take a bullet, it would be him. The thought of Piper getting hurt or worse… He shoved the idea out of his mind.

Inside Harmony's bedroom, Piper rushed to the side of the curtain. "You aim the gun, and I'll open the window."

"Piper, I can't see out there."

"You'll see a red dot, won't you?" Her face paled and her eyes flashed with fright, but her brave and cool exterior overshadowed it.

"Yeah, but that won't help me see the shooter. If he's even using a laser now."

Harmony moaned and collapsed to her knees. "I don't think I can make it."

"I just saved your life! You suck it up and move." Piper pressed her back against the wall and glared at Harmony. "Who is that out there?"

"I told you. I think it's Chaz." Harmony's breathing was labored. Luke tore her shirt where the bullet went through.

"Harmony, I think it's a flesh wound, but we have to find something to apply pressure with or at least cover it."

"My bathroom." Harmony grunted.

"Luke, we're running out of time. Chaz could already be in the house. He's that quiet." Piper peeked out the window. Rain slashed against it. Too dark.

Pilfering through the bathroom, Luke found a bath towel, ripped it in strips and hurried into the bedroom, wrapping it tightly around Harmony's shoulder. She jerked. "I know it hurts. Hang on."

Time was running out.

"On three," Piper said.

Luke's stomach roiled, but what choice did they have?

"I'm gonna lift the window and kick out the screen." Piper gave one solid nod.

Sweat slicked Luke's back, beaded around his upper lip and temples. "One...two...three..."

Piper swung in front of the window, moving like a

high-speed rail train as she flipped the locks and raised
the window. She darted back against the wall, her chest
heaving. With a shaky breath, she pivoted and side-
kicked the screen out of the window then ducked below it.

"Nice job, Pip." Luke's grip on his gun turned clammy.
It wasn't just himself he was trying to save. This was
Piper. This was different. "I'm going to go first so I can
cover you and Harmony. Send her out, and you come
last."

Piper nodded. Luke stood at the hem of the curtains.
Somewhere out there, someone was working stealth-
ily to take them down. This might not turn out as well
as he hoped.

He faced Piper. "I know this isn't fair, but fair is off
the table right now." He leaned down, cupped Piper's
cheek and pressed an urgent kiss to her lips. "Be careful."

Piper touched his hand resting on her cheek. "I will."

Harmony cried out again. After all she did, Piper
hadn't let her die. She'd stepped in and saved her. Ten
years ago, she might not have. But something was
changing in her. Stepping out of God's way had made
room for Him to work, and Luke had peace that God
would finish what He had started.

He surveyed the darkness—no lightning. Time to
strike while it was hot. He nose-dived out the window,
landing on wet mulch and azalea bushes. Springing into
a crouch, he scanned the woods. Listened. Not much
could be heard over the beating rain and thunder.

"Harmony's coming."

A swatch of blond hair poked through the window.
Harmony muffled her cries with her hand, then looked

at Piper. "Why would you save me? After everything I've done to you?"

Only Piper's shadow showed in the window. "It's called mercy. I've been getting a heavy dose of it lately. Now get out the window and let's get through this."

"I'd rather die than go to prison."

"Night's young," Luke quipped and grabbed the trunk of her body as Piper eased her through the window. Careful not to injure the bullet wound further, Luke gently laid her behind the azalea bushes.

"Piper, come on!"

Piper moved to the window and launched herself out, landing on Luke. "Sorry."

"Not a problem."

"Now what?"

"We sprint behind the oak tree. Take cover, then book it through the woods to the nearest house where we can call in backup. Harmony, how far to your closest neighbor?"

Harmony gasped and shoved hair from her face with her uninjured arm. "Mile, maybe, but they travel a lot."

"Then, Piper, you'll have to teach me a lesson on breaking and entering, and we pray they have a landline since you don't."

Or Eric might come. Where was he? Every second the ball of dread grew wider, heavier.

"I can't feel my arm and I'm cold." Harmony shivered in the rain.

Luke shrugged off his soaked jacket and threw it across the yard as a decoy. Nothing. Either the shooter hadn't figured out where they were or he was checking the house. Any minute he'd discover they'd gone out the window. "We gotta move. Now."

"Harmony, can you run?" Rain pelted Piper, her hair matting to her face and neck.

"I can…can try."

Luke heaved a breath. "I'll help her and cover us best I can in the dark. Piper, you stay behind me."

"Luke, I can run faster and—"

"Behind me! I can shield you, so stay right on me."

"Okay."

Luke put one arm around Harmony for support, helped her up and ripped across the yard toward the oak tree. Wind howled, the pressure working to blow them over, and rain stung his face like freezing needles. He hoped Piper was on his tail. Too much thunder. Too much noise.

The tree was five feet ahead.

Four…

Three…

One…

Luke clung to the large oak as if it were life. Harmony whimpered next to him. Piper slammed into the tree, gasping.

"We made it."

For now.

"Piper, I'm so sorry. I really am," Harmony whined.

Sorry or sorry she got caught? Either way. Piper sighed. "Can we make it into the woods?"

Luke scanned the perimeter. Lightning cracked, giving him a floodlight view of the woods. "I don't know. I don't see anyone. Could Chaz have made that shot? The woods were a stretch from the kitchen. That would have been the kill shot if you hadn't intervened."

Piper shivered. "I don't know. He had a few guns, but I've never seen anything like that."

"Well, we can't sit here. It won't provide us shelter for long. Harmony, how you holding up?"

"I don't know if I can make it. Just…just leave me. I'll be okay and if I'm not… I deserve whatever I get."

Piper reached over Luke and gripped Harmony's face. "You're right—you deserve a lot, and when this is over you'll have to face the consequences, but right now…you get mercy. Nobody's leaving you." Piper peered up at Luke, squinting in the rain. "Right?"

"Right." Luke wasn't sure what Piper had been wrestling with the past few days. But one thing was for sure. God was working inside her heart. "Harmony, if you can't run, I'll carry you."

"Then give me the gun." Piper's eyes held steady determination.

"No. You stay to my left. We'll sandwich Harmony. Now! Go!" Clutching Harmony with one arm, Luke grasped his gun in the other, ready for whatever was about to come.

Ten feet in, Harmony dropped to her knees. "Go! I can't… Leave me!"

Luke snatched her, threw her over his shoulder and hollered, "Go, Piper!"

She dashed to the tree line.

A crack sounded!

Piper tumbled to the ground.

Chapter 17

Piper sprawled on her stomach, a burning sensation reeling on her right side. She pressed her hand to her waist and brought it up. Rain smeared the blood from her fingers.

She'd been hit.

Another bullet hit the tree above her. Bark splintered around and on her. She drew into a ball when another boom broke through the atmosphere.

Not gunfire. Thunder.

Army crawling through the pine needles, mud and leaves, she butted up against a tree to catch her breath and shield herself from the man bent on destroying them. She lifted her T-shirt and inspected the wound. Grazed her. She sighed and leaned her head on the tree.

The shooter knew her whereabouts, which meant if Luke tried to beeline it to her—and knowing him, he would—he'd never make it. Not that his chances alone were prime, but with Harmony on his shoulder it would be impossible.

Piper touched her lips where he'd planted a frenzied kiss before ducking out the window. To see him shot down would kill her. But he was an open target where he was. The oak tree would shelter them for only so long.

Bait. Piper needed to lead the shooter through the woods, giving Luke and Harmony a fighting chance. He wasn't going to be happy about it, but if they made it out alive he might be grateful later.

Glancing toward the oak, she hoped Luke would know what she was doing. Take his door of opportunity and haul it into the woods.

Another splitting crack reverberated through the towering pines. She haphazardly pushed her hair from her face. Goose bumps raised on her drenched chilly skin. Her moccasins had soaked in the rain, and they squished when she moved, but the soles were rubber and kept pinecones and other debris from piercing the bottoms of her feet.

God, please continue to show me mercy and keep us alive.

Piper sprang up, ignoring the burning in her side, and blasted east toward the neighbor's home. About a mile, Harmony had said. Either way, she had to get the focus off Luke.

Hovering darkness and the freezing storm battering her head deafened any other noises in the woods.

Branches toppled from the trees as they arched and strained from the howling wind. *Don't think about bullets. Don't think about the shooter. Run. Just run.*

A shot piggybacked a booming explosion of thunder. Piper screeched as bark chipped off the tree, and she zigzagged. Chaz may want her dead, but she wasn't going to make it easy for him. Like sharp figure eights, she looped around and through the trees, barely making out the next one.

Piper tripped over a branch and flung forward onto her knees. Crawling and scratching through the saturated muck on the woodsy floor, she crouched behind a large tree.

Where are you, Luke? Did you run? Are you here?

Lungs burning, Piper focused on breathing. In. Out. In. Out. Her calf muscles ached and her hands wouldn't stop trembling. Her chin quivered no matter how hard she bit down on her bottom lip.

If she could track the shooter…if she could come in from behind without that gun in her face, she had a fighting chance to save them all. But he kept to the shadows, and with a rifle he could be hundreds of feet away.

A beacon of lightning flashed. A dark blur moved about fifteen feet north of Piper and disappeared behind a large tree with a branch hanging low, split from the power of the lightning or wind.

Up.

Running made her a target, and Chaz would be hunting her from the ground. Piper lifted her chin and made a quick study of the branches. Reaching up, she couldn't grasp the first branch of the pine. Her stitches on the left side pulled, and the fresh wound on her right burned and throbbed.

Could she make the jump? She forced back the pain, focused and put everything she had into the power of her legs. *God, I've done my part, but I can't do it with-*

*out You. I know that now. I'm weak. I need You to be
strong for me.*

Never had she asked God to be her strength.

She'd been her own strength.

But it hadn't been enough, and it wasn't now.

Piper crouched low then sprang, clasping the branch
with one hand. Swinging her left hand up, she grabbed
the branch, but with slippery hands she was having a
hard time hanging on. Dangling from the tree branch,
she might as well be a piñata.

"God," she whispered through gritted teeth, hot tears
mixing with the chilled pelts of rain, "I need You!"

Renewed strength filled her body, and she hoisted
herself onto the sturdy branch. She heaved a sigh and
thanked God. Like a gymnast, she climbed up until
she was on the fourth branch, about ten feet from the
ground.

Under the heavy pine branches, she found shelter
from the constant downpour. Earth, musk and spring
filtered into her nose. Hanging on to the limb above for
balance, she surveyed her surroundings. Where was
Luke? Harmony?

Chaz?

A flicker of lightning graced the inky sky. To her
left. Luke! If only she could holler for him. Let him
know she was okay. And close by. Relief flooded her.
He was safe. Tucked behind a tree. Harmony leaning
against it, her hand on her wounded shoulder.

Did Piper make the right choice? Should she have
kept on and tried to make it to the nearest house?

A shadowy figure skulked from one tree to the next.
Big—or the night was playing tricks on her. He darted

to another tree, moving with stealth. Six more trees and he'd find Luke. But he had to pass under her first.

The urgency to signal Luke was overpowering, but she focused and kept her mouth clamped shut. Good thing heights didn't scare her. Spiders—spiders she ran from, but heights were okay. Down below lay the biggest spider she'd ever seen, and she was about to be one big shoe. No running.

Inching onto the branch, she kept her balance, poised to pounce.

Just a few more feet left.

Now that he was closer, she spied his gear. Rifle on his back. Smaller gun in hand—pistol, she guessed. Guns weren't her thing. Dressed in black from head to toe. Looked as if a ski mask had been rolled up, using it as a hat. Unfortunately, Piper couldn't make out his face.

Three more feet was all she needed and he'd be directly under her. She'd catch him off guard, smack the gun from his hand and knock the stuffin' clean out of him. Anxiety and fear morphed into a fiery blue blaze, the kind that rested under the licking flames of a fire. Hotter than red.

This man had finished haunting her dreams. No more poking her head over her shoulder. It was over.

Starting now.

Piper dropped from the tree, colliding with the attacker, but she didn't quite make her mark. Instead of dead center, she landed on his shoulder. The hard edge plunged into her sternum, stealing her breath. The gun skittered a foot or two away.

The hulking man turned.

But it wasn't Chaz.

* * *

Luke watched in horror as the motion from the trees stole his attention. It took a few seconds for it to register. Piper was falling from a tree. No. Not falling.

Jumping?

"Harmony, stay put. You'll be safe."

Harmony gave a weak nod, and Luke sprinted toward the action. He had to get to Piper. Whoever this was, he was moving like military. Luke let the scene replay in his head when they were run off the road, and even the dojo fire.

Professional.

Couldn't have been Chaz. He might be sneaky when it came to burglary, but he'd never murdered anyone that Luke was aware of.

And Luke's apartment. It was disturbed, not destroyed. Someone had made it look like a burglary, but the way he'd attacked, as if lying in wait—that person wanted him dead. Why?

Everyone else associated was either in prison or in a grave. Everyone except… Only one other person from that night could have known he and Piper were going to see Sly Watson in prison and could have easily put a hit out on him, followed them without Luke catching it.

Only one other person could have known about the jewels.

No.

No way.

Luke's breath hitched, and he powered his legs forward. Piper wasn't battling an old thug. Piper was fighting someone who knew how to fight, military combat style. Someone with tactical skills and years of experience taking down bad guys.

She was in serious danger.

From his old partner, Kerr Robbins.

Piper had plummeted ten, maybe twelve, feet from above, throwing Kerr to the ground, but he rolled over quickly and threw a punch. Luke moved faster. If he hollered out, Kerr might shoot her.

Piper dodged it and leaped to her feet.

Luke darted left, maneuvering behind Kerr.

"You've misjudged your opponent, little girl," Kerr hissed.

Piper danced on her legs as if this were a sparring match. She kept her eyes trained on Kerr. "I remember you. And you might want to take a better look. I'm not a little girl anymore." A dare rode through her tone. Now was not the time to make challenges.

The rain let up, only small rumbles of thunder in the distance, but the wind beat at them.

"You didn't fare so well the last time we did this. Seems I left you in a heap of books. This time, I'll finish it."

The revelation gave Piper pause. Kerr lunged, and she seized his arm, slid under it and made a direct kick to his ribs, but he grabbed her leg as it made contact, dropping her to the ground, pinning her legs and arms. "Whatcha gonna do without your extremities?"

She spit in his face.

Luke aimed his gun at Kerr's head, no choice but to reveal his presence. "Up and move slowly."

Kerr tilted his head and grinned. "Hey, friend."

"Don't you ever call me that again. Get off of her. Hands in the air." Luke glanced at Piper. "You okay, Pip?"

Kerr eased off Piper into a squatting position. "We

could share the money, Luke. I meant it when I said this one couldn't be trusted. I really was looking out for you."

"You knew exactly who you were chasing that night." Chaz must have run with the jewels. "You caught him after all and killed him for them."

Kerr's icy eyes stared at him, his hands out to his sides, rifle on his back. Kerr was tricky. Luke kept his eyes locked on his face and hands.

"So I caught him. An opportunity arose. Punk had all these rubies and diamonds. We make peanuts and put our lives on the line every day because of scum like him." He nodded toward Piper. "Like her. I thought it was high time I got mine. And I'll give you a cut. You can keep doing what you love and have a cushion for when you retire. And if you're smart, like me, you can have a little extra now without calling attention to yourself."

Luke's blood boiled. "You're a murderer, and you are under arrest."

"I've saved your life. You're going to repay me by this? And I didn't murder anyone who didn't deserve it."

"What about me? At my apartment? The dojo? Or when you tried to run me and Piper off the road?"

Kerr's eyes narrowed. "You gave me no choice! When you pulled those files, started digging. I knew you'd eventually put it together. I had to take drastic measures." Luke had trusted him, and it hadn't dawned, until now, that Kerr never mentioned the great-granddaughter reporting the jewels missing after Luke left the theft division. He'd kept it out of the case files and from Luke, then killed anyone involved in that night to keep his own behind safe.

"Are you in on it with Harmony Fells?"

"Hardly."

Kerr must not have known she was there the night he killed Boone. "Where's Chaz's body?"

"Rotted and gone somewhere in the Mississippi."

The betrayal cut deep. "I know you didn't do it on the scene."

"I'm not an idiot. I told him he could go, but I kept the jewels. Told him I'd split them and we met later."

Chaz had been the idiot. All these years he hadn't been in hiding. He'd been dead.

"He was a crook. And Sly? He nearly killed that old lady. Boone Wiley? Harmony? They were the ones who killed Baxter and Baroni, and hurt her granny, hunting for what's mine."

Piper's entire body shook. "You burned down my dojo! You tried to kill me then frame me for Boone Wiley's murder, then kill me again!"

Oh no.

"Piper, don't!"

She rammed a foot into Kerr's side with a force that sent him two feet over and onto the ground. Kerr came up with a pistol in his hand and fired.

Luke dropped to his knees, fire racing up his right leg where the bullet landed.

Kerr aimed the gun at Piper. "Like I said, a dumb little girl." He wiped his cheek with the back of his hand.

Piper slid in front of Luke and touched his bloody leg. "I'm sorry."

"I know, baby. It's okay."

"I'm touched, really," Kerr said with a deflated tone. "You can't say I didn't give you a chance, Luke. I was willing to bring you in at this point."

"You're just going to kill us and think you'll get away with it?" Piper clung to Luke, her hand trembling over his as he applied pressure to his leg. Could have been worse. Could've hit an artery.

"That's exactly what I think. Let dead ole Chaz take the fall. He ran away with the jewels that night. Been lying low. No one will be alive to say any different. Sly won't make it this time. And Harmony Fells? Don't think I don't know she's hiding behind one of these trees, Luke. It's over."

"I don't think it is." Eric's voice boomed from the shadows. "Drop your gun, Robbins. You know the drill."

Sirens. Was that…was that sirens? Luke puffed his cheeks and released a breath. "I am so glad you're here. Where've you been?"

"Oh, you know, the usual—gettin' pistol-whipped and left for dead." Eric read Kerr his rights. "Good for you, I have a really hard head. Not so great for you, Robbins."

Sirens grew louder and probing lights lit up the woods. Flashlights. Luke collapsed onto his backside, Piper clinging to him, her face buried in his neck.

"It's over, Luke. It's really over." She kissed his cheek, his ear, his neck. "I thought we were gonna die."

So did he. "When I saw you drop to the ground… I've never been more scared in my life."

"Just grazed me."

"I didn't know that." He'd wanted to roll in a ball and die right then, but she popped up and ran. He wasn't sure if she'd been hit or not. All he knew was he had to get to her as fast as he could. "You were amazing."

"God saved me. Saved us both. And it helps that I

liked climbing trees and not playing with Barbie dolls when I was little."

Had Luke heard that right? Piper was giving God credit over her own ability? Over Luke's? Hope ballooned in his chest.

Eric cuffed Kerr, and several uniforms hauled him off. Paramedics headed their way.

"I didn't mean your bobcat move from the tree." He peered into irresistible hazel eyes, dirt and blood crusting her face. Hair hung limp down her shoulders. "I meant for showing Harmony mercy. You could have let her die, but you put your life at risk for her."

Piper brushed her hand along his cheek. "As Mama Jean would say, I had a Come-to-Jesus meeting these last few days. I betrayed Him. We've all betrayed Him, and He died anyway. Shown me more grace and mercy than I could even express. Has to be His grace giving me strength to do that for Harmony."

Was this God's way of letting Luke know that he wasn't going to have to give Piper up forever? What if he'd chosen not to let her go? Would things have turned out differently? Would she still be trying to fly with a broken wing? *God, thank You for showing me that letting her fly means letting You mend her wings.* It wasn't Luke's job to push her from the nest or catch her if she fell. It was his job to trust God, and maybe one day, he could fly beside her.

Lord, whatever You ask, I'll do. You know how much I love her.

She let out a strangled laugh through a few tears. "Luke?"

"Yeah."

"I love you. I know it's not fair to tell you that.

Wasn't going to because it'd make things tougher for you, but—" she grinned "—fair's still off the table."

"Sir?" Paramedics stepped in, taking vitals, placing oxygen masks on them. Again. Might be a good thing they'd been interrupted. Luke was about to kiss her senseless and he wasn't sure that would have been the right thing.

Separate ambulances carried them away. God had done some pretty big and amazing things this past week.

One of which was administering healing balm to their wounded hearts and using this horrible night to do a lot of it.

Now for the hospital to administer healing to their physical wounds.

In Piper's words, he was *sick* of hospitals.

Chapter 18

Luke had been released after a two-night stay at the hospital. Bone hadn't been shattered, but the muscle in his thigh had some damage. Doctors removed the bullet and were positive that he'd fully recover and could return to active duty. He'd been in and out for those two days, but he was pretty sure in his fuzzy awake moments, Piper had been sitting with him.

But she hadn't been there when he left the hospital. Eric had. Was here with him now, snoozing in Luke's recliner.

Kerr had lured Eric from his post that night, clobbered him on the head—enough he had a concussion—and the doctors said it could have killed him. Eric could blame it on a hard head, but they both knew God had been protecting all of them.

When Eric had come to, he'd phoned in backup and figured out Kerr had sent the Durango with a passed-

out Eric down the ravine, across from Harmony's, trying to make it appear as if he'd hit his head in a car
accident. He found his way into the woods. And in the
nick of time. Thank God.

Luke closed his eyes and settled on the leather couch.
He'd been given the promotion. Found out this morning. After his display of courage and closing out not
one case but two, he was well on his way up the ranks,
but Piper was going back to Jackson.

After the episode in the woods, it was obvious Piper
was on the mend without any help from him. When he
wasn't on pain pills, he'd prayed about whether it was
the right time for another chance with Piper. Now that
he didn't want to fix her and she knew whom to look
to for her strength.

He couldn't get back the past ten years, but they'd
grown, matured. It was time to start a new life. If that
meant transferring to Jackson, starting out as the new
guy, then he'd do it.

For her.

Because the time was right. But the fact Piper hadn't
been there when he'd been released from the hospital
needled him. Had she already gone back to Jackson?
Did she think leaving without saying goodbye would
be easier for her? For him? He'd talked himself out of
calling. When—if—she was ready to talk to him, she
would. He hoped. It had to be ideal for them both.

A knock sounded on his door, and Eric jerked awake.
"I got it. Don't try to get up, man." He rubbed away the
sleep from his eyes as he stumbled to Luke's front door.

"Hey, hey, it's Kung Fu Piper. You bring food? I'm
starving."

"Actually, I did." Piper handed him a pack of Twizzlers and smirked.

"I could kiss you," he teased.

Luke cleared his throat. "I think you better not."

Eric winked at Luke and wrapped Piper in a brotherly hug.

Then she set those eyes on Luke. He lost his breath, and his heart tripped. Good thing he couldn't stand for the bum leg; he'd gone weak in the knees.

"Hi," she whispered.

Piper swallowed hard. Luke's unruly hair and few days' worth of growth on his cheeks and chin only made him appear that much more rugged. Blue-green eyes beamed; a lopsided grin covered his face. Her stomach backflipped.

"Hi," he said through a husky voice.

"Well," Eric said and clucked his tongue in his cheek. "I'm feeling some zings in the air here, so that's my cue to take a walk. Seeing as I have two legs, I actually can."

Luke rolled his eyes, and Piper chuckled.

"Hey, before I go, I heard you went all Tarzan on that piece of dirt—seriously, jumping out of trees. Nice. So I got to thinking, you got real skills. You oughta come over to our side. It worked for Steven Seagal. He's even got his own reality show. Going all cop in Jefferson Parish, Louisiana. Think of it, me on TV—I mean you, *you* on TV. Roughing up bad guys."

Piper smothered a laugh and stared him down with a disapproving glare.

"No?" Eric shrugged. "Maybe it's the concussion talking. You know, the one I got saving your life...so think about it. TV." He tousled her hair and winked, then shut the front door behind him.

She sighed. "He never quits, does he?"

"It's his way of saying he cares about us."

"He could just say he cared."

Luke flashed a brilliant grin. "Come to me."

Piper's insides quivered as she made her way to the couch. He scooted closer to the back, giving her room to snuggle up next to him. He smelled like fabric softener and a clean-scented body wash. She crunched down on her bottom lip, her mouth turning dry.

Piper had needed a few days to think. As she sat by Luke's bedside while he slept from surgery, listening to his mumbling, applying a damp, cool rag to his head during his fitful sleep, she'd prayed. Prayed more than ever before. Prayed for Harmony, who was recovering from her injuries, praying mercy on her. Consequences were coming.

She'd prayed for Luke and Eric, for Mama Jean. And now she was here, after some time alone without seeing Luke or smelling him. She didn't want anything to sway her prayerful thinking.

"I missed seeing you when I left the hospital." Luke laced his fingers in between hers. "I was afraid you'd gone without...without telling me goodbye."

Piper rubbed his thumb, callused at the end. "I needed to see Mama Jean, and I had to make a few calls to Jackson. Checked in with Ms. Wells."

"How's Tootsie?"

"Still pooping in my yard, I'm sure."

He laughed, and then his eyes turned solemn. "And to call your Realtor?"

"Yes."

"I need to tell you something, Piper."

She pressed a finger on his lips. "Me first."

He nodded and kissed her finger. A thrill raced up her arm. "I know I've done a lot of things throughout the years to lose your trust. To hurt you. We've both been hurt. And you were right when you said that you couldn't fix me, that if we were together you'd try and fail. That I'd be disappointed in you."

Piper swallowed down the anxiety. "But I can't go back to Jackson, Luke." Tears burned the backs of her eyes. "I can tell you that God is doing some things in my heart, but I've lied to you before, and I don't want you to think I'm just saying that so we can be together."

"Pip—"

"No." She held her hand up. She had to get this out while she had the strength. She'd prayed intently about this and believed it was the right thing to do. "Let me finish." Taking a deep breath, she continued. "But it is true. So, I talked to my Realtor and I leased a place. Yesterday. Drove down and signed the papers, but Braxton is going to run it."

Luke's eyes grew wide. "And where are you going?"

"Home. Here. Mama Jean agreed to the assisted-living center, finally. It's really nice, too." She cleared her throat. "I'm gonna start house hunting in the meantime and look for a building to lease. Start a second dojo."

She closed her eyes, opened them. "And I'm praying over time you'll see that I've placed my trust in God. Not me. Not you. You were right—I'm not invincible. I have the bullet wound to prove it."

He kissed the back of her hand but said nothing. Good, she wasn't done yet.

"And when you believe it, when you know it in your heart, then I want to start fresh. If you can. If seeing me won't remind you of pain and heartache." A tear pooled in her eye and she blinked, letting it roll down her cheek.

Luke scooted up, wiped it away with the pad of his thumb. "Piper, you don't have to do all this for me, to show that you've changed. I know you have. I know God is healing you. I saw it when you gave Harmony mercy."

He had? What did this mean?

"I was going to decline the promotion and tell you I was coming to Jackson. It's not as important to me as you. I love you, Piper. Since the moment you blew out the flame on my lighter. There's nothing I wouldn't do for you. You're my world."

Piper laid her forehead on his. "You're mine," she whispered.

"Hold that thought." He struggled to sit up. Piper slipped off the couch as he took his crutches and winced.

"Where are you going?"

He hobbled across the living room, down the hall and back, then eased onto the couch, tugging Piper down with him. "I've been looking at this a lot lately. Took it out of my dresser drawer the day you stormed into Mama Jean's hospital room."

A black velvet box rested in his hand. "I had this in my pocket that night at Ellen Strosbergen's."

He was going to propose that night? Piper's lip trembled. She refused to feel guilty. Some regret, yes. But she'd been forgiven for the past. And she'd forgiven herself. No more condemning thoughts.

Luke opened the box. A princess-cut diamond twinkled on a thick gold band. Another band of diamonds nestled behind it. "Piper Regina Kennedy, will you marry me…finally?"

Piper brushed her finger over the diamond. "Yes. Yes, I will."

Luke slipped the engagement ring on her finger, closed the box and ran his fingers down her battered and bruised cheeks. "I love you," he whispered.

"I love you, too."

Sliding his hand through her hair to the back of her neck, he gently led her to his lips. His kiss revealing his tenderness toward her and renewed trust as well as the declaration of his devotion, his loyalty. Even his vulnerability. All poured out with a sweetness that brought fresh tears to her eyes.

God had given her far beyond anything she deserved. A merciful God with so much more tenderness, loyalty and devotion toward her than even this man thrilling her with a slow-burning, glorious kiss.

And she was ready to keep discovering this divine love for her. As well as the enduring love from her future husband.

Luke broke the kiss. "Piper?"

"Hmm." Her heart hummed and sputtered.

"Happy birthday, my love. I didn't forget. I just wasn't sure where you were or where we stood." He brushed a soft peck to her nose. "Now will you tell me what you wished for all those years ago?"

Piper savored his scent; a longing tightened her stomach. She was home. In so many ways. "I wished for you. For the rest of my life."

He hooked her chin with his finger, a sparkle in his eye, an impish grin turning her inside out. "I told you every birthday girl deserves a wish. Aren't you glad you made it?"

"I'm about to make another one." She leaned down, pressed her lips to his. "I wish for a big family."

"And a dog," he murmured.

"I thought this was my birthday wish."

Luke chuckled. "Fine. We can do this all over again in three months when it's mine."

Piper sighed and nestled against Luke's chest, listening to it beat, embracing the moment.

And thanking God for unending mercy.

* * * * *

Get 3 FREE REWARDS!

We'll send you 2 FREE Books plus a FREE Mystery Gift.

FREE
Value Over
$20

Both the **Romance** and **Suspense** collections feature compelling novels written by many of today's bestselling authors.

Get 3 FREE REWARDS!

We'll send you 2 FREE Books plus a FREE Mystery Gift.

FREE
Value Over
$20

Both the **Harlequin Intrigue®** and **Harlequin® Romantic Suspense** series feature compelling novels filled with heart-racing action-packed romance that will keep you on the edge of your seat.

HARLEQUIN
PLUS

Try the best multimedia subscription service for romance readers like you!

Read, Watch and Play.

Experience the easiest way to get the romance content you crave.

Start your **FREE TRIAL** at
www.harlequinplus.com/freetrial.